NECROPOLIS

THE NECROMANCER THANATOGRAPHY
BOOK ONE

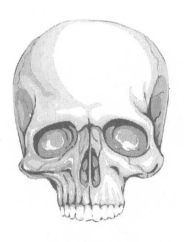

SHANE SIMMONS

ISBN: 978-1-988954-00-4

Necropolis
Copyright © 2017 by Shane Simmons
All Rights Reserved.

Published by Eyestrain Productions
eyestrainproductions.com

Prologue

Waking the Dead

I'D BEEN IN BED ten minutes when I heard the phone ring in the next room. I was tired, drifting away, not quite asleep but not easily roused. Gladys picked it up after the first ring. She was working late. She was always working late, sitting at the desk in my home office, taking calls at all hours. Grateful for it, I ignored the late interruption and let myself fade a little more. One distant ring wasn't enough to pull me out of my slow descent into unconsciousness. Gladys's shrill voice was another matter.

"Phoon!" she bellowed at me through the wall.

"I'm sleeping!"

"Yoo tak in yoo sleep? Ansa da phoon!"

I didn't know which I found more irritating at eleven-thirty, Gladys's grating tone or her impossible accent. There was no getting around it. She'd badger me until I took the call. I sat up with a long indisposed groan and reached for the extension I always kept on mute. The caller I.D. told me who it was—another woman in my life who would not be ignored. Whatever she wanted at such a late hour, she'd just keep calling until she got it.

I hit the "talk" button, but all I could do was listen.

Chapter One

Curtain Call

I T WAS HARD getting me out of bed, I admit. The idea of putting on fresh clothes and cabbing it to the city core for a midnight show seemed like a lot of time, effort and expense for something that was probably going to amount to a splitting headache at best. I like to be made aware of new talent when it comes to town, or rises through the ranks of mediocrity, but I had low hopes for any of the acts that were going to break up the otherwise relentless assault of noise pollution generously billed as "music" at Gallery Nowhere that night.

I'd been to the gallery before and it made me more and more nervous each time. Every visit to the venue seemed to feature one less load-bearing wall. Structural integrity was suffering an extinction event in the old three-level tenement. Everything deemed superfluous by the management had been torn out to create more open space to pack in more bands and more paying customers bent on drinking their weight in cheap booze. The building dated back to the city's industrial boom, and after a century, an extra decade, and a few years of spare change, it was lucky to still be standing at all. The metal bands, the speakers at maximum power, and the jumping, flailing, stomping fans all seemed determined to rectify this. I fully expected Gallery Nowhere to be levelled by some cataclysmic drum solo one night, flattening it like all the other period houses it had once been attached to that had since been turned into pay-by-the-hour parking lots. And I didn't want to be present when it happened.

Despite its reputation for offering sets to unbookable garage bands that should have left the car running and the doors closed during their last practice session, Gallery Nowhere was designated, on paper filed at city hall at least, as an art gallery. As such, they were required, often reluctantly, to open their doors to other acts that didn't sell quite so many drinks, including unspeakably bad spoken-word raconteurs, indecipherable modern-art junk-pile vernissages, and more than a few old-school vaudevillian novelty acts and freak shows that had been rebranded "performance art." Some might question just how much art is involved in a man with a pierced scrotum lifting chained weights with his balls, but you couldn't deny that that sort of thing packed in the drunken teenagers almost as reliably as the battle of the bottom-feeding bands. It had become common for Gallery Nowhere to break up an evening's entertainment by staggering band sets and solo routines. Ten minutes of stage time with a contortionist or a sideshow geek would give the audience an opportunity to refresh their drinks and stop their ears from bleeding.

I met Rebecca lingering outside, having a smoke by the curb. Some band, destined for merciful obscurity, was going at it full throttle inside. Even through stone walls and wooden beams, all the way across the street I could feel the thump-thump-thump beat arguing with the rhythm of my heart, trying to force it to reset its pace. If you looked at the façade of the aging venue closely enough, you could see crumbs of mortar dust trickling out from between the rows of brick with every over-amplified note. I think the building was only still standing out of a misplaced sense of pride. But nothing lasts forever. Erosion will get Mount Everest in the end. Everything dies.

"You made it," Rebecca said, like I ever had an option. Rebecca will not be stood up.

"Despite my better judgment," I grumbled, just in case the sour face wasn't communicating my displeasure obviously enough.

"You won't be disappointed," she assured me, "There's somebody you have to meet."

The fact that she needed to assure me at all convinced me that disappointment was in the cards—loading the deck as we spoke, hedging the bet by stuffing a few more disappointment cards up a sleeve.

"It's not a card act, is it?"

I had cards on the brain. I'd been burned before—guaranteed I'd be shown something that would blow my mind, only to see some fraudster with wide palms and quick, agile fingers get up on stage and pull out a deck of cards. Fucking card tricks. Is there anything more boring, more asinine, more transparently sleight of hand?

I'm not a talent scout. I'm not looking to represent somebody's act or audition them or sign them to a contract so I can shave ten percent off the top. I just like to be informed about who's out there, and who has the goods. The real goods. Magicians are about as common and scuzzy as meth-whores in this town. The only difference is the nature of their addiction—magicians crave attention rather than methamphetamines. Plus they usually have a nice set of teeth so they can flash their admirers a winning smile after turning a trick. The meth-whores, not so much.

"Come on," she said, taking me by the arm and cutting the line, "I'll buy you a beer."

A flirtatious wink and a nod of recognition at the doorman was all Rebecca needed to slip us both in ahead of the dull normals who had to wait their turn because they didn't have the looks or the cash to make the line go faster. There was a cover charge to get onto the third floor where the bands were. Rebecca made me pay for both of us, but the ticket girl seemed reluctant to take my money or stamp the back of my hand as proof I'd paid. I figured I didn't look sufficiently trendy. Rebecca received no skeptical glances as she got rubber-stamped through the door. But, of course, she has a style that's up-to-date and easily categorized.

I tried to guess how long my green smiley-face brand would be with me as we sat down at the bar. These rotating stamped codes were only ever good for one night at one venue, but the ink, doubtlessly toxic, was semi-permanent and needed to wear off gradually since it always refused to wash off in a timely fashion.

Rebecca didn't have to buy me a beer. She never had to buy drinks at all. If there was alcohol being served, she could rely on smitten suitors to send her a bottomless supply of freebies, hoping to win her favour or at least earn her attention for a few short moments. Rebecca passed any beers from her haul on to me, concentrating instead on downing the rum-and-Cokes, vodka-and-limes, and gin-and-tonics one after the other. I sipped at my third bottle quietly, taking it slow. As Rebecca's designated wingman, it was my job to stay sober enough to keep her from going home with anyone below her station and, if necessary, hold her hair for her while she puked up the evening's beverage buffet into the nearest available gutter.

We'd been in Galley Nowhere for twenty minutes when Rebecca started tugging on my sleeve excitedly, making me spill the neck of my freshly opened fourth beer.

"Oh, check it out!" she said, hopping in her seat, "You have to see this!"

Rebecca was in the giddy sweet spot I'd come to know and dread. Having had my thoughts drowned out by consecutive interchangeable bands, I was slow to figure out what she was so thrilled about. After collecting six drinks and eight phone numbers, with perhaps one viable romantic prospect among them, it could have been anything. And then the crowd joined in, reflecting a similar anticipatory excitement.

"Barf-O, Barf-O, Barf-O!" they chanted in frenzied unison.

For a moment I thought they were calling for Rebecca to let loose with the mixed-drink cocktail of doom sloshing around in her stomach. But no, the chant had risen to greet the next act taking the stage.

The performer was young, probably mid-twenties, but dressed in an anachronistic tuxedo that I couldn't imagine ever looked fashionable, even when new. Doubtless it was recovered for a paltry sum from some thrift shop, and pressed into service for the act to give him an ironic appearance of respectability. He wasn't wearing a top hat, so apparently he hadn't gone all-in for the retro magician look. His only apparent prop was a vintage carpet bag he set down on the floor and then ignored.

The act was self-consciously mannered and pantomimed. The performer never addressed his audience, but engaged them with a mute flourish of gestures and body language, exaggerated for comic effect. For his opening, he reached into his tuxedo jacket and produced a length of twine about a foot and a half long, stretching it out and snapping it a couple of times to show the audience it was intact and unremarkable. He then proceeded to tie three knots in it, several inches apart, and again pulled the twine taut to demonstrate what he'd done. Satisfied everyone had had a good look at his handiwork, he bunched up the twine into a ball, popped it in his mouth, and swallowed it with the aid of a glass of water.

The performer opened his mouth wide and pivoted in place so that everyone assembled could see his mouth was empty and that the length of twine had indeed been swallowed. When he closed his mouth once more, he stood up straight and made a series of small contortions, twisting his neck, clearing his throat, and puffing out his chest. Once he was done, he made a fist and thumped himself in the ribs twice. One end of the twine poked out between his lips and he grabbed hold of it. Throwing his head back, he slowly extracted the entire length, revealing that all three knots had been untied while they were inside his stomach.

Everyone was amazed and applauded accordingly. I, on the other hand, was deeply disinterested and found myself longing for a good card act.

"You brought me to see a regurgitator?" I muttered at Rebecca, who was one of the enthusiastic applauders. Regurgitation is a parlour trick. It's not a school of magic any more than sword swallowing or fire breathing.

"What's a regurgitator?" she asked.

Ah, sweet innocence. Sometimes I wish my mind wasn't polluted by so many of the things I know.

"You're looking at one," I said simply.

It's true, some people vomit for a living. Not so much to be disgusting, although it is definitely that, but as an amusement for others. The tradition goes back centuries, but it's become something of a rarity in modern times. A certain subset of performers, be they the stage or street-corner variety, would train the esophageal muscles to bring common objects up or down their throat at will. In doing so, they could employ their stomach or, in rare medical-oddity cases, a protruding esophageal pouch, to temporarily hold these objects for dramatic effect. Common feats of astonishing regurgitation included tried-and-true staples like the swallowing of a quarter cup of sugar, followed by the downing of a tall glass of water, climaxing with the upchucking of the sugar, still miraculously dry. Any regurgitation act could also be relied upon to feature the ingestion of a handful of coins followed by the vomiting of the exact change as requested by a random audience member.

A variation of this would precede or follow, involving as many as a dozen numbered balls that would be swallowed and brought back up in any numerical order the assembled crowd wished.

One by one, Barfo hit all his marks. Each gastrological trick brought a round of thunderous applause from everyone in the room, me being the only exception. My sole reaction was to cross another standard from the regurgitator repertoire off my mental list. Admittedly, Barfo was a proficient showman and accomplished vomiter, but the pioneers of his field had done it all at least a century before. I kept waiting for him to have some contemporary take on the material—swallowing somebody's smartphone and texting himself from inside his own stomach perhaps—but by the time he brought out the goldfish bowl, I knew there were no innovative ideas forthcoming.

If I'd had to guess which overdone regurgitator trick Barfo would choose for his grand finale, I would have gone with either The Fisherman or The Fireman. The Fireman was considered a rather advanced maneuver for a regurgitator, reserved for the higher echelons of the trade. But having seen the polished ease Barfo brought to his act, I thought he might be up to it. And I didn't expect the management would have any issues with The Fireman trick considering the dilapidated state of the building. In decades long past, vaudevillian venues declared a moratorium on The Fireman. It wasn't that the stunt involved fire, which always has the potential for disaster in a theatre setting. It was another sort of property damage that concerned them. The routine for any performance of The Fireman followed an identical pattern with only a few variations depending on the individual showman. A small structure would be brought out on stage. A typical example might be a steel-frame approximation of a building—about the size of a large dollhouse. Flammable material would already be stuffed inside. Oily rags worked well, but anything would do provided it could be relied upon to produce a convincing inferno for the next few minutes. Once it was set ablaze, the "fireman" would spring into action. While the fire burned, the headline regurgitator would pound back an inhuman amount of water. Brimming glass after brimming glass would be poured down his throat at breakneck speed. Only someone with well-trained throat muscles, who didn't even need to swallow, but could rather tilt his head back and pour the water directly into his distended stomach, could accomplish this. The preamble to the finale was impressive enough, but what followed never failed to amaze and horrify. The regurgitator, now stuffed with several gallons of water, would walk back across the stage to his miniature inferno. Standing several paces away, a safe distance from the roaring flames, he would assume a wide stance, place his hands on his hips, and proceed to vomit copious amounts of water through the air in a fountaining arc. After several lengthy dousings, the regurgitator would be empty and the fire completely extinguished. Generous applause would follow. Sometimes there would be a standing ovation.

Despite the popularity of such a spectacle, and its reliable ability to pack in a crowd, one by one every theatre on the vaudeville circuit banned the act. The open flame wasn't the problem, nor all the spilled water. These could easily be handled by an attentive cleaning crew and a mop. It was all the gastric juices that came up with the water and splashed everywhere. It ruined the hardwood stage floors, leaving an unsightly yellow film before the booking finished playing its first week. That simply wouldn't do. Once the climactic show-stopping trick of the top regurgitator acts was universally banned, the rapid decline of the art form was officially underway. At least until the next breed of vomiting neo-vaudvillians brought it back from the dead.

It was a brave new world for the likes of Barfo. Everything old was new again, like a renaissance fair for forgotten freak shows. Unfortunately, The Fireman act would have to wait for a renaissance man a little braver than Barfo, because he was opting to end with The Fisherman instead—a trick considerably safer, but arguably much more disgusting.

At last the carpet bag's purpose was revealed. That was where the fish bowl filled with tap water and a lone goldfish was stashed. Barfo lifted the bowl from its hiding place and placed it on a small table that had been set out for him on the stage. He unscrewed the top and set it aside, exposing the surface of the water. His tuxedo jacket proved to be home to the last of his props—a pet-store fish net. There was more wordless visual comedy in the offing as Barfo made a production of chasing the goldfish around the barren bowl with the net. Finally cornering and capturing it, he scooped the fish out and plopped it into his free hand.

Barfo juggled the wriggling wet fish, pretending he might accidentally drop it at any moment. Suddenly, as if to avoid such an accident, he popped it into his mouth for safekeeping. The move was so quick, the audience wasn't sure if he'd really done it or had merely hidden the fish up his sleeve. There was a smattering of uncertain laughter that was quickly replaced with howls of revulsion as Barfo let the flicking tail of the fish slip out between his lips and wave at the audience. Hearty laughter was the final, intended reaction, as the audience responded to its own initial sickened response. After swilling the fish around in his mouth and allowing it to poke out at the audience head- or tail-first a few more times, Barfo swallowed in exaggerated fashion and opened his mouth to show the live goldfish had made the final plunge.

The now-familiar routine of bodily contortions began, half of them practical, half in the name of theatrics. They ended, once more, with the obligatory double chest-thump, at which point Barfo casually spat the fish back into its home bowl like a cowboy hocking a wad of tobacco into a saloon's spittoon. The fish dove straight to the bottom but didn't resume swimming as expected. Instead it remained momentarily motionless before slowly tilting over onto its side and drifting back up to float at the surface. The applause that had begun at the reappearance of the fish quickly dissipated and was replaced by confused murmurs from the crowd. When Barfo noticed the state of his aquatic assistant, he took a curt bow and snapped the lid back on the bowl. With his back to his audience, Barfo quickly packed his props away in his bag and retreated from the stage.

"The Amazing Barfo," bellowed the evening's announcer, taking the stage and covering for the performer's abrupt exit. There was applause and a few hoots for the end of the act, but nothing that came close to the fervour Barfo had effortlessly commanded just a few short minutes ago. The next band was encouraged to start playing as soon as possible in an effort to smooth over the fact that Barfo's grand finale had bombed.

"So what do you think?" asked Rebecca, as a trio of electric guitarists started tuning their instruments or playing their biggest hit—I couldn't determine which.

"I hate you," I told her. She took it in stride and passed me another gifted beer that had just arrived at our table.

Barfo was the last of the performance artists that evening. At Rebecca's insistence we suffered through the final set of the final band, and its uncalled-for encore, lingering past closing so she could introduce me to her recent discovery.

"Stay here," she said, as the place slowly began to empty out. "I'm going to go see about arranging a meet-and-greet."

"Really, don't put yourself to any trouble," I told her. "Let's just finish our drinks and go."

I tossed down the dregs of my beer.

"See? Finished. Let's go."

"Come on, when have I ever steered you wrong?" she said, wearing her best doe-eyed expression of innocence.

"I think the problem comes from your trying to steer me at all."

But I made no further move to get up and leave. Rebecca seized my implied consent and filtered into the departing crowd, slicing through the mob on her way to the backstage area where they kept the bathrooms and dressing rooms.

The lines for the toilets must have been unbearable. Women were openly using the men's room in order to empty their bladders and vacate the venue as efficiently as possible. By the time Rebecca returned, there was hardly anyone left in the place. The only remaining customers were the ones who had poorly timed their final round and didn't want to abandon the last couple of fingers of their overpriced and watered-down beverages.

Rebecca plopped herself in the chair opposite me and gave me an ashen stare. She looked a bit ill. Maybe all the free drinks were finally catching up with her.

"I need another drink," was the next thing she said.

"Really? You're going to pay for a round yourself?"

"No. This one's on you," she insisted so firmly I didn't dare deny her.

Rebecca said nothing as we waited for her stiff double to arrive. She sipped at it persistently once she had it, like a baby with a bottle. And still she said nothing, lost either in thought or one of her trademark mood swings. I couldn't determine which. Either way she made for lousy company once she drank herself into this sort of stupor.

"Look, I'd love to sit here all night and talk each other's ears off, but I have some work I have to get up for by the crack of noon. If your guy isn't interested in this social engagement you have in mind, I'll just be..."

"My guy? Right. Him," muttered Rebecca, as if vaguely recalling the whole purpose of this outing.

She looked around at the dwindling signs of life. It was a quarter past three in the morning, and the stragglers left in Gallery Nowhere were mostly staff, the friends of staff, and a few of the evening's acts who had no place better to be. Now that the paying customers had thinned, the performers were filtering out from their backstage cubbyholes to pack up their gear and grab whatever drinks the house was still willing to comp them. The regurgitator was among them. His tuxedo was rolled up and tucked away in his carpet bag, and he'd changed into some regular street clothes. Rebecca flagged him over and there was a flash of recognition on his face. I still didn't see much benefit in having a formal introduction, but Rebecca insisted, and few people had the strength of will to refuse her. Me least of all.

"Be nice," she said, a plea rather than a command. "Don't do anything too fucked up, okay?"

"I'll try to restrain myself," was the only promise I was willing to make.

The regurgitator arrived at our table with a small entourage. I knew them all by sight, a few by name—bookers and managers associated with the gallery. One of them stretched out an arm and proudly proclaimed, "May I present The Amazing Barfo."

Handshakes were exchanged all around. Since I was the only complete stranger at the table, the regurgitator took an extra moment to get familiar.

"You can just call me 'Barfo.'"

"I'm not calling you 'Barfo,'" I told him.

"Okay. 'Tom' will do," he reluctantly compromised.

"This is Rip," Rebecca said, referring to me, "Rip Eulogy."

Look, I never said my professional name didn't have its fair share of cheese.

"Oh, yeah?" said Tom, recognizing an obvious alias when he heard one, "What sort of act do you do?"

"I don't have an act," I stated coldly.

"Shtick then."

"I don't have a shtick either," I replied, adding some additional frost to my tone.

"You totally have a shtick," Rebecca laughed at my expense, suggesting a much more intimate familiarity with my trade than she actually possessed. She had slipped into her social-drinking mode. In such circumstances, some people were the designated driver, some the designated table-dancer. Rebecca always cast herself as the designated conversation lightener. She took it as her sacred duty to keep the mood at a table frothy and fun. This involved filling awkward silences with giddy chatter, linking non sequiturs back to the topic at hand, and defusing tension between people set on disliking each other. She was masterful at it, although this night she seemed off her game, unable to summon her usual verve.

It was made clear that Rebecca thought Tom and I might mutually benefit from knowing each other. How or why was never explained to me, but Rebecca was quick to remind me of my disorganized but extensive database of all sorts of magicians, tricksters, and soothsayers that had passed through local theatres. Many of them had showed little promise or talent, so why then wouldn't I want to add a proficient young vomiter of undeniable ability to my collection? Before I could articulate any of my numerous good reasons, Tom took his cue.

"Let me give you my card," he said, pulling one out of his breast pocket and handing it to me. I was reluctant to take it, but was grateful, at least, that he didn't puke it into my lap.

"The Amazing Barfo, Regurgitator Extraordinaire, Vomitorious Expert, Master of Expectoration," announced the card in flowing type, followed by contact information that included phone, email and URL. The reverse featured a cartoon approximation of Barfo himself, hurling a torrent of green sick into a puddle at his feet. The artwork was cute in an ironic sort of way, and ironic in an irritating sort of way. I resisted the urge to tear it up immediately, stuffing it into my pants pocket instead as a token gesture of politeness.

A sharp poke in the ribs with her elbow informed me that Rebecca thought I should reciprocate. I retrieved my own silver-plated business-card case and selected one to pass back to Tom. He studied the white-on-black text carefully, though there was little to read.

Rip Eulogy, Necromancer

That was all it said. I'd made sure to give him the version with no contact information. I rarely answered my own phone, but I didn't want to burden my secretary with calls from people I never wanted to hear from again.

"You know, I can't say I've ever seen a necromancer act," said Tom after much consideration.

"That's because it's not an act. It's a profession," I told him.

"Necromancer, huh? That has something to do with death, right?"

"It has a lot to do with death."

"I guess I could have used a necromancer tonight. I totally died on stage," said Tom, attempting a joke.

"You're not the only one."

Tom stared back blankly. He was so busy feeling like a victim, he'd already forgotten about the real casualty of the evening. I nodded at the open carpet bag resting at his feet. Inside, next to the wadded up tuxedo, was the sealed fish bowl with its dead occupant still floating on its side.

"So what happened to your little friend?"

Tom looked genuinely embarrassed about his performance gaffe. He'd had the audience in the palm of his hand and lost them to a moment's error in stagecraft.

"I fucked up. I wanted to hold him half-way down, but I slipped and sent him all the way to my stomach. There wasn't enough water to buffer him from the acid. Even if they're not down there long, they can go into shock and die in just a couple of seconds."

"Have you tried swallowing something a little more hearty? A turtle perhaps? Or maybe a small dog?"

Tom ignored the fact that I was trying to tweak his balls.

"I like to stick with the tried and true. Fish get a good audience reaction. The act works better with a fish."

"Unless you're the fish."

Rebecca tried to defuse the tension I was purposely building for my own amusement.

"Who's up for shooters?" she suggested, hoping her mock enthusiasm for more drinks would be contagious. "I bet Tom wouldn't mind swallowing something he doesn't have to bring back up."

I was having none of it, and resumed poking Tom in his bruised performer's ego.

"Look, if you're not one hundred percent with your live-animal act, strap on some training wheels and work with a pet rock. You won't have to go down to an Aquarama outlet after every show looking to recruit a new assistant."

That bit of prodding seemed to work. I thought I saw Tom wince, wounded.

"It was the first time this ever happened to me. On stage."

"What's your body count including rehearsals?"

"You're not going all PETA on me, are you?"

"No, not at all," I said. "You can drag a barrel of fish onto the stage and start unloading a shotgun into it for all I care. I'm just saying killing little critters in front of an audience will turn them on you pretty damn fast. It's not like an escape act with a guy in chains dunked in a water tank. The audience half wants him to fail so they can be shocked and horrified by a real death during a live performance. That's a story they'll tell their friends. But killing animals? They'll be shocked. They'll be horrified. But they'll also be angry. That's no good for repeat business."

"Rebecca tells me you're some sort of magician," said Tom. "Have you played many venues in town?"

"I've been to them all. I see every act that comes through here. But I've never been on stage in my life."

"So you're not speaking from experience," Tom jabbed back.

"I'm speaking as a connoisseur," I replied. "Look, I've seen my share of magic-show fatalities over the years. A dead dove or two, probably suffocated while they were waiting to appear in a puff of smoke. One magician killed his trick rat in front of everybody when it bit him. Then there was the rabbit, which wasn't even the magician's fault. I think it just got stressed out for no apparent reason and died of a heart attack. You want to see an audience turn against an act fast, kill a bunny. That one got ugly."

"I'll keep that in mind for when I'm selling out stadiums."

Tom tried to cut our chat short, turning to someone else, eager to change the subject. I decided to draw him back in. I folded my arms and looked up at the rafters, contemplatively.

"No, there's only one way you can pull off killing a cute little animal on stage and not have the audience want to lynch you."

My tone was purposely rhetorical, as though what I was considering was for my own benefit alone.

"Do tell," said Tom, with as much skeptical disdain as he could muster. But his curiosity was piqued.

"You bring it back."

Tom spent a long moment looking confused. It suited him.

"What do you mean, 'You bring it back?' Back from where?"

"Back from the dead."

"What, like you have an identical one in your back pocket or something and you make the switch after some hocus-pocus?"

"I'm not talking smoke and mirrors. I'm talking resurrection."

"Like a Lazarus act?"

"Yeah, but for real. No faking."

Tom laughed and looked around at the others at the table for support. No one else was laughing. If they didn't know me, they knew my reputation.

"You think I should have performed CPR on my goldfish?"

"That I'd pay to see. But no, heart massage and some mouth-to-mouth is not going to raise your fish from the dead."

"What then?"

"A simple incantation. Nothing fancy. It's just a fish."

Rebecca knew this conversation wouldn't stay theoretical for long. She'd seen me engaged in this sort of pissing match before and it nearly ruined our friendship. Memories of that outcome still give her the occasional sleepless night.

"Rip, don't," she warned.

Neither of us was willing to back down now and we both ignored Rebecca's plea for civility.

"Please, you know so much about showbiz," said Tom, dripping contempt, "show me."

Tom reached into his bag and pulled out the bowl. He popped the top off and held it out towards me like a beggar's cup. The dead fish floated limply on its side, staring up at me with a single profiled eye. Tom sloshed the contents around in circles, like he was trying to tempt me with the scent of a delicious bowl of hot noodles. I knew I should let it slide, but the sarcasm in his voice, the sarcasm in his gesture, had the desired effect and I let myself be baited.

"As you wish."

I played it cool, but I was eager to slap that smug look off his face. Tom was sure I'd bullshitted my way into a corner, and he wasn't going to let me out until I'd made a fool of myself.

I reached into the bowl and scooped out the dead fish. Holding it by the tail, I gave it a sharp flick to relieve it of any excess moisture, and then laid it down across one of the cardboard beer coasters on the table. As the moist fish stained the logo of some obscure microbrewery, I retrieved my kit of short-notice essentials I kept in my jacket pocket. I often stepped out without a phone, but never without my kit. Everything I was likely to need on a call was stuffed into the many pockets of a single zippered leather case that was the size and shape of a lady's wallet. In fact, it was probably designed to be a lady's wallet, but years of use and abuse had left the leather a cracked and well-worn tan colour, rendering the design neutral and non-descript. I set it out on the table and spread it open like a book.

"Your hand, please," I said to Tom, holding out my own.

He took my hand without comment. Whatever trick I was pulling, he was willing to play his part as volunteer, assistant or stooge. He knew every act has its routine. There was no need to question the details.

Once I had his hand, I selected a sewing pin from my kit and jabbed it into the tip of one of his fingers. He wasn't expecting it and struggled to withdraw his hand.

"Ow! What the fuck?"

I held on tight—long enough to squeeze a single drop of blood from the wound. It fell onto the head of the soggy fish, dissipating across the wet scaly surface and seeping into its gills. That, I figured, would offer enough penetration to begin. I released Tom's hand.

"Sorry. Normally I'd use my own blood, but he's your fish. I'm not binding him to me."

One of the pockets of my kit contained a selection of Band-Aids. I offered one to Tom but he declined, opting instead to suck on his pricked finger with an annoyed expression on his face.

"I'll have that drink now," I told Rebecca.

"A shooter?"

"No. Straight shot. You like Sambuca right?"

"I do," she confirmed. "Anyone else?"

The others at the table shook their heads. They weren't drinking. Rebecca turned back to me.

"White good? Or a red?"

"Whatever they have. I don't care."

Rebecca ordered two shots of white Sambuca which were delivered in moments. The other customers were gone now and the gallery was deserted, but the remaining staff was still willing to serve a regular. Rebecca paid for her first round of the entire evening and passed me one of the two shot glasses. She immediately downed hers in a single gulp and, only then, noticed I wasn't joining her.

Instead of drinking my shot, I dipped my thumb and first two fingers into the alcohol and drew a wet circle around the fish on the coaster. I had to dip my fingers a couple more times and go over the line again to make sure it was unbroken. On my last dip, I drew a simple sigil on the table between myself and the fish.

"Here. You can have the rest," I said, pushing the shot glass with the remaining Sambuca towards Rebecca.

"I don't want it after you dipped your fishy fingers in it!" she balked, picking up the glass and moving it to a neighbouring vacant table. Such a waste. I knew I wouldn't need the entire shot, which was the only reason I ordered one of her favourites. Any drink with a high enough level of ethanol would have done.

I've never smoked, but I always carry a lighter—another kit essential. Being able to make fire on short notice is handy, even when you're not conducting an arcane ritual.

"Mortem resuscitet," I said to nobody in particular. Flipping open my lighter, I touched the flame to my alcoholic table art. It ignited with a soft poof. Everyone at the table leapt back, startled, whether they were expecting it or not. Chuckles at their own reaction followed as the low circular blaze licked the air and made a permanent scorch mark in the laminated wood.

"Was that, like, your version of 'Abracadabra?'" joked the talent booker sitting across from me.

"As incantations go, this one's a little more specific."

The flames died out quickly, consuming the thin sheen of Sambuca but finding no viable fuel in the flat, dense hardwood below. As the last hint of fire burned away there was movement on the table. It was almost imperceptible, but if you looked closely you could see the goldfish's gills starting to rise and fall, gasping for air it couldn't process and didn't need. Most of the people at the table missed this initial sign of life, but everyone took notice the first time the dead fish flipped over on the coaster. They all jumped in their seats. One grown man cried out like a frightened little girl. I'll be generous and call it a yelp rather than a scream.

"Holy fucking shit!" was the general consensus as the fish continued to flop around with ever increasing vigour.

Before it could get too restless, I picked up the coaster by one corner and flipped the fish back into its bowl. It splashed around for a few moments before finding its equilibrium, and then proceeded to swim laps around the glass globe in a frenzy.

"What's the trick?" one of the Barfo entourage wanted to know.

"No trick," I told him. "You saw what I did, you heard what I said. Simple, really."

"Just don't try this at home," I felt obliged to add.

"It's all fun and games until somebody starts a zombie apocalypse, right?"

Rebecca's snide comment inspired a few worried looks on the other side of the table.

"She's kidding," I assured them. "A resurrection incantation can't start a zombie apocalypse. But seriously, don't try this at home. Very bad things can happen."

The fish ricocheted around the bowl like a rifle bullet, gaining energy and velocity with each impact against the glass. Tom hurried to clamp the lid back on to keep it from flying out the top. He needn't have bothered. The same moment he got the top secured, the fish blew through the side of the bowl, shattering it and sending water and broken glass splashing across the table.

"How the hell do you stop it?" yelled Tom over the growing commotion at the table.

"You don't. Which is one of the many reasons you shouldn't try this at home."

Any deceased creature newly resurrected is bound to have some birthing pains, but it soon became apparent that this specimen was more agitated than usual. I'd never done a goldfish before. The problem, I discovered, with bringing back a creature that has only a three-second memory capacity, is that all it remembers from life is its dying moments in horrible agony. Now that it was back from the dead, physically reanimated but incapable of forming new memories, its entire existence was made up of an endless three-second loop of boiling to death in the Amazing Barfo's stomach acids. No wonder it was freaking out. Oh well, live and learn. I decided that the next time I resurrected some lower life form, I'd try to choose something that would return with a few fond recollections of what it was like to be alive.

Tom seemed badly shaken. This wasn't the sort of chicanery he'd been expecting. While the others merely watched the fish flop about violently with varying degrees of aghast looks on their faces, Tom chased the fish all over the table, through puddles of water and shards of broken glass, trying to wrestle it under control. Perhaps he felt responsible. It was his fish, his victim.

There was no holding it down. The goldfish would not be contained, subdued, quelled or quashed. Tom couldn't keep a grip on it for more than a moment, and his futile efforts only made things worse. The fish's violent thrashing was eventually met with equal violence from Tom himself as he started to pound the table with his fist, trying to mash it in place. The fish wouldn't hold still for a moment, and it was like watching a sick variant of a whack-a-mole game at the carnival. Despite making contact a few times, there was no hint of it slowing down, and the fish finally ended up on the floor where it continued thrashing.

Tom looked around for something to beat the fish back to death with and finally resorted to kicking off his own shoe and hammering away at it like he was trying to drive a nail through the floorboards. I knew it wouldn't work. The fish was alive again, not just in a single-entity sense, but on a full-bodied cellular level. Mere abuse wasn't going to do the trick, but I didn't bother trying to tell Tom this. His manic efforts to usher his pet back to the void were too damn amusing. I don't often get a good laugh in my line of work. Mostly it can be pretty grim. But sometimes… sometimes it has its moments.

Rebecca couldn't see the humour it.

"Okay, I'm ready to call it a night," she said wearily, rising from the table. Nobody else took any notice of her. They were too busy watching the merciless beat-down happening on the gallery's floor. Tom outmatched his opponent by a hundred IQ points and nearly two hundred pounds, but he was losing just the same. That fish was going to outlast him and outlive him. Probably by centuries.

I joined Rebecca as she made for the stairs.

"That's the last time I take you out for drinks and a show," she informed me.

"Promise?"

We were out on the street a few moments later. The thump-thump-thump of the music was gone now, replaced by the thump-thump-thump of the Amazing Barfo futilely trying to flatten his fish into something that would die, or at least stop moving.

"That was you being restrained?" asked Rebecca.

"Hey, I'm not the guy who went freaky on the fish. I just brought it back to take a bow."

"You didn't make a very good first impression."

"That's fine because it was also a last impression."

"You're not going to use him?" Rebecca sounded genuinely surprised.

"What makes you think I would have any use for a god-damn regurgitator?"

"I don't know. I thought it was a pretty cool talent."

"Your definition of 'talent' is looser than mine."

In my line of work, people tossing their cookies is a problem, not an asset. I can't tell you the number of times I've called in an assistant or a consultant on a job, only to have them sprint off to the nearest sink or toilet with their hand clamped over their mouth as soon as they had a look at what I was working on. I need to be able to rely on people with unique and applicable gifts. And I need them to be able to keep their lunch down.

"You'll keep his number though, right?"

The card was still in my pocket where I'd stuffed it. Just to let Rebecca believe the evening was somehow productive, I agreed to hold onto it.

"I'll file it with Gladys. She keeps track of all this shit."

Even though we were headed in the same general direction, Rebecca decided we weren't going to share a cab. We'd had enough of each other's company for one evening.

Chapter Two

State of Being

NECROMANCY GETS A BAD RAP. It's the redheaded step-child among the many schools of magic. It creeps people out, pure and simple. The sorcerers are the ones who get all the attention with their flashy spells that light up the night and glow pretty colours as they shoot through the air and make things go boom. Illusionists get all the pussy, those smarmy showmen who always need a lovely volunteer from the audience to help them weave their webs of mass distraction—a volunteer who will inevitably join them in their hotel room after the show has left her drunk on adulation.

But there's no love for the necromancer.

Maybe I'm bitter because there's nothing in my own bag of tricks that can easily translate into a viable stage act. I'm not a medium. I can't select random people in the crowd and put them in touch with their deceased loved ones. Oh sure, I can talk to the dead just fine. But I need to be in the room with them. And wheeling some stinky, maggoty old corpse onto the stage for a post-mortem interview isn't likely to play well with the audience—or the municipal board of health.

Some people think being able to speak with the dead is a gift. Some consider it a curse. It's neither. Mostly fucking boring is what it is. The dead go on about the same tedious crap the living do, only more so. Usually they want to know what they've missed, and they don't have to be dead long to have missed a lot. What's been happening on their favourite soap operas, which B-grade celebrity got divorced from or married to which C-grade celebrity, and did their hometown team make the playoffs? I don't even follow sports, so when they ask me about a team, I rarely know which game they're referring to. I just tell them they're on a winning streak and that puts them in a good mood. It's easier for me to get what I need from the dead if they're in a good mood, so I'm happy to tell them lies. It's not like they're going to crawl out of their graves to check the sports page and see that I'm bullshitting them.

The dead are usually in a pretty pissy mood. Being dead is a major factor in this. Wishes unfulfilled, promises unkept, lives unlived. Regrets, regrets, and more regrets. Given enough time to sum it all up, who wouldn't be in a poor mood? And the dead have plenty of time on their hands. Time enough to fume and simmer and grow deeply bitter. Then I come along. I'm not necessarily the first person to talk to them since they got planted in the ground. People do still swing by gravesites to have a one-sided chat with their deceased loved ones. But I'm the first in years who can actually listen to them. And boy do I get an earful.

It was a corpse interview that took me to a stately funeral home the next afternoon. After a late night at Gallery Nowhere, I was barely able to crawl out of bed by half-past one. I skipped breakfast and a shower and was still nearly late to the party. By the time I met my client in the reception hall, the funeral was only five minutes away. It was barely enough time to get the job done, but I was determined to try. I didn't want to hang around for the ceremony. I wasn't appropriately dressed, and all that praying and sermonizing gives me the heebie-jeebies.

"You're late, Mr. Eulogy," my client told me, checking his watch like I billed by the hour.

"Don't call me the late Mr. Eulogy in a funeral parlour," I said.

"Bad form?"

"No, bad pun. I hate puns."

"Well I hate tardiness, so that makes us even."

Yeah, my client was a dick. Clients often are, but this one had been enough of a pain in my ass that I wasn't interested in any repeat business from him, no matter how large or rich his family was or how many of them already had one foot in the grave. Whatever service you're offering the public, it's inevitable that some of the people who hire you are going to be high maintenance. If they're paying you for a job, they think they own you, even though all you're selling them is your expertise and a bit of time. Jeremy Saunders was one of those task masters who didn't know where the line was and kept crossing it so often it was starting to feel intentional. The preliminary consult had been an endless barrage of questions and queries. He wanted all sorts of credentials and references, which are things I never provide. My other clients expect confidentiality, and they don't need some newbie skeptic asking them probing questions about what I did for them. As for the credentials, there's nothing I do that I'd care to put on a résumé, and there aren't any schools of higher learning that hand out diplomas with pretty gold seals, guaranteeing I'm qualified to go probing into eternity.

With our unpleasant pleasantries out of the way, Saunders led me to a viewing room where the closest family members were packed in thick and tearful. The dead man had kicked off at the ripe old age of ninety-four, so it could hardly have come as much of a shock to anyone. Still, the hankies were out, meaning at least some of the kids and grandkids and great-grandkids must have liked him. Jeremy Saunders was one of the few who didn't give a shit. I understood this was his uncle through marriage, so I guess you could excuse him for not being particularly choked up about it. What I couldn't excuse was the outright glee he could barely contain when I told him over our first meeting that yes, I could obtain the information he wanted from his late uncle. For a retainer and a finder's fee.

The corpse was lying in state at the head of the room in a very pricey open casket, with enough wreaths to make the room stink like a perfume factory. Maybe I was being a sentimentalist when I attributed all the sniffling and blowing to genuine grief. It could have just been an allergic reaction that ran in the family. Mourning or not, they'd all have to leave if I was going to get the job done. That was one of the reasons I usually prefer to handle this sort of interview graveside, after everyone has dispersed and gone home. Making contact through six feet of dirt can be challenging, but I like the privacy and extra time a late-night visit to a cemetery offers. And if I find I'm dealing with an uncooperative corpse, or I'm getting poor reception through too much earth, there's always the shovel.

This was one of the cases that necessitated a trip to a funeral parlour or a morgue. Samuel S. Higgins, deceased, was going from his thickly attended funeral straight to the crematorium where the oven would undo all the fine and expensive work the embalmers and makeup artists had accomplished on his remains. That alone didn't screw me up too badly. I can talk to ashes, I'm that good. But Mr. Higgins had a busy day ahead of him. From the crematorium he was going straight to some scenic vista his family had selected for him, where his ashes were to be scattered into the wind.

Ashes are challenging but doable. I can't do shit with them if they're scattered, though.

"Excuse me, everyone, can I have your attention?" I said in my loudest, most commanding voice. "The funeral will commence shortly. Perhaps you can start making your way towards the chapel."

That got the most mobile mourners heading for the door. The old and infirm lingered with their handlers.

"I'll have to ask you to please clear the room," I told them in a softer, but no less commanding voice once the numbers had thinned. "We'll need a few moments alone with the deceased."

I was still wearing last night's club clothes. I'm not a fancy dresser, but my ensemble was a bit loud for a funeral. Since nobody recognized me and I wasn't dressed as a mourner, I let them all assume I was somebody connected with the funeral logistics—a casket salesmen making sure they got the model they paid for, or a manager from the hearse company confirming the embalming job wouldn't leak and spoil my upholstery. Whatever incorrect conclusion each of them was formulating to explain why they were being kicked out of their viewing room by a stranger, they were all convinced to take their tears and tissues elsewhere for the next few minutes.

I shut the double doors behind the last of them and locked the top and bottom doorjamb bolts in place so we wouldn't be disturbed. As always, my kit was close at hand, but it looked like there was nothing I required from it on this call. With the body on display, I didn't need the key. The so-called casket key is more of a winch really, with a handle on one end and a hexagonal head on the other. It's like an Allen key for coffins, one-size-fits-most. They're used to lock the casket before burial, or crank the corpse up or down for viewing. I don't have to open a box to make contact, but if it's closed I like to take a peek inside just to make sure I'm dealing with the right remains. You'd be surprised how often funeral homes wheel the wrong bodies into closed-casket services. I can understand families opting for a closed casket. Not everybody wants to look at their loved one made up like a Kewpie doll and stuffed in a box. But between you and me, here's an insider tip: always have someone in the family check to make sure you got the corpse you paid for. Assuming you care, of course. Many don't. Dead is dead, gone is gone, and funerals are for the living.

Hovering over the body of Sam Higgins, I recognized him from the photo in the online obituary. I usually just scan obituaries for anything that's specifically relevant to a job, but this one I read properly. Higgins had accomplished a lot in his life. Self-made businessman, entrepreneur, philanthropist—all the titles you would expect from his public stature. More anecdotally, he liked to paint landscapes, was an avid golfer, and also something of a mountaineer. Well, at least he climbed a mountain once. Kilimanjaro, which I understand you can just walk up if you have a few days to spare. Still, it's a real mountain. I'll never climb one.

What the text didn't mention was how much money he'd made, but it must have been considerable. Movers and shakers of his calibre never land in a pauper's grave. I don't know what the will said, but there was a lot of money to spread around, and a lot of inheritors waiting on a cheque. With a complex estate like this, the executor would have his hands full of paperwork and legalese for the next two or three years before anyone saw a dime. Saunders wasn't the patient sort. He probably had a good chunk of money coming, but he wanted the estate to start paying off immediately. That's where I came in.

"Mr. Higgins," I said aloud, "Mr. Samuel Higgins."

Simply saying the deceased's name is usually enough to get a response if you're tuned to the right wavelength, which I just happen to be. This time, though, I got nothing. Nothing at all. The ether's version of a dial tone.

I tried again, repeating his name in both formal and familiar terms. He didn't answer to anything. Not "Samuel, Sam, Sammy" or, "Hey, Higgins!"

"Problem?" asked Saunders. He was getting the same sinking feeling I got from the first non-response.

"There's nothing I can do. He's not there," I told the client.

"What do you mean, 'He's not there?' He's lying right in front of you."

"There's tissue to work with, but nobody's home. Was there an autopsy?"

"I don't know that!" he barked at me, like it was somehow an offensive question.

I loosened the stiff's tie and took a peek down his neckline. I could see the shabby stitch job at the tips of the tell-tale V-shaped scar that ended at his collar bones. They usually don't bother cutting up somebody this old. The cause of death is often age-related pneumonia or some other lesser ailment they were too weak to fight off. But sometimes there's a lingering question or two, or the medical examiner is bored, or he's breaking in some intern and it's been a slow death day.

"Yeah, they cut him," I pronounced, and made a cursory attempt to straighten the tie.

It turned out the casket key had a use on this call after all. I stuck the key end in its slot on the side of the box and cranked the upper half of the body higher so I could get a look at the top of Sam Higgins's head. The incision was mostly hidden by the hair that had been carefully combed back down, but pushing aside a couple of tufts, I saw where the skin had been cut and the bone had been sawed through.

The skull cap had been returned, stitched back in place, masked and made up for the funeral, but the damage done was obvious on close inspection. I cranked the body back down to its original position.

"Just as I thought," I announced. "I can't make contact if he hasn't got his marbles."

Every autopsy it's the same deal. Whether it's called for or not, they cut into the skull, scoop out the brain, measure it, weigh it, and enter the data. What good any of that does, I have no idea, but for my purposes it's incredibly destructive. If only they popped it back in, it would give me something to work with. But more often than not, they toss it, along with any other internal organs they saw fit to remove and examine. I don't give a shit if it's a kidney or a liver, but a missing brain really narrows my options. I figured the dead man's mind was probably roasting in some medical-waste incinerator while I was stuck trying to make contact with an empty shell.

I knew Saunders wasn't going to take the news well, so I started working on my departure right away. I didn't feel like lingering to hear my soon to be ex-client piss and moan about my coming up empty. Sometimes clients are understanding in these situations. If they already had low expectations about getting what they needed from their dead relatives, they're at least glad I didn't try to string them a line of crap or make something up on the spot. We depart amicably, and they never call with work again. No hard feelings. That's how it goes sometimes. But I knew Saunders wasn't going to be one of the understanding ones.

"That's it? You're giving up?"

I was already across the room, unbolting the doors.

"There's nothing I can do. Not with what they left me."

I barely listened to the barrage of entitled indignity that was hurled at me in the time it took to let myself out of the room. Despite my better judgment, I tried to leave Saunders with a metaphor that could help him grasp the situation.

"It's like if you hired a mechanic to fix your car. I can put air in the tires, I can align the steering, I can tune the brakes. If you want, I can even wash it, wax it, give it a new paint job. Whatever. But if it doesn't have an engine, it's never going to run again, and there's nothing I can do to change that."

Saunders stared back at me. My little parable wasn't getting through to him, but at least it made him shut up for a moment. I took the opportunity to turn and weave my way through the family of mourners lingering just outside the door.

"You're a fuckin' fraud, you know that?" is the last thing I heard him shout at me across the reception hall of the funeral home.

I made a mental note to deposit Saunders's retainer cheque in the nearest available bank machine before he could try to cancel it. Even if I didn't get the job done, I'd earned my retainer. I didn't need some dissatisfied douchebag trying to screw me out of it because he thought he got conned. Bad word of mouth would probably end up costing me much more than his measly down payment anyway.

Sometimes the job gets ugly, and normally I keep the hell away from funeral parlours in order to avoid public spectacles like that. When I'm scrounging up work, which is pretty much always, I don't like to peddle my wares at funerals. I know that sounds counterintuitive, but I find it to be tacky and ill-timed—like the lowlife lawyers who hang out in emergency rooms waiting for a juicy negligence-injury case. You don't want to get a reputation as a hearse-chaser. Most people who hire a necromancer need enough time and space to realize they could use the services of one on their own. Funerals are for grief and sorrow. I wait for all that raw, tearful emotion to dissipate, and strike once the greed sets in. Will readings and estate sales are where I go to pass out my business card. Once a mourner's mind switches to cashing in on the deceased, they're ready to talk shop with the likes of me.

Few are the people who go to their graves without any secrets. And a lot of these secrets are ones that the living left behind are dying to know. Often, it's answers to personal questions they're after. Who was my biological father? Did you ever really love me? Why didn't you believe me when I told you uncle Bob was touching me inappropriately? I can help with these for a fee. But the real payday comes from discovering the location of off-shore bank accounts, squirrelled-away cash and jewellery, and backyard-buried bullion. Extracting this sort of information from beyond the grave earns me my usual fee plus a percentage of the recovered wealth. It doesn't amount to much if all I find is a penny jar stuck up in the attic of some dead retiree's bungalow, but I can make out like a bandit if I score a hitherto unknown tax shelter in the Cayman Islands. That's what Saunders had been after—a suspected tax-dodge account in some foreign land, so secret it wasn't even in the will. With the right numbers, he was hoping to cash in on some hefty funds he wouldn't have to share with the rest of the family. Just with me. Losing my finder's fee on this one hurt, even if I didn't know what was in the account, or if the account ever actually existed. I missed the thrill of the hunt and that charge of excitement I got from digging up lost treasure. It had been a long time since I'd had a sizeable score. My last bit of successful forensic accounting only managed to turn up a dog-eared stamp collection overlooked and forgotten on the top shelf of a linen closet. The client unloaded it at a hobby shop for a hundred bucks. Who the fuck collects stamps anymore? I waived my percentage on that one. I was too embarrassed to go chasing after ten bucks.

"Another satisfied customer?" a familiar voice called to me as I pushed my way through the funeral home's front doors.

I looked back for the source. A lot of mourners were looking at me uncomfortably after Saunders had made his negative customer feedback so publicly clear. I almost didn't recognize Tracy in the sea of black, she melded into the mix of mourning so well. I was only able to spot her by expression alone. She was smiling, pleased to see me.

"You on a job?" I asked her.

Obviously she was. Tracy was in full-grief attire, conservative, tasteful, jet black. She wouldn't be at a funeral home otherwise. What I was really asking was if she was coming or going.

Tracy lifted the netted veil that hung from the brim of her hat so I could better see her face. Her eye makeup was streaked and ruined. Twin rivers of dried mascara ran down her cheeks. She'd been crying, but looked so cheerful you'd never notice without the tracks left behind by her tears.

"Just done," she told me.

"Coffee and shop talk?" I offered.

"Screw the coffee, you can buy me an ice cream."

Θ

I may not work funerals, but that doesn't mean I don't have a source of insider information. Tracy Poole is a professional moirologist who knows the scene back to front and can mourn in any religion, faith or orthodoxy. She's a goth girl, complete with the raven dye job, raccoon makeup, and tattoos up and down her arms and legs. But she cleans up well and will show up at your funeral looking very proper and respectable, complete with restrained lipstick, subtle eye shadow, and prim mourning attire covering all of her spider- and demon-themed ink.

Moirology is a dying art, which is probably what attracted Tracy to it in the first place. Back in the old days, mostly in the old world, professional mourners would hire themselves out to publicly perform acts of grief when someone prominent passed on. They were usually wizened women of incredible stamina who could wail and keen all night long, for days on end, keeping the level of sorrow at a fever pitch until all the family assembled from far and wide for the funeral. Following certain dogmatic religious doctrines, prayers and tears would be kept flowing throughout the period between the death and the burial, ensuring that pleas for mercy and forgiveness for the departed soul would be heard and impossible to ignore. The moirologists would only fall mercifully silent after the body was interred, everyone had gone home, and they had received their fee. By the time they had completed their duties, I'm sure they had little problem collecting the bill. Even if a client tried to stiff them on their payment, the whole village would have been willing to pass a hat and gather enough to get them to shut up.

Modern moirologists are a rarity and serve a somewhat different function today. Mostly, they're employed to keep up appearances by making a scene. Some families are simply too uptight, too restrained, to engage in any public displays of affection or anger, pleasure or pain. In most circumstances, this is fine. I've met a few families that should take lessons on how to tone down the high drama in public places. But often these restrained, uptight families are so self-conscious, they worry that their distant demeanor will come across as coldhearted at a funeral for one of their members. A moirologist can fix that, putting on a memorable display for any outsiders in attendance who might otherwise assume the deceased was unloved and the family indifferent. With a moirologist drawing all the attention, casual observers would go home remembering that at least one person at the funeral seemed deeply upset. They may even end up assuming that there were plenty of other sniffles and weeping going on that went unnoticed because of that one demonstrative mourner stealing the show. In time, their whole memory of the funeral will be skewed by that single anonymous moirologist, leaving an indelible impression of the heart-wrenching grief the deceased had inspired that day.

Tracy and I had hit it off a few years earlier during one of my rare funeral appearances. We were both on the job. For dramatic purposes she chose my shoulder to cry on, mostly by convenience of proximity, turning the sleeve of my best suit into a glistening slick of mucus. She apologized afterwards and paid for the dry cleaning. When she came by my apartment to deliver the freshly pressed jacket, I made a joke about leaving it in the dry cleaner's plastic wrap in case she felt another flood of tears coming on. She responded with a fondly remembered story about how her sister, who had always aspired to be an only child, used to give her plastic bags to play with as a kid and then suggest a game of Little Red Riding Hood. The sister would play the Wolf, Tracy would play Red, and the plastic bag would fill the role of Hood. Many hours of fairy-tale delight and near suffocation would ensue.

We kept in touch because some of her clients were likely candidates to be my clients next. I tried to reciprocate whenever I could. As it turned out, I knew plenty of unloved assholes who could have used someone squirting out a few crocodile tears at their wake. I hooked Tracy up with a long list of contacts who might have otherwise gone unmourned without her services. She made the rounds and secured a good number of retainers. All she had to do now was wait around for them to die off.

In her regular life Tracy is a bit of an emotional flatline, not particularly sad or happy, and never loud or hysterical.

But at a funeral, she lets it all hang out. In stark contrast to her understated mourning attire, she will weep and wail on command. She'll beat her chest, sob uncontrollably, and fill any number of funeral-home-brand tissues with snot and tears. For an extra fee, she'll throw herself onto the coffin in a fit of high drama, even going so far as to casket-dive into an open grave if that's what the client wants. I've had the privilege to see her at work on a few occasions, and she's absolutely convincing, even when she's taking it so far over the top it pushes the boundaries of plausible grief. The reason she's so good at what she does is that all the tears and anguish are genuine. They're not for the deceased stranger in the box. Tracy once shared her deepest trade secret with me—her take on method acting. Whenever she needs to do her thing at a church, in a funeral parlour, or at a gravesite, she digs deep into her own childhood trauma and dredges up the one memory that always pushes her over the edge into inconsolable convulsions. She thinks about *Charlotte's Web*. And that does the trick.

"You weren't at the parlour for the Higgins show, were you?" I asked Tracy over a couple of bowls of butterscotch ripple and a pair of plastic spoons.

"No," she said, "I was next door in Salon B. Petersen was the name. That show was a pre-deceased booking I've had it in my ledger for years. Booked by the corpse-to-be himself, back when he was still in fine health."

"Petersen, huh? Was that one of my referrals?"

"No, I scored him on my own. No finder's fee for you," Tracy winked, as she scraped at a promising canal in her ice cream. "I think the idea was to make his shrew of a wife jealous by having some young, gorgeous thing like me wailing over his coffin. You know how that one plays. Everyone assumes I'm the mistress he's had tucked away all this time, the widow is humiliated, and revenge is his…even if he's not there to enjoy it."

"Or maybe he was," I pointed out. Some souls linger to attend their own funerals. It's rare, but it happens. The body may die, but narcissism lives on.

"Well then, I gave him his money's worth, because the dagger-eyes were flying thick."

"Oh good. So not all the nasty looks back at the funeral home were necessarily directed at me."

"Get a helmet, Rip," Tracy scolded. "It's a tough business dealing in death. The people left behind can be a real bitch."

"Believe me, the dead ones can be just as bitchy."

"It's funny us running into each other like this. I just had a guy asking about you the other day at a funeral."

"Client?" I asked, trying not to sound too hopeful.

Tracy shrugged, uncertain.

"Just a guy, all in black."

"Of course he was in black. It was a funeral."

"This one really committed. I couldn't even see his face for all the black. Of course, I had my veil on. I can't see shit in that thing."

"Did he leave a number or an email address?"

"Nope. Just asked if I'd seen you around lately."

"It's not like I'm in hiding. I'm trying to run a business."

"You're a man of mystery, Rip," Tracy said, the sarcasm running thick. "Unknowable, unapproachable, unfathomable."

"And yet here I am, sitting in an ice-cream parlour with all the dull normals. Present company excepted," I was quick to add.

Tracy saluted me with her spoon and continued the onslaught against the scoop in her bowl.

"So does the mystery man have any good anecdotes to share?" she asked.

Tracy liked occupational horror stories. Not just from necromancers, though mine always seemed to amuse her. She'd be all ears if you had a juicy story about waiting tables, or washing windows, or toasting buns at a burger joint. Her only caveat was that it needed to be morbid. The grislier the better. Not too many people have a stomach-turning tale about their summer job as a filing clerk, which is why she liked to keep tabs on friends who worked as paramedics, addiction therapists, or necromancers. They could be relied upon to supply the goods.

I didn't have to think long to come up with a good one that had happened since last we spoke.

Chapter Three

Statute of Limitations

I WAS BETWEEN SECRETARIES, a couple of weeks short of hiring on Gladys, stuck dealing with my own calls. I hated being a slave to every incoming ring and would use any excuse to cut a conversation short, even a ring from another source I found only slightly less troublesome. In this case, it was the door buzzer interrupting one chat for another.

Rebecca was the one who had been nattering away on the phone. About what I have no recollection. The only reason I remember it was her I'd been on with, was the parting exchange of ritualistic banter. Sometimes the ties that bind old friendships are thin, but you cling to what works.

"I gotta go," I told her. "It's the door."

"You entertaining?"

"I try not to be."

"It must be work."

"Client," I confirmed. "I've got a rabbi coming over."

"Thinking of converting?"

"From what?"

"Right. I forgot," she said. "You're nothing."

"I just don't play for any team."

A second buzz announced a degree of impatience from my guest downstairs. I didn't want to be rude and keep him waiting, so I was rude to Rebecca instead, stepping on her next volley.

"Seriously, I have to get this. I won't call you back."

"Yeah, that goes…" was as far as she got before I disconnected.

I confirmed who my visitor was over the ancient crackling intercom that was first connected to the building's front hall when such technology was new and innovative. In my line of work you need to be careful about who or what you're inviting into your home. There are strict rules about this sort of thing, and you break or ignore them at your peril.

A couple of minutes after leaning on the button that remotely unlocked the main entry, I heard the elevator clunk to a halt on my floor and its gate rattle open. Through the spyhole of my apartment door, I saw the black hat and bushy grey beard of the man who had travelled a great distance to consult with me.

"Mr. Eulogy, what is your opinion on evil?" he asked, after we had exchanged greetings and I had made us both a pot of tea.

"Am I pro or con?"

"Do you believe it exists?"

"Only as a concept to explain actions most people can't or won't empathize with," I said.

Such chit-chat was a bit too theological for my tastes, but I figured it came with the territory when talking to a holy man. Members of the clergy didn't often seek me out. They usually think they have the whole life, death, and afterlife field cornered and don't want somebody like me intruding on their monopoly.

"I believe in evil, Mr. Eulogy, though I've never personally confronted it myself. I found my belief in the eyes of my father. He was a good man, a kind man. But when I looked in his eyes I could see what they had done to him. More than his stories or his scars, his nightmares or the number tattooed on his arm, it was his eyes that spoke of true evil. He had seen it in the ghettos and the camps and the mass graves. All of it was burned into them, as if he'd stared too long at the sun, or hell itself."

"There is no hell, Rabbi Reubenski. I've looked for it and it just isn't there."

"All the more reason to deliver punishment to the wicked ourselves," said the rabbi. "I am a Jew with no concept of a Christian hell. I believe in the tradition of *Gehinnom* for the lowest among us, as is our custom. But there are those who deserve far worse."

I had done some rudimentary research on my guest when he first booked an appointment, and I could guess what sort of person might be on his "wicked" list.

Aharon Reubenski's family name had been Reuben until shortly after the Second World War. When his father arrived at Ellis Island in 1947, he added "ski" to it. In a time when so many Jews around him were changing their names to something more western and Christian—an attempt by many to avoid further discrimination and abuse—Chaim Reuben went in the opposite direction. He wanted to wear his Judaism like a badge of honour. This was no yellow Star of David sewn into his overcoat by the Nazis, a brand for the cattle to be slaughtered, this was a statement of pride. "Reuben" was no longer Jewish enough for his tastes. When people heard his name, he wanted there to be no doubt; Chaim Reubenski was a Jew. Capital "J." Pushing his only son into rabbinical school was probably an extension of that, but Aharon becoming one of the world's foremost Nazi-hunters was his own doing. By the time he took up that cause, his father was already several years in his grave and had no say in the matter.

"I'm not in the justice business," I told Rabbi Reubenski. But he only sipped his tea, unmoved.

"We are all in the justice business, Mr. Eulogy. How we behave to each other on a daily basis, who we choose to love and trust, who we choose to mistreat and ostracize. These are all determinations we make based on our own sense of morality, and what we view as just and deserved treatment."

"I can accept justice as a concept," I said. "But I don't involve myself in doling out punishment."

"Do you not think there are those deserving punishment? The wicked, the evil?"

"I just don't think I'm qualified to be the one to judge."

"To judge their punishment, or whether or not they are evil?"

"Both, I guess."

"Are you sure you cannot pass judgement on the man behind this?" he said, sliding a manila envelope across my coffee table at me.

"What is it?" I asked, knowing from the size and shape it was almost certainly a collection of eight-by-ten photo prints.

"This is horror," he told me. "Unspeakable horror committed by a man who has already been judged and who has earned his punishment."

"Murder victims?"

"Mass-murder victims," he stated.

I took the envelope and slid the photos out into my hand. I knew he wouldn't be satisfied until I'd had a look.

"I've seen dead people before," I said.

"Not like this."

I flipped through his stack of photos to make him happy and to make me a little more miserable. I suppose it was shocking, unspeakably horrific and all that. But it wasn't anything I hadn't seen before. One stack of emaciated nude corpses looks about the same as the next. It's all about context, and some old snapshots from the evidence file of a forgotten war-crimes tribunal didn't offer much. I had worked long and hard to become this jaded, and it wasn't something I could turn off at will just to be polite to a guest.

"Yeah, I get it," I said. "He was a bad man who did bad things. I'm guessing this man—the one responsible—is long dead by now."

The rabbi nodded sadly.

"Dead and buried. Him and too many of his kind. From the time I was a young boy, I dreamed of joining the other Nazi-hunters who travelled the world seeking satisfaction—bringing these men to their long-delayed trials and executions. When I was finally able, I offered what help I could, but I came late to the hunt. By the time I was able to get out with my own team, running my own operations, there were only scraps for us to find. A low-level camp guard occasionally, or a child soldier who had been pressed into service in the last months of the war. If we looked hard enough, we could find one or two who had taken to the brutality of their criminal orders with a zeal above and beyond the call of duty. But the big fish, the real monsters, had already been snatched up or killed off by age and illness."

"You still managed to make a name for yourself. Some of your captures and convictions were pretty high profile."

I'd even heard of some of them in the years before I needed to do any research on Aharon Reubenski. He may have missed the heyday of Israeli agents kidnapping war criminals and spiriting them away to the tribunal they had narrowly dodged decades earlier, but he still ranked among the most respected latter-day hunters. It was men like him who continued to seek a public catharsis in the courtroom, even in the face of diminishing returns. His ilk still earned grudging respect for stubbornly refusing to let bygones be bygones. Some crimes simply could not be forgiven, and there was no statute of limitations when it came to the villains who had engineered and participated in the Holocaust.

Aharon Reubenski was not the least bit appeased by my modest offering of banal flattery.

"I cannot be satisfied with such petty victories. Not when so many of the monsters remain unpunished. Like this man we speak of. The one who made such photographic testimonials possible."

I took another glance at the loose photos lying on my coffee table. Whoever we were talking about certainly had an ocean of blood on his hands. Reubenski separated one of the photos from the rest and tapped his finger above a figure in the image.

"Him, that one there."

It was a new print made from an old photo that was cracked and faded. Even when it was a brand new negative, it wouldn't have been a very good shot. The focus was soft and there was a great deal of motion blur. But the image itself was compelling. A row of men, all Jews most likely, were kneeling in front of a ditch they themselves had probably just been forced to dig. They were moments away from each receiving a bullet in the back and a hasty burial by the soldiers who held them at gunpoint. On the left of the frame stood three men. I couldn't make out the face of the darkest one of the three.

"Who's the guy in the black coat and hat?" I asked.

"Gestapo, probably. The Nazis would send observers to the east to make sure their Axis brethren were adhering to their high standards of slaughter."

Figuring more prominently in the photo were the other two men. There was the one Jew of the bunch still on his feet, defiant and dignified to the end. He was also dressed in dark clothes, but his beard stuck out prominently in the black and white picture. Reubenski saw me looking at this man.

"A fellow rabbi, very much like myself," he said. "Killed along with all the rest just moments after this photo was taken, no doubt."

And in front of him, a uniformed officer, the one being pointed out to me. His face was a faint smear at best, but the anger and the hatred was evident in his body language as he swung a rifle butt at the defenceless victim before him. The camera, always such an impartial witness to history and horror, had captured this split instant in time before the first drop of blood was spilled on what was to be a very bloody day.

"Who was he?" I asked, staring at this forgotten moment of execution from so many years ago on the other side of the world.

"His name, at least at one time, was Csaba Szabo. Not a German this one, but a Hungarian, allied with the vile deeds of the Axis. 'Szabo' means 'tailor' in his dialect, but he was misnamed. The man was a butcher, make no mistake. By all accounts he was an enthusiastic anti-Semite before the war, and leapt at the opportunity a uniform and an officer's rank afforded him to murder my people en masse once the spectre of genocide was unleashed. His many victims remain uncounted and unavenged. Details of his escape are scarce, and he vanishes from all records with the collapse of the eastern front. He was presumed dead for many years. Despite his crimes, no one so much as looked for him. It was assumed, if he survived the war, that he likely died soon after in the Soviet prisoner-of-war camps along with millions of surrendered soldiers. Years later, when sightings were first reported, they weren't even believed. Nobody thought he could have made it out of Europe alive, let alone re-establish himself overseas with a new identity.

"I understand many war criminals did just that."

"The Germans, yes. The Hungarians, no. They didn't have the same network of connections and contacts the Germans had to smuggle men out and set up a new life elsewhere. What we didn't anticipate was Szabo being able to pass himself off as German to plug himself into this network of Nazi sympathizers and use them to help him vanish. He fooled us and he fooled them as well. We didn't even know he could speak German. Certainly not fluently. But he must have been convincing because when he approached the Nazi smugglers with a stolen uniform and someone else's identification, they gave him the same assistance they would have offered to one of their own."

"So where did Szabo end up?"

"As far from his home and his origins as he could get. The name he went by for the rest of his days was Werner Albers. And this was never questioned by his fellow war-criminals-in-hiding. They knew the name was false—just like their own new identities—but never suspected he wasn't even a German. He died in Argentina in 1979. A mundane drowning accident in his own pool. Hardly the vengeance he deserved."

"I don't suppose he deserved the Argentinian villa with a private pool either."

"He certainly did not," said Reubenski. "Once we determined the sighting reports had merit, we sought him out. We hunted him for fifteen years after his death before we found it had all been a pointless task. Oh, we could tell the families of his victims that the monster was gone at least. He had escaped our judgement, yet still had much to answer for in the face of God. But only the truly devout can find the comfort they need in that."

"And not even all of them, it seems," I said.

"It is true. My confidence in a final judgement for all has waned over the years. How many of these fiends have I searched the globe for, only to find old men who had lived full lives, and died peacefully in bed surrounded by loved ones who knew nothing of their crimes? Dozens? More? I'm afraid to count."

"But you haven't given up on Szabo yet. Even now, decades dead. You still want a piece of him."

"It was only recently I learned a man such as yourself might be able to help."

"Where are the remains now?" I asked, hoping an all-expense-paid trip to the sunnier climes of Argentina was in the offing.

"They're local," he answered. "He has a son here who repatriated the body so it could be buried in a family plot. That is why I have come to you. Had he been interred in another city, I would be hiring locally there."

"Necromancy is a rarefied occupation, rabbi. You can't just land in any city and ring up one like a plumber. If you want to hire me, hire me for my skills, not because I don't have to commute to work."

"I did not mean to offend you, Mr. Eulogy. You come well recommended."

"By who?" I asked. "I like to keep track of my references."

"Someone. You would know him if you saw him, but he wishes to remain anonymous."

"So I've met him?"

"He said you had. Long ago. He wouldn't be more specific than that."

"And you trust the opinion of this man?"

"He is known in certain circles."

"Religious circles?"

"Among others," said Reubenski.

The vagueness was giving me a vague headache, so I dropped the subject. Somebody threw work my way and didn't want thanks or credit. Fine. That meant they didn't want a cut either.

"Well, I'm your corpse wrangler, if you can cover my fee," I said.

"Is that all that is important to you? Payment?"

"This job isn't a calling. It's a business. My clients can worry about whether they have their principles in order. I'm just here to facilitate. I'll get you your war criminal, rabbi. The vengeance end of it is all on you."

"I accept those terms," he nodded after brief reflection.

"When do you want this done? I'm free this weekend. I suppose the Sabbath is out..."

"Tonight."

"Tonight? A little short notice, don't you think? There are things to prepare, rituals..."

I was blowing smoke. I had one bag and it was already packed.

"Time grows short."

"What's the hurry? He's been dead and buried for years."

"Ever since we identified him and traced his remains here, controversy has been brewing. An injunction to deport the body back to Hungary was filed by several concerned citizens who do not care to have a war criminal resting in the same ground as their own loved ones. A number of people from my own organization were among the plaintiffs."

"Yourself included?"

"I am afraid so. This was before I learned there may be other—options—at our disposal. After years of being kicked around by various courts, a ruling has been issued at last, and the body of Csaba Szabo is to be exhumed and shipped out of the country in three days' time. As you might imagine, no nation is pleased to welcome the mortal remains of a known war criminal, even if that is where he was born and raised. There is every indication that the remains are earmarked to be quickly and quietly disposed of. Either buried at sea, or purposely misfiled in some customs house and entombed for all time under a mountain of unread paperwork. Whatever the circumstances, we can be sure that anything left of Szabo will be placed out of reach and wilfully forgotten in short order. I might have been content with that before I learned of your particular trade, but now that I know more can be done, I see I must act quickly. It is my understanding that you need to make contact with the deceased, personally?"

"I don't have to lay hands upon as such, but proximity is required, yes."

"Then I ask you again. Can you be ready to move tonight?"

I was ready to cash a cheque. That's always ready enough in my book.

Θ

We met at the gates of a large venerable cemetery that was known as Algonquin Fields, though any signage that once identified it as such had decayed and vanished like the people it was named for. It had served the municipality so long, the graveyard had once been well outside the city limits. Back then, it was always a good idea to bury the latest cholera victims far from well-travelled streets. Now that urban sprawl had spread and surrounded it on all sides, the cemetery was sitting on a lot of prime real estate developers would have loved to plop a bunch of cookie-cutter condos on. Bids had been made, but they were all shot down. Too many mayors and councilmen and former masters of industry were planted under the oldest rows of headstones. Cultural-heritage and historical-significance issues would always crop up whenever someone suggested moving graves for the sake of a quick buck. As a result, acres of green space nobody living wanted to spend any time in persisted as an economic dead zone in the middle of town.

Our meeting had been set for after sunset, once the gates were locked and the grounds were closed for the night. Breaking into a cemetery is rarely a feat that requires much skill. I'm handy with a set of lock picks, and popping open a padlock on a chain is a small task that doesn't even require any sort of property damage. It took a few minutes of working the pins inside the mechanism to get them properly aligned so I could turn the tumbler. If I hadn't had an old man with me, I might have opted to climb the fence instead.

Once we let ourselves in, I left the chain on the gate with the padlock open but hooking the links together. It sufficed to hold the gate shut, and from a distance it would appear locked as normal. I wasn't expecting any security to make the rounds and check it this soon after closing.

"Will the age of the body be an issue?" Reubenski wanted to know. After too many years of justice denied, he was second guessing what might yet go wrong.

"If you want the kind of contact that involves conversation, the brain needs to be present. Or whatever's left of it. Rotten, decayed, or dust, it doesn't matter."

"As far as I know, he was buried whole."

"Then we're golden."

The paved path took a curvy, scenic route around the yard, but the layout of the graves was orderly, row upon row, and easy to count. To save the groundskeeper any unnecessary pestering from the bereaved, the cemetery's homepage included a search engine to help visitors locate the final resting place of whoever they wanted to come and see. Hunting through a cemetery's online mapping feature drained much of the mystery and adventure out of a late-night search through ten thousand graves, but I'm always willing to trade a bit of atmosphere for a lot of convenience.

It had been a simple matter to find Szabo's grave online. Szabo wasn't exactly a common name. He was the only one in the whole city, living or dead. Once present in the cemetery itself, it wasn't much harder to work the grid and find our target mixed in with a few layers of marble markers that were fashionable in their day. Grave aesthetics change almost as often as clothing fashions, but the differences are more subtle. If you have as much experience as I do, you develop an eye for it. When I'm on my game, I can look at any random tomb and pinpoint the decade it was set in the ground and often the masonry company that chiseled it. Szabo's grave was late '70s, early '80s high-end. This was no small memorial plaque set at ground level, fighting off the grass's annual attempt to spread and grow right over it. Someone went all-out and sprung for a fair-sized obelisk marker that left no doubt that this was a man of some importance we were trodding on.

"Nice stone," I commented. "Somebody cared."

"The family has money," explained Reubenski, with enough contempt to suggest he considered it all ill-gotten gain. If he'd had his way, the family line would have stopped at the end of Szabo's noose after a speedy and concise trial within the first year of the end of the war. As things played out, he lived long enough to father plenty of children who inherited all the money he should never have lived to earn.

Money and modesty rarely go hand-in-hand. What should have been a disavowed black sheep of the family was, in death, memorialized like an upstanding community leader. The stone itself, however, offered scant information about who it was set for. There were no sentiments, no dates etched into the marble face. Just a name—"Csaba Szabo"—as though that were explanation enough, and any additional details might dredge up the unpleasant history nobody cared to remember. His offspring had grown up with the safely anonymous assumed name of Albers. It was easy to distance themselves from the original family name, even when they were the ones who had paid to have it immortalized in stone.

The attempt at a marker that was at once garish and low-key failed to keep Szabo in his carefully cultivated place of obscurity. He'd been found out, and before long his grand monument, shuffled among so many others in the field to avoid undue notice, would be pulled down and stuffed into storage someplace where his chiseled name would never be looked upon again. Just as the memory that he had ever been granted refuge in Argentina during his later life had faded, so too would the memory that he had enjoyed refuge in this city in death. Our local embarrassment at having unknowingly housed his remains for decades was only peripherally covered by the local media. Who would even remember the story a year from now? Who would even care? Perhaps generations from now, some future developer, finally permitted to build on this land, would uncover the disused marker stuffed into the back of a tool shed on the grounds. If he even took a moment to read the base of the obelisk, and assuming he could still make out the name "Csaba Szabo," would he know enough about the history of the Second World War to recognize its significance? And if he did, would he care enough to preserve it, or would it just get tossed onto the back of a truck with all the other debris from a demolished graveyard and unceremoniously dumped into a landfill where so many cemeteries themselves are laid to rest once they've outlived their usefulness? My interest was purely academic, and barely even that. To me, a graveyard is a work environment. I look at them the same way an office drone must look at a cubicle. It's a claustrophobic space where I'm willing to do a job for money, but I have no desire to spend any of my free time there. Certainly not eternity.

"He's not down there," I told Reubenski, after a few moments staring at the stone. "This is just a monument."

Simply standing in the presence of the grave, I could already tell there were no trace elements of Csaba Szabo lingering in the vicinity except for the man's name.

"I was assured this was the place. His remains must be here!"

Reubenski had been expecting things to go wrong, and now his pessimism was seeking to validate itself. But I wasn't so easily put off.

"We'll check the niches. He may have been cremated after all and this is an open-air memorial the family wanted."

It happens. Not every grave in a graveyard has an occupant. People go missing, bodies are never recovered. Token personal artifacts are buried in lieu of real remains. But we knew Szabo had left a fully intact, easily identified body behind at the bottom of his swimming pool. He might have been cremated in South America before his remains were ever sent here. Ashes are cheaper to ship. It wasn't that uncommon for a family to want a more public marker for their loved one on the grounds, while the actual remains were more discreetly tucked away in a wall of a nearby columbarium. At least, I hoped that was how the burial had played out. I didn't want to have to track down all of Szabo's kids, looking to see which one might have dear old dad's ashes collecting dust on their mantel.

Aside from maintenance buildings, a reception hall, a chapel, and a few dozen above-ground family tombs, there was one other structure of note in the cemetery. Cremation had come a long way since its days of being dismissed as a sacrilegious means of disposing of the dead, suitable only for ancient pagans. Now it was every bit as common as a full-body burial, and most of the world religions had backed off their former hard-line condemnation of the practice.

Columbariums could be found in most cemeteries, ranging from a simple wall of niches built outdoors, to an elaborate vault the size of a small cathedral. We had a moderately sized building housing the niches, which pleased me. Outdoor niches are often cemented shut, which means a chisel and hammer to break in and additional vandalism charges if caught at it. Interior niches usually have four standard one-size-fits-all locking bolts, one in each corner of the marble plaque, that can be opened with their own equivalent of a casket key. Of course I always keep one handy in my kit, but since I was on an actual cemetery call, I came armed with my entire tool shop.

It was all packed into a canvas satchel I had slug over my shoulder. Rebecca, in particular, liked to taunt me by calling it my "murse" or "man-purse," but I was never able to figure out a better way to carry the larger equipment I often needed. My wallet-sized kit and jacket pockets had most common eventualities covered, but there was no room for, say, the army-surplus contraption I would never cross the threshold of a graveyard without. Six feet of mud densely packed by years of weather is not something you want to have to dig through without a proper shovel—or an entrenching tool that offered the additional convenience of folding up and fitting into a satchel.

The columbarium was locked for the night, but the door was short work for my picks. Once inside, it took us another fifteen minutes to find the right niche by flashlight. They were all clearly numbered, but the numbers bore no relation to whose urn was filed away inside. Generally, they were clustered together by date of death, though some families threw that small amount of order out of whack with pre-need purchases, or some fussy desire to have their loved one entombed on an east wall as opposed to a north, south or west wall. Finally we located Szabo's pigeon hole, more or less surrounded by other fatalities of the late 1970s. I dropped my satchel on the floor and selected the appropriate instrument. Niche key in hand, I had the four long screws out in short order and was able to lower the stone face to the floor without cracking it.

"Pepper spray works on the dead?" asked the rabbi, peering into my satchel as he watched me work. My tools were piled inside in complete disarray—another reason Rebecca called it a man-purse. The pepper spray happened to be on top of the pile.

"Not at all. But it works great on the living," I explained. "That's for if I run into a night watchman who takes his job too seriously and tries to call the cops."

The urn inside the niche was simple, standard—tastefully bland for something that was meant to be locked away forever and never looked at again. I lifted it out of its stone cupboard and presented it to Reubenski.

"Here's your man," I said. "What's left of him."

"Can you make contact? Is he..." Reubenski trailed off. Even holy men have trouble wording it when faced with the practical reality of what was once abstract dogma to them.

He tried again, "Is his spirit...his soul in there?"

"No, but the remains work as a conduit. Like a physical phone line, I can use them to give him a ring."

Reubenski swallowed hard, bracing himself.

"Do it," he said.

I set the urn down, crossed my arms, and took a firm grip of the bridge of my nose, tilting my head down and squeezing my eyes shut. It was a position that didn't really help me concentrate, but it certainly helped make me look like I was concentrating. Clients appreciate signs of effort and focus, even if they're completely contrived.

"Szabo," I said aloud, "Csaba Szabo."

The response came, instant and irritable.

"Albers. Werner Albers," the voice corrected from the beyond, a whispered hiss that echoed through the columbarium. Rabbi Reubenski looked unnerved by the voice from the grave. I might have warned him in advance, but it slipped my mind. Usually I try to have these graveside chats on my own, with the client safely out of range of the weirdness. It's never a good idea to show fear in the face of a raised spirit. It gives them the advantage, and when they sense they have an advantage, they tend to show you a lot of attitude. I tried to defuse it by keeping my tone casual and routine, letting him know who was in charge without being too rude or demanding about it.

"We're dispensing with the aliases today, Szabo," I told the voice. "We know who you are. Come on out, I've got somebody here who wants to have a word with you."

When spirits manifest themselves in the physical world, they're not some transparent puff of smoke, or a recognizable translucent image. We perceive them in ways that touch on all of our senses. You can smell them, taste them in the air, every bit as much as you can see them as some irregularity in your field of vision, or hear them as a distant echo of a whisper. When they're present, you'll know it. Even if every piece of high-tech monitoring technology in the room swears otherwise, registers nothing, draws a flatline, the creeping sensation tickling its way up your arm hairs will convince you. I've been in rooms like that before—a million dollars of surveillance equipment and half a dozen skeptics. At the end of the session, the equipment remained unconvinced, but none of the people who carried it all away left with any doubts.

The immortal essence of Csaba Szabo leeched into the cold stone chamber of the columbarium like a noxious gas. It was everywhere and nowhere, hinted at by a fleeting whiff or an oscillating wave in our peripheral vision. It circled the room, rippled across the ceiling and floor.

"Szabo, be still!" I commanded, hoping to keep him a bit more contained and cohesive so my client would have something focused to talk to.

For a moment, all that remained of Csaba Szabo came together, hovering over his ashen remains where I'd left them sitting on the floor. The twisting vortex of diffused light and stink rolled and boiled a few feet in front of me, as perceptible and present as a spirit could manage on its own. Although it had no physical form, it seemed to lean in towards me, like it was having a closer look. It wasn't the rabbi Nazi-hunter he was interested in. It was me.

"I know you," wheezed the spirit.

I have a reputation among the dead.

"I know what you've done!" it howled and fled straight through the nearest wall in a puff of foul, oozing mist.

It's not always a great reputation.

A distant curse echoed from the void, "Bastard!"

"We've got a drifter," I informed Rabbi Reubenski.

This happens sometimes. An uncooperative spirit makes a dash for it rather than hang around to chat about an uncomfortable subject—war crimes for instance. I'd call them "runners," but that doesn't seem apt. You need feet to run.

"We must go after him!" declared the rabbi and turned for the door.

"No point," I told him. "You just saw him drift away through solid stone. What little perceptible presence manifests itself can easily give us the slip—pass through walls, sink underground, fly into the air. You might as well chase after a faint smell or a slight breeze. If you want him, we're going to have to hold him someplace he can't get away from so easily."

"Like where?"

I looked down at the urn on the stone tiles at our feet.

"His mortal remains."

"You can do this?"

I wasn't sure I could. Cremains can be tough, there's so little to work with. A nice semi-intact rotting corpse is simple—kid's stuff. A full skeleton offers few complications. Even a handful of bones is perfectly doable under the correct conditions. An impromptu bind with an urn of ashes was dodgy, but I saw no other option.

"I can stuff him back into his cremains. Bind him to them. That should keep him in place for a while."

I bent down and picked up the urn. The lid sat loosely on top. I pulled it off and handed it to the rabbi. Without further ceremony, and certainly with no respect for the deceased, I upended the urn and dumped the entire contents onto the floor. The ashes and soot that had once been the body of Csaba Szabo rained down on the stone and scattered everywhere. Small clouds of him washed over our feet, coating our shoes and pant legs in dust. I crouched back down again, set aside the empty urn, and started poking through the pile with a finger. It was a rush job. Szabo's essence lingered nearby, but he wouldn't stick around long. And it would be much harder to draw him out again now that he suspected an ambush.

People assume that when they have a loved one cremated at a mortuary, their body is reduced to a fine powder, completely beyond recognition. This isn't quite true. Despite the high temperatures corpses are subjected to in the crematorium ovens, there are always some things that won't burn. Immediately following the cremation, as the ashes are gathered to be boxed up and shipped out to the next leg of the funeral arrangements, someone at the mortuary will have the task of picking through the scant remains. Metal objects like pins from past bone breaks, artificial hips and surgical staples will be set aside if any are found. No use having those things noisily rattling around inside an expensive new urn, chipping away at the interior finish. There will also be plenty of fragments of bone left over—some quite large. In bargain crematoriums, these get pounded down by a special mallet which, for all practical purposes, looks and handles just like a meat tenderizer you might buy in a kitchenware store. Only once all the larger bits of bone have been hammered into flakes, so they won't look quite so bone-like to any customers who might sneak a peek, are the cremains approved for final dispensation.

Bone flakes were of no help to me. I needed something a smidge larger. Something more along the lines of a decent shard or splinter of a bone. In a quality cremation, you'd almost never find a piece of bone as large as that, especially if it had been passed through a modern grinding machine. But quality products, customer services—these things erode everywhere in time. Mortuaries are no exception, and the oven operators in crematoriums are just as likely to be lazy and half-assed as any other underpaid technician doing a dull repetitive job.

It only took me a matter of seconds to discover exactly what I needed amidst all the grey ash. The splinter was less than half-an-inch long. Discoloured from the flames and the body fat that had boiled away all around it, it looked more wooden than bone. I only hoped it was brittle enough to break easily.

"Pulvis redimio," I announced, and snapped the bone fragment in two between my fingers.

Truth be told, I can make an incantation work in any language. I usually go with Latin when there's somebody around. It plays better to an audience.

I held the two halves of the splinter of bone tightly, one in each hand. I could feel them heating up as they vibrated—not enough to burn, but enough to feel them being drawn back to each other. Had I set them within a few inches of each other, they would have fused together. That was something I couldn't let happen if I was to keep control of the reanimation.

From inside my bag, I retrieved two thumb-sized clear-glass jars. I always kept some on hand to hold ingredients or collect samples. They were exactly the same sort you might find in an arts-and-crafts store, used for small quantities of oil-based paint. I liked them because they were conveniently tiny, with extra-thick glass that would reliably keep them from breaking if mishandled. I stuffed the two halves of the bone shard into one jar each and screwed the lids tight. The splinters rattled around in their individual prisons, seeking to merge again, even though that was now an impossibility.

"Okay, Szabo, let's try that again," I said to the mound of ashes on the floor.

And suddenly I could feel he was back in the room with us. I'd agitated his remains, imbued them with a need to draw close and become whole again. Unlike a reanimated corpse, there was little a collection of ashes could do to pick itself up and become mobile again. But just giving a single bone shard the shivers compelled the former corporeal occupant to return to the fray.

"Begone and let me be!" demanded Szabo when he realized he was fixed to a single location in the mortal world where he had no desire to be.

The ashes began to shift, rippling and rolling in dusty waves. Tiny peaks and valleys formed. The effect was subtle at first, but the longer I stared at the circle of soot that used to be Csaba Szabo, the more I could make out the distinct features of a human face. I'd never laid eyes on the man beyond the single blurry photo Reubenski had showed me in my apartment, but I knew immediately that I was looking into the empty ashen sockets of an accurate recreation of a dead man's likeness. The ashes continued to flitter about, making the grey death-mask of Szabo appear animated, expressive. The mouth even moved when he spoke. I'd seen reanimated cremains move incrementally before, form impressionistic images, but never anything so complex. I was honestly impressed. It was a masterful display of physical control for a nebulous spirit, long departed.

"Haven't you done enough already?" spat the spirit with contempt.

"I'm just getting started," I replied, refusing to acknowledge the garish expressions he was accomplishing with only a handful of dust and a mountain of hate.

"Bah!" the ashes appeared to exclaim before folding over on themselves and forming what at first appeared to be a narrow, swirling, horizontal vortex. The cremains stopped churning once they'd rolled themselves into a tubular structure that looked like half-a-foot of soiled, blackened garden hose. Csaba Szabo simply refused to be contained and was now trying to leave the building, bound to his ashes or not. In a determined, palpably enraged fashion, this densely packed cylinder of incinerated human remains began inch-worming its way across the floor of the columbarium, aiming itself at the door. It was at once pathetic, grotesque and fascinating.

"Wow," I commented, tracking its progress with my flashlight, "That's sheer willpower. You don't see that too often."

"I have never seen anything like it at all," gasped the rabbi in awe.

"Exactly."

"So what do we do with him now?"

"Well, he's still not cooperating," I said. "We're getting the silent treatment and he's just trying to leave again. I suppose we can try to get him in a finger hold."

"Is that some kind of wrestling move?"

"Sort of. Except the pain and the blood are real. It's a way to grapple with the dead."

"And you do this with your finger?"

"Yeah. Exactly," I said hesitantly. "Only there's a catch."

"And what is this catch?"

"The finger can't be attached to the rest of you."

I looked at the rabbi and his gnarled old fingers, any one of them a candidate. Reubenski caught me staring at his hands.

"Why does it have to be my finger?" he asked, withdrawing his hands and cupping them close to his chest.

"It doesn't. But I don't see any other volunteers. And you're not paying me enough for a self-maiming."

He opened his palms and looked down into them.

"I...I am not certain..."

Szabo was still inching his way towards the exit. At this rate, he'd be running free and clear through the cemetery grounds in another hour. Or two.

"Your call," I told him, "but he's getting away. Very slowly. How bad do you want him?"

Reubenski considered the abomination creeping its way across the stone floor, grunting with each flex of its dusty body.

"If it is the only way it can be done, then it must be done."

I handed him a pair of wire cutters from inside my satchel. I was never without a pair for just such an occasion, or any of a dozen similar situations that would crop up on the job. These were clean and new, fresh from the hardware store only a few weeks earlier. I was always replacing them. The filthy things you have to cut through in my line of work.

The Rabbi stared at the blades in his hand and contemplated how he was going to go about mutilating his other.

"Does it matter which one?" he asked, a fair question.

"It's entirely up to you. They're your fingers."

I watched him play eeny-meeny-miny-moe with the fingers of his left hand for a while before finally sliding one between the scissor blades of the wire cutter.

"Interesting," I commented.

The rabbi was distracted from the moment of truth before he could squeeze the grip of the cutter together.

"What is?"

"I've seen people make this sort of choice before. They always choose the pinkie. You went ring finger."

"Arthritis," he told me. "It bothers me most in this finger."

"I guess it won't anymore."

Most people who have to remove a finger go for the joint. Joints make for a natural target. There's more gristle but less bone to get through. The rabbi chose a spot midway between the knuckle and first joint. I guess he figured he might as well amputate the arthritic hot spot completely, but it wasn't going to make his task any easier in the moment.

To his credit, he didn't piss away valuable time contemplating what needed to be done, psyching himself up, mustering his courage. He bore down on the grip as hard as he could, trying to get the job done as quickly and cleanly as possible. I could hear the bone crunching between the blades. It was a sound that might have made me nauseous if I hadn't heard it so many times before. Reubenski winced hard, gasped once, and the finger came free, dropping to the floor. He'd done well, but looked woozy, like he might pass out at any moment.

We had a good pumper for an old man. I grabbed him by the wrist and held him firm. He was already trembling, going into shock. I body-checked him into the nearest wall of niches to keep him steady and aimed the spurting finger nub at the slithering mass of ashes. Individual streams of blood fired out of the stump with each beat of his heart, drawing wet curving lines across the marble slabs of the floor. I finally got a few jets on target. Spattering squirts of blood fell across the serpentine length of the reanimated cremains and locked them in place like shackles. Szabo writhed and twisted and bellowed complaints, but he could make no further progress towards the door.

I was ready to rifle through my kit for something to stem the bleeding and dress the rabbi's wound, but he already had a handkerchief out and was applying pressure. Since he was doing as much triage as I could offer, I instead focused on finishing the finger bind of Szabo's physical and spiritual remains.

Another piece of regulation equipment in my treasure-trove kit of handy tools is a standard-model Dustbuster I always kept fully charged and ready for action. In my business, there's no end of residue that needs collecting or cleaning up. A simple, vacuum device like this may seem more at home in the hand of a hotel maid, but it really is tremendously useful for practitioners of the dark arts. I've recommended them to everyone I know in necromancy and related fields, but I'm the only one who comes armed with one on calls. I think most of them understand the usefulness, but are just too embarrassed to carry one around. It looks silly and not at all cool.

The Dustbuster made short work of Szabo, sucking him and the rabbi's coagulating blood into a refuse chamber I kept lined with a clear-plastic Ziploc bag. Once I was sure every powdered trace of the cremains was off the floor, I opened my hand-held vacuum cleaner and removed the bag. All that was left of Szabo was inside, howling and shrieking and scrambling to get out. I retrieved Reubenski's amputated finger from the floor and threw it into the bag with the ashes. Instantly they became calm and Szabo's complaints were silenced. So long as the finger, willingly offered, lay amidst the cremains, they would stay still and behave themselves. I zipped the bag shut, sealing in its imprisoned occupant.

I checked on Reubenski, who was still soaking up the blood with his handkerchief and squeezing off the stump of his missing finger as hard as the knobby fingers of his free hand would allow. He seemed to have it under control. A trip to the nearest emergency room and a few creative lies to the staff would see him patched up and released by morning.

"Not so bad?" I asked.

He looked a little pale, but nodded. His eyes were on the ziplocked ashes of Szabo, now rendered inert by the presence of the finger rustling around inside with them. I held up the bag so he could have a better look.

"Well, you can do this nine more times, max. Choose wisely."

"I think just this one will satisfy me for now."

The last key elements were the bone fragments in their twin jars. These I also gave to Reubenski. The two splinters of bone stood on end in their individual containers, vibrating, swaying, twisting, like metal filaments reacting to a magnet.

"Keep these apart and he's all yours."

The rabbi nodded, understanding. With his hands otherwise occupied, I stuffed the jars into his coat pocket.

"Can you hang on a bit longer while I tidy up?"

Again he nodded. The cleanup was quick, slap-dash, but simple. A few individually wrapped pre-moistened napkin-wipes I'd collected from a frequented greasy-spoon diner eliminated any traces of the rabbi's spilled blood. The empty urn was replaced in its niche, the plate refastened like it had never been disturbed. I locked the door of the columbarium behind us and did the same for the padlock on the gate once we were off the property.

Although the bleeding hadn't quite stopped, it had slowed considerably and some colour had returned to Rabbi Reubenski's face. I offered to escort him to the hospital, but he wouldn't hear of it, so I helped hail him a cab to take him to the final stop of his night's adventures. The cab driver didn't even blink at the sight of a wounded holy man climbing into the back seat during his late shift. Cab drivers in this city see that and so much worse when the sun goes down.

That was the last I saw of the Nazi-hunter as he drove away with the remains of one of the most reviled war criminals of the last century distributed in various pockets of his heavy dark coat. I did hear from him again some weeks later, however. There was a long-distance phone call one afternoon. I recognized the voice right away.

"How's the finger, or lack thereof?" I asked

"Healing nicely, thank you."

"And your guest? How's he enjoying his..." It took a moment for a word to occur. "Sequestration?"

"Perhaps he can best tell you himself," said the rabbi. I heard steps across the floor as he carried the phone with him, then the creak of a door opening. I'll never forget the sound I heard next.

They weren't screams, like cries of pain or torture. This was something far worse. It was sobbing—mournful, inconsolable sobbing. Not of remorse, regret or grief, but of exhaustion. Terrible, relentless exhaustion. This was the sound of a creature that had simply had enough—more than enough, far far more than enough. And yet there was no conceivable end in sight. It was brutal to listen to. I nearly dropped the phone rather than hear more than a few seconds of it. As you might imagine, it takes a lot to rattle me. This rattled me.

I considered hanging up without another word, but there was another noise in the background—faint compared to the torment that filled the room, but distinct once I identified what it was. It was music. Very clearly music.

The rabbi came back on the line with the sound of the door shutting. The commotion in the closed room was reduced to a background muffle.

"Twenty-three days he has endured so far. He begs me to stop, as I am sure his victims once begged him to stop. From me, he shall receive the same absence of mercy."

"Then I'll assume you're satisfied?"

"That I can never be. But I am content that some small justice remains always within our grasp."

With that, we hung up on each other, and severed all ties. The rabbi's follow-up call had provided me with the answer to the only question I had concerning the case. How do you punish a dead man who no longer possesses a physical body, cannot feel pain or suffering or anguish as the living do? A man who persecuted Jews by the thousands, torturing and murdering with impunity for years. A man who escaped the law, never felt guilt for his crimes, never faced denouncement or exposure, never served time. A man now beyond any form of earthly accountability. What do you do with a man like that when all you have is his tainted soul, stuffed in a bag?

You can't torture him as such, but you can make him listen to klezmer music all day and all night, relentlessly and without end. It's not much, but maybe that's hell enough.

Chapter Four

Earning a Living

TRACY MUST HAVE ENJOYED my latest bit of shop talk. She'd let the last couple of spoonfuls of ice cream melt to pudding at the bottom of her bowl, untouched.

"Klezmer music, huh?" She sounded a little skeptical to me.

"You don't need to be an anti-Semite to hate klezmer music, but I'm sure it helps."

"True enough," she said, and tipped up her bowl to drink down the dregs of butterscotch slime.

"You have anything for me?" I asked when she was done.

"Like what?" she said, setting the bowl down and licking her lips.

"Stories, anecdotes, tales of woe."

I tried to start her off light before digging for the goods.

"All moirologist stories are tales of woe."

"Come on, amuse me. You're not the only one who enjoys the lighter side of death."

Tracy thought about it for a moment before offering, "Well, last week I had a guy who wanted me to show up at his dad's funeral and pee myself during the viewing…"

"Pass," I stopped her. "I don't want to hear about your sicko clients unless one of them needs me for a gig."

I skipped to the point.

"I need work, Tracy, things have been…"

"Slow?" she finished for me when I tapered off.

"Glacial," I told her frankly. "It's been so bad, I let Rebecca talk me into seeing a regurgitator act last night."

"For fuck's sake, why?" Tracy sounded genuinely alarmed.

"I didn't know it was going to be a regurgitator. She didn't even know what a regurgitator was. She just thought he could do some cool tricks."

"So these tricks of his, were they cool?"

"No. They were typical. Proficient, but typical. So I showed him a cool trick of my own."

"You didn't."

Tracy had picked up on the sly amusement in my voice, the slight curl of my lips.

"You did! Christ, Rip, what did you do?"

"Never mind. It was just a little trick," I said in my defence, and demonstrated how little by holding my thumb and index finger apart. "Small one."

"It was some super-creepy supernatural shit, wasn't it? You know you need to keep that sort of thing under wraps."

"That's the problem today. Everyone with real talent is keeping it under wraps. It's hard to network."

"We're networking now, you and me," said Tracy, wagging a pointed finger between the two of us.

"It's not the same. There's nothing special about what you do."

Tracy exaggerated the offence she'd taken at my words.

"I beg your pardon? Let's see you do what I do."

"I wish I could do what you do," I assured her. "I might make some money. But let's face it, crying on command isn't exactly taking control of the beyond and bending reality to your will."

"Point taken. But at least I don't have to perform a bunch of freaky rituals with dead chickens and the first menstrual blood of a virgin born under a full moon and shit like that. I can turn the waterworks on and off whenever I want. Wanna see me cry?"

She looked at me with an expectant broad smile, like a playground kid trying to solicit a dare.

"I've seen you cry," I reminded her in my least encouraging voice which completely failed to stem her at all. The challenge was on.

With no buildup whatsoever, Tracy suddenly let her head hang as if to hide the look of strenuous sorrow that had instantly distorted her face almost behind recognition. After a sharp, quivering intake of breath, she let out a mighty sob and followed it with a torrential downpour of tears that cascaded across her cheeks. It took her a few moments to work up to a wail and then top it off with a full-blown Gaelic keen, deafening in the small parlour, and an instant draw for all eyes and ears in the place. For good measure, she let her nose run freely, which, I had to admit, was a nice touch of authenticity.

Despite my best efforts to remain stoic, I could feel a twinge of red embarrassment creep up my face, and I couldn't stop my eyes from darting to the looks of concern coming from the other tables.

"Okay, quit it. You're making a scene," I said.

Tracy accepted my concession and shut off any trace of despair in an instant. She retrieved her spoon and quietly scraped at the bottom of her bowl for the last hints of flavour, like the blubbering ugliness had never happened.

"Making a scene is my bread and butter, baby. That one was free. Next time, I'll charge you."

Θ

When looking for work, the important thing is that I get to my potential clients before they turn to a medium. Not only are mediums competition, but they're the bane of my profession. Chit-chatting with the departed is disputed no-man's-land between our fields, and the mediums think the necromancers should keep to our reanimation rituals and decomposing body parts and let them act as the line of communication between the living and the dead. And for the most part they're right. I don't particularly care if some flashy medium with a fake turban perched on their big hair poaches the lonely-hearts from me. I'm no good at providing solace and comfort to people anyway, and frankly I get bored relaying messages of love and longing across the ether. But they seriously need to keep their grubby paws with long, painted fingernails off the salvage gigs. First of all, it's no use turning to a medium in order to recover practical information like account numbers, safe combinations, or the location of hidden keys. Even if you're lucky enough to employ a medium who isn't a total scammer, the few genuine examples are really only good at tuning in to emotions or simple sentiments. If a client is looking for cold, hard, verifiable facts, they're out of luck. And they'll come away from the experience thinking we're all a bunch of con artists. A bad medium experience makes it twice as hard for me to swoop in, pick up the pieces, and convince a client I can deliver the goods.

Over the course of the past year, I'd had five solid gigs and a few more promising leads yanked out from under me by mediums. All but two of them I lost to one particular medium. His homepage, and pretty much every other bit of multimedia social-networking self-promotion, billed him as Reynaldo the Wise. I called him Reynaldo the Fuckhead behind his back because I'm petty and childish that way. It would be a lot easier to hate him if he was one of the scam-artist mediums, but unfortunately he's the real deal. He has the gift, and he knows how to use it, market it, and profit from it. The bastard.

I hadn't run into Reynaldo in months, and was enjoying my Fuckhead-free stretch. In retrospect, I should have realized I was pushing my luck that day by crossing the threshold of Wilbur's Wonderama, but it was on the way home and it had been a long time since I checked out the newest arrivals at the neighbourhood magic shop. I usually avoid magic shops, but sometimes even real practitioners of the dark arts need a garish prop or two. Atmosphere sells, and a bit of showmanship makes good business sense. Need a wrought-iron candelabra or the guttering candles to go with it? Wilbur's was your place. Caught shorthanded without a hand-sized scarab mounted in a glass box, or a fiercely posed taxidermied rat? Wilbur's would fix you up. The only other place in town that could offer you such a variety of macabre crap was the wiccan shop, and I never, ever went there. Those people give me the willies.

Wilbur's Wonderama had been a staple of the local showbiz scene for decades. Home to all sorts of magical trickery, it had your act covered whether you needed a new box for sawing someone in half, or a marked deck to irritate friends by forcing them to pick a card—any card. The "Wilbur," whose name adorned the flowing-script sign over the door, was known as Wilbur the Wizard to generations of children who tuned in to his variety show that ate up a ninety-minute block of time on select network-affiliates every Saturday morning. He'd been retired for many years now, but still turned up at his shop regularly to greet customers, shoot the shit, and pull a coin out of some unsuspecting kid's ear. Anyone younger than thirty wouldn't remember his TV show, but the Wonderama kept him in the public eye. I doubt the old ham would have lived this long without some form of celebrity to keep him going.

"Rip, my boy! You made it," said Wilbur, as he abruptly rose into view from behind the counter. Given the state of his knees and his bad back, this appearance was a magic trick unto itself.

Wilbur was always friendly towards me. He was friendly with everyone, but he put some extra effort in when I visited his shop. He was still grateful for the time I helped extract the location of his heart medicine from his late wife. His prescription ran low at an inopportune moment and might have driven him into an adjoining grave if I hadn't discovered where she stashed a backup bottle of slightly expired pills. Once the emergency was over, I sealed the deal by also finding out where she'd hidden his medical marijuana. He paid me with store credit, which I'd long since used to help furnish my apartment—mostly in the black curtain department. When he was in a good mood, he still offered me a modest discount. I appreciated the gesture, but other than some basic furnishings, he didn't stock anything I needed and little I wanted. Even with a reliable twenty percent off retail, my cash flow of late wasn't exactly impulse-buy friendly.

"Hey, Wilbur, how's tricks?" I asked, trying not to make a face as I got the worst pun in the business out of the way. If I hadn't said it, Wilbur would have, and it would have been even more cringe-inducing coming from him.

"Can't complain," he said. "And if I did, who'd listen?"

"Not me, that's for sure."

"You're looking much improved. You've got some colour back, I see," said Wilbur, giving me a familiar wink. I tried to think back to when we last saw each other and what state I might have been in. Even if I could remember, it didn't mean Wilbur's recollection was accurate. Celebrities, major or minor, tend to be kind of spacey. In recent years, Wilbur's eccentricities had been further compounded by age and memory loss.

"Thanks," I told him, accepting his compliment, whatever it meant or didn't mean.

"Oh Rip," he said, looking like another sudden recollection had jarred the previous vague memory out of the way, "there was a fella in here a couple of days back asking after you. He was already inside when I unlocked the door. At first I thought it was a break in, but nothing was broken, nothing missing. I told him you hadn't been around in months."

"Who was it?"

"Couldn't say. But he knew you. Said you two went way back. Said you'd met before, but it was never the right time, and now things have changed and you two have to talk. Something like that, I didn't quite follow. I gave him one of your cards. Was that okay?"

Like half the other talent in town, I'd left a stack of business cards with Wilbur to distribute as he saw fit. The good ones— with an address and phone number.

"That's fine. It's what they're for. But I don't know who it could be."

"He left his own for you, but it doesn't say a thing."

Wilbur retrieved the card from under a stack of twenties in the cash drawer of his register and handed it to me. It was solid black, featureless. Only when I looked at it from an angle that allowed light to reflect off the glossy lettering on the matte background could I make out two words.

Charlie Nocturne

Another damn stage name, no doubt. Some upstart magician looking to pick my brain. Maybe he'd heard of me, maybe we'd been introduced, but he didn't realize I wasn't a performer, didn't have an act, wouldn't represent him, couldn't book him a show if I tried.

"What did he look like?" I asked as I pocketed the card.

"Black coat, black hat, dark glasses."

"What about his face?"

"That's just it. I don't seem to recall."

"His face?"

"If he had one."

Wilbur was being cute. His eyesight was as shot as his knees, his back and his ticker. The poor guy couldn't even do card tricks anymore because he couldn't tell the difference between hearts and diamonds, spades and clubs. They all blurred together; red blobs and black blobs.

"Say, Rip, did you hear the one about the magician who performed an amazing feat of magic on stage one night? A guy in the audience yells out, 'How'd you do that?' and the magician says, 'If I told you, I'd have to kill you.'"

I cut Wilbur off before he could prattle his way through the rest of the joke.

"And the guy says, 'Okay, then. Just tell my wife.'"

Wilbur was visibly disappointed. "You heard that one before?"

"No."

"Then how'd you know the end?"

"I figured it out. It's easy if you know the key to all good punchlines."

"Surprise?" asked Wilbur after a moment's thought.

"Inevitability," I told him as I walked away.

I didn't have the desire or the disposable cash for a kitschy prop, and browsing finger traps and miniature guillotines can only hold my attention for so long. Predictably my eyes drifted to the collection of pinned notes, cards, playbills and ticket stubs that covered nearly an entire wall by the counter. The colossal collage was always my final stop.

"So it's come to this?" I asked myself like it was the first time it had come to that.

I found myself perusing the bulletin board at Wilbur's Wonderama almost every time I'd been there, if only to see if there were any new business cards posted. If I had work, my interest in the board ended there. If work was scarce, I'd linger a little longer, giving the rare job offerings a quick glance on the very slim chance that there was a task or problem my skill set could help with for a fee. Mostly the help-wanted ads were night-club auditions or people who were too lazy to call around, trolling for a party magician. Necromancers don't play a lot of birthday parties. We tend not to have any appropriate tricks up our sleeves—unless maybe it's an orphanage calling, asking us to raise Mom and Dad from the dead for a little boy or girl's special day. I never held out much hope of seeing that gig up for grabs.

Of course it was at that exact moment, just when I was slumming for the shittiest of the shit jobs, that a voice, familiar in pitch and pomposity, let me know I'd been caught in the act.

"Give up on the classifieds, or can't you afford a newspaper?" said Reynaldo, in the sort of taunting tone familiar friends use with each other. Considering we were neither familiar nor friends, it was a wildly inappropriate tone that made me want to punch him in the face, even before I turned and saw his puffy mug gawking at me with a self-satisfied grin that cut across his bulldog jowls. Business-acumen-related jealousy was only a small part of the problem I had with Reynaldo. The lion's share of my issues with him was based on the fact that I thought he was an asshole.

"I was just on my way home from a job. Thought I'd check in, see what's new," I said as casually as I could manage. "Yourself? Aren't you booked most afternoons? Little old ladies wanting you to contact their dead cat or parakeet and such?"

"Just a business errand," Reynaldo replied. "Looking for some new wares. I needed a replacement."

He held up a hefty crystal ball he was carrying to the cash when he ran into me. I could see my face reflected back at me, upside-down in the clear curved surface.

"Oh? Did somebody break your balls?"

"Too much manhandling," he said, caressing the crystal as he might do in front of a client. "Over time it fogs the glass. Rings and fingernails and even dust rags leave scratches and marks. I like a nice, clear view."

"And what do you see?"

Reynaldo rotated the glass sphere so he could read the price tag stuck on one side.

"A sixty-percent mark-up."

"You should shop online."

"And miss these chance encounters with fellow travellers? I think not. Buy you a drink?"

The question came before I could disengage myself from further conversation. Generosity was not among Reynaldo's few strong points or his many faults. I was curious why he might want to spend any more time with me—even so short a time as it would take to throw back a single beverage. He took my hesitation to refuse as an acceptance.

"If you'll just wait a moment while this is rung up, we'll pop out for a quick one."

I decided to roll with the invitation, remembering how I'd just been bitching to Tracy about the lack of networking going on in town these days. Reynaldo made sure his transaction at the Wonderama took an infuriating amount of time. Probably just to test my resolve to see what he was after.

"Did you really have to have it gift wrapped?" I asked him as we left the shop and strolled down the sidewalk together, a plastic shopping bag stuffed with his freshly boxed and colourfully decorated crystal ball in his hand.

"I like opening presents. Especially ones from myself. I always seem to know what I want."

"What's the point if it's not a surprise?"

"Nothing surprises me. I'm psychic."

The fuck he is.

"I heard that."

"I didn't say anything," I told Reynaldo.

"I heard your mind say it."

"That so? Repeat it back. Verbatim. I'll tell you if you're right."

"I never use such appalling language."

It didn't take psychic powers to tune into what people generally thought of Reynaldo and his line of crap. Still, he was surprisingly spot-on about certain facts some of the time. More so than any other medium I'd ever met. I'll admit I made a point of not thinking too hard about things like passwords and PIN numbers in his presence.

There was a bar around the corner from the Wonderama that was always open early enough to cater to late-lunch drinkers, evening head-starters, and twenty-four-hour alcoholics. Once the sunlit door shut behind us and our eyes adjusted to the abrupt darkness we found inside, we selected an open table in the middle. The patronage was sparse at that time of day and we had our choice of seating at the bar or in a booth. We both knew our exchange wasn't going to last long enough to get cozy in a booth, or involve enough rounds to perch ourselves under the bartender's nose. A table offered the least amount of comfort for the shortest amount of time and allowed for a quick exit once we'd decided we'd had our fill of one another. We were already past that point, but had yet to determine if there were any fruitful facts that could be pried out of our competitor.

Reynaldo had an Irish coffee. I didn't particularly want a drink, but I ordered something harder and more expensive since I wasn't paying. Whatever I chose, he was going to want more than his money's worth. Scuttlebutt or cheap shots, he'd make sure he got value for his dollar.

Reynaldo bored me with some small talk about recent rain and the chill in the air, but he got around to the point once the drinks arrived and there was no threat of a waitress interrupting us again until we were at the bottom of our glasses.

"I have a new client," he announced. "Very new, in fact. I think you know him. Saunders is the name."

So that was it. Reynaldo wanted some backstory for the cost of a round of drinks. It made me wonder if our meeting was so happenstance after all.

"Called you already, has he? That was quick," I said and sipped my drink. "The son of a bitch only fired me a couple of hours ago."

"So he mentioned. Not by name, of course. He was more discreet than that. But when he described a low-life crook who disrupted an otherwise perfectly tasteful funeral and tried to con him, I naturally made the connection."

"Naturally."

"Fair warning, you might want to cash his cheque. He mentioned calling the bank and issuing a stop payment."

"Already covered, thanks."

Reynaldo let me take another sip before he began fishing for facts in earnest.

"So other than fostering an unproductive working relation-ship that ended in bitterness and tears, how was Saunders as a client?"

"Unethical," I stated simply.

"Him or you?"

"You for asking."

Reynaldo ignored my accusation. Ethics in our business was nebulous, subject to moment-by-moment interpretation depending on context or timing. There were few guidelines for what we did professionally, certainly nothing written down or generally agreed upon.

"I'm not certain client confidentiality applies. I already know all the details. I'm just asking for an honest opinion."

"Okay," I said, and gave Reynaldo a look up and down. I told him, "That tie is hideous, the comb-over isn't fooling anyone, and your cologne makes you smell like a budget prostitute."

"Aren't we in a mood?" he said indignantly. I could tell he wasn't nearly as insulted as I'd hoped. Reynaldo appreciates bitchiness, even when he's the target.

"Why don't you do something productive," he suggested, "like direct that anger inward where it belongs? I didn't steal him out from under you, you know."

"I'm not saying you did. I dropped the ball, you picked up. Run with it as far as you can."

Reynaldo looked skeptical. He didn't trust my invitation to continue from where I left off.

"What's the catch? If you're angling for a referral fee, you're way out of line. You and Saunders were done before he ever called me."

"No catch. He's all yours. Enjoy."

I toasted him and took another swig of my drink. Reynaldo followed my lead, taking a lesser sip of his own. I was gratified to note he looked concerned, perhaps even a tad worried.

"High maintenance?" he asked.

"No more so than you, yourself."

That really seemed to trouble him.

"Oh, dear," he said. "Well, if I recover his inheritance for him, it will be worth the time spent holding his hand and whispering sweet reassurances in his ear."

"He's not the touchy-feely kind. He's just looking to squeeze every dime he can out of the present circumstances. Try holding his hand and you might not get yours back."

"Duly noted and I thank you for the heads-up. It may not be worth a referral fee, but let me buy you another round."

Reynaldo started to wave the waitress back to our table, but I stopped him.

"Thanks, but no. I need to get back to the office."

"You mean home?"

"Home office, yeah."

Reynaldo worked out of his home as well, but he liked to remind me that I could never swing the rent for a dedicated place-of-work. He could afford it, of course, but he was too lazy to commute more than twenty feet after crawling out of bed first thing in the afternoon.

"How's the new secretary working out? Better than the last two or three, I hope."

"Three or four, actually," I corrected, rising from my chair. "But yeah, she seems to be handling things all right. She hasn't gone and quit on me yet at any rate."

"Pleased to hear it. But, of course, how could she?"

Reynaldo leaned back in his chair and smiled, making no effort to see me out. He would finish his Irish coffee all by himself, in the company of his favourite person. We were both glad to watch me leave.

Θ

I got home from the ice-cream summit with Tracy and the gin-and-bullshit abyss with Reynaldo in the late afternoon. I could hear Gladys in the back office, nattering away on her headset in some language I couldn't even guess at. She was probably calling home, wherever that was, running up my long distance bill. I stuck my head in and interrupted. Every once in a while I like to remind her she's on the clock.

"You have any new messages for me?"

"No," she said. It was the only English word she could nail. Gladys was well-practised in telling me that one.

"Nothing?"

"No," she insisted. A pulsating dot of red on the phone's cradle disagreed.

"What's this blinking on the machine?"

"Is meessage."

"I thought you said I had no messages."

"I haff no meessage for yoo! Meechine haff meessage for yoo!"

"When I ask about messages, I mean any messages. Whether you took them, the machine took them, or they got stuffed under the door, it doesn't matter."

"Fak yoo Reep! I no car abat yoo fakkin meesage!"

Gladys's tone became more civil, if no less frantic, as she returned to her overseas conversation like my rude interjection was already a distant memory. I left her to it and picked up a remote extension in the living room. Thumbing through the call log I recognized the number of my missed connection. It was the police. The actual message was a curt, impatient "Call me back." There was no other information offered, but I knew who it was and what it had to be about.

I remotely disconnected Gladys's call, for which I was treated to a lengthy barrage of obscenities that might have been genuinely offensive had they been the least bit comprehensible. I then dialled the number for a nearby police precinct by memory. It only took me a few minutes to navigate the digital switchboard at the cop shop and get my man on the phone—Detective Alan Frenz. We skipped the pleasantries. Frenz and I always kept things strictly professional. I was his occasional necessary evil, and he was a signature on an infrequent cheque.

"What have you got for me?" I asked.

"Murder. No witnesses."

"There's always a witness."

"None we can talk to. That's why we need you."

The other regular work that gets mediums and necromancers stepping on each others' toes are the cop jobs. Most police forces dismiss what we have to offer in the missing-persons and unsolved-murders department as laughable hokum, even when our tips turn out to be right on the money. Failures and inaccuracies only reinforce the widely held assumption that we're full of shit. Successes are usually dismissed as coincidence at best, or admission of criminal culpability at worst. It's not a terrific career move to pinpoint the location of a body dumped in the woods if the cops are only going to turn around and accuse you of being the one who dumped it. I mean, why else would we know where to find it, right?

It's important to be aware which municipalities have true believers in positions of authority within the department—overseers who are willing to give us the benefit of the doubt in light of positive outcomes and arrests that turn into convictions. Mediums have an easier time getting their foot in the door. All they have to do if show up and say they have a feeling about this, or an impression about that. If they offer enough specifics, the cops are duty-bound to follow up on the tip. And if they get it right a few times, they're in. The cops will start calling them to see if vibrations in the psychic realm or some such crap are telling them how to solve their caseload. Even a total skeptic will follow the advice of a random fortune-teller if it improves their arrest record and increases their chance of promotion.

Earning an inroad like this with the police is more challenging for a necromancer since we deal in actual physical remains rather than vague psychic impressions pulled out of the air. Although we can get infinitely more verifiable information from a murder victim than a medium could ever hope to, the cops are very touchy about letting outsiders play with their first degrees, second degrees and manslaughters. Building trust with Frenz took a very long time and a tall stack of bodies, but we had finally arrived on the same page. I could help. For a fee.

"Okay," I told Frenz, "let me have the particulars."

The particulars sounded like your usual boring mugging-gone-wrong. Someone had been found beaten to death and ditched behind a restaurant dumpster. No wallet, no I.D. It was the sort of crime that went unsolved all the time in every major city. I guess more cities could use a local necromancer. It's a shame we're so scarce.

"You need to see the crime scene?" he asked, even though he should have known better by now.

"Why the hell would I want to do that?" I said, sounding indignant.

Crime scenes are messy, awful places. They're usually spattered with all sorts of blood and tissue, and stink of gunpowder and released bowels. They're best avoided whenever possible.

"I thought you might want to have your own look at the evidence."

"I don't do evidence. I skip straight to the end results."

I've always found cops and their little evidence baggies of shell casings and cigarette butts and fibres tiresome. I suppose it's all necessary if you want to prove your case in a court of law, but that's not my department. Someone else can sort through all that DNA splashed around by any number of suspects. If that's what floats their boat, good luck to them.

Me, I'd rather just get the scoop from the murder victim personally. They usually know who did it. Figuring out the ballistics of which bullets were shot from what gun at whatever angle is academic masturbation.

"Who has the body?" was all I needed to know.

Now that I had my in with the police, you'd think I'd have it made. Surely there are enough unsolved murders every year to keep the jobs coming. That's true enough, but every department has a budget, and the discretionary funds are meagre. They can only pay out so much to freelancers who speak with the dead before they have to answer for what they've been spending their money on. The bean counters will rubber-stamp all sorts of absurd expenses, from youth-outreach programs to PTSD counselling, but they tend to freak if they see "necromancer" on their itemized list of payouts come audit time. It doesn't matter if someone sits them down to explain where their highest profile collars came from, it's all about public perception. So long as my fees are small enough to get lumped in under "miscellaneous," we're fine. In other words, no matter how often I do their job for them, I can't ever be paid more than what they spend on donuts in a single year. And, despite the cliché about cops and donuts, that's not as much as you might think.

Police work pays shit, but it's saved me from not making rent more than a few times. I've occasionally found myself hoping for a good murder spree when there are bills due. I don't wish anybody dead, I just wish the people doing all the killing would learn to pace themselves better. Sometimes these homicide droughts are hard for a guy like me to survive. The new stiff on the coroner's slab was welcome, but I hadn't been called to consult in so long, I was worried my fee wouldn't come soon enough to pay a couple of bills and keep the lights on.

Once I was off the phone with Frenz, I took a moment to shuffle through the mail I'd brought up from the lobby of my building. I was only halfway through the invoices I couldn't afford to pay when the phone rang. I heard Gladys pick up in the next room.

"Yooloogee, wat yoo want?"

After a pause so brief, I doubted she even listened to a word the caller said to her, "Uh-huh, uh-huh, ya, yoo hole da phoon."

"Reep, is for yoo!" she bellowed through the door.

"Of course it's for me. Who is it?"

"Why I no dis? Why I car? Is sum asshool for yoo! Peek ap da fakkin phoon!"

It was prudent advice. I grabbed the extension before another round of broken English with Gladys convinced my caller to hang up.

"Rip, I hear you're coming over for a visit."

It was Louie Cramer, one of the city's morgue attendants the coroner trusted with murder cases. Frenz had just told me he was in charge of the body I was supposed to look into.

"Frenz gave me the broad strokes," I told him. "I was just about to call you, but you beat me to it."

"The stiffs are stacking up down here. I need you to come by ASAP."

"I'm only on this one mugging case, Louie. I can't help with the rest of your inventory."

"Anything to free up a drawer, man. When can I expect you?"

Before I could be pinned down to a specific time, Gladys cut in on the line with a pressing office emergency that clearly warranted her interrupting a business call.

"Reep, I nid mar stapples! Stapples an papper-cleeps!"

I was friendly enough with Louie to be able to break away from our conversation and be as irritable with Gladys as I wished.

"For fuck's sake just order some more from the office-supply store. You know how to do that."

"How I no theese? I no no thees! Yoo shoe me now!"

"You've done it before. Just use the same account number. It's in the office-supply file folder."

"Yoo git it for me! I cunt reech!"

"Of course you can reach it. It's a file folder on the computer."

"I no see theese."

"It's on the goddamn desktop where it always is! Just look for it yourself and don't bug me with this shit when I'm on a call!"

"Fakk yoo too, Reep!" she yelled and fumbled to disconnect, making sure I heard her mutter, "Fakkin madder fakker" before the line cleared.

"Who's your assistant?" Louie wanted to know. "She sounds hot."

Louie was always a sucker for an exotic accent.

"She's more room temperature, really."

"You should introduce us. I could show her the town," he suggested.

"She doesn't get out much."

"She shy?"

"She doesn't do public places."

"I could come over."

"She's busy."

"Don't tell me she's washing her hair or some shit like that," said Louie.

"No, that's not an excuse I would go with in this particular case. How about we just say you're not her type and leave it at that?"

"Not her type? What the hell type am I supposed to be?"
"Breathing," I told him and hung up.

Chapter Five

Sudden Death

G LADYS HAD BEEN in my employ for the last six months and things seemed to be working out. She possessed a bad attitude and a terrible temper, and as a secretary she was barely adequate. She had poor language skills, weak communication skills, and she was bar-none the slowest typist I'd ever seen in action. But she hadn't walked out on me yet, so that put her ahead of all her predecessors. I'm incredibly disorganized when it comes to keeping track of files and contact information, so having some sort of secretarial assistance is a rare business expense I can justify on my tax return. Without someone to keep my records straight, there simply wouldn't be a business at all. For years I'd tried hiring a variety of interns and students and placement-agency peons to do the heavy lifting, but none of them had lasted.

If you worked for me long enough, you were bound to see some creepy shit that would shake you. And I don't just mean turn your stomach. I mean chill you to your core in a spiritual, existential sort of way. On average it took one week. My new secretary would be coming along fine, more or less, keeping things organized, more or less. There would be questions, sure, odd looks at moments, but things would be going smoothly. And then they'd see something—

something they hadn't expected to see, not at this job, not on this earth—and they'd quit. Sometimes they'd take a moment to submit an official resignation. Most of the time they'd just flee the premises, usually screaming, occasionally driven mad. And then I'd be stuck doing my own filing again, making my own phone calls, trying to find at least one temp agency that hadn't blacklisted me yet.

I came to realize that I was kidding myself thinking that a secretary shuffling papers for me in a home office would be insulated from all the grotesqueries I have to deal with on the front lines. I tried not to bring my work home with me and keep my assistant's exposure strictly in the realm of confirming appointments, sending out invoices, and making coffee. But inevitably, some element of the job wouldn't rub off so easily. It would follow me home, clinging to me like the stench of rotten meat, or tracking across the floor like shoes still muddy from an open grave. Some horror from the beyond would crop up and reveal itself in full view of the help. I often wouldn't even realize what the problem was until the shrieking and the panic began. By then it was too late and I'd find the position vacant once again. What I needed was someone who wasn't going to be scared off by the weirdness. I needed someone who was part of the weirdness. Someone who would fit right in. That's when I met Gladys.

I first laid eyes on her online. Not on any sort of match-making site—romantic, employment or otherwise. I picked her up on eBay. Fully articulated human skulls can be had for about a thousand bucks if you want one in good shape with all of its teeth. The item condition is always described, un-ironically, as "used." Most of them come from the private collections of doctors, dentists and biology teachers. When they kick the bucket, the families can't get rid of their collections of medical oddities fast enough, and usually sell them for a song to the first dealer who makes an offer. The dealers flip them for a quick profit to other medical professionals, morbid weirdos, or people like me who qualify as both. The internet has become the world bazaar of the bizarre. I wish I'd been active back when these sorts of deals happened between shady people in dark places. Organizing a clandestine exchange of goods and cash would have been so much more colourful, if less convenient, than signing for a package at my own front door.

Although I'm always interested in an intriguing parasite sealed in a jar of formaldehyde, a preserved birth defect frozen in a fetal position for all time, or a cancerous organ that's more tumor than organ, articulated skulls are an artwork unto themselves, and I'd never be without one. The skulls themselves are usually from the poorest shitholes in the world and are mostly young females. If you're unlucky enough to be hit by the double whammy of being born a girl in a dirt-poor third-world nation or failed state, your family may well end up selling your dysentery-ravaged corpse for a few bucks to someone who tells them they need it for medical research. These seemingly well-meaning Westerners or their intermediaries are only half lying. They're not interested in doing any research that might involve finding cures for what ails and bettering the lot of the suffering poor in the aforementioned shitholes. They're interested in recruiting fresh corpses for medical schools back home, and they're willing to pay bottom dollar.

The World Health Organization, Red Cross, UNICEF and, of course, the Catholic Church all have workers or volunteers who are operating their own little businesses on the side. They keep the supply coming for whoever has a demand. Packed in ice and shipped out on the next available cargo plane with a bit of spare space, the bodies arrive back home fresh as the catch of the day, ready to be signed for as "medical supplies" by a go-between with all the nearest teaching hospitals and universities on speed dial. Aside from being dead, the otherwise healthy corpses, with their pink and perfect organs, end up being autopsy subjects for students and future surgeons still learning the ins and outs of the human body. Anything sick and possibly still contagious goes to one of the facilities that specialize in stripping down a corpse to its bare basics. This involves a lot of dismemberment and boiling until the bones are stripped of every morsel of flesh and muscle. Particularly nice examples are wired together to create full-bodied skeletons for anatomy studies and lecture halls. But few of the boiled bodies come out of their sterilizing broth looking so fine that all the bones get to stay together and hang at the front of some biology classroom forevermore—or until budget cuts end their tenure early and they're sold for scrap. Recruits from the third world usually come with all sorts of imperfections, including broken limbs that never healed right, spinal curvatures, and horrendous teeth. There's some demand for interesting abnormalities, but quality generics are the bread and butter of the osteo-industry. Bones of similar sizes can often be mixed and matched to help fill out an incomplete skeleton, but there are always bins brimming with spare parts.

I didn't have the funds to invest in a complete skeleton. Once you factor in the cost of the bones plus all the necessary ingredients for a full-blown reanimation ritual that won't fade away or sputter out after a month or two, we're talking tens of thousands of dollars. Sure, it would be cheaper and easier to just steal a fresh corpse from somewhere. Raising something fresher than bones is always simpler and less costly since you don't have to worry about all the bits and pieces staying attached once it starts moving around on its own. But even the best reanimator out there can't do much about the smell after the first few weeks. I know a fellow necromancer in London who has a reanimated corpse that's been with him for years. "Shambler" is what he calls the corpse, named for his pitiful gait as he drags himself around his master's quaint little row house, performing menial tasks and duties. Shambler was fairly well preserved and maintained, even after those many long years unburied, but the stench could be awful on warm, humid days. Last I was there, he was decorated like a Christmas tree, with a dozen air fresheners, several ampules of scented oils, and a pungent soap-on-a-rope necklace. The combination muted the stink, but couldn't hope to mask it entirely. The neighbours still complained.

Properly prepared bones, on the other hand, have a completely neutral scent. And a single skull was within my means. After the lengthy ritual of summoning a consciousness to the remains and trapping it inside the skull, I introduced myself and explained what I required from her.

"Fak yoo!" were the first words Gladys ever spoke to me. It quickly became her favourite greeting, response and sentiment.

I have no idea what her name might have been, and I probably wouldn't have even been able to pronounce it if I did. So I call her Gladys. Her English is atrocious. When she answers the phone, she sounds like a telemarketer at a call centre in Mumbai. In her old life, she may have been exactly that. I've never asked, out of basic politeness. Disembodied, reanimated skulls don't care to be reminded of their former lives. No matter how badly they may have sucked, they still tend to get wistfully nostalgic about the good old days of having a body, flesh, and a life.

In the months since entering my service, Gladys had been sitting on my desk like a set of novelty wind-up Chattering Teeth—only you didn't have to wind her up and the novelty wore off quickly. Technically, the chattering-teeth effect comes from telekinetic residue as the sound of her voice forces itself through the ether and into the empty conduit that used to be a head. I'd tried to explain it to some people, but it was usually easier to agree with visitors that I had a talking skull and wasn't that cool, or creepy, or sick or whatever adjective they cared to append. In fact, most of the sound she makes actually comes out through the empty sockets of the eyes and nose, making her voice, already insufferably alien, sound like it's coming from inside a sea shell you're holding up to your ear. Clients on the phone just assume it's a bad connection.

Gladys, apart from manning the phone and working the computer, is an integral part of my filing system. The cap of her skull is detachable, and can be pivoted back on a hinge that was installed as part of the articulation. I stash all the business cards I accumulate in the vacant space, turning her head into an ossified Rolodex of contact information. Gladys despises my using her empty cranium for storage, but nothing I do pleases her, so I can't tell in the grand scheme of things where this particular transgression stands on her list of my offences. I don't do it to be mean, or to humiliate her, but it's a convenient container, and stuffing her with so much card stock helps muffle the echo-chamber effect of her voice.

"Git yoo fakkin hends off me, fakker!" bitched Gladys, as I removed her telephone headset and cracked open her skull long enough to deposit the jet black calling card of Charlie Nocturne, with its complete lack of any useful information whatsoever.

I wasn't interrupting one of Gladys's personal calls. At that moment, she was surfing the web, looking at the latest spring fashion designs she could never hope to wear. My bit of filing didn't get in the way of her browsing, but she made sure I knew it pissed her off regardless.

I was just checking my other pockets for any more slips of paperwork I needed to tuck away, when I heard a knock at my door. There had been no ring from the lobby, I hadn't buzzed anyone in. This didn't make me particularly suspicious. Sometimes visitors walk right in while someone else has the door open, neighbours occasionally swing by to complain about unearthly noises or, all too often, it's the superintendent coming to bitch about a late rent cheque or investigate the source of a leak somewhere in the building.

I left Gladys to her fashion fantasies and strode across the length of the flat to greet my guest. Purely out of routine rather than paranoia, I hunched over to peer through the fish-eyed lens of the spyhole to see who it was. I couldn't make out the face behind the barrel of the gun that was poised less than an inch away from the other side of the glass. Then I saw the muzzle flash. The last thing to pass through my brain, other than the bullet, was the thought, "I've just been murdered. Fuck."

Chapter Six

Dying Young

I WAS FOUR YEARS OLD the first time I died.

I choked to death on a hot dog at a barbeque, which I thought was a damned foolish way to go, even at four. Paramedics were summoned, and one of them happened to have just the right set of tongs to reach deep into my throat and pull out the big bite I'd taken eighteen minutes earlier. By that time, I had turned blue, my pulse had stopped, and my brain had shut down. I was a DOA if ever there was one, but the ambulance crew went through the motions anyway—if only for my parents' benefit. No one likes to give up on a four-year-old kid.

I remember watching them work for a long time until I got bored and my attention began to drift. It was a simple matter of just stepping back into my body and I was alive again. My chest was sore from all that CPR, but otherwise I was fine—maybe a bit loopy with so many oxygen-starved brain cells, but that passed in time. Everyone hailed the miraculous recovery and thanked the paramedics, but I was left with the distinct impression that they knew something was off. In their line of work, I imagine they see all sorts of oddities, unexplainable deaths, and seemingly impossible recoveries. But they also would have known just how far gone I was when they arrived on the scene. My recovery didn't thrill or delight them like it did everyone else at the barbeque. They looked disturbed.

It was another four years before I died again. By then I had almost convinced myself that the first incident had been a childish delusion—something I'd dreamed. Nevertheless, I possessed a sense of immortality beyond what most children, still innocent concerning the fragile facts of life, naively assume. I was considered fearless, a daredevil, up for any danger. Idiotic was what I was. I felt I had something to prove, and it was child's play, quite literally, for the other kids to goad me into doing reckless things. I would agree out of a misplaced sense of pride. Tempting fate, risking life and limb, was something I was called upon to do every time school friends and neighbourhood kids wandered out of the eyeline of watchful parents. In this way I was dared to dangle off a train trestle while a passenger express roared by overhead, double dared to sprint across six lanes of rush-hour traffic without looking, and triple dared to pick a fight with Flunk Wilson, the biggest kid in third grade, who had already been held back two years due to "slow development" issues that didn't extend to his muscles or height.

It was while stepping up to the comparatively banal challenge of climbing to the very top of an ancient oak that I met my very literal downfall. Every kid in town climbed that tree, but few ventured higher than the lowest branches, which were as thick and sturdy as the trunks of most other trees. I was pitched the idea of scaling all the way to the very top and poking my head out of the leafy canopy. It sounded like a great idea, not just for the admiration it would earn, but for the view it would offer once I was up there. I didn't account for how thin and brittle some of the uppermost branches—twigs more like—would be. I quickly ran out of viable foot- and hand-holds as I ascended, but I kept going regardless, higher and higher until I committed to a branch that couldn't have hoped to support half my weight. The dead branch snapped off in my fist and I carried it with me all the way to the ground despite impacting on every other branch jutting out between me and the gnarled roots at the base of the tree.

I heard the snap of my neck as I landed on my head, and I knew in that instant before unconsciousness swept over me that my reckless behaviour had finally succeeded in getting me killed.

When I opened my eyes again, it was dark. All the other kids were long gone, having fled the scene of the peer-pressured crime. The dead branch from the tippy-top of the tree was still clutched in my hand. I had almost made it, had almost managed to get my head through the thick growth of oak leaves that blotted out the sky, had almost treated myself to the best view of the world offered for many miles in all directions. Almost. Yet somehow I still had a memory of that view—as though I had been up there, floating for hours, even higher than the upper reaches of the tree would have permitted.

I tried to sit up, but my was neck was sore and it was so much more comfortable to remain lying flat on the ground, staring up at rustling leaves and twinkling stars. Eventually I tried again and managed to pull myself into a sitting position. My head, however, hung off my shoulders limply, unnaturally. I grabbed myself by the ears and tried to set my skull straight. I could hear the loose bones crunching in complaint. It took a while, but I finally managed to prop my head back onto the peak of my spine in a way that felt correct. I held it there for several long minutes before slowly letting go and removing my hands. It didn't feel very stable, but eventually I felt my fractured neck fuse back into something that could support the weight of the head perched on top of it.

I rose to my feet with careful poise, like I was trying to balance a tall stack of books. What I was really trying to keep balanced was my skull. I took it easy on the walk home, allowing everything I'd broken in the fall to settle back into its proper place. By the time I arrived, only to be informed I was very late and had missed supper, nothing about me appeared unduly amiss. I was back to being just another dirty boy, with dishevelled clothes and the usual variety of scrapes and bruises after a day of play and roughhousing.

My classmates were genuinely surprised to see me at school the next morning. I'd been dead for hours and didn't even take a sick day. Surely that was worth a doctor's note and time off. I acted like nothing was wrong, nothing was different. But I was the only one. After that, nobody dared me to do anything ever again. Nobody talked to me again, either.

The next time I died it was less than a year later. That time it was on purpose, to prove a point. I leapt off the roof of my house and made sure I landed on my head. I didn't just break my neck that time. My skull split open and there were little-boy brains all over the place. Or so I'm told. I lost consciousness instantly. When I became self-aware again, I was no longer in my body. I didn't even know where my body was. I roamed the neighbourhood for days, just a consciousness on the prowl, drifting wherever I cared to, through solid walls and closed doors, spying and eavesdropping at will, then floating away to whatever captured my fleeting attention next.

It was through sheer happenstance that I found myself at my own funeral. I'd followed some local kids I knew but no longer spoke to as they piled into the family car, wearing their Sunday best on a day in the middle of the week. I'd been curious about where they were going, and drifted alongside them until they pulled into the parking lot of the town's only funeral home.

I discovered a familiar face lying at the head of the chapel, in front of an audience of weepers. That was me in the box, or at least what was physically left of me. My shattered skull had been reassembled, the broken skin sewn shut, plastered over and made presentable. They'd dressed me in a suit and tie I didn't recognize and had certainly never worn while alive. I looked like a proper little gentleman, hands clasped over my heart, dozing lightly like I might wake up at any moment. And I thought that's exactly what I should do.

The service hadn't begun yet. There was no priest stealing the show by leading grievers in prayer and song. In theory, the deceased at a funeral should be the centre of attention, but they rarely are. Friends and family who haven't seen each other in years get busy chatting, and before long they forget all about who they've gathered to bury and why they're all dressed in black. It took several long minutes before someone in the front row noticed my pale stiff hands had started to move, working the rigor out of the finger joints. That's when the screaming started. And once others saw what had inspired the screaming, they joined in. The effect was not unlike the chorus of prayers or songs typically heard at funerals, only not so melodic and with more stampeding panic.

To their credit, some of my relations didn't immediately bolt when I first rose from the dead. But I did manage to clear the room when I started convulsing violently and vomiting up tremendous amounts of embalming fluid. By the time I had emptied my system and turned the boy-sized coffin into a bathtub of formaldehyde, I found I was alone in the building. I had the run of the place for two hours before anyone dared enter to confirm what they thought they had seen. Not that I did much running. Mostly I was stiff and ravenously hungry. In the family room, a special chamber set aside for those closest to the deceased, I found a spread of complimentary tea, coffee and biscuits. I'd eaten them all and drank every drop by the time the funeral home staff cautiously breached their place of business and found me sitting alone in a chair opposite my own coffin. My suit was ruined by the gallons of embalming puke, creased and stained, but almost dry by then. I was still dazed after such a lengthy period of death and didn't turn to greet them. They approached me from behind, slowly making their way up the red runner between the rows of chairs. They were careful not to make a sound, but I could hear the breath of one of them whistling through his nose. I don't know what they expected to see when they so hesitantly stepped in front of me to have a look. A zombie or a ghost maybe. If that's what they were anticipating, they must have been sorely disappointed. What they got was a sleepy-eyed kid, natural colour quickly returning to his made-up face, looking like hell, but also looking very much alive and relatively normal despite all the stitch-work poking out from under the hairline.

"Oh," I said slowly, my first words in days. "Hi."

That was a difficult death to recover from, and I was sick in bed for weeks. The more food and liquids I got into me, the quicker I healed, but that cocktail of preservative crap they'd pumped into me after sucking out all my blood was a real hurdle. I spent the first few days expelling the remaining embalming fluid from my body through every available orifice. I literally had to sweat it out night after night, waking up in a pool of stinking chemicals and soiled sheets each morning. It was awful and gruelling, but eventually I bounced back. By the end of the month, you could never tell I'd been sick at all, let alone dead for days. At least there were no physical signs of my demise and resurrection. Socially, however, I'd laid waste to my parents' lives. It was no longer a matter of the other kids not talking to me at school. The rest of the family refused to take their calls. Some even changed their numbers. Word got out to the community at large and we were openly ostracized everywhere. My father was laid off from work for no convincing reason, mail was no longer delivered to the house, and every local business turned our patronage away. My mother had to drive two hours to get to the nearest grocery store that would sell us food to stock our fridge and pantry. On the rare occasion anyone said anything to us, it was an accusation of witchcraft, devil worship, or general heresy. We came to believe that if we stood our ground much longer, we'd all end up burned at the stake, and I wasn't so sure that was a death I could come back from. I knew my mother and father couldn't manage the feat. In the end, it was easiest and best to sell the house and move a thousand miles away to a new home where nobody had ever heard of us.

I gave death a good long break after that, partly to spare my parents the anxiety and grief and general misery, but mostly because dying was a painful experience and I didn't see much point in it. As stunts went, this was a pretty spectacular one, but it would be a long time before I thought any good could come of it.

My eventual vocation may seem like a natural step, given my childhood experiences with death, but drawing obvious connections like that is work best suited for quack psychologists. No, my path to necromancy was more convoluted, and included many side trips down dead ends of study and employment. It wasn't until my second year of facilitating graveside communication as a freelancer that my ability to enter the realm of the dead, rather than merely act as a conduit, became useful. Sometimes it's just easier to get things done when you're deceased. Chasing down uncooperative spirits through the afterlife for one, accessing places that are otherwise mortally inaccessible for another. There are usually workarounds to all these problems a necromancer faces, but simply dying to finish a challenging task offers me an advantage over the competition. I've met other necromancers with a few freaky talents hidden away for special occasions, but I've never met one who can do what I do.

From time to time, the ability to die and come back has been very handy indeed, although I'll try just about any other option before resorting to this final trick up my sleeve. It's not so bad if I can do it in a controlled situation. Lying down on a couch with a handy overdose of pills is easy and simple to bounce back from. Some discomfort, but no real pain, and I'm off in the netherworld taking care of business. My corpse lies around in relative security, waiting for my return. If I'm gone for more than an hour or two, there's rigor mortis and lividity to deal with, but they're no biggie. Another few hours to work out the kinks and get the blood flowing again and I'm fine. But it's rare that I can plan ahead like that. Unfortunately, when the moment arises that I need to resort to a quick demise to accomplish the otherwise impossible, it's because circumstances have spiralled out of control. Something has to be done immediately, on the spot, or the contract blows up in my face and I don't get paid. That's when I go with the derringer.

The derringer is one of those items in my kit I like to keep at the bottom of the bag. I know it's there, but I don't like to be reminded of it. I don't even like to see it when I'm rummaging around for some other tool. I've had to use it on half-a-dozen occasions, always on myself of course, and I don't have any happy associations with it. Small but deadly, it's a late-issue model with the standard twin-chambers in the over-under barrel design. I always keep it loaded with a double round of hollow-point bullets. Hollow-points flatten on impact and cause more catastrophic damage as they push through meat and bone. I'd prefer not to make such a mess of myself when I have to do the deed, but I need to make sure I get the job done right if it comes to that. There's no point mortally wounding myself and lingering near death, while doctors make heroic efforts to keep me alive, hooked up to a battery of machines and monitors. I need to set my consciousness free in an instant and be on my way.

This, of course, leaves an untidy body behind, often in an inconveniently public place. To deal with this problem, I've left strict instructions in my living will that my organs are not to be donated, that I'm to be kept on ice, untampered with, for as long as the morgue will permit, and that under no circumstances am I to be embalmed. Once was enough of that shit. I carry identification with me at all times so whoever discovers my body will know who I am, understand my wishes, and give me enough time and space to return intact and unmolested by well-meaning coroners and morticians. The real hassle is the paperwork. If my body has been through the system, there are police reports and death certificates to undo and it can be a tedious affair. The bureaucracy of resuming life as normal can make you wish you were dead. Luckily I now have a few connections who can help things along by losing inconvenient paperwork behind filing cabinets, shredding incomplete forms, or hitting the delete button on intrusive data that might otherwise play havoc with my bank account and credit rating. When it comes to the legal and financial systems, being dead is like being a persecuted minority. You don't want to deal with anal-retentive bureaucrats who are sticklers for details like who's dead, who isn't, and who used to be but might not be anymore. Avoid it if at all possible. Trust me on this: if you die, stay dead. You don't need the hassle.

Although I'm willing to put a bullet through my own head when circumstances and paying work dictate, I'm not pleased to have someone else do it for me by surprise and without permission. Especially when I'm on a schedule. That's probably why I felt so cranky when I finally opened my eyes after spending days dead on the floor of my apartment, lying in a pool of my own blood and brain matter. That, and the fact that my nice Turkish rug was ruined. Some stains never come out.

I'd been so surprised by my abrupt assassination, it took a long time for my mind to focus itself and realize what just happened. Had I gotten my act together quicker, I could have astrally projected myself out of my apartment and had a look at who pulled the trigger on me. Instead, it took me until nightfall to gather my consciousness back into one cohesive whole, and by that time it was hours too late to play whodunit.

With nowhere else to go, at least not as a spirit, I drifted around my apartment, concentrating on remerging with my corpse and jump-starting my heart. The damage was severe, and it's always a lot harder to get back inside when there aren't enough brains left in my skull to let me think. It didn't help that the very nature of this particular demise had me so distracted. It was such a bold, premeditated murder. The suggestion of malicious intent rubbed salt in my massive head wound. I don't operate under the delusion that I'm well liked, but I didn't think anyone hated me quite so much.

Who was it, I wondered. A dissatisfied customer or one of my nefarious associates? With the door between us and nothing but a view of the gun barrel through the spyhole, I'd seen nothing helpful whatsoever. I guess sometimes there really are no witnesses.

Once I finally wormed my consciousness back inside and raised my eyelids, I had something to focus on—ceiling tiles. It wasn't much, but I used it. It helps to have a tangible sensation to work with. A sight, a sound, a smell. Anything that gets me to reconnect to the land of the living. Once I'm in, the healing can start. Mobility returns soon after. Speech takes a little longer.

"Gladys? How long have I been down?" were my first words, weak but distinct. Gladys was in the next room, but the door was open and she was close enough to hear.

"Reep? I tot yoo deed."

"How long?"

"Why yoo no deed?"

"I was dead. I got better."

"I weesh yoo deed!" she yelled, disappointed.

"Thanks, Gladys. Love you, too."

"Thees no possabal!"

I hadn't died once since Gladys entered my employ. She'd never seen this particular talent of mine, and I hadn't bothered to enlighten her.

"It's just a thing I do. No big deal. Did you see who shot me?"

"No. Nobaddy cam in. I jas heer beeg bang. Gon go ka-pow, yoo fall don, stay don lung time."

"Yeah, but how long?"

"Abat tree days."

You'd think somebody would have heard the shot, or noticed the scorched bullet hole in my door. But that wasn't the nature of my building. People who lived there kept to themselves, expressed little curiosity about their fellow tenants, and almost never said "Hello" when passing each other in the hall or encountering someone at the mailbox. It wasn't much of a community, and it suited me.

"Three days. Feels about right. What time is it?"

I slowly rose to my feet and staggered into the back-room office. I could feel loose brains and bone fragments shifting around inside my skull. They hadn't anchored to where they needed to be yet and the sensation made me nauseous. I steadied myself on the corner of Gladys's desk with one hand and reached for the window blind with the other.

The sun was out, hanging low over the skyline. Day. Afternoon. I'd been shot on a Friday and lost the weekend. That made it Monday, still an hour or two away from the evening shift. Newly resurrected or not, I had bills to pay and work to attend to. Louie would be at his station soon and there was time I needed to make up.

"I gotta go," I told Gladys, and braced myself for the mechanical effort it would take to change into a fresh shirt that wasn't spotted and soaked in my blood. The task seemed monumental. A short nap before the attempt seemed prudent.

"Reep?"

"Yeah, Gladys?"

"Is god yoo no deed."

I nodded an acknowledgement to the talking skull on the desk.

"It was a passing phase. I'm over it."

"I glad yoo no deed."

It was the most civil tone she had ever used with me.

"That's sweet of you to say, Gladys. You going soft on me?"

"Fak yoo."

Chapter Seven

Bring Out the Dead

I T'S HARD TO KEEP TRACK of the time when you're dead. Time doesn't count for much when you find yourself on the other side of eternity. But three days out of the loop with the living and you can miss a lot. The world keeps spinning without you and much can happen.

After wasting the entire weekend lying around on the floor, I had finally regenerated enough to regain consciousness and make the long, arduous climb to my feet. I was ambulatory enough to get to the fridge, guzzle all the milk and juice I had on hand—about three litres worth—and then climb into bed for a few hours of sleep. Regular sleep, not the sleep of the dead. My liquid diet gave me enough vitamins and proteins to finish growing back the lost tissue and heal over the massive head wound. When I woke up again, I checked myself out in the bathroom mirror to make sure I was presentable. The bullet had entered just above my right eye, but the hole was now fleshed over. The skin was still quite pink and new, but a pair of sunglasses would cover it nicely until the hole was done healing in another day or so. The back of my head was another matter. That was where the exit wound was. The fractured plate of skull was still eggshell fragile as the cells grew back to replace what was missing. A fresh layer of skin had grown over the exposed bone like a layer of cobwebs spun by invisible spiders. It grew thicker by the hour, but it was still far from ready to make a public appearance. Once the new flesh started sprouting hair again, any evidence of the wound would be covered up while it finished mending. No one would be able to detect anything amiss by the time the next weekend rolled around, and I'd be completely healed come the start of the following week.

I didn't have much time to lounge around the apartment and recover in privacy. I had people to see, appointments to keep, murders to solve. My own for one. So when I left my home an hour later, I wore a hat. I cocked it far enough back on my head to cover the wound from sight and protect the tender new flesh from what was left of the setting sun.

Hillside General was the unimaginatively named general hospital that was built into the side of a hill. Its most notorious feature, other than a corrupt administration misappropriating funds, was the confusing elevator system. What was the first floor on one side of the building was a sub-sub-basement on the other. If you entered the hospital reception area on your way down the hill and walked straight through the main corridor, you would find yourself with an impressive fifth-storey view of the downtown core from the window at the end of the hall. During visiting hours, no one seemed to have any idea what floor they were on, or where they could find the friend or loved one they were trying to visit. No two elevators agreed on which floors they were servicing, because it was all relative, and changed at hundred-foot intervals as you travelled through the various wings.

I never got lost at Hillside because I was only ever headed to one point of interest—B8, the morgue. Even with the sub-most sub-basement as my target destination, I still had to walk up the Hillside incline to get to the lowest available entrance. Hiking up there was a bitch, especially in my still-delicate condition. Fifty more feet of dirt and rock perched on top and the hill would have officially qualified as a small mountain. Once upon a time it was, but the last creature to see it in its full-blown mountainous glory would have been a stegosaurus or a brachiosaurus or some other saurus that had been indigenous to the area back when it was all part of one big happy Pangaea.

What was the main floor at my point of entry was actually level B4 as far as most of the rest of the building was concerned. That meant I only had to descend another four B's to get where I was going. Each of those levels was accessible to hospital personnel only, and even then, only the authorized few with a key that had to be turned in a lock at the bottom of the service elevator control panel. I happened to have one on my keychain, right alongside the ones for my apartment, my mailbox, and any random caskets and niches I might encounter.

One more key to the kingdom of the dead. At least I didn't need to pick this lock. Years ago I'd seized an opportune coffee break at the hospital, when certain staff were away from their posts, to slip out and get a copy made of the master elevator key. It saved the hassle of dealing with reception and having someone with an officially sanctioned copy of the key and a laminated hospital ID badge to come all the way up just to escort me back down. This way I could come and go as I needed. The morgue staff must have realized I'd procured my own key by now, but nobody seemed to care. It was a convenience that ran both ways, and they were always happy to see an outside face down in the meat locker, provided it was alive and animated and could talk back to them.

Louie Cramer was my favourite of the morgue-men, and I liked to time my visits with his shifts whenever possible. It wasn't that the rest of the corpse-patrol gang were bad people, but there's something about the work in a morgue that fosters a certain bad attitude. Not grim, but ghoulish. I'm all for gallows humour where appropriate, but some of the slab jockeys wouldn't let up. You need to keep the mood light in a place like that, but after a while jokes at the expense of burn victims and car-wreck fatalities stop being funny and start getting icky. It's not the inappropriateness, it's the relentlessness. They should really switch up their material, tell the occasional knock-knock joke that doesn't have a dead body as the punchline. There are perfectly hilarious sex stories that don't involve necrophilia. They need to look into it is all I'm saying.

Louie wasn't like that, though. He was one of the few you could talk to and immediately get a sense of his life outside the morgue. To him, it was just a job. He did it well, he had the stomach for it, but he wasn't interested in talking about it outside the context of work. He'd rather chat about sports or politics than the most surprising thing extracted during an autopsy that week. Admittedly, he'd always throw his five bucks into the pot to see who could accurately predict what that thing might be, but he wouldn't dwell on it. It was the difference between cynical and morbid. I get my fill of morbid, but I appreciate a good cynic. Cynics are well informed. That's what turns them into cynics.

I pulled the elevator key out of the lock and pocketed it again as soon as the doors slid open on B8. As usual, there was no one in sight to question why I had a key, but I like to keep discreet just in case. Louie was at his post at a desk in the hall. He had the entire floor to himself. With no new bodies on the way, everyone else on the night shift was elsewhere. The hospital had a games room for personnel on break. They were probably heeding the siren call of discount vending machines and a worn-out ping-pong table until the next patient in the hospital flatlined and interrupted their fun.

Louie stayed behind, earning his keep by filling out forms no one would ever read.

"You're late," he reminded me needlessly, looking up from his desk.

"I am."

"You're three days late."

"Who's counting?"

Louie didn't ask for details or excuses. He knew things came up. And when it came to me, he knew very strange things came up. If he didn't need to know, he didn't want to know. Another reason I liked Louie.

The small talk taken as read and the bullshit skipped, we entered the storage room and were standing at the row of corpse drawers a minute later. With no fanfare, Louie pulled out the relevant drawer so I could take a look. There was no sheet to pull aside, no bag to unzip. The body lay exposed and naked on a slab that would simply be spritzed with a bleach-based spray and wiped down before it was given a new customer to support. Hospitals and ambulance crews don't waste perfectly good body bags on corpses unless they're a horrible mess—violently mangled and bloody, or putridly septic and weeping fluids. This one wasn't too bad, as back-alley slayings went. Pale grey, typical; contusions, few; head wound, fatal but unremarkable as smashed skulls go; age, old; beard, bushy; fingers, nine.

"He's still filed as a John Doe. No idea who he is," Louie told me.

I was caught off guard but didn't let on. This was the first time I knew the body in the drawer by name.

"His name is Aharon Reubenski. He's an eighty-year-old rabbi. Not local."

"That was quick. You made contact already?"

I didn't keep Louie in suspense and gave him the particulars.

"No. I recognize him. He was a client. I haven't seen him since he handed me a cheque for one night's work. I had assumed he left town, went home, wherever that is."

"Cops seem to think it's a botched robbery. Some stupid kid looking at a mandatory ten for manslaughter. No suspects."

"Manslaughter my ass. This is a Murder One. Rabbi Reubenski had enemies. Too many for this to be a random mugging fuck up."

"Who murders an eighty-year-old man?" wondered Louie aloud.

"Somebody impatient."

"And a rabbi at that."

"An impatient anti-Semite. When did you get him in?" I asked.

"Four nights ago."

So while I was out carousing with Rebecca, drinking cheap beer and watching a grown man puke for a percentage of the door, old Aharon Reubenski was getting himself beaten to death across town. I'm not sure who had a worse night out.

"You're lucky we even still have him," said Louie.

"True enough," I agreed. According to Jewish tradition, he should have already been in the ground. "I wonder if he's been reported missing. He must have family."

"Must have. So ask him."

Louie looked at me expectantly. He knew what I could do. He didn't understand it, but he knew. I'd shown him results and helped clear his stock of unidentified remains in the past. Louie appreciated that. He liked to keep a tidy morgue, and he didn't like freeloading corpses stuffing his drawers for days past their welcome.

I stood over the old man who wouldn't be getting any older and concentrated. In the intervening days, his consciousness could have drifted off anywhere. But standing next to the body like this, I could draw him back easily enough. Getting the goods on Reubenski's murder promised to be a simple task. I wouldn't even have to introduce myself. But after a few moments of getting no hint of anything from the beyond, I knew something was amiss.

When I opened my eyes again, I found Louie looking at my furrowed brow with an expression that switched from expectant, to disappointed, to guilty. I instantly knew why.

"Did you cut out the brain?"

Louie hung his head, ashamed, and muttered, "Yes."

"What the hell is it with you pathologists and performing indignities on bodies? If one of you isn't slicing and dicing, then another's sexually interfering with the latest Jane Doe."

"I'm sorry. I didn't think they'd give this one to you."

"Tell me you've still got some brain tissue lying in a tray somewhere," I said, looking around pointlessly.

"It all went to medical waste days ago. It's been burned by now."

"You don't make my job any easier, you know that Louie?"

"Sorry."

I wasn't listening to Louie's apologies. My mind was racing, considering what I could do with what I had on hand. I'd never been to the hospital's medical waste dump. Anything there would have been a hopeless mix of biohazard bins, all of it earmarked for incineration. And this many days later, the rabbi's organs and brain would be long gone. Torched and trucked off to some dump along with the ashen remains of amputated limbs, tumours, blood samples and biopsies that had already been tested and cleared for disposal. But then I remembered there was another department on B8 that could still help me out. Laundry.

I left without another word. Louie thought I was going home angry and dogged my steps, throwing more apologies at me for mishandling the meat. When I walked down the hall, right past the elevator, he knew something was up.

The laundry room was through a set of swinging doors at the far end of the hall. Rows of washers and driers were running on synchronized settings. With all the machines somewhere in the middle of their cycles, no one was hanging around to watch the linen spin. The steady mechanical grinding was only broken up by the occasional soiled bedsheet or vomit-stained pillow case that would drop down the chutes that jutted out of the ceiling. All of those stains and spills would land in one of the giant hampers that were stationed at regular intervals down the bowling-alley layout. There they would wait for the next wash cycle, when workers would return to move things along, from washer to drier and finally back into service.

There were carts stacked with folded laundry, ready to be bused upstairs to the supply closets of the patient wards on floors high above us. I started helping myself to one of almost everything, scoring a set of scrubs, a medical gown and a lab coat. This was also where the hospital stored packages of items meant for one-use wear, so they could be distributed along with the freshly washed reusables. I grabbed a couple of plastic baggies containing a pair of paper slippers and a shower cap I thought might come in handy.

"Rip?" I heard Louie's voice behind me. He sounded like he had questions for me, but hadn't quite managed to form any yet. I tried to explain.

"I can't afford to lose my commission on this one."

He finally vocalized the most obvious question.

"What are you doing?"

"Exhausting my options."

A moment later I was marching back to the morgue with an armful of everything I could find that was readily available and qualified as clothing.

"I can't pump him for information if he hasn't got a brain," I told Louie, as he hurried to keep up with me, "but the carcass can still be of some help."

We stepped back into the morgue. Aharon Reubenski lay in the open drawer where we'd left him.

"Is he cleared for release?" I asked.

"Yeah," confirmed Louie. "The autopsy was three days ago. Written up, signed-off, and filed. Nothing's keeping him here, other than a lack of interest."

"So nobody will miss him?"

"Not until we get in touch with the family."

"Hold off on that, will you?"

"Rip, I'm babysitting enough stiffs here as it is. I want to move this one along. We need the drawers."

"Don't worry about saving space," I said, approaching the body with my improvised wardrobe. "I'm taking him with me."

I dumped the clothes on the floor and tore open the tiny plastic bag with the folded shower cap inside. Once I got it out, I placed it over Reubenski's head. It didn't exactly make for an appropriate hat, but it was bigger than a yarmulke and would mask the head wound from prying eyes.

I needed the body out of the drawer and on one of the autopsy tables if I was going to get the rest of the clothes on him. I scooped my hands under Reubenski's shoulders and started to prop him up. He'd been dead long enough for the rigor mortis to have worked itself out. The body was malleable, but surprisingly heavy for a skinny old man. I tried to press Louie into service.

"Help me pull him out and get him dressed."

Louie made no move to help. "What for?"

"Well I can't very well take him out on the town wearing nothing but a toe tag."

"Rip, what the hell are you talking about?"

Louie was going to need a moment of explanation if he was going to allow me to walk out of his morgue with one of his patients. I didn't blame him. It was asking a lot and might land him on unemployment insurance if things didn't go well.

"Tell me," I said, trying to ease him into the idea, "have you ever had one of your lodgers get up after they've been laid out on a slab?"

"We get interesting post-mortem muscle spasms sometimes. Twitches, stiffs with a hard-on. Once or twice a year we'll get one that sits right up. The interns take a shit when that happens. It's hilarious."

Morgue anecdotes told at hospital-staff Christmas parties weren't what I had in mind. I tried another approach.

"Louie, how long have we known each other?"

"I don't know. Years. Not double-digit years, but a long time."

"And how much do you know about what I do?"

"You talk to the dead. Everybody knows that. Everybody in the loop, at least."

"I do a lot more than that," I said, and knew I was going to have to sit Louie down for a serious talk about the facts of death.

Θ

In the end, it took over an hour to state my case. For the first time, I used the term "necromancer" with Louie and elaborated on what it was I did, not only for the police, but for paying clients with some highly unusual needs. I threw in a few of my shorter war stories to help flavour this pill I was asking Louie to swallow, and give him a sense of what my daily work experience was like. He laughed at a few of my tales, so it wasn't all horror and freakiness to him. I knew if there was any uninitiated civilian in my life who could handle hearing the gory details, it was Louie. By the time I was done talking, he had helped me stuff the late rabbi into an unflattering costume of mismatched hospital wear—part patient, part nurse, part doctor. Louie didn't look too sure whether or not he believed it all yet, but he hadn't run from the room or fainted. That was something.

Inevitably, we circled back to the topic of exactly what it was I needed from the body in his charge.

"The crime scene? What the hell are you looking for at the crime scene?"

"Evidence," I shrugged.

Louie knew I didn't deal in evidence. At least, not the same kind the police do, and certainly not for the same purpose. But this case had left me with few options, and having a look at the crime scene was the only thing I could think to do at this point. I didn't care what the evidence could prove, just where it might lead.

"Frenz mentioned they found the body dumped behind a restaurant." I elaborated. "'Dumped' usually means 'moved.' I want to see where the murder actually happened. At the very least, I can point out the spot to the cops when I find it. They can dust it for prints or sweep it for fibres or whatever the hell it is they do. It's not a slam dunk, but maybe a location to search will be worth a few bucks to them."

At this point I was trying to salvage a percentage of a fee that was already too low to settle my outstanding bills. But every little bit counts. Besides, I felt I owed it to Reubenski to at least try my best to offer him some justice, even if his spirit was already too far gone to ever know if justice was done in his name or not.

"So how's he supposed to get you there?" said Louie, looking down at our freshly dressed decedent.

"It works kind of like a homing pigeon, except this pigeon isn't looking for its roost, it's looking for the place it died. Once I get him mobile, brain or not, he can lead me right to the spot where it happened."

"Like an instinct?"

"More like a magnetic attraction. Even with the soul, the spirit departed, there's something left over in the body that wants to be reunited with the location where it was last a living, breathing organism. It clings to it. It's a memory residue that exists in its decaying cell structure, like the last hints of DNA before it all rots away to nothing."

"That's creepy. And kinda sad."

"Is it? I haven't really thought about it. Mostly I just find it useful."

I had low expectations of my ability to spot any leads in a murder mystery once I got to the scene of the crime, but one step at a time. First I had to get Reubenski up and walking again, then I had to set him loose in a city of full of people who would totally lose their shit if they spotted him for what he really was. Walking or not, he was going to look like a corpse, and it would draw attention. All I had succeeded in doing with the hospital uniforms was to make sure he wasn't going to draw attention for being a naked corpse plodding down the street. Reanimated cadavers aren't popular with civilians, but nobody likes to see a reanimated nudist cadaver. Even I'm not cool with that. Prudish I suppose, but we all need our hang-ups. I could probably do with a lot more.

I had my pocket kit with me and spread it open on the nearest table top.

"Your hand, please," I said to Louie, holding out my own.

"What do you want my hand for?"

"Nothing," I lied. "Just give me your hand for a second, will you?"

"You're going to stick a needle in me to draw blood or something like that, aren't you?"

"No," I said, palming the pin I had ready so Louie wouldn't see it.

"Use your own damn blood for your Satanic mumbo-jumbo."

"It's not Satanism."

"But it's mumbo-jumbo, right?"

"Fine!" I grumbled and stuck the tip of one of my own fingers with the pin.

I've died many times before. Often violently. Occasionally horribly. I like to think I've faced my own death with a certain bravery each time. But I still hate needles. The thought of them poking through my skin, finding a vein, drawing blood... I go weak in the knees. I think I'd rather take a bullet. I *know* I'd rather take a bullet.

I thumbed open the rabbi's eyelids in turn and pinched off a single drop of blood into each of them. Once that business was done, I looked around for a handy product I knew I would find within arm's reach. Rubbing alcohol has a million uses and is well stocked in every conceivable ward of a hospital. The morgue had a convenient bottle on hand for cleansing purposes. I grabbed it and carefully poured a thin line around the circumference of the autopsy table, outlining the late rabbi's body.

"Don't stress out about this," I told Louie, "but I need to start a small fire."

I pulled my lighter out of the kit and got ready to touch the flame to the trail of alcohol.

"Don't stress out? Rip, you're going to set off the sprinkler system! There'll be alarms, they'll have to evacuate the whole hospital!"

I tried to calm Louie's fears, knowing this had to be done, but also knowing he might well be right.

"It's a bit of rubbing alcohol burning on a stainless steel table. There won't be any smoke and I'll put it out in just a few seconds."

Louie looked uncertain. I decided to interpret that as consent and set fire to the table. The line of flame whipped around the rabbi instantly and flickered on top of the polished silver surface. Despite my best efforts to pour the alcohol as far from the body as possible, some of it had trickled towards the middle of the indented surface. Flames licked at the rabbi's wardrobe and there were a few small plumes of smoke forming.

I didn't want to smother the fire with a sheet in case the fabric got scorched and made more smoke. Instead, Louie and I ran around the table, blowing out the flames before they could spread. Smoke trails continued to rise off the corners of the burnt cotton, twisting towards the ceiling and the sensitive detectors that were attached to the dozen sprinkler heads above us. We stared up at them for a long time, anticipating a sudden shower and blaring alarms. Louie fanned the air with a file folder to dissipate the sparse smoke as much as possible. After a long minute of suspense, we were confident that we'd gotten away with our petty act of arson and continued.

"Shit," I said, considering the next step in the ritual.

"What? What's wrong?"

"I can't remember the incantation in Latin."

"Does that mean we abort?" asked Louie, hopefully.

"Nah. It works fine in English. It just sounds kinda dorky when you can understand the words."

I rambled off the incantation in a hurried, indifferent monotone, feeling faintly embarrassed by the whole song and dance.

"Arise departed, arise and walk the earth anew, bound by blood, bound by fire."

Louie looked decidedly underwhelmed.

"Believe me, it's a lot more impressive in Latin." I told him, trying to excuse myself.

I don't know who originally came up with these rituals untold centuries ago, but from "abracadabra" on, magic words have always struck me as kind of silly. You can't argue with the results, but they could all use a major rewrite for modern audiences. Admittedly, I hadn't given it a very good line reading. It's the words themselves that count. You don't actually need to perform them with overwrought bravado for the incantation to work, but the clients like a show. They want an operatic wizard bellowing their soliloquy to the cheap seats. Louie wasn't a client, so I didn't put on a show. In retrospect, I wished I had. It all seems rather foolish without the theatrics.

"That's it? Seriously? Sounds like anyone could do that."

"Well not just anyone is a fucking necromancer, are they? You need to have the gift."

Louie considered this a moment.

"I get it. So, like, anybody can go to the hardware store and buy a wrench. But that doesn't mean they can fix a leaky pipe. What you really need is a plumber."

It was as good a metaphor as I'd heard.

"Okay," I agreed.

"Gah!" was the next thing Louie had to say when he turned around again.

It wasn't a scream, but it was close. In the time we had spent discussing the apparent lameness of the ritual, it had worked its magic. The empty shell of Rabbi Reubenski was now sitting upright on the table with its paper-slippered feet dangling off the side, over the cold tiled floor.

Louie composed himself quickly. He hadn't quite known what to expect, but once he'd had a moment to think about it, this matched the results I had promised.

"So, uh, this is what you meant to do, right?" asked Louie, confirming this wasn't some horrible mistake. A reasonable question. When first encountering a raised corpse, most people—at least the ones who don't immediately run away—want to make sure it's not going to try to eat their faces off. Pop culture has cultivated all sorts of unrealistic expectations of what shenanigans the reanimated dead are likely to get up to. Generally, they behave themselves like good little deceased boys and girls. Bitey ones are very rare, and face-eating almost never happens. Of course, an isolated instance here or there and it gives all zombies a bad name.

"Yeah. We're all set. He's good to go."

Reubenski tipped forward and slid off the table. His feet slapped on the hard floor like a couple of frozen steaks. Once he had his footing, he stood erect and awaited instructions. In the face of the rabbi's newly discovered mobility, Louie wavered. Me walking out of the morgue with one of the bodies was no longer a theoretical proposition.

"Are you sure this is the best way to do this? This resurrection thing?"

"It's not a resurrection, it's only a reanimation. And yeah, I'm sure. We have a long way to go and do you know a better way to transport a corpse? I'm not carrying him."

"I don't know," said Louie, looking the poorly dressed specimen up and down as it stood there, jaw agape, eyes open and unseeing. "It just seems disrespectful."

"He's walking around on his own two feet. It's empowering."

Louie wasn't buying my attempts to soft-sell it.

"Let me grab my coat," was his verdict after much consideration.

"Why?"

"Because I'm coming with you."

I knew I wouldn't be able to talk him out of it. Until the family claimed him, Rabbi Reubenski was municipal property that was not to be damaged, stolen or misappropriated. Louie had an overdeveloped sense of responsibility. He could be relied upon to stretch the rules when appropriate, even break a few, but he was psychologically incapable of throwing the rule book out. Not completely. Whether I liked it or not, the rabbi and I were going to have a chaperone that night.

Θ

Getting out of the hospital with a stolen body was the easy part. I had the rabbi take a seat in a wheelchair once we were out of the elevator. Together, Louie and I wheeled him through the corridors like he was a patient, and nobody gave us a second glance. The rabbi looked dead, but with only a quick peek within the context of a hospital, people in the halls dismissed him as merely looking terminally ill. Outside on the street, I knew it would be another matter.

With our fatal head wounds and both of us sporting ridiculous hats to obscure this fact, we were quite a pair, Reubenski and I. We were two dead men walking, one considerably more dead than the other, but reanimated corpses both. I was on the mend and could pass myself off as normal, but we were going to need some way to usher the rabbi nearly forty blocks with as little scrutiny as possible. Louie and I decided to try our luck with a cab and hailed one at random.

The three of use squeezed into the back together. Louie and I sandwiched the rabbi and gave the driver a cross street near where the body was discovered as our destination. I sometimes think cab drivers in this city see more peculiar things on the job than I do. They can usually be relied upon to be too world-weary to ask probing questions or take notice of things better left ignored. But by the time we hit the second stoplight, I noticed this driver checking us out in his rear-view mirror too often, too closely. He had his eyes on us more than he did on the road, studying Reubenski much more thoroughly than I would have liked.

"That is the best zombie costume I have ever seen," he stated at last, genuinely impressed.

Louie and I looked at each other, not quite sure how to respond on Rabbi Reubenski's behalf.

"Uh, thanks," replied Louie.

"You guys doing the Zombie Walk this year?"

I rolled with it, letting the driver draw his own conclusions, embellishing the narrative he'd already invented to explain the corpse in his back seat.

"Why should the kids have all the fun?" I said.

"I don't see the point in it, myself," commented the driver. "Walking around like it's the end of the world and everybody's dead? We'll get there soon enough. And it won't be much of a joke when we do."

"Well, sometimes you just have to laugh in the face of the inescapable."

"I guess you're right," agreed the cabbie. "It's that or spend all your time crying."

Θ

Mercifully, the end of town Reubenski got himself murdered in was crappy enough that there weren't too many people walking the streets at night, and the types who were prone to walk those streets knew to mind their own business. Once we had our crime-scene magnet positioned on the sidewalk, we let him orient himself. He shuffled around in his paper slippers, like a compass needle finding north, and then began to walk slowly and deliberately towards the spot where he met his end.

It was slow progress following our reanimated homing corpse, like walking a small dog that wanted to sniff at every telephone pole, parking sign, and fire hydrant. Most of the journey was spent keeping an eye out for other pedestrians and making sure the zombified rabbi didn't wander into traffic. There was time to kill, so Louie killed it by trying to get me to hook him up.

"So how long has Gladys been working for you?"

"Give it a rest, Louie. She's not interested, and if you met her you wouldn't be interested either."

"How do you know she's not my type?"

"She isn't anybody's type. She's beyond types."

"Is she a big girl?" Louie speculated. "You know I'm not put off by big girls. I'm not shallow like that."

"She isn't a big girl. Quite the opposite."

"Eating disorder?"

"She doesn't eat at all."

"Poor girl. Is she all skin and bones?"

"Mostly bones."

"Well, I'm not necessarily interested in her for her body," claimed Louie.

"Good, because she doesn't have one."

"Flat-chested doesn't put me off either, you know."

"How about no-chested?"

"What's her personality like?"

"Angry, vindictive, poisonous."

"I like a girl with a fiery temper," Louie sighed. "Twisted, unhealthy, I know. But it kinda turns my crank. It tells me she has a real passion for life."

"I'll let you know when she gets one."

"You'll introduce us, then?"

"Only if you piss me off and I think you've got it coming."

We'd been down half a dozen streets and as many service alleys. I'd lost track of exactly where we were, but the spot we were looking for was taking its sweet time revealing itself. I'd become so bored sauntering after our slow, laboured tracker, I almost didn't notice when his last left turn kept turning in on itself, resulting in a full circle that repeated. Reubenski was stuck like a tetherball, orbiting the same spot over and over again. The rabbi's corpse would go no farther.

"This is it. It happened here," I announced.

Louie had the foresight to bring along a copy of the paperwork that arrived in the morgue with the body. The file contained a number of details that had no relevance to the coroner, but proved useful to us on our field trip. Among those details was an address and a hand-sketched map of the alley and adjacent streets made by one of the responding officers.

"The report says this is exactly where the police found the body," said Louie.

There was no sign of a chalk outline on the pavement, no police tape cordoning off the crime scene. Nobody had bothered. The murder had appeared too mundane, too petty-street-crime, for the cops to put in much effort beyond re-moving the body and hosing down the pavement so local commerce could continue as normal.

"So much for your moved-and-dumped theory," said Louie. "Maybe it really was a mugging."

"It doesn't make any sense. What was Reubenski doing here, in this end of town? What was he doing back in town at all?"

Louie stepped out into the street that lay beyond the mouth of the alley. Looking around the corner, he spotted the neon sign that was hanging off the front of the building we'd found ourselves behind.

"Grabbing a bite?" he suggested. "It's a kosher deli. Rabbis gotta eat too."

If this really was the scene of the crime, the police had already been over it. I doubted I could find any great revelations among the usual back-alley trash that they hadn't already picked through themselves. My billable fee was diminishing by leaps and bounds, but I was just as glad to not have to root through dumpsters looking for a murder weapon. The whole area was filthy and full of rusty, pointy things lying in wait, plotting to give me a good dose of tetanus or a virulent blood disease if I dared disturb them. I could hear the broken glass crunching underfoot as the rabbi ran the circuit of his tiny patrol over and over again.

"Did he meet with somebody over dinner?" I wondered, trying to exhaust any leads that didn't include me poking into trash bags full of rotting restaurant plate-scrapings.

"An evening of brisket and homicide? Could be," Louie encouraged. I'm sure he was just as eager to avoid rummaging through garbage for clues.

"Strange," I commented after another moment's observation of the scene.

"What part of tonight hasn't been strange?"

"Look at him," I said, nodding at the rabbi, still on the march and going nowhere fast.

"I've seen enough of him, thanks."

"The way he's shuffling around in circles."

"Yeah. Right around the spot where he died. That's what you wanted from your homing pigeon, isn't it?"

What I wanted, but not quite the way it should be.

"He shouldn't be circling the spot, he should be standing right on it," I explained. "The place where he died is the final destination, but he's not holding still. It's like he's close, but he can't quite arrive."

"You think he'll be okay here for a few minutes while we go inside and ask around?"

"If I owned a car, I wouldn't want to leave it parked in this end of town. But I guess I can park a zombie rabbi for a few minutes without some local punks stealing him for a joyride."

Θ

"Yeah, I seen him," the kid behind the deli counter told us.

Once we explained we weren't hungry but were willing to feed his tip jar for some answers, he got talkative. The place was open into the wee hours, catering to the late-night drinkers who might want a bite once the bars had to shut their taps off in accordance with municipal bylaws. The bar crowd was still a couple of hours away from rolling in, so there weren't many customers filling the meagre number of booths. The few present were nursing coffees and drug habits, and weren't the chatty type.

"We don't get so many rabbis in here, but we had one that night."

"Was he with anyone?" I asked, stuffing a five-buck bill in the paper cup taped next to the cash register with the word "TIPS" and a smiley face suggestively etched onto the side in heavy black marker.

"No," he replied, but then elaborated after a moment's thought. "Well, not at first. But I think he was waiting for someone. He got up and left when a guy came to the door."

"You know this guy?"

"Never seen him. He just stood there for a few moments and then walked back out. The rabbi followed."

"What did this guy look like?"

"I can't really say. He was a black guy."

Louie and I exchanged a glance. Thwarted by the vagueness of racism.

"And all black guys look alike to you?" Louie felt compelled to ask.

"No, I mean he was a *black* guy." The deli boy was adamant. "Black coat, black hat, black face. He had on dark glasses too, but I couldn't make out a single feature on him. Hell, I couldn't even see the nose those glasses were perched on."

I looked at the flickering fluorescent lights overhead. They were dim and made everything look slightly green and unhealthy. Under them, we all looked sick, the food all looked inedible. But the deli wasn't dark.

"Was he standing in a shadow?" I suggested, hoping for a reasonable explanation and worried I wouldn't get one.

"It wasn't bad lighting. It's like he wasn't even there. I could see him, sure, but it was more like looking at a hole in the ground instead of the ground itself, you know?"

While I was rifling through the roster of what we might be dealing with in my head, Louie kept probing.

"And this...hole. It was shaped like a man?"

"Yeah. A man wearing a black coat, a black hat, and dark glasses."

"And you didn't say anything, do anything?"

"Like what? He was in, he was out, he didn't order a sandwich. After dark in this neighbourhood, I don't say shit about anything I see unless somebody points a gun in my face and asks me to empty the till."

I didn't speak again until we were back outside and heading around the corner to the alley.

"I like clear answers, something definite." I told Louie at last. "This isn't it."

"We know for sure he met somebody. And it's a fair bet they came back here to have it out about something, and then that somebody bashed his head in."

"Maybe."

"You think it wasn't this guy who did it?"

"I'm thinking maybe it wasn't a guy at all. Not a living, breathing human guy. Something else."

"Like what?"

"That's the inconclusive bit I don't like. This doesn't sound like anything I've dealt with before. I'm not sure how I should proceed, and I'm not sure what I might need to do if I come face to face with it."

"Maybe you should step away from the case. Just tell Frenz you came up empty. Blame it on me. I'm the guy who cut out the rabbi's brain. I'll take the heat."

I thought about the all-black business card sitting at home inside Gladys's skull. Charlie Nocturne. Who or what was a Charlie Nocturne? Was he the last one to see Rabbi Reubenski alive? Did he kill him? Did he kill me?

"I don't think it's going to be that easy. I think this man in black is already on *my* case."

Wilbur told me he'd given him one of my cards. One of the good ones, with all my contact information, including my home address.

"And I think he knows exactly where to find me."

"Look," said Louie, interrupting my worries about a netherworld stalker, "he's stopped."

Like a watch that's finally wound down, the rabbi was standing still where we left him, staring out into space with glazed eyes that could sense but couldn't see. His ponderous orbit of a single point on the pavement had ended and he had become an inanimate part of the urban landscape.

I walked over to the rabbi and inspected him, noting that the long shuffling stroll had worn through the bottoms of his paper slippers. His shower cap was also missing, blown off by the currents that whipped through the service corridor behind restaurants and shops. Except for the rustling of his hospital gown, he was so still he could have been one of the telephone poles spaced at regular intervals down the length of the alley.

"I guess he's finally decided on a spot," I concluded, although his earlier indecision still seemed odd.

"So what do we do with him now?"

Releasing the rabbi, letting him resume a normal death, was an option. But I had lingering doubts, questions he might yet help me answer. Inevitably his family would want him back for burial, but they still didn't even know he was dead. There would be paperwork and bureaucracy before the body was finally shipped to whichever city was going to be his final resting place. This bought me some time. Not much, but enough to keep my options open.

"Louie, do me a favour and stash him back at the morgue for me."

"Like this?" Louie asked. He wasn't used to housing corpses that were quite so vertical.

"Just stand him in a corner and throw a sheet over his head."

"Other people work in the morgue, you know. They'll notice."

"Stuff him in a closet then. Or a locker. Someplace cool and dark so he doesn't spoil. I'll be around in a couple of days to put him down or take him for another spin."

"Rip, you are seriously pushing it."

"I freed up one of your drawers, didn't I? You're welcome."

I pointed a finger at Louie and told the zombie rabbi, "Follow."

Technically he couldn't see who I was pointing at, couldn't hear me issue the simple command, but on some primitive level he still understood and obeyed. He placed one foot in front of the other and slowly, stiffly, began to walk towards Louie. I noticed the lost shower cap, blowing around between the dumpsters with other paper and plastic refuse, and grabbed it before escorting the pair to the nearest main drag that might offer us a ride.

At that time of night, in that neighbourhood, it was a long wait to hail one cab, never mind two. I let Louie and the rabbi take the first one to come along to be nice. We might have shared, but I was headed in the opposite direction, and a second cab meant I wouldn't have to listen to Louie grouse about the burden I'd saddled him with.

As Louie bent the reanimated corpse into a sitting position in the rear, I leaned down to explain the situation to the driver through the passenger-side window.

"Makeup for that Zombie Walk thing."

"I wasn't even going to ask," barked the driver, waving a dismissive hand at me.

If only everyone were this disinterested, it would make my job so much easier.

My head was throbbing from my healing wound. I took off my sunglasses to massage my temples.

"What happened to your eye?" asked Louie, when he saw me without my clever disguise.

"I got punched."

"Knocked the colour right out of it, huh?"

I looked at myself in the side-view mirror of the cab and saw that the iris of my healing eye had turned a milky white. It looked horribly mismatched next to the green of my left eye. I hoped it wasn't permanent.

"It can happen," I said, and put my glasses back on.

"Rip, I work in a hospital," Louie reminded me. "No it can't."

"I'm going home to get some sleep. I have a splitting headache."

I handed Louie the shower cap and helped him shut the cab door. He took a moment to fit the cap back on Reubenski's head, covering the violent indent in his skull.

"Not as bad as his, I bet," he remarked.

I tapped the roof of the cab, letting the driver know he was clear to pull away.

"You'd be surprised," I said.

But then again, after our night on the town, maybe not.

Chapter Eight

My Soul to Keep

"J ESUS RIP, I HAVEN'T BEEN ABLE to reach you for days. I thought you were dead."

"Well, as a matter of fact…"

I didn't bother finishing my sentence. Rebecca worries about me. Thus the late calls. She's sweet like that.

"Rip?" she asked, after a few moments of phone silence.

"Never mind. What's up?"

"It's night and something's going bump."

Unfortunately, Rebecca expects me to reciprocate on the worry front. I find that difficult. Not because I'm a cold-hearted prick, although I've certainly been accused of being that. I just have a hard time getting on board with Rebecca's petty anxieties. We're both worriers in our own way, but different things weigh on us. She worries about little things that probably won't happen. I worry about big things that definitely will happen.

"Don't sweat it," I told her, "It's probably just rats in the wall."

"This doesn't sound like any rat," she said.

After a moment of silence to let a new worry seep in she added, "Why would you even say that? Do you think my building has rats?"

"No," I lied.

"Come over," she said. "Please."

"You said it yourself. It's the middle of the night."

"Of course it's the middle of the night. I wouldn't be scared if it was the middle of the day."

"Why are you the one who's always getting me out of bed just when I'm getting comfortable?"

"I'd feel bad if that creepy-ass thing was a bed. Or comfortable."

Okay, let me get this out in the open and done with. Now's as good a time as any to mention I sleep in a casket. No, it's not a coffin. That would be weird. Coffins have six sides. Caskets have four. Yes, technically they both get used as vessels to bury the dead in. Given my chosen professional and general demeanor, people assume that this is some purposely morbid choice on my behalf—an over-the-top attempt to be dark, mysterious or, I shudder to think, goth. It's a conscious choice I've made, true, but it's a chiropractic one. I've tried all sorts of beds, and none of them offer the sort of narrow-spaced, flat-back support I get from my casket. Not to mention, I've always felt snug and secure in an enclosed space. The air can get a little thin after a night with the lid down, so I have to close the top half on a ball-point pen I keep handy. The pen keeps the casket cracked open enough to let the interior breathe and to keep me from suffocating. Sure, it's odd. Maybe even eccentric. But it's not crazy as some have suggested. The results speak for themselves every morning when I spring out of my not-so-final resting place with no lower-back pain to fold me in half and make me hobble around for the rest of the day. The story of how I discovered the comfort and back-pain relief to be had from sleeping in a casket is convoluted and not particularly interesting. Suffice to say that when you find yourself locked overnight in the display room of a funeral home with a set of broken picks and no phone, you try to make yourself as comfortable as possible while you wait for the staff to let you out in the morning.

"Are you coming over or not?" said Rebecca, cornering me for a simple yes or no. I already knew "no" wasn't an option.

"This better not be the building settling or an insomniac neighbour walking the floor."

"You're a doll," she told me before hanging up.

Just knowing I was on my way made her sound less afraid. Actually showing up at her place seemed redundant. If I went back to bed, she'd probably doze off herself before long. She'd wake up to a new day and bright sunshine and forget all about whatever nightmare got her out of bed in the first place. But then I'd still catch hell for not making a personal appearance, so the decision was made. I grabbed my pants and a fresh shirt and was out the door a few minutes later. Sleep—what little I'd managed—had helped me heal up some more. A quick look in the mirror had confirmed that I was at least able to dispense with the dark, wound-masking glasses. Colour had not returned to my eye, however.

Rebecca's place was a short ride away. I knew it well— had even helped her find it when she needed to get out of her last rental. But I rarely visited. In turn, she rarely visited me. She thought my place, or at least everything in it, was troubling. I think she secretly harboured a dose of apartment envy—or at least rent-control envy. When we got together, it was usually in a neutral third location, where we'd both have no opportunity to criticize each other's personal space.

Apartment hunting with Rebecca had been a chore I deeply regretted getting myself roped into. Everything in her price range seemed to have termites, active mould colonies, or sick-building syndrome. By the second week of trying to judge which shoebox had the best view of a neighbouring brick wall, I was feigning enthusiasm for any place that didn't appear to be the base of operations for a drug cartel or a human-trafficking ring. Rebecca finally grabbed a fourth-floor walk-up with a crumbling plaster ceiling that let in all the noise from above, cracked floorboards that let in all the smells from below, and a permanent draft of unknown origin that made the place feel damp and chilly even when it was hot and dry outside. The apartment was shitty, but the closet was a walk-in. Rebecca was sold. I gave it my seal of approval just to make the nightmare end, and skipped town for a fictional job I made up on the spot when it came time for the actual move. I figured I'd already put in my time. Friendship, trust, loyalty—these things go a long way, but I have to draw the line at wasting my Saturday dragging couches and chairs up four flights of narrow stairs. After exhausting her recruitment efforts, Rebecca ended up paying to hire movers. Then she borrowed money from me to settle the bill. Six years later, she still hadn't paid me back.

"What?" was all I said in greeting after Rebecca buzzed me in and opened her apartment door.

"That's what I want you to tell me. It's in the bedroom."

"What are you? A child? You think you have monsters under the bed now?"

"I didn't say it was under the bed. But it's definitely in the bedroom somewhere. That's why I can't sleep."

"And that's why you won't let me sleep."

"I can hear it every time I turn the light off."

"But when you turn it on, it's like there was never anything there."

"That's it exactly," said Rebecca hopefully, like I had some special insight. "What do you think?"

"I think that might be because there was never anything there."

Rebecca gave me a scowl of too little sleep and too little patience.

"You're here now. Just check it out, okay?"

I gave her a grunt instead of a scowl, but the sentiment behind it was the same.

There was a thin strip of light shining under the bedroom door. I opened it and saw Rebecca had left a single bedside lamp on. She stood behind me, looking over my shoulder at the same bunch of nothing I saw.

"Didn't you bring your murse?" she asked, noticing I'd arrived unarmed, without my call-kit in hand. Leaving home without it was usually a bad idea, but in my sleep-deprived stupor I'd forgotten to grab it on the way out. I had already dismissed Rebecca's insomnia as baseless, had expected to resolve the issue with some hand-holding and coddling, but that was no excuse for sloppiness. I didn't let on that I'd made a mistake by showing up for what, to her at least, was a professional job, without the tools of my trade.

"Don't worry," I told her, a pointless suggestion to a worrier, "I've got this covered."

I made a grand pantomime of searching the room high and low, tipping unwieldy pieces of furniture forward so I could see behind them, dropping to my hands and knees to look under the bed. Finally, I got up and grabbed hold of the switch on the lamp.

"Ready?"

Rebecca nodded warily and grasped onto my free hand. I flipped the switch and the room fell into instant darkness.

There was nothing for a very long time. All I could hear was Rebecca's shallow breathing as she tried to make as little noise as possible, hoping there would be a sound to confirm her fears with a witness present, dreading there would be a sound to confirm her fears at all. I let the moment play out, to assure her I gave her phantom all the time it would need to reveal itself. That's when I heard it for myself, somewhere in the corner of the room. Which corner I couldn't say. It started at a very low volume, nearly too faint to hear, but escalated quickly until it was unmistakable, jarringly loud.

It sounded just like a death rattle. Never heard a death rattle? Lucky you. If you do, you won't forget it. It's not a rasping or a wheezing or any sort of noise a living person might make. It sounds more like a heavy wooden door slowly swinging shut on some very old and rusty hinges. Except the noise goes on and on and on and that damn door never does seem to close. It's unnerving, very horror-movie. If you ever have to sit up with a dying person and hear a death rattle, you'll know the end is at hand. And no matter how much you love that person and don't want to lose them, you'll want it to stop and be done with as soon as possible. Because the sound is unbearable.

I immediately snapped the light back on. Illumination revealed nothing and the sudden brightness ended the noise, but I knew what we had just been listening to.

"Okay, that I heard."

"Now tell me that was a neighbour snoring or a dripping tap or a tree branch blowing in the wind and knocking on my window."

"That's not what that was," I conceded, and found myself longing for my kit and the comfort the arsenal inside gave me in moments like this. And yet I knew there wasn't a single item in the satchel that would have been much help anyway, had I thought to bring it. This wasn't a job fit for a necromancer. The spirit in question was malevolent, dangerous, difficult, but it wasn't dead. I had no natural or supernatural power over it.

I dropped to the floor again to take a second look under the bed. With the lights out, the entity had come out into the open. Now that the lights were back on, it would have retreated into darkness. I had to make sure it wasn't hiding in the obvious places I had already checked.

"Please don't tell me that thing we just heard is under my bed."

"No," I told her, finding nothing more than a couple of small tumbleweeds composed of dust and Rebecca's own hair. "It must have found a better place to stash itself."

And then I remembered the other door in the room. It was thin, flimsy, and fitted with dozens of slats that would allow quick exit and entry points every time the light was toggled. It had to be there.

"Did you look in the closet before you called me?" I asked of Rebecca's beloved walk-in, now likely defiled.

"No."

"Why not?" I asked, just as glad she hadn't.

"Because I was scared shitless of course."

Fair answer, reasonable response. I knew the feeling. Now I was scared to look in the closet. Not because I didn't know what was in there, but because I was sure I did.

"Turn on the overhead," I instructed Rebecca.

She snapped on the ceiling light. I wanted as much illumination in the room as possible. The closet's occupant coveted darkness and if I was going to open the door, I needed the room I was standing in to be uninviting and out of bounds.

I didn't bother to give Rebecca a heads-up about my next move. I didn't want her talking me out of it, and at that moment I could have very easily been talked out of it. Necromancer or not, wrong field of discipline or not, this needed to get done. Somebody was going to have to take care of this thing tonight and there was no one around to subcontract to before the sun came up. I threw the closet door open and braced for impact.

Nothing happened. No horror came spilling out to claim my soul or flay my flesh off or commit any number of other indignities malevolent spirits are apt to do when cornered. All I could see was a deep dark space and too many outfits for too many occasions dangling from too many coat hangers. I noted that a lot of them still had price tags pinned to the sleeves and made a mental note to bring this up with Rebecca the next time she tried to borrow money.

Rebecca looked into the walk-in abyss over my shoulder, equally concerned for her immortal soul and her wardrobe.

"Is it in there?" she asked, like I knew. A process of elimination dictated it was, but I wasn't sure. I couldn't hear it, I couldn't sense it in any way.

Slowly I reached forward with my hand, careful to make sure it stayed in the light the whole time. The overhead was shining brightly enough to illuminate inside, just to the point where the wall of clothes blocked any illumination from penetrating deeper. My fingertips passed through the frame of the door. A second later I withdrew them like they'd been electrically shocked. There was a terrible chill in the air just inches inside. The air was as icy as a meat locker.

"I...hunger..." the thing in the closet announced.

I shut the door and pushed the dresser up against it for good measure.

"Don't go in there," I advised Rebecca.

"What is it?"

"A harbinger. And quite a nasty one if I'm not mistaken. Where you might have picked it up I have no idea, but we'll look into that once I deal with the immediate problem—how to contain it."

"Why is there a harbinger—whatever the fuck that is—in my closet?" asked Rebecca.

"They hate the light but they find the dark nice and cozy. Your closet is the darkest spot in the whole apartment."

"But why does it have to be *my* closet?"

"It must have followed you home from somewhere."

"What, like a lost puppy?"

"Exactly like a lost puppy, provided that puppy is a malignant essence that consumes and thrives on the pain and suffering of the dying."

"Who's dying? Is somebody dying?"

"If there's a harbinger hanging around, you can bet your ass somebody hasn't got much time left."

"Who is it? Is it me? It's not me, is it? I'm not ready to go yet! I have so much more I want to avoid doing! Years' worth!"

Rebecca wasn't panicking, but she was frightened witless. I didn't try to console her. Fear is good. Fear is handy. Fear keeps people out of trouble.

"Let's worry about who's snuffing it after we've contained the thing. Harbingers don't do any killing themselves, but they've been known to give the victim a push in the right direction to make sure they get their kicks."

I made for the door. There was no more time to waste.

"Where are you going?" Rebecca wanted to know. "You're not going to leave me alone with it!"

"I have to go out and get supplies. Don't worry, you'll be perfectly safe. Unless there's a power failure and the lights go out."

"What the hell do I do if the power goes out?"

"Run. Very fast. And keep running. Apparently it's decided you're the key to its next meal and it's going to latch onto you until it's satisfied. Harbingers are very stubborn and tenacious about these sorts of things."

"Where am I supposed to run to?"

I thought about it for a moment.

"Airport. Hop the first flight north and keep heading north."

"How far?"

"All the way. You'll need to be somewhere where the sun never goes down. Right now, that would be the arctic. It should buy you some time."

"Holy shit, Rip. I don't even have a good winter jacket."

"Look, our power grid is a little iffy sometimes, but the chances of it going down in the next hour are minimal. You'll be fine."

"You're sure about that?"

"Pretty sure. A solid ninety percent."

Rebecca looked genuinely panic-stricken, poor thing. It was one of those awkward situations that called for a touch of comfort and compassion—two things I'm pretty poor at. But since it was Rebecca, I made the effort and gave her a little squeeze and an awkward kiss on the forehead. It struck me as transparently insincere, but it seemed to do the trick. Worry lines remained deeply etched in her face, however.

"Stay here, keep all the lights on, and for fuck's sake don't talk to it," were my final instructions as I turned to the door.

"What happens if I talk to it? Do I die?"

"Of boredom. Harbingers are terrible conversationalists."

Θ

Spending the entire weekend dead, I'd missed laundry day. That was the only convenience to come out of my untimely murder. It meant I was still wearing the same pair of pants from the week before and wouldn't have to go back home to dig through Gladys's vacant skull for a single slip of paper. The business card I needed was stuffed in my pant pocket where I'd happily forgotten about its existence until now. Consulting the crumpled cardstock, I found there was an address mixed in with all the other contact information. I didn't bother phoning first. I figured a personal appearance would be harder to ignore or shun.

I asked the cab I flagged down to wait for me outside once it delivered me to my destination. It was going to be a short visit one way or the other. Either I'd get kicked out before I even got through the door, or chivalry would prevail and I'd be back on the road with my recruit, eager to save Rebecca from the slice of evil that had taken up residence in her closet.

As expected, the address on the card was an apartment and not some commercial building that would have already been locked up for the night. The buzzer was broken, as was the lock on the front door, so I let myself in and took the elevator to number 704—suite 704 according to the card, a vain attempt to make the mailing address sound business-like.

I pounded on the door long enough to wake up the occupant and all his neighbours as well. Finally, at long last, I heard the chain unlatch. Tom opened up, bleary-eyed and only moments awake. I noted with amusement that he wore actual pyjamas to bed instead of underwear and a t-shirt. It struck me as a tad precious for someone who vomited for a living.

"Rebecca needs your help," I told him, before he'd had a moment to recognize me and slam the door in my face.

"What? Who?"

"Gallery Nowhere. Pretty girl. She was very insistent we meet."

The synapses were firing slowly. I decided this was a conversation better had inside. There was less chance Tom would be rude and get rid of me if I was already a guest in his home.

"Can I come in?" I asked and stepped inside, well ahead of any response.

"Nice place," I commented, as I looked around at Tom's flat, no sarcasm intended. It was a typical run-down bachelor pad for a guy his age, but it was much better than you'd expect for someone in his line of work. I guessed he was still collecting an allowance from a parent or guardian, likely more out of sympathy than love if they were aware of his one and only talent.

Tom struggled to remember how to be a genial host at such a late hour.

"Uh, you want a drink or something?"

"Sounds good. How's the water?"

"Brown. The plumbing is shot. But I have some filtered in the fridge."

There was no need to ask for directions. The kitchenette opened directly into the living room. Tom tried to shake off his sleepiness and get up to speed.

"So wait, what's going on? Why are you here? It's 'Rip,' right?"

"That's me."

I noticed my own business card stuck to the fridge with a plastic ladybug magnet. It was one of many cards, clippings and photos arranged all over the off-white door in Tom's own lame filing system. It made me feel organized.

"I asked around about you," said Tom. "After we met. Not too many people knew you. Those who did wished they didn't."

"I'm not in show business. I don't have to be liked. It's not about popularity, it's about the quality of the services rendered."

"The ones who did know you had some crazy things to say. I wouldn't have believed any of it if I hadn't seen some of that craziness for myself."

"A practical demonstration here and there goes a long way. Word of mouth is my bread and butter."

I opened the cupboard to look for a glass. The selection was sparse and mismatched—a few novelty mugs, a couple of beer-branded pint glasses liberated from a local bar, and a plastic sippy cup minus the toddler-friendly pacifier-style top. I reached for the one visible plain glass on the upper shelf, but stopped when I saw it was already full of water. And something else. Floating near the surface, doing a pathetic little sidestroke, was a pulverized goldfish, flattened and broken with shredded fins and tail. Its one remaining ruptured eye stared straight up, unseeing, from inside a crushed skull.

"Tom, why the fuck do you still have this thing?"

"It won't die. I don't know what to do with it."

"Throw it away," I told him.

"I can't do that. It's cruel."

"Like swallowing it and throwing it up three shows a night isn't?"

"Didn't you say it was bound to me?"

"That was bullshit. I just didn't want to prick my own finger."

"But it's still my..." Tom searched for an appropriate term. "My responsibility. Isn't it?"

I could see now I'd saddled Tom with a real guilt trip. It wasn't fair, and apparently I was the only one who could lift the curse I'd laid on him. Without further ado, I marched into the bathroom and pitched the entire contents of the glass into the toilet. A flush later and the fish and its stagnant cup of spoiled water were whirlpooled out of sight and hopefully out of mind.

I handed the empty glass to Tom.

"I recommend you give this a good wash."

Rather than relieved and thankful, Tom looked appalled.

"You didn't just do that! I mean, won't it go on living down in the sewers? Forever?"

"Yeah, probably. Who cares? It's a just a fish. Forget it, move on."

"But that's horrible..."

"Look, if you want an undead goldfish so bad, ask a pet store to give you a free floater and I'll bring it back for you. You won't have to feed it or change the water or anything.

And it'll look normal enough that you can keep it in a bowl out in the open, instead of hiding it away behind some coffee mugs."

"That's not what I want! I mean...well... Shit."

It wasn't the kind of closure Tom was looking for, but it worked fine for me.

"So, the reason for me dropping by..." I began, hoping to put the fish incident behind us.

"Yeah, why are you here?"

"I can't believe I'm about to say this, but..."

I took a deep breath and let it out.

"Something's come up, and I could really use the services of a regurgitator."

Θ

"Wait, is that Barfo? As in The Amazing?"

Rebecca had buzzed us in a few minutes earlier. She was surprised by the company I'd brought with me. When I'd said I was going out for supplies, she had probably expected me to return with a bazooka.

"It's Tom. But yeah, the regurgitator. Him."

"I'm happy to see you two working together, but why's he here?"

"He's the tool I needed."

"So he knows what's up? He knows what to do?" asked Rebecca hopefully, knowing my talent for skipping vital information when I needed somebody to do something for me.

"I briefed him on the way over," I assured her.

Just then, our resident harbinger took the opportunity to utter a bone-vibrating dirge from inside its dark, unhappy place. Rebecca had filled the place with light, making sure every bulb in the place was on. She had multiple flashlights out and pointed towards her bedroom, which she had not re-entered. Her smart phone, tablet and laptop were all on with the screens set to an all-white page for maximum brightness. She'd even turned the burners on her stove to full so the glowing red coils would add just a bit more light. With the whole apartment lit up like the Vegas strip at midnight, the harbinger had been cornered in the closet for nearly an hour. It was growing impatient. It was nighttime, and it wanted to be out and about, feeding off tragic deaths and arranging for them to happen when it could.

"What the hell is that noise?" said Tom, the uninitiated.

I'd briefed him, sure. Basically. Vaguely. I didn't want to get too specific. I was afraid he'd stop the cab and leap out.

"It's a death rattle," I said. "Sort of. More like an impression of one. Harbingers like the sound of a death rattle. They find it soothing, comforting, like a cat's purr. So they mimic it, often poorly, but the effect is the same. It announces the end of a life and assaults everyone in earshot."

"So why am I here?" Tom wanted to know, suddenly realizing that although he was chivalrous enough to put himself in harm's way for a woman in need, this wasn't the sort of danger he had anticipated. "I mean, you're the necromancer, right? Isn't this sort of shit right up your alley?"

"Yeah," I said, "except it's not really. This is a demon we have here. Demons aren't dead. They were never technically alive either. They exist in an existential grey zone that's outside my usual area of expertise. If you have demon problems, you need to call a demonologist. I'm a necromancer. You call me if you have bodies that won't stay buried, or dead things that need to be up and about and made useful again."

"So call a demonologist."

A reasonable suggestion, but impractical. I had a few phone numbers, but they were all long distance. And I wasn't about to let this harbinger stew and plot in Rebecca's closet while I waited for the cavalry to arrive with a super-soaker full of holy water and a Bible—or whatever demonologists arm themselves with these days. There were local demon-ologists to be had, sure, but none of them were the real deal. Most self-appointed demonologists are devil-worshippers with delusions of grandeur. If you want to listen to a bunch of hackneyed Aleister Crowley quotes and "Do what thou wilt" bullshit while they try to get in your pants, knock yourself out. But if any of these jokers ever saw a real demon, they'd crap themselves and call a toll-free Christian hotline for abso-lution.

"We don't have time to ship one in. Not with a hungry harbinger hanging around."

The troops looked frightened, skittish.

"Don't worry, we can handle this," I assured them. "Har-bingers are lesser demons. In the demonic hierarchy, they're way down the list, but you still don't want to mess with one."

"Isn't that exactly what we're about to do?"

"Well, yeah. But in a controlled sort of way. I have a plan."

Rebecca looked confused about something.

"Didn't you once tell me there's no hell?"

I thought it was a tad off-topic at the moment, but I don't like to shy away from the big questions.

"Yeah. I've spent enough time dead to go hunting and there was nothing to find."

"So if demons are real, where do they come from?"

"That's the wrong question. It's not a matter of where they're from, it's where they're trying to get to. That's the issue."

"So where do they want to go?" asked Tom, an ominous question if ever there was one.

"Inside."

"Inside where?"

"Inside all of us."

"That doesn't sound good."

"It isn't. Which is why you want to get rid of them. Whether they're inside you, or just inside your closet, they have to go, no matter how lesser they may be."

"So how do we do this?" Rebecca asked, shoring up her courage.

"We need bait."

"What sort of bait?" Rebecca wanted to know. "Don't say dead bait."

She was always vaguely suspicious I was going to bring random corpses into her home.

"No, no nothing like that. A harbinger won't go for somebody dead. We need somebody who's dying. Someone in the process of snuffing it."

This was the crux of my plan. The only thing that made me the least bit confident I could take on any sort of demon was the common area of interest we shared, the harbinger and I. It wanted to gloat over the dying, and I dealt exclusively in the dominion of the dead.

"Why are you looking at me like that?" said Rebecca, suddenly paranoid.

"I need to take care of the harbinger when it comes after the bait," I explained.

"What about Tom?"

"I need Tom's help with the trap I have planned."

"What the hell are you asking me to do here, Rip?"

"Die," I shrugged. Rebecca looked horror-stricken, so I tried to pitch it better. "Just a little. I'll stop your heart for bit. You'll only be clinically dead long enough to grab the harbinger's attention and we'll take care of it while he's distracted."

"No way." Rebecca was firm.

"I'll get your heart going again right after. Promise."

"Nope."

"I took a CPR class. Once."

"No fucking way, Rip!"

She'd gone from firm to angry. I hadn't really expected her to cooperate with my A-plan, but it was worth a shot. It was her problem, I was dealing with it. Was spending a minute dead really too much to ask?

"You're going to make me do this myself, aren't you?"

"But you're so good at it," Rebecca told me, like she was paying me a compliment.

"That doesn't mean I like it."

"I'm sorry," she said. And indeed she sounded genuinely sorry. "But this one's your idea, not mine."

"What's my part in the plan?" Tom wanted to know.

"I'll tell you when the time comes."

"Won't you be...dead?" he asked. My plan was beyond him, but at least he'd been listening. There was hope for the kid yet.

"Not for long," I said, removing my jacket and kicking off my shoes.

I went into the kitchen to pour a glass of water and find a fork. The fridge door had been left hanging open, offering still more light, even as the milk and eggs went bad. With my weapons in hand, I collected everyone at the bedroom door.

The lights were all on in the bedroom, but just to be sure, I gave the place a quick survey before shutting the door behind us. I highly doubted the harbinger would have braved the light to relocate and catch us off guard, but you can't be too cautious with these devious little buggers. I pulled the plug on the sole lamp, but the overhead light kept us safe for the time being. Tom, armed with a flashlight, manned the light switch. Rebecca had her phone set on a super-bright LED app she'd just downloaded for a token fee. The camera flash on the phone burned brightly—blindingly if you looked right at it. I pushed the dresser away from the closet and carefully pulled the door open, leaving it yawning, the dark interior exposed, the path clear for the intruder inside. A faint mist rolled out across the floor as the frigid air seeped out.

"If this goes wrong, get out of the room fast, back to where there's light," I instructed my companions. They nodded in acknowledgment but looked pale and perturbed.

I dumped the glass of water on the floor next to the end table and stepped into the resulting puddle. I should have removed my socks as well. This was likely going to burn some holes in them. I heard the harbinger again, reacting to the water, sensing something was up. Its death rattle rose to a deafening pitch, sounding like hunger pangs from a rumbling stomach. Appropriate enough, I suppose. Dinner was about to be served.

"Lights out!" I commanded.

Tom flipped the switch, plunging the room into darkness, offering the harbinger passage from its lair and a free run beyond. At that same moment, I jammed the prongs of the fork into the empty plug socket behind the end table. Electric current fired through my body, scorching my hand at the entry point and burning a hole through the soles of my feet as it sought to ground itself. Along the current's path was my heart, which sputtered violently with the sudden jolt and stopped in mid-beat. I saw bluish-white sparks fly for a moment before my body collapsed out from under my consciousness, leaving it displaced and hovering over a spastic corpse. After a few reflexive kicks from my charged muscles, my body lay still. I was technically dead. Swift medical intervention could still bring me back, but Rebecca and Tom knew better than to offer assistance. I had instructed them to keep their lights off me, no matter what happened, no matter what they heard. They had to let the harbinger feed.

What came scurrying out of the closet was small and ill-formed. It hadn't been in this world long and was still unnourished and lacking a firm shape. Mostly it appeared to be a collection of wiry-haired insect legs dragging themselves across the floor, ever changing in length and number, with no actual body to support or head to command them. The harbinger was as black as the shadows it hid in. Rebecca and Tom couldn't have hoped to spot it in the dark, but as a disembodied soul, the lack of light couldn't mask it from me. I watched from above as it crawled up my leg and grabbed at my shirt, pulling itself towards my face where it could have a closer look at my staring eyes, where it could wallow as they glazed over and dilated.

Rebecca and Tom stood still. They could hear the harbinger in the room with them, fawning over my corpse as my blood flow stilled and my body temperature began its slow, steady decline. They kept their twin beams of light fixed on the wall, waiting for my signal, ready to swing them onto the demon and expose it, but terrified of what they might see when the moment came.

The foul thing was perched over my face, sucking in my last breath of air as the vapours leaked from my still lungs. While it was distracted, taking in all the joys that were to be had from my sudden demise, I let my consciousness drift back into my fresh corpse. Once I was inside, I found I could sense a distinct emotion from the harbinger: reluctance. It wasn't enjoying its meal much. It was feasting just the same, but not with the relish I would have expected. It's like I wasn't good enough for it. I tried not to take offence and instead concentrated on revival.

Although there were some burns that would trouble me for the next few days, the actual damage wasn't extensive— nothing like being shot in the head, and so much easier to bounce back from. This wasn't a resurrection that would take three days. More like three seconds. I had to be quick about it. It wouldn't take the harbinger longer than a few moments to realize I had miraculously returned from the dead and spoiled its repast. I had to make sure it didn't run off.

The demon may have been a malevolent spirit, but having manifested itself in the physical world, it had assumed a semi-physical state. Physical enough for me to grab hold of it the instant I jump-started my body and came back to life. I seized it firmly in both hands, bunching its awful collection of limbs together like some shaggy, oily bouquet of writhing seaweed. It twisted and contorted with surprising strength and violence, rasping and groaning in anger and disappointment.

"Light! Give me light!" I yelled.

Rebecca and Tom swung their beams over to the wrestling match on the floor and the harbinger squealed in pain. Tom leapt over to the wall to turn on the overheads and further weaken the harbinger.

I heard the light switch clicking up and down several times, but there were no results. The room remained black. Rebecca threw open the bedroom door to let light flood in from the rest of the apartment. Too late she saw the rest of the apartment—the rest of the building—was in blackout.

"Oh, shit," she gasped. "Rip, I think we blew a fuse!"

That's what I get for stuffing silverware into the old wiring of a crummy building.

One flashlight and a phone's camera flash weren't going to offer enough of a focused assault on the demon as it thrashed around and refused to stay in one place.

"Help me!" I demanded, although there was nothing either of them could do to aid me as I rolled around on the floor with a creature that only wanted to break free and go hide in a deeper, darker, safer place. What I really wanted was for Tom to get a few steps closer so I could spring the trap.

"What can I do?" he asked in a panic, unable to hold his flashlight steady on the grotesque thing in my hands.

Squeezing the harbinger close to my chest, I struggled to get my footing and stand. Once I was up, I stumbled forward to narrow the distance between Tom and myself. With as much strength as I had left in my recently dead arms, I launched the harbinger into Tom's face, straight at his slack jaw and dumbfounded expression.

"Here, hold this," I said, clamping a hand over his mouth.

There was only one available route left for the inky, black soul of the harbinger and it took it, peeling apart Tom's lips and crawling into the dark cavity it found just beyond as it sought shelter. I can't imagine the essence of a harbinger tastes very nice, and I knew the sooner Tom could get it out of his mouth the better it would be for him. But I wasn't about to let it escape.

"Swallow!" I commanded Tom, "Swallow! All the way down, you can do it."

Tom struggled with the writhing foulness in his mouth. I was sure he'd swallowed a great many larger things, but nothing so vile. Despite his obvious discomfort and distaste, he forced the toxic soul deep down inside himself and clamped it off in his iron stomach for safekeeping.

"Now hold it," I said, and slowly withdrew my hand from his mouth.

Tom sat down heavily on the edge of the bed and bounced up and down on the springs for a moment. I took the flashlight from his hand and pointed it at his face, making sure there was no sign of anything coming back up and poking out between his lips.

"What did you do to me?" Tom asked, in a state of shock.

"Nothing at all. I'm just using you as a temporary means of transportation. Like a grocery bag, or a padded envelope."

"Get it out! Get it out!" He was panicking.

"You're a regurgitator. You should be able to bring it back up whenever you want. But what I need you to do right now is hold it down."

"This was your plan?" asked Rebecca. She probably thought it was unscrupulous to involve Tom like this without sharing all the details. She was probably right, as usual, but results are results.

"I think I'm going to be sick," Tom whined.

"No you're not! You're here because you can be sick or not sick at will. Now do your job!"

Tom held his hands over his stomach. He looked like an indigestion sufferer from an antacid commercial.

"It feels like it's running laps in there."

"It's just a little pissed off right now. Clamp off that esophagus. Nothing gets past, understand? Not until we're ready to deal with it."

Tom fell silent for a minute, assessing the state of his internal organs.

"Okay, it's slowing down. It's not roaming around so much."

"It's dark and warm in there. That should keep it calm for a while," I assured him.

"So what now?" asked Rebecca.

"The priority is to get that thing out of Tom before it sets up shop and takes over."

"Well what the hell are we waiting for? Let's get it out!" said Tom.

"It has to come out in a controlled environment so it doesn't scurry off somewhere to make more trouble. You're containing it for the moment, but that's only temporary. I need to prepare something permanent. Not just a holding cell, but an eternal prison."

"How do we do that?"

"First off, I'll need something biologically viable. Dead and fresh. The fresher the better. I don't suppose you've seen any cockroaches running around lately?" I asked Rebecca hopefully.

"What makes you think my building has roaches? Have you seen any here before?"

"No," I lied.

I went into the kitchen to look for anything organic that used to be alive and well and walking around. The fridge was still hanging open, but the light was out. I shone the flashlight inside to take inventory. Aside from an expired jar of mayonnaise, a six pack and some spoiling dairy, there wasn't anything of use.

"What's in your freezer?"

"Ice," answered Rebecca.

"Any steaks? Raw chicken?"

"No, just ice. Cubes and frost."

"You should take better care of yourself," I warned her.

"I eat out a lot."

"And drink alone at home?"

"That's not true. I drink out with people too."

"Um...excuse me," said Tom, raising a hand like he was waiting to be called on in class. "But could we get on with doing something about me being demonically possessed?"

"Don't be silly, Tom. You're not demonically possessed," I informed him.

"I'm not?"

"Not yet." He didn't look reassured.

"Okay," I told Rebecca, "we're going to hit the road and take care of this thing. I'll give you a ring tomorrow. Maybe then you can tell me what dark paths you were wandering to have this nasty critter latch onto you."

I grabbed Tom by the shoulder and hustled him towards the door.

"Sorry I fucked up your whole building," I added. "I'm sure the superintendent will get it fixed by morning."

"Can't we just take care of this thing here and now?" pleaded Tom.

"Elsewhere and shortly," I told him.

"Hey, Rip?" Rebecca called after me.

I paused in the doorway.

"Thanks for dying for me."

"Let's not make it a habit," I said, departing.

Θ

I flagged a cab at the curb and helped Tom get in the back with me. He didn't look so good. It must have been something he ate.

"Where are we going?" he asked, when the passing street lights caught his attention and pulled him out of the dazed funk he was in.

"Back to your place."

"My place? Why my place?"

"Because you're not feeling well and you're going to need to lie down after we're done with your late-night snack.

"Why couldn't we do it back at Rebecca's place? I just want this over with."

"This is going to take a lot out of you. And I don't just mean the contents of your stomach. You'll want to be close to a familiar bed so you can crash once it's all over."

I don't think I'd ever seen someone literally turn green from nausea. Tom was green.

"I feel awful," he said, looking awful indeed.

"I don't doubt it."

"I feel like I just ate a dozen burritos and they were all stuffed with botulism."

"That sounds about right."

"I'm really going to be sick."

"Hold it down. You can do it. You're a professional. Act like it."

"I don't know if I can…"

"Tom, you're the best goddamn regurgitator I've ever seen. That's why I recruited you for this job. No one else can do what you do."

"Really?"

"Really," I lied. I could make some calls and come up with half-a-dozen viable regurgitators within the hour. But I didn't have the time and none of them were in town.

"You no get sick in my cab!" barked the cabbie supportively. "You make sick in my cab, I kick you ass out!"

"He's fine," I assured the driver. "We're nearly there."

I really didn't want to prolong the conversation with Tom, but he needed something external to focus on so he wouldn't think too hard about what was going on internally.

"Look," I explained, "something's not quite right with this whole harbinger thing. It wasn't satisfied with my death. It's like it was waiting for something else—someone else, dying some other way. And since Rebecca seems to be the key to it getting its fix, I want to put some distance between them. You want to help me keep her safe, don't you?"

Tom nodded, unable to speak, holding the harbinger down like a bad case of gas. I was concerned that if he nodded too firmly, he'd bring everything up in the back seat and give the cabbie something far worse than soiled upholstery to complain about. But Tom hung in there, fighting his own body's natural instinct to purge.

"I just noticed…" said Tom weakly.

"What?" I asked, wondering if there was some relevant insight I should be aware of.

"Your eye. It's all fucked up."

Tom fell silent and said no more for the rest of the trip.

When we were finally back at the building where I'd first picked him up, I took Tom by the arm and led him carefully, delicately, up to his apartment. I found his keys in his pocket and opened the door for him. Once inside, I led him to the couch and lowered him onto the cushions. Getting another cushion to support his shoulders, I leaned him back into a half-lying position I hoped would be comfortable, soothing, and settling for his stomach.

"Apparently Rebecca hardly eats, but you look like a strapping young lad. You must have some sort of meat tucked away."

I tried my luck with Tom's fridge. Given all the crap he put in his body in the name of show business, it didn't seem likely he was a vegetarian.

"Yeah, actually," answered Tom weakly. "I have a chicken breast and a leg I picked up at the butcher the other day."

It was a possibility, but not optimal. I contemplated making a quick run to a 24-hour supermarket, but it was unlikely they'd have anything much better.

"I don't suppose they had any whole chickens? Unplucked with the heads still on?"

"Gah, no! Gross," groaned Tom, swallowing heavily. "I wouldn't shop there if it did."

I laid off the butcher imagery. Tom didn't need any mental images that would turn his stomach more.

"Yeah, I figured this end of town was a little too white-bread for that."

It might have been worth a break-and-enter to get my hands on a whole chicken. Or a pig or goat or something. Some of the local butcher shops catered to the more exotic tastes of various immigrant communities and were known to hang a few carcasses in their windows that would offend more assimilated citizens who ventured into the district.

Unfortunately they were all deep in the west end and the clock was ticking.

"Too far to make a run," I muttered to myself. "And you don't have much time left."

"I don't?"

"No. But don't worry. Some raw pieces of chicken should suffice. Probably."

I dug the chicken dinner out of the freezer and tossed it onto the counter. It sat in a white Styrofoam tray, wrapped in cellophane and frozen solid. It touched a finger to it, melting a small circle in the layer of frost that coated the wrap. It did nothing to warm up the icy chicken underneath.

"I wish it was a bit more thawed."

"Why? Does that matter? Does it screw up getting it out of me?"

Tom was justifiably concerned but I didn't want to give him more cause to worry. Worry is bad for digestion.

"No. Getting it out won't be the hard part. Getting it to accept a new host is the trick. Hopefully it won't be too put off by this block of ice."

"Do you need anything else?"

"Lighter fluid would be good. Or cooking oil. Something that will ignite easy and burn hot."

"Matches?"

"Covered," I said, patting the lighter in one of my pockets.

"You're going to start a fire?"

"More of a pyre. It's not a barbeque, it's more of a ritualistic cleansing. Once we get our harbinger set up in his new home, we'll need to burn it to a crisp."

"Will that destroy it?" Tom asked hopefully.

"Not really. But it should keep him trapped and out of our hair for a few centuries."

I looked up and saw there was a standard fire detector screwed to the ceiling over the kitchenette.

"We should probably pull the battery on that. It's bound to get pretty smoky in here what with the fire and the brimstone and your chicken-dinner inferno."

I climbed onto a chair from Tom's tiny dining table and twisted off the cover of the detector. The nine-volt battery dropped out into my hand, disabling the alarm. At least now the neighbours wouldn't be woken up by my half-assed attempt at an exorcism.

"You owe me half a chicken," Tom told me from the couch.

"Hey, this is your harbinger I'm binding and burning here. Be happy I'm not charging you my regular fee for taking out the trash. The least you can do is cover a few basic expenses."

"You're the one who put it in me, asshole."

He didn't really sound that cross at me. He'd been a good sport about the whole thing. Prevailing on his sense of decency only worked because he actually had one. I had to give him that much credit.

"All for a good cause, right?"

"Rebecca seems nice," he said.

"She's a lot of things. I suppose 'nice' is somewhere in the mix."

I stepped down off the chair.

"Are you two a couple?" Tom asked me out of the blue. Sick as he was, dying as he may have been, his immortal soul in very real peril of being consumed and corrupted by some ancient denizen of the pit, Tom was sniffing around for a date.

"Us? Nah. We're friends."

I started to rummage through the various cupboards and cabinets of the kitchen, hunting for fuel.

"Friends with benefits?"

"Sure," I shrugged, not quite sure what qualified. "She benefits from my ability to save her from the demons in her closet."

"And you? How do you benefit?"

I had to think about that one for a moment.

"I get to have somebody talk to me like a regular human being. It kind of gets on my nerves, but it's probably a healthy thing, you know?"

"I guess it would be."

Tom fell silent.

"You think she likes me?" he asked more directly. Rebecca drew them like flies.

"I'm sure she thinks you're very brave for coming to her rescue on such short notice."

Tom stared up at the ceiling, right through it. "Nobody's ever thought of me as brave before."

"Yeah, well she's a poor judge of character."

He looked back at me again.

"What about you? Do you think I'm brave?"

Tom was sounding more distant by the second. Delirious. I was losing him.

"You're either very brave or very stupid. Given your pants-shitting reaction to a reanimated goldfish, I'm going to have to go with 'stupid.'"

I'd searched through every drawer and nook in the kitchen and had come up empty. There was nothing easily flammable, not even vegetable oil I could heat up on the stove. I was beginning to regret relocating from Rebecca's apartment. At least she probably had a bottle of scotch stashed somewhere.

"Don't you have anything in this place I can use as fuel?"

"I might have something in the medicine cabinet," Tom said. "I'll look."

Too eager to help speed the process along, Tom rose off the couch before thinking things through. He wavered and bobbed on the balls of his feet, trying to find his balance, waiting for the room to stop spinning. He turned towards the bathroom and tried to focus on the path to the door. I didn't think he'd make it more than two steps without falling on his face. I was about to offer to go myself when he made a sudden dash, sprinting across the room like someone had just fired a starter's pistol.

Tom threw the bathroom door shut behind him. I heard the toilet lid clack against the water tank, followed by violent retching and a splash that sounded like somebody had just dropped a bowling ball into a swimming pool.

I wanted to give Tom his privacy in such a delicate moment, but I was also compelled to see what sort of demon-spawn he'd unleashed so I could assess the danger. Approaching the door, I could hear the echo of Tom's breath, panting into the bowl after such a vicious gastrointestinal upheaval. Things had calmed down in there. But then the high-pitched screeching began and I recognized Tom's voice. I turned the knob and burst in.

I found Tom kneeling in front of the toilet, his hands gripping the rim of the bowl, staring down at the flailing tendrils of the harbinger as it splashed around in the water and vomit below. He was screaming, too terrified to pull himself away. The lights were on and the room was brightly lit. White tiles on the floor and walls helped illuminate the situation and keep the harbinger contained in the relatively dark bowl. But it wasn't happy. It was cornered by the light, enraged, pained, and doing its fair share of screeching as it sought an escape route. I reached over and pushed down the plunger on the water tank, ending the show. The harbinger scrambled to grab hold of the porcelain as it whipped around in the cascading whirlpool, but the surface was wet and smooth and offered no traction. With a gurgle and a final angry squeal it disappeared down the drain and was gone from our sight.

I put a hand on Tom's shoulder and helped him to his feet. His eyes remained fixed on the toilet, so I lowered the seat and lid and flushed a second time for good measure.

"Here," I said, handing him a bottle of mouthwash that had been sitting on the back of the sink. "A swig and a spit and you'll be as good as new."

Tom did as he was told, but he remained shaky, troubled.

"That's bad isn't it? That's really bad. We didn't take care of it properly. We didn't bind it and burn it and trap it forever and now it's free."

"Yeah, that's true. But hey, at least it's gone," I said, staying positive. "Gone is good. It may be a less than ideal solution, but I'll take it."

It wasn't my preferred outcome, but I was content to call it quits for the evening. It was late, I was tired, and Tom's breath still stank of vomit despite the mouthwash. With a bit of luck, the whole harbinger incident was over and done with.

As if to disagree with this optimistic sentiment, the walls of the bathroom groaned, flexing inwards ever so slightly— enough to crack a few tiles and pop out strips of grout that crumbled to the floor. This was followed by a metallic rending noise and a vibrating rattle as the pipes behind the walls tried to shake themselves out of their moorings.

"Does your plumbing usually make that noise?" I asked, trying to sound casual about it.

"I said the plumbing was shitty, not possessed."

We waited and listened as the sound continued, off and on, for several long minutes. There was nothing to see, but we kept turning our heads to look at the walls, the floor, the ceiling, every time there was a new disturbance. No two noises seemed to come from the same direction. The harbinger was spelunking its way through the pipes, working through the system, hunting for a way out. Or a way back in.

After there had been a long enough stretch of silence to suggest the harbinger had either moved on or settled down, I left the bathroom.

"Still not contained, still on the loose," I declared. "But we've removed it from Rebecca's vicinity, so that's something. I'd say we've done a solid night's work."

"You're not leaving it here, are you?" Tom called after me. He sounded a bit delicate, but he was a big boy. He didn't need me to hold his hand till morning.

"It's fine. We've driven it twenty blocks from where it wanted to be. Once it realizes it's been displaced, it'll probably crawl down into the sewers where it's nice and dark and it can amuse itself tormenting the rats."

"You're sure?" asked Tom, unconvinced.

I wasn't any more convinced, but "Yeah" is what I said. "Just leave the light on in the bathroom, keep the lid down on the toilet, and always make a pre-emptive flush before use. The water flow will help usher it on its way."

"But what if it tries to come back up? Should I call you?"

"Me? Why me? I told you demons aren't my department. I was winging this for Rebecca's sake."

"Should I call one of those demonologist guys then?"

"Nah. Most of them suck."

"Who then?"

I gave Tom a parting shrug.

"Under the current circumstances, try a plumber. He can snake your pipes, which is the only thing I can suggest at this point. It might work, it might not. Either way, you can send a plumber's bill to your landlord. A demonologist, not so much."

I left before Tom could raise any more concerns I couldn't alleviate, or questions I couldn't answer. It had been a long night, my back was starting to ache, and there was a flat, hard casket-bed waiting for me at home. Master of the dark arts, raiser of the dead, immortal for all intents and purposes, I had my limits. I was pooped.

Chapter Nine

Danse Macabre

SOMETIMES YOU HAVE to sit back and take stock of your life. I didn't care for the sum total I was left with. Despite running errands for everyone, I was still looking at a stack of bills and nothing to invoice for. The loose ends were piling up and no one was paying me for the pain in my ass, not to mention the residual discomfort from being shot in the head.

I had a zombie rabbi stashed somewhere in a hospital sub-basement waiting to give me more inconclusive evidence about his murder; a homicide department asking me to do their jobs for them at a slave-wage consulting fee I was about to lose; a hungry harbinger blocking the pipes at a two-bit showman's dive apartment; and one nagging question: who murdered me the other day?

There was only one possible solution. Throw a party. I started making the necessary calls late the next evening after I'd spent the afternoon making certain other essential preparations.

"A party? You?" was Rebecca's gut response as soon as I extended an invitation. She had gone through all the motions of asking me how the harbinger issue worked itself out in the end, but I could tell she just wanted to move on and forget the revolting thing had ever invaded her home. She was all too happy to roll with the change in subject when I brought up my proposed party. She knew I hated parties. And socializing. Socializing at parties most of all.

"Yeah," I told her, flying in the face of all logic.

"Why?"

"Because I want to hang out with my friends."

"Rip, you don't have friends. You have associates."

"Okay, maybe I want to schmooze with my business associates."

"You, schmoozing? That'll be the day."

"Okay, cut the crap, Rebecca. Are you coming or not?"

"Would I miss this train wreck for anything? I'm so there."

With all the questions and conundrums I was currently faced with, there was one that was weighing on me heaviest of all. I felt like I couldn't proceed until I had at least one satisfactory answer. Who had it in for me? Or, failing that, who didn't have it in for me? I needed to know which of my compatriots I could still rely on, and that meant vetting everyone on my shortlist. My plan, sketchy as it was, was to get them all into the same room at the same time and then see if I could determine if any of them were capable of blowing my head off at point-blank range.

"Louie, how's our guest? Behaving himself, I hope."

My call was able to catch Louie at work, which was good because I didn't have a clue what his home number was.

"You know him, the life of the party."

"Speaking of parties..."

"Yeah," said Louie, "I got your email."

I had announced this party without the normal social fanfare. There was no time for a formal invite, but I did get one mass email out to make the occasion sound more official. I doubted anybody on the list would already have plans. They were a more active bunch than the people I often deal with professionally, but that didn't mean any of them got out much.

"I dunno, Rip. My last few shifts have been wearing me down. You know how it is, gallivanting around town with the living dead and all. I was thinking about taking it easy this evening, catching up on some games I recorded on my PVR before somebody tells me who won."

"Come on Louie, it's a party. How often do I throw a party?"

"Never, by my count."

"It'll be fun," I promised. An empty promise. I immediately realized I'd have to offer better bait to seal the deal. "Gladys will be there."

"Yeah? You invited your secretary?"

"Not really. But it's not like she's going anywhere. She'll be around."

"And you'll introduce us?"

"Sure," I agreed. I knew Louie would show up for sure now. I also knew he'd hate me for it forever.

I got Tracy on her cell phone next. She wasn't home, and by the sound of things she was just wrapping up a point of business with a client. She excused herself for a moment while I held the line. I could hear her finishing the negotiation in the background.

"Normally I'll throw myself on the casket while it's still above ground, but if you want a grave dive there's a surcharge. What kind of casket is it?"

The person she was with was standing too far away from the phone for me to make out the voice.

"I mean what's it made of?" Tracy clarified. "The wood."

"Oak costs extra," said Tracy when she got a response she didn't care for. "Oak hurts like a bitch. I don't like working with it, so if you go oak there's a surcharge on the surcharge."

Again I couldn't hear the response, but apparently the client decided that the floor show at the funeral was more important than the quality of the casket.

"Pine's good. I like pine," agreed Tracy. "Pine is a nice soft landing. I'll write up the agreement. You can look it over and sign once you've discussed it with the next of kin."

Tracy had a free moment and got back on the phone.

"I fucking hate oak," she told me by way of explanation. "I cracked a kneecap on an oak box once."

"Forlornly throwing yourself on some stranger's casket soon?" I asked her.

"Client wants me to wait until it's been lowered all the way down before I jump."

"Why the hell does he want that?"

"It's more of a spectacle. And it eats up time at the graveside ceremony. Somebody has to climb down to pry me off the box, at least two have to help me back up. Sometimes volunteers are slow to step forward. It can go on and on. It's a much longer affair than a simple coffin toss at a parlour or a church."

"But isn't it dangerous?"

"What, doing my own stunts?" laughed Tracy. "Yeah, a bit, which is why I demand danger pay. But ever since I banged up my knee, I show up at this sort of gig in a longer dress to cover the pads. The dress makes me look like a grieving schoolmarm, but I can hide enough protective gear under it to play hockey."

"Did you get my email?" I finally asked.

"No. It's been a crazy morning. I haven't checked my messages."

"I'm having a party at my place tomorrow, around seven. I know it's very last minute..."

"And you want to know if I'm willing to cancel everything and come over."

"It's sort of an informal dinner."

"So you're feeding us?" said Tracy.

"Actual food."

"Not just chips and dip?"

"An actual meal."

"Count me in." Tracy liked to eat. She liked to eat free food best of all.

Wilbur didn't have email. Or a computer. Or a cell phone. He had a landline, though, so I called that. I seem to remember he once mentioned having to pay the phone company an extra fee every month just to retain his rotary.

The phone rang forever. Apparently he didn't have any sort of answering service either. I was about to give him up for dead when he finally came on the line.

"Hey, Wilbur, what's up?"

In truth, Wilbur wasn't high on my list of suspects, but I had one extra chair. Just one. And sometimes I felt bad, thinking of poor old Wilbur, a widower alone every night, eating alone, sleeping alone. Or maybe he just reminded me of myself, and this was self-pity masquerading as sympathy. Either way, I thought I'd extend an invite to my unheard-of soiree.

"Not much," he confirmed at last, after we spent five minutes between my question and his answer establishing who it was calling him. Add call display to the list of modern conveniences that didn't adorn his ancient telephone.

"Look, I know this is very last minute, but I'm having a dinner party tomorrow and I was wondering if you could help me fill out the table."

"Oh yeah? What's on the menu?"

"What do you mean, 'What's on the menu?' I'm offering you a nice meal, nice company."

"I'm picky about what I put in my body. I'm off salt now. Doctor's orders. Salt is the devil and I gotta stay healthy."

"Aren't you over eighty?"

"Don't age me, boy. I'm not there yet. And I won't get there if I'm blowing my blood pressure through the roof with plates full of salt, will I?"

"Eighty or eight hundred. We all get there in the end. Alive or dead, we all get there."

"That's profound," declared Wilbur.

"Thanks."

"You going to be filling the air with profundities like that all night at this party of yours?"

"Probably not."

"Then I'll be there."

Tom took a long time to pick up after I dialled his number from the Barfo business card. When at last he did, he sounded distracted.

"You get my invitation email? I guess I should have printed up something fancy for the occasion, but you know how it is. I'm lazy and cheap."

"Do you hear that?" Tom asked, completely ignoring my effort to be charmingly self-deprecating. Since he mentioned it, I did hear something. I had assumed it was a bad connection at first, but this wasn't static or dropped data.

"Oh, yeah. How's that harbinger problem going? Any more weird noises?"

The noises I heard in the background were indeed weird. Faint but disturbing.

"I can hear it," Tom said in a hushed tone. "Mostly at night. It's still in the pipes, rattling around in there. It whispers to me. When I'm in the shower, when I'm brushing my teeth, when I'm on the toilet. I can hear it through the taps. It tells me things."

"Anything interesting?" I asked, expecting not.

"Something's changed." Tom sounded haunted. Literally. "It's not after Rebecca anymore. I think it's still interested in her, but it doesn't want her the way it once did."

"Ah, well that's good. Sounds like an improvement." I like to keep upbeat when talking to someone with a severe case of the shivers.

"It wants me instead. It wants back inside. It's always asking, especially in the dark. It won't let me sleep, it won't let me rest..."

"But Rebecca is in the clear?" I wanted to confirm, just to be sure.

"Why does it want to be inside me?" Tom whined, his voice quivering. "It says we're linked forever now. It says I just have to accept it and we'll be together always."

He paused and then asked aloud, like he really didn't know the answer, "I don't want that, do I?"

"It doesn't sound like a super idea, no. I'd keep my distance," I replied, offering the sagest advice I had on hand.

"How can I keep my distance? It's here with me all the time. In my pipes, in my head. The pipes run everywhere. The pipes..."

Tom trailed off, lost.

"Have you considered breaking your lease?"

"I hear it now. It's calling to me. Always calling... I have to go to it."

"But you'll be at the party right? Sounds like you need to get out, take a break."

"Yes. Yes of course."

Tom's voice was distant, muted, like he'd stepped away from the phone and wasn't talking to me anymore. I decided to take it as a solid RSVP. Then the line went dead.

"That's the last of them," I told Gladys. "Everybody is coming."

As soon as I'd arisen in the morning I had set her to work composing a suitable email invitation to go out as a preliminary salvo before my phone-call follow up. Typing isn't her thing, so it took Gladys until noon to complete a first draft. In her defence, she's probably still a better typist than any other disembodied skull you might encounter in the secretarial pool. It took me until 1:00 to correct the spelling, add punctuation, fix the typos, and rewrite everything. She had managed to butcher every single word and mangle the structure of each one of the half-dozen sentences in the brief note. The office would probably run a lot more efficiently if I just did some of these petty tasks myself, but what's the point of having a secretary if I don't delegate?

"Yoo aye look fanny," was Gladys's only comment following the news that my party was on.

"So I've been told."

Like I needed a talking skull making me feel self-conscious.

"Is gat no calla."

"What's a calla?"

"Calla! Calla! Yoo no. Reed, bloo, yella. Calla!"

"Right. The colour's gone. One eye is white. I'm sure it's just temporary."

"I no tink so."

"Every time I've ever come back from the dead, all my wounds have healed. This should be no different."

"Is nat woond. Is mak."

"You think it's a mark? A mark of what?"

"How da fak shood I no dis? Is mak. Yoo bin makked."

"You talk a lot of shit, Gladys."

"Is my falt? I spose to be deed. Yoo da wan make me tak."

"You're right. It's my fault," I agreed. "That and so many other things."

$$\Theta$$

Rebecca was at my door an hour before the stated start time, and at least two hours too early to be fashionably late. I'd given her credit for being enough of a socialite to know how these things work. Even I know enough not to show up that early to a party.

"I came to help you set up," she announced.

Apparently she didn't trust me to handle the logistics of my little gathering. Or maybe she just wanted to be the first to gloat over my disastrous mishandling of the event.

"That's nice," I told her, "but I have it covered. We're good to go."

She looked around at the apartment, which was almost exactly as she remembered it from the last time she was over. The only addition was the dinner table. I'd set up three collapsible TV-tables end-to-end and thrown a table cloth over them to create an unconvincing single unit that was flimsy but functional. Barely. Six folding chairs were placed around the perimeter, a mix of economy vinyl and repurposed outdoor deck seating. It wasn't exactly black-tie, but I figured it would do.

"This is your set up?"

"What do you want?" I asked. "Balloons and a band?"

"An open bar would be nice."

"Over there," I said, pointing to my coffee table that I'd shoved into a corner for the evening. There was half a bottle of leftover vodka, five of a six pack, and something green. I don't know what the green stuff was—the label had peeled off years earlier—but it stank. I was a solid ninety-percent sure it came from a liquor store and not, for instance, a chemical lab.

"I take it all back, it's perfect," said Rebecca, and beelined to the bar to get a head start. She'd brought her own bottle to add to the drinks table. Generous, though she probably intended to throw back twice as much by evening's end. I hoped some of others would bring booze. Rebecca could be an angry drunk, but never so angry as when there wasn't enough to drink.

I'd left Gladys sitting next to the bottles, hoping she might scare some of the guests off overindulging. No such luck with Rebecca. She and Gladys exchanged pleasantries.

"Hey, Gladys."

"Heyloo, Rebeequa," answered Gladys in a tone that was the closest thing to chipper she could manage. Everybody loves Rebecca. Even Gladys who, as best I've been able to determine, hates everyone.

"How's the new help working out?" Rebecca asked me once she'd poured herself three fingers of vodka neat.

Rebecca had met Gladys briefly a few times before and they'd spoken on the phone at length. Gladys would tie her up with all sorts of girl talk when she called. She should have been patching Rebecca directly through to me, but I was starting to believe I wasn't the one Rebecca really wanted to chat with when she rang.

"Bad attitude, bad at pretty much everything. But don't worry, I'm not thinking about firing your favourite phone friend."

"You could try being nicer to her. Works for me."

"You mean like buy her flowers on Secretaries' Day? She has no sense of smell."

"I mean do something to brighten her life—such as it is—a bit. It can't be easy for her, far from home, working long hours. And her disability. I guess her current condition qualifies as disabled."

"On many levels," I agreed.

"And what's with that name? Gladys? A little old fashioned don't you think? She certainly doesn't sound like a Gladys."

"I don't know. I just picked a name. I had an aunt Gladys. She was very skinny and bitter, so it seemed to fit."

"Did you ask her what her name was after you jump-started her noggin or whatever it was you did to the poor girl?"

"She may have mentioned it once. You think I could pronounce it? It's quite a mouthful. I'm surprised she can even say it without lips or a tongue.

"Or vocal chords, or lungs?"

"My time is valuable. I'm not struggling through some giant contortion of a name every time I need to tell her something. She gets two syllables, max."

"Wow. Two syllables. Nobody can say you're not a generous boss."

"I offer benefits."

"What? Dental? She's a bit beyond health-care insurance."

"Retirement," I said. "I have a nice little ossuary picked out for her somewhere down the road. But as for right now, I can't spare her."

The rest of the guests took their time arriving, but once they started to trickle in around half past seven I found myself buzzing them in every few minutes. When I opened the door for the second arrival, I was slightly surprised by who it turned out to be.

"Ah, Tom. I half-expected you not to make it."

After our last conversation, I gave him even odds that his harbinger hanger-on would talk him into a sad, lonely suicide. Probably by cutting his wrists in a warm bath that would give the demon quick access to Tom's dying moments through the drain.

"A bit overdressed, but welcome," I added.

Tom was wearing his stage tuxedo.

"It's my only suit," he explained.

"Classy," I said, taking in the whole ensemble, complete with a high polish on the loafers and a pocket-watch chain looped through a button hole of the vest. He looked shockingly together for a man who probably hadn't slept a wink since his own personal hex had begun.

"Is Rebecca here yet?" he asked. I suppose a one-track mind helps keep you focused.

"She's over there, working on her stupor," I said, pointing out the drinks table where Rebecca had been hovering for the last hour. "Go say 'hi' while she's still capable of speech."

Louie was next, also eager to begin sweet talking a special lady.

"Is she here?" was all he wanted to know as he passed me his token offering of a bottle of cheap scotch. I knew Rebecca and the scotch would get on well. I was less hopeful for Louie and Gladys.

"Oh, she's here all right," I confirmed.

"Where is she?" said Louie, scanning the apartment over my shoulder.

"Laying low. Come on in, pour a drink and I'll introduce you in a bit."

"Be cool about it," he said. "Play it casual. Get us on a first-name basis and I'll take it from there."

"Have that drink first," I told him. "Or two."

I had hardly ushered Louie inside before Wilbur was at my still-open door. He was cradling two more bottles, one under each arm.

"You never told me what we were having, so I brought a red and a white. One of each." He studied my face more closely, and commented, "Not unlike those eyes of yours."

"Oh, that. Yeah. I woke up like this a couple of days ago."

"A relapse, huh? I'm sure they make drops for that."

"It's a one-time thing," I said. "This has never happened to me before."

"You sure? Looks like the same condition from last time I saw you."

"At the Wonderama?"

"No, not the store. At my place."

Wilbur was mixing up his dates and places again. If it wasn't for his schedule at the magic shop, he'd never be able to tell you what day of the week it was. Had I not invited him to the party just last night, he probably would have arrived the following Wednesday looking for a meal and music. Before the conversation could get any more lost, Rebecca came over to greet Wilbur and his wine. She'd known him through me for years.

"Wilbur, you're my saviour."

"Which do you want me to pour, dear?" said Wilbur, spotting the bottle opener I'd left on the drinks table.

"Both I hope. You want something harder before it goes?" said Rebecca, tilting a clear-glass bottle and swirling around the dregs of what used to be the half-full vodka so recently.

"No," said Wilbur. "I'll just start with the white."

"More for me," announced Rebecca, who uncapped the bottle and looked about ready to finish it off without the inconvenience of a glass.

"Enough for you," I said, taking it away from her.

"Party pooper," she called me.

"My party to poop. Pace yourself. At least stay above the table until we're through dinner, please?"

"I'll have you know I'm used to passing out under a much higher calibre of table than that sad display. You have some kids coming over? Where are the adults eating?"

"Wilbur, will you play bartender to Rebecca and keep her from drowning herself before the appetizers come out?"

Wilbur took her by the arm.

"Come along, sweetie, and tell me all the latest," he said.

Switching her to wine after all that vodka would make her ill sooner, but keep her coherent longer.

Once Tracy made her appearance, she was less interested in the other attendees than what I'd done with the place since she'd last been by.

"You know there's a big hole in your door, right?" she said.

"I noticed."

"I thought I'd mention it in case it slipped by you."

"It didn't."

"You used to have a rug right here," Tracy noted, staring down at my bare living room floor.

"I did," I confirmed.

"What happened to it? It was nice. Just about the only bit of decoration in this place that had any colour."

"I spilled something on it."

"Wine? That's a bitch to get out."

"Brains."

"That's probably a bitch to get out too," she nodded knowingly.

Rebecca came over again. Not to greet Tracy, although they knew each other well enough, but to complain about one of the other guests.

"It's here!" she hissed.

"What's here?"

"That thing! That harbinger thing!"

"Where?" I asked, masking my alarm.

"Tom! Tom brought it with him. And he didn't even bring a bottle!"

I figured I'd better check it out before the party was ruined by people dropping dead before it even started. I hoped the harbinger sighting was merely a bout of alcohol-induced paranoia from Rebecca.

"Tom," I said simply as I approached. It was enough to startle him. "Did you bring a crasher I should know about?"

"It wasn't my idea!" Tom exclaimed, like my simple query was twisting his arm. "He made me bring him! He wouldn't let me out the door unless I took him with me."

I grabbed Tom by the lapels of his antique tux and manhandled him into the hall closet where I kept coats and boots.

Ignoring the odd looks from the other guests, I pulled the door shut behind us and yanked the string on the bare bulb to illuminate the narrow space as much as possible. I didn't relish the idea of locking myself in an enclosed place with Tom and his piggybacking demon, but it would be worse if the harbinger made a break for it in mixed company.

"Where? Where is he?" I demanded.

Tom's eyes shifted down and I followed his gaze to the fine silver chain that was looped through his button hole. I followed the string of links to where they disappeared deep down inside a bulging breast pocket. I grabbed the chain and reeled it in, ill-prepared for whatever I might find on the end of it.

"Behold, mortal! For I am Qixxiqottltoq, loyal servant to the Lord and Master, Dagon. And I am reborn!" the demonic entity bellowed at me through its puckering mouth once it was exposed to the light and staring at me with its single glassy eye.

I tried not to laugh in relief. It was the harbinger all right, but it had found something undead to merge with, much as I had intended for it at Tom's apartment before the frozen chicken failed to pan out. Somewhere, deep in the recesses of the building's plumbing, it had discovered the reanimated goldfish, moved in, and then used its new body to swim its way back up the pipes and pry its way into Tom's life.

Safely ensconced in its new fishy form, the harbinger was no longer light-sensitive. It didn't recoil from the bare bulb in the closet. That was the one advantage it had in possessing the body it now inhabited. But I couldn't see many other pluses—certainly nothing that made it particularly dangerous. Apparently it could talk a good game if it so easily turned Tom into its humble servant, and maybe that was enough to get it what it wanted, but I was no longer concerned about it being able to orchestrate deaths for its own amusement. This body was rather limiting for such a purpose. From sheer accident of proximity, it had found its stature reduced from an ancient malevolent demon to a chatty pet nesting in Tom's pocket—still evil, but utterly ineffectual.

To better suit the needs of the harbinger and its new form, Tom had taken an antique open-face pocket watch—one of his props meant to be swallowed and regurgitated—and removed the time-keeping mechanism. Filling the empty chamber with the small amount of water it could hold, he'd stuffed his undead companion in last and screwed the reverse plate back on. The end result was a miniature aquarium for his used and abused fish, pressed into permanent profile, offering just enough space for it to flick its shredded fins and pump its crushed gills as it stared out of the glass face with its one semi-good eye.

"It was his idea," explained Tom. "He said he could function as my totem."

"Totem my ass. You're going to tell me your power animal is a squashed goldfish? Be careful with this one, he's trying to con you."

"He guilts me into things. I feel I owe him."

"You want to make it up to him, buy him a new bowl, some coloured rocks, a plastic plant, and a mermaid that blows bubbles. That ought to balance the books. Even Steven."

"I'm sorry. I didn't mean to endanger everyone by bringing him here. But when he tells me to do things, it's like I have no will of my own."

"It's all in your head, Tom. He's powerless now. Just ignore him."

I pulled the string on the bulb again, plunging the closet back into darkness, and opened the door.

"Pardon that embarrassing scene, everyone. It's all under control," I said to my guests, who had all been standing in place, watching the closet door while I questioned Tom. "I thought we had a situation, but we only have an unexpected guest. Tom, would you like to introduce your little friend to everyone?"

The fish dangling from the watery capsule at the end of the watch chain didn't wait for Tom to present him.

"I am Qixxiqottltoq," he announced thunderously, "vassal to the Mighty Lord, Dagon! Bow before me as you would before him!"

Conspicuously, nobody bowed.

"That's quite a mouthful," I told the fish. "Mind if I call you 'Moby-Dick' for short?"

I don't know if he ever read Melville or was a fan, but he seemed to take offence at my flippancy.

"Foul hu-man, you shall submit before me and pay proper reverence, for I am Qixxi…"

I cut him off there.

"Moby-Dick it is," I told him. "I'm Rip, this is Tracy, Wilbur, Louie. And I think you already know Rebecca."

The possessed fish eyed Rebecca with his only available eye.

"Yes, the woman," he said civilly, thoughtfully. "The woman is the path to the watery grave…"

He still had a thing for her. And not at all in the same way Tom did.

"We'll have a talk about that later, you and I," I told him.

"She must lead the way!" blurted out the fish.

"Now behave or I'll take you for a swim in the piranha tank down at the pet store."

That shut him up. Immortal demon-fish or not, nobody wants to get chewed on by piranhas—ugly, toothy things. Tom tucked the encapsulated monstrosity back into his pocket for safekeeping.

The flow of party chatter resumed and Tracy and Rebecca took the opportunity to catch up.

"That's Tom," Rebecca told her.

"Uh-huh," said Tracy. "And what's the deal with Tom's friend?"

"Undead fish. Rip's doing."

"I didn't kill it," I said in my defence.

"No, you did way worse to it," said Rebecca. "Tom was on stage. There was a mishap."

"Wait, is he that guy you dragged Rip out to see?" Tracy asked.

"What guy?" said Rebecca, suspicious of how much Tracy knew about our evening at Gallery Nowhere.

"The regurgitator."

"Oh, him. Yeah, I guess so. That's what Tom does for a living. He…" Rebecca twirled her finger in a rolling motion and made an ill face, suggesting vomiting without being so gauche as to actually say it out loud in mixed company.

"The stupid shit people do for cash, huh?" said Tracy, shaking her head knowingly.

"Tell me about it," agreed Rebecca.

Despite my assurances that everything was cool, Tom had suddenly become the wallflower of the party. Everyone gave him a wide berth as he busied himself picking over my spread of hors d'oeuvres that offered a choice of cheese on a saltine cracker or a strip of cold cuts on the same brand of saltine cracker. Only Wilbur was willing to strike up a conversation with him.

"Ventriloquist act, huh?" Wilbur said, cornering Tom. "I seen plenty of dummies in my time, worked with quite a few. Gets so you end up talking to them like they're a real person. Never seen a ventriloquism act with a dead fish before, but I guess you gotta give the kids today a fresh twist on the old corny routines so it seems new. New and—what do they say now—edgy? I remember when that used to mean nervous and fidgety."

"I'm not a ventriloquist," explained Tom patiently, "I'm a regurgitator."

"How's that work then? Instead of making him talk while you drink a glass of water, you make him talk while you puke one up? Well, it's original, I'll give you that."

Wilbur tried to feed himself one of the cold-cut crackers, but the topping rolled off before he could get it in his mouth and plummeted to the floor. With an old-bone grunt, he bent down to retrieve the fallen morsel, but misjudged where it had landed. Instead of a rolled-up length of thinly sliced ham, Wilbur found a different chunk of meat and stacked that back onto the cheese spread and cracker. Watching from across the room, I wondered what it could possibly be until I recognized the tell-tale hue. I thought I'd scraped up all the blood and brains when I was cleaning the apartment earlier, but apparently I'd missed a small piece of my murder.

"Um...Wilbur?" I started to say.

Wilbur popped the grey-matter cracker and turned to see what I wanted.

"Mmm?" he asked, chewing politely with his mouth closed.

"Never mind."

I figured that probably absolved Wilbur of the murder. Whoever had pulled the trigger on me would know better than to eat random mystery meat off the floor of their crime scene.

"Are we safe with the fishy thing?"

Rebecca had returned to my side. Despite my assurances, she was still worried about the newly merged entity that had Tom in its thrall. Goldfish don't have much personality or sense of self, so the harbinger that had menaced her in her apartment was the dominant presence. I didn't blame her. Without much experience in this sort of thing, it's hard to adjust from being terrified of something, to finding it pathetically comical. It can be a real leap. I should have said something to quell her fears.

"Who brought rosé?" I said instead. Rebecca was nursing a wine glass with a pink beverage swilling around inside.

"Nobody," she said. "I was drinking red and topped it up with some white."

"Of course," I agreed. There was no point discussing it. Why drink anything straight if you can turn it into some horrible mixed cocktail?

"So is it safe?" she asked, insisting on an answer.

"It should be," was the most reassurance I was willing to commit to. "Your harbinger may have possessed it but he's stuck in there now. And how much harm can a goldfish do? But the same rules apply. Don't get chatty with it. He's up to something, that fish. I don't like the look in his eye. Keep your distance until I figure out what he wants."

"You know what it wants. It wants to watch somebody die."

"True," I agreed. "But not just anybody. This one seems to have a specific death under specific circumstances in mind. Some harbingers have a preferred diet. Most of them are pretty meat and potatoes and any death any which way will do. But there are others with more refined tastes. They can still get off on anybody's demise, but there are certain types of death they really enjoy. And they'll chase them down whenever they get a sniff of one coming."

"What kinds of deaths are we talking about?"

"Could be any variety. A lot of harbingers really enjoy executions. They like the ritual, the ceremony of it. There's even been a few notable cases where harbingers have interfered with phone lines to stop any last-minute gubernatorial re-prieves from robbing them of their kick. But individual tastes can vary greatly. Air harbingers like skydiving accidents and airplane crashes. Cancer harbingers look for promising tumours and encourage them to metastasize. Pervy harbingers seek out autoerotic asphyxiations and other sexual mishaps."

I was starting to enter into speculative territory, but I figured Rebecca had a right to know. This demon had been drawn to her specifically.

"I think what we have here is an aqua-harbinger. They're into deaths involving water—anything from sinking ships to tsunamis, they're all over it. It explains why this harbinger merged so easily with an undead fish. A reanimated creature of the sea is a natural vessel for it to inhabit. It would also explain its apparent fealty to Dagon, who is one of the fishier ancient gods of the east."

"I won't argue with your diagnosis, doctor, because I don't know shit about any of this crap. I just want to hear what you think we should do."

"I still say burn it," I stated, erring on the side of caution. "If nothing else, it might at least get him to shut up."

I looked at Tom in the corner, where he was still getting his ear talked off by Wilbur about the good old days of stage magic.

"But hey, if Tom wants to accessorize with a lesser demon, that's his choice. As long as he ignores all the bad advice he's likely to hear from his scaly friend, he should be safe enough."

Rebecca didn't seem convinced. I didn't sound particularly convinced either. A watch-and-wait policy was rarely a prudent choice when dealing with a supernatural force of ill-will bent on mischief. But basic curiosity made me want to let it play out before I went through the indignity of wrestling Tom's pocket aquarium away from him and ritualistically torching it.

I was still waiting on one final arrival. I couldn't proceed with the plan to expose the possible killer in the room until we were all together. As a preliminary line of inquiry, I decided to make the rounds of my gathered suspects and scope out each of them individually. Perhaps by addressing them face-to-face, one of them might let slip a hint of guilt or unease. I kidded myself that I'd be able to pick up on any subtle displays of emotion brewing beneath the surface. I usually don't pick up on people's feelings unless they're displayed in grotesque, cartoonishly exaggerated fashion. Even then, I've been known to confuse anger for fear, crying for laughter, Emotions can be messy, ugly things and I've developed a blind spot. Mostly on purpose.

Going around the room and offering everyone fresh drinks promised to get expensive and deplete the meagre bar, so I played it cheap and retrieved Gladys's skull from the coffee table. She, of course, protested being picked up. Gladys didn't care to be treated like an inanimate object to be carried from one location to another regardless of her wishes in the matter. Nevertheless, I pressed her into service as a convenient prop for my social rounds. The top third of her skull was fastened to its base by a pair of hooks on either side of the crown. Unhooking them allowed me to hinge back the bone bowl, revealing the treasure inside. For the party I had replaced the usual collection of paper slips and business cards with something more festive.

"Bon-bon?" I offered the first guest on my list.

Gladys hates it when I keep sweets inside her. She also hates being used as a Rolodex, but she's particularly offended when I employ her as a novelty dish for candies and chocolate. I think she's secretly jealous. I suspect she had a sweet tooth when she was alive, and having all those confections stuffed in her skull when she can't taste any of them must be torture.

Tracy dipped her hand into the skull without hesitation. She hadn't been introduced to Gladys yet, but I didn't think she'd be the least bit put off by a real human skull. Even a reanimated one.

"It's chilly in there," she commented, as she withdrew her fingers with a mint square.

"Must be a draft."

"Yoo tink is coold? Yoo try been me!" Gladys chattered. "I coold all da fakkin time!"

"It speaks," observed Tracy.

"It does. And often. Never anything nice."

"Creepy supernatural shit?" Tracy asked.

"Yeah," I confirmed. "Or just 'Gladys' as I call her."

"Weren't you telling me the other day you needed brains —or something that used to be brains—to reanimate and talk with the dead?"

"Ah, the class was listening," I said. "I'm always gratified to know I'm making some headway in illuminating the dull normals about the reality that's happening all around them, right under their ignorant noses."

"Watch who you're calling 'ignorant,'" said Tracy. "Or 'normal.'"

"I'm kidding."

"Even in jest," she cautioned.

"He asshool wid yoo too?" Gladys asked Tracy.

"Oh yeah," Tracy said, more to me than the skull.

"He alweez asshool wid me!"

"If you could get Gladys up and chit-chatting away in whatever language that is…"

"English," I said.

"Really?" Tracy seemed unconvinced.

"Of carse I spakkin Angleesh! Wat fakkin lingwage yoo spakkin, beech!"

Tracy ignored the skull's burst of outrage.

"I guess you're right. I've never heard English sound so foreign before."

"Gladys was an osteo-reanimation," I explained. "It's a completely different process. Much more complicated, much more involved, and a lot less animation when you're done. It's impractical for any time-sensitive job, plus there's one other complication."

"It puts them in a piss-poor mood?"

"Other than that. No, the real problem is there's no guarantee you'll summon the original skull's owner."

"You mean this might not be Gladys's actual skull?"

I shrugged. "Might be, might not be. I'm just glad I managed to reel in a human spirit. An osteo-reanimation is like setting a bear trap. You'll probably catch a bear, but just about anything can wander into your trap. There are no guarantees what you'll get, so you proceed with caution."

"What sort of precautions do you take for that?"

"It took eight days to reanimate this skull. Every night I slept with a hammer under my pillow. Just in case I had to, you know..." I wondered how to put it delicately in front of Gladys. "Smash her to pieces."

"I smush yoo to peesez, fakker," Gladys muttered.

"But it all worked out in the end. I got a perfectly harmless spirit to inhabit the skull."

"I shoe yoo who hamlez, kaksacker!"

"Rude, but harmless," I added.

"Where'd you learn how to do all this crazy shit, Rip?" Tracy asked, suitably impressed. "Is there some book I can order, or a correspondence course I can take?"

I smiled in what I hoped was an obnoxiously enigmatic way and moved on. I don't mind teasing people with the occasional trade secret, but some things are far too dangerous for a novice to know anything about. A good magician never reveals his best tricks for fear of losing his audience. A good necromancer never reveals his best tricks for fear of throwing the balance of life and death out of whack and destroying reality as we know it.

"Who thees owld fakker?" Gladys wanted to know as I stepped up to rescue Tom from Wilbur's nostalgic tirade.

Wilbur was immediately taken by Gladys and smiled in delight.

"That's a neat gimmick you got there," Wilbur commented on the uncouth candy-laden skull in my hands. "What's the trick?"

"No trick," I assured him.

"Don't bullshit the bullshit king, boy. How's it work?"

Wilbur knew from experience that my abilities stretched beyond the norm. But other than collecting information only the dead could know, he hadn't seen much of my work. That was on purpose. I didn't think his heart could take it.

"Smoke and mirrors," I told him, "smoke and mirrors."

"Go on then, be like that!" he grumbled. Wilbur was disappointed. He still wanted to know how all the tricks were done, even this many years after retirement. I decided I'd let him stew about what complex puppetry rigging made my talking-skull gag work. He'd be weeks trying to figure it out. Cruel? Maybe. But it would keep his creaky old mind more active than crossword puzzles and Sudoku.

"Something sweet before dinner?" I asked Tom, offering him the contents of Gladys's skull. "Sorry I don't have any fish flakes for your pal."

"Curse you, necromancer!" spewed a muffled voice from inside Tom's pocket.

Tom reached for a sweet. His hand hovered over the selection indecisively.

"Peek a fakkin candee!" Gladys blurted out impatiently.

Tom snatched one at random and scurried away.

Louie approached on his own before I could even finish my rounds.

"So where is she, man? You have another bathroom in this place where she's hiding?"

"Who?" I asked, forgetting why he'd agreed to come in the first place.

"Gladys. Who do you think I'm talking about?"

"Oh. Her."

"Who he meen? Me?" Gladys asked.

The conversation stopped so suddenly, I could almost hear the brakes squeal.

"Did that skull just talk?" Louie asked at last.

I wasn't sure what answer could keep the situation civil, so I merely said, "Yes."

After what was the single longest socially awkward pause of my life, Louie enthused, "That is the coolest thing I've ever seen in my whole life."

"Really?"

"It's a hell of a lot cooler than a zombie rabbi."

I didn't question this unexpected common ground of interest. Gladys was a talking skull, Louie somehow thought that was fascinating. The door buzzer offered me a quick exit from this match made in—not heaven, not hell—let's simply say "purgatory."

"Here," I said, offering my bony candy dish to Louie, "you two get better acquainted. I have to let somebody in."

"Finally," I said, as I pushed the button to unlock the front door downstairs. My attempt to read the guilt or innocence of partygoers had proved futile. They were all too alive. I have much better luck with the deceased.

"Who's that?" asked Tracy.

"Our final guest," was all I had to say.

Rebecca did a quick tally and noticed that just about everybody I was on good terms with was present.

"Who else could you have invited?" she asked.

I heard the elevator clunk to a stop on my floor. The gate rattled to one side and heavy footsteps echoed in the hall. I didn't wait for the knock. I opened the door and let him in with no introduction needed.

Reynaldo was fashionably, irritatingly late. Of course.

Chapter Ten

Medium Rare

THE DAY BEFORE, in the early afternoon, as Gladys sent out the party announcement by email, I had left to secure my most important guest. Without him, the whole gathering would be about pointless socializing and camaraderie, and I couldn't let that happen.

The decision to invite Reynaldo into my home was not made lightly. It's not like I was concerned about the competition snooping around and conducting acts of home-office espionage. I was concerned about the competition snooping around and making a bunch of snide comments about my standard of living, my decorating decisions, and my taste in everything from dishes to the door mat. Reynaldo was the sort of snob who thought he had supreme taste in all areas and would delight in criticizing anything anyone considered to be their personal style or preference. He was a real bitch that way. He'd probably find an excuse to work his disapproval of my couch into the conversation every time we encountered each other from now until the day he dropped dead—possibly from me strangling him for harping on for the millionth time about the colour of a couch I once owned. If he did the job I needed him to do, it was a price I was reluctantly willing to pay.

Reynaldo's was the only invitation I needed to extend in person. It was going to be an uphill battle to get him to come. I didn't call ahead, didn't want to announce my imminent arrival. My best bet was to ambush him, catch him off guard, and get him to agree to my plan before he had a chance to think of all the reasons to say no.

Reynaldo lived in a three-storey greystone, sandwiched between many identical twins, on an old street that showed off its original cobblestones whenever it developed a new pothole. His neighbourhood marked an abrupt upturn in real-estate value and earned annual income. It taunted me with a success I might have enjoyed had I been as good as Reynaldo at monetizing my profession. I might have chosen one of those grand old greystones myself if not for two important considerations—I'd need an extra zero or two appended to the end of my annual income to swing it, and the idea of having Reynaldo as a neighbour sickened me more than the most putrid maggoty corpse I ever had to dig up on the job.

As I walked up the steps of his building, I could see the heavy velvet drapes were all drawn. Reynaldo wasn't as fond of the gloom and darkness as, say, myself. He liked to let the sunshine in, which meant he was either still in bed, or manufacturing mood for a client. Either way, he wouldn't be pleased to be disturbed by the likes of me. I pressed the doorbell regardless and took my chances. He'd either invite me in or kick me out. I'd know one way or the other in a few minutes.

It ultimately took more than a few minutes. I had to ring a couple more times to get a response. Reynaldo knew there was somebody at his door and likely even knew who it was. I was sure I saw movement at the curtains. Someone had sneaked a peek. I didn't try to hide my face. I knew my best chance of getting in lay in piquing Reynaldo's curiosity. Once he knew it was me at the door, he'd have to know why I was there. That didn't stop him from making me stand on the porch for as long as he thought I was willing to wait. Sure enough, the very moment I turned and acted like I was about to walk off the property, I heard the door bolt unlock with a sharp clack.

The front door swung in and Reynaldo stood in the vestibule, looking me up and down like a special-delivery package he didn't know if he wanted to sign for. He was dressed, if you could call it that, in a smoking jacket over a purple silk shirt. Whatever I was interrupting, it wasn't his sleep. Once he'd silently made his disdain obvious, Reynaldo chose his opening salvo.

"What on earth have you done to your eye?" he asked as insensitively as he could manage, the moment he spotted the remnants of my fatal wound.

"Occupational injury."

"Oh," he replied, sounding vaguely disappointed. "For a moment I thought you'd splurged on one of those dreadful coloured contact lenses."

"Why would I get just one?"

"A fashion statement for the impoverished? I'd assumed you couldn't afford a pair."

"Are you going to invite me in?"

"Are you going to tell me why you're paying me this visit?"

"I'll tell you inside."

"I thought you might," Reynaldo smiled, humourlessly.

He stepped aside but left the door yawning open as an unspoken invitation.

"I hope I'm not tearing you away from anything important," I said, hoping I was tearing him away from something important.

"No, not yet. We haven't begun."

An unfamiliar face descended the stairs from the master bedroom. The face was chiseled on top of a body that looked like it was carved from a single slab of marble during classical antiquity. He was wearing a pair of borrowed sweat pants that modestly covered parts of him that were probably as muscled and hairless as the rest.

"Really?" I asked. "Because it looks like you've only just finished."

Once he arrived on the landing, Reynaldo ran a finger up the young man's abs like he was playing the bars of a xylophone.

"Sleep well?" Reynaldo asked his evening's entertainment.

"Did you let him sleep at all?" I asked.

"Only once exhaustion took its toll," smiled Reynaldo.

A formal introduction didn't seem forthcoming.

"So who's the boy beefcake?" I asked, to be impolite.

"I think his name is Andre," said Reynaldo, right in front of the statue, not caring whether "Andre" heard or not. "I brought him home with me to share a bottle of wine because he got carded at the club and they wouldn't serve him alcohol. Isn't that delicious?"

"Reynaldo's been a total sweetheart," Andre assured me.

"He's not too old for you?" I asked Andre.

"No, of course not."

"Too fat? Too ugly?"

"No!" Andre was quick to protest.

"Too obnoxious?"

"Ah," I exclaimed, when I didn't get the same immediate knee-jerk response, "he paused there, didn't he? You saw it."

Andre looked down at his sugar daddy apologetically and was met with silent displeasure.

"Awkward," I labelled the moment.

Reynaldo turned and stared at me like he was doing math in his head. He gave Andre a pat on the ass and sent him on his way.

"Run and get dressed. My plans for you involve more appropriate attire."

Andre did as he was told and climbed the stairs again to retrieve whatever outfit he'd arrived in last night.

"So," Reynaldo said, "you're here. Tell me what you want and perhaps I'll tell you what I have in mind for you."

I knew there would have to be some sort of tit for tat. Reynaldo had already leapt ahead in our chess game of give and take. He didn't know what I was after, but he'd already decided what he wanted in exchange.

"May I?" I asked, nodding at an adjoining room. I thought it might be a more comfortable place to discuss terms than the hallway.

Reynaldo ushered me into his parlour, "By all means, take a seat. Don't make yourself comfortable. We haven't established if you're staying."

The room was filled with antiques—the sort a collector hand-picks over years rather than the type heirs get handed down and keep for convenience, not taste. I sat in a love seat that was of a style probably named for some numbered monarch or other, I couldn't say which. Reynaldo sat opposite me in a dark leather lounge chair that sighed and farted as his heft pushed all the air out. Once he was settled in and his seat had stopped protesting, he assumed a relaxed but attentive pose, as though he were holding court on the one day of the year the serfs were allowed into the castle to state their business and plead for satisfaction.

"I'm listening," he announced.

Reynaldo almost looked serene. He was enjoying this. I launched into my pitch immediately to cut his basking-time short.

"You noticed my eye," I said.

"The occupational hazard? How could I not?"

"Want to guess how that happened?"

He paused a moment to consider.

"No."

So much for guessing games.

"I was shot," I said.

"Dead?"

"Of course dead. I got shot in the eye. It went right through."

"Oh goodie," Reynaldo sounded delighted. "Did it hurt?"

"Mostly my feelings."

Reynaldo knew far more about my unique abilities than I would have preferred, but it's challenging to keep things from a genuine psychic—especially one with no particular moral qualms about poking around in other people's thoughts and emotions without an expressed invitation. I should have guessed, the moment I spotted him as the real deal, that someone with his skill set, versed in speaking to the dead, would be able to recognize me as someone who had died repeatedly. It left me feeling exposed, which I hate, in front of someone I intensely dislike—which I hate even more.

"So do you want me to kiss the boo-boo and make it all better?"

"I want you to help vet suspects."

"Intriguing. A mystery!" exclaimed Reynaldo. "I haven't turned my talents to a task quite like that before. I expect I'd be superb at it. So who is on your list of prime suspects? I'm all ears."

Reynaldo was acting like I was dishing juicy gossip rather than discussing the events surrounding my being shot, execution style. I tried, and failed, to not be offended.

"You know the circles I walk in. You know who I associate with?"

Reynaldo placed a couple of fingers on his right temple, closed his eyes and frowned in deep concentration. He came out of this trance a few moments later.

"I do now."

I'll admit, he got me. I probably looked alarmed.

"Totally messing with you," he said, laughing it off. "Yes, I know the names and faces of your various peers. I'd ask after them if I cared at all."

"One of them may have murdered me, and I want to know who."

"So you have trust issues. Ah, don't we all?"

"If it was a disgruntled client, I don't care. I'll take it as a bad review and move on. But if it was somebody I work with, that's a problem. I can't afford to have one of them backstab me while we're in the middle of a job. Who knows what forces it could unleash if they try to take me out again when I've got something going that I need to keep a handle on."

"And how do you plan to accomplish this great confrontation of all those who fall under suspicion?"

Reynaldo the Fuckhead was every bit as grating as I expected him to be and then some. My expectations for how well this proposition would go had been low. Reynaldo was exceeding them. We seemed to cross paths far more often than either of us could stomach. This was the second time in one week we'd come face-to-face, and it was stretching our patience to the breaking point. My suggestion of a third encounter was shattering our patience into little pieces and spraying the shrapnel all over Reynaldo's luxury digs.

"I'm throwing a party. Tomorrow night."

"A party? You?" Reynaldo forced a laugh even though he wasn't really amused. A condescending chuckle was simply the quickest and most detestable way for him to exhibit contempt.

"Nothing fancy," I assured him. "Dinner, drinks and a short list of guests. I could try putting the screws to them myself, but it'll be too obvious coming from me. I figure you could cut through the bullshit and read between the lines, so to speak."

"So you need me to sort through all these people you're unsure of and tell you which one has it in for you," said Reynaldo, summarizing my request as he saw it. "Please don't tell me I'm your only real friend."

"Don't worry, we're not friends. I can't stand the sight of you, but right now you're the only person I can trust."

"Why? Aren't I a suspect in this heinous deed?"

Reynaldo sounded offended that he might not be.

"I figure not," I told him. "Everyone knows we hate each other. If someone finds me lying around dead with my brains blown out, you're the first guy the cops are going to consider a person of interest. You know that as well as I do."

"But of course you're not lying around dead. At least, not anymore. You're up and about and more or less on the mend, I see."

"That's the other thing. You know gunning me down isn't going to do you any good. I'm just going to get up and walk it off. So what's the point?"

"Fleeting satisfaction? The cathartic thrill of pulling a trigger and splitting your head open like a melon? Even if it's all for naught, I can certainly see the entertainment value in the experience."

"Fair enough. But the shooter didn't stay to gloat. Never saw the damage done. Never even confirmed the kill as such. I was shot through a closed door that was still locked when I woke up three days later. Not much catharsis to be had in that. So you're off the hook for it."

"I'm so relieved to be exonerated of this crime I've only just this moment learned of. Although I doubt my lawyer will be as pleased. Perhaps he did the deed in order to swing suspicion my way so he could rack up some more of his exorbitant hourly wage."

I remembered Reynaldo's lawyer. He'd threatened legal action against me more than once and I had to back down each time. My only consolation was that every time he got in my face, Reynaldo was running up the tab. I like to think I've cost him more in legal fees than he ever made poaching my clients.

"So how about it? You drop by my place around seven, have a drink, a bite to eat. You point a finger and go. Simple."

Reynaldo took his time considering my request and then began, "As your duly appointed nemesis…"

"You're not my nemesis," I cut him off. "You don't qualify as a nemesis. A nemesis needs to be some sort of actual threat. You're my duly appointed pain-in-the-ass."

"Do I not routinely whisk paying clients out from under you? Do I not constantly eclipse your abilities with astounding feats of clairvoyance? Do I not…"

"Yeah yeah," I cut him off. "But some lost work and a few lucky guesses don't make you more than a blip on my radar."

"Lucky guesses, are they?" Reynaldo clicked his tongue at me dismissively. "If you truly thought that, you wouldn't be here now."

He had me, so I tried to push him towards a simple yes or no answer.

"We both know you won't do it as a favour, so you either want something from me or you don't. Name it or I'm out of here."

Reynaldo smiled. Playtime was over. It was to business at last.

"As it so happens, I'm having a spot of bother with a client."

I didn't need a sixth or seventh sense to figure out who.

"Don't tell me. Saunders."

"Indeed. Recovering the hidden assets of his late uncle has proved problematic. Aside from personality conflicts and high-maintenance issues with the client you, yourself, warned me about, the departed spirit of Samuel Higgins has proved elusive. I've made two attempts at it so far with no discernable results. I believe the late Mr. Higgins is reluctant to manifest himself because he holds his nephew in about as low a regard as we do. Your arrival is fortuitous because I was just about to make a third do-or-die attempt at contact. I would have written off the case already, but it's my under-standing Mr. Higgins was well and truly loaded, so every avenue must be exhausted—even if one of those avenues is a cul-de-sac with you standing at the end of it."

"I already came up empty once. What makes you think I'll do any better this time?"

"Nothing at all. Set to the task alone, you'll only fail again. But, perhaps, with our talents combined in one con-certed effort..."

"You're saying you want to tag-team a ghost into coughing up an account number."

"It might work," said Reynaldo. "I think I could talk Mr. Saunders into letting us try."

"Good luck with that. I'm sure he doesn't want anything to do with me."

"Let's see, shall we? He's waiting in the next room. He'll be so thrilled to know it's you who's wasting his time. Again."

I looked at the double sliding door that separated the parlour from what was once the house's dining room—now Reynaldo's official séance central. Dozens of tiny square windows were set into the doors, but they were all frosted, allowing little more than a bit of light to filter through. Looking closer, I could make out movement from someone fidgeting impatiently in a chair in the adjoining room. It could only be Jeremy Saunders.

I didn't want to give the man one more second of my time and never wanted to lay eyes on him again. But I let greed speak for me.

"Am I going to get a cut of the take?"

"I think not," said Reyanldo. "That ship has sailed. This is my recovery contract now. I might, however, consider offering you a consulting fee."

I shook my head no. "Peanuts."

A consulting fee would amount to whatever Reynaldo thought my consult was worth. Knowing him, he'd calculate it as being worthless, undercut that amount, and then shave off another twenty percent for good measure.

"Or..." countered Reynaldo, leaving the word dangling in the air between us.

"Or what?"

"Or I could swing by this party you're planning and find your culprit for you," he shrugged casually.

I considered and countered, "How about that consult fee and the personal appearance?"

"One or the other. Choose."

So I chose. Probably poorly.

Θ

Abruptly sliding twin doors open makes for a more dramatic entrance, which is probably the main reason Reynaldo repurposed the dining room as his prime venue to host clients. Once they were seated and kept waiting at the table in the middle of room for a suspense-building allotment of time, he would finally make his appearance in full medium regalia. I'd watched him prepare in the parlour, shrugging off his smoking jacket and replacing it with a far grander and more colourful cloak, applying eye liner in a mirror so the whites of his eyes would pop every time he stared into the beyond, and topping it all off with the turban. It wasn't a real turban. I doubt Reynaldo had the patience or know-how to wrap one around his head properly. This thing was more of a turban-shaped hat, permanently fixed in its shape, and purportedly pinned together with a bejeweled brooch where the wrappings criss-crossed at the forehead. The ruby jewel was likely just as fake as the brooch's duty as an instrument of binding, but the theatricality of the ensemble created an undeniable mood of exoticism. I probably should have been taking notes, but the idea of putting on such an absurd show for a client gave me the giggles.

Throwing aside the doors and revealing himself in all his splendour, Reynaldo failed to impress Jeremy Saunders. He'd already been through this song and dance twice before, and Saunders was a man who was only impressed with results. Reynaldo had failed to give him any thus far.

"Reynaldo the Wise is ready to make contact," he announced anyway.

"Why the hell is he here?" was all Saunders had to say on the matter.

Whatever atmosphere Reynaldo was trying to create in the room was probably undermined by my unenthusiastic saunter as I strolled in behind him. Saunders immediately recognized me and, as expected, wasn't happy about our reunion.

"Mr. Eulogy is merely here to assist as a courtesy. There will be no additional fees or charges for his participation here today."

"That son of a bitch already stole plenty from me."

"I cashed your retainer," I said in my defence. "You retained me."

"Now now," Reynaldo said, trying to soothe his client, "Mr. Eulogy may have overcharged you for lackluster work, but he's here to make amends by helping out in some small capacity. We all want a happy resolution, do we not?"

"Yes," grumbled Saunders.

"Then let us use all available ammunition at our disposal to bring this final attempt to a successful outcome."

Reynaldo turned to me.

"As you see, I have everything we could possibly need at our fingertips."

The room was filled with glass cases and cabinets stuffed with all the props of the trade, some of them actually useful, most just for show. Rather than take inventory, I focused on the printed wooden slate resting on the table. Apparently this was what Reynaldo was about to resort to before I arrived and offered a better option.

"Wow, a Ouija board. Really?" I said. "From the makers of the Easy-Bake Oven and Play-Doh."

Reynaldo was quick to defend his last desperate bid after transcendentalism and a marked-up crystal ball had failed him.

"Current copyright-holders aside, Ouija dates back more than a century, and psychography a thousand years before that. Such methods of contacting the spirit world have a long tradition and remain useful to the modern medium."

I wasn't letting him off the hook.

"That's some serious occultism you've got there, Reynaldo. Maybe after we commune with the late Samuel Higgins we can invite him to join us for a rousing game of Monopoly. I get to be the top hat."

"I think we'll dispense with Ouija in this instance," said Reynaldo, folding up the board and putting it away. "Now that you've agreed to join us, we have enough for a foursome."

"I've heard about your foursomes, Reynaldo. Not my scene, sorry."

"Ha!" barked Reynaldo at my cheap shot. "May this party you're planning prove so merry. No, I was merely suggesting we sit down and have ourselves a proper séance."

"Oh I see, a séance. So unlike one of your usual foursomes, we'll only be holding hands?"

Saunders looked displeased at the mention of a séance, though I couldn't imagine anything short of unambiguous success would please him at this point.

"I don't understand why we didn't try a séance right from the start," he said. "Isn't that what you people do?"

Saunders was referring to both Reynaldo and myself, but I didn't try to differentiate our techniques for him. I very much doubted he gave a shit.

Reynaldo was a little more patient and explained, "Séances are really only necessary for groups of clients. For one-on-one encounters I prefer to use direct channelling or automatic writing. But since we've been having difficulty and we currently have the numbers, we should try to focus all our psychic energy to the same end."

"Andre, are you decent?" Reynaldo called, loud enough to be heard upstairs.

I could hear Andre trot downstairs at the summons. He entered the room a few moments later, appearing much less the beefcake in a trim, tailored suit he must have been wearing at the club the night before when Reynaldo picked him up.

"We're lucky to have with us Doctor Andre Dupont, a preeminent parapsychologist, highly regarded in his field," said Reynaldo, making the introduction to his client.

"Who, me?" asked Andre, who didn't recognize the title, description or name assigned to him.

"Yes, you," confirmed Reynaldo. "Don't be so modest, Doctor."

Reynaldo spared me a firm glare that told me I shouldn't challenge the qualifications of our fourth member that he'd just made up. I figured it wasn't in my interest to expose him as a one-night-stand boy-toy hookup. Saunders already thought I was a dodgy character. He didn't need anyone impugning the spotless reputation of the preeminent Doctor Dupont as well.

"Okay, just tell me where to sit and let's get on with it," I said.

Instead of offering me a chair, Reynaldo waved me over to one of his cabinets.

"Mr. Eulogy, I have the necessary equipment for you here."

I went over to see what he wanted. Whatever he had to give me was under lock and key in a drawer. A moment later, Reynaldo pulled out a small vintage tin, the kind loose tobacco used to be sold in. He pried open the lid and revealed the contents resting on a folded handkerchief inside—a dozen clear capsules that looked like vitamin supplements, or perhaps cough drops.

"What flavour are they?" I asked.

"Instant-death flavour," said Reynaldo in a low voice so the others couldn't hear. "They're cyanide capsules. KGB surplus. Very rare. A souvenir from the cold-war spy game."

"Where did you get them?"

"I have my sources. You're not the only one who collects morbid artifacts."

"And what do you want me to do with these?" I asked, although I figured I already knew damn well.

"Just one will get the job done," he said, handing me a single capsule and locking the rest away again. "At the correct moment, simply bite down. The cyanide will do the rest. The effect should be virtually instantaneous."

"I said I would help out on this gig. I never said I was willing to die for the cause."

"Why else did you think I wanted your assistance? I can summon the spirit in question, but he's been uncooperative and I need you to go have a more direct conversation. Anyway, what are you complaining about? It's quick, relatively painless from what I understand, and much cleaner and more efficient than that derringer you carry around with you."

Reynaldo had a point. Cyanide was quick and lethal and, more importantly, simple to bounce back from. I'd wanted to get my hands on some capsules just like these for quite some time. It would have made my job so much easier. But they were very rare, highly illegal, and staggeringly expensive on those scarce occasions when some came to market. Reynaldo had to know how much I'd like some at my disposal, which was exactly why he'd never tell me where he'd found his. Sharing a single pill for his own benefit was as much generosity as I could expect.

"How do you know these are still good?" I asked, turning the lone capsule over in my hand.

"I guess we'll find out," he said, and went to take a seat at the head of the table.

I popped the capsule in my mouth and tucked it under my tongue for safe keeping. There was no danger of it dissolving. Most cyanide capsules were tiny glass ampules, designed as an air-tight non-degrading seal for long-term storage. I only hoped that meant it sealed in the deadly freshness all these years.

"Doctor, if you could lower the lights for us..." said Reynaldo.

It took Andre a moment to respond to his new title, but once he realized Reynaldo was talking to him, he hunted for the light switch and found the dimmer on the wall. He muted the overhead chandelier until we could barely find our chairs around the table. Reynaldo struck a match and lit a large candle set between us for a little more light and a lot more atmosphere.

With Reynaldo at one end of the table, I sat opposite him. Saunders was to my left and Andre to my right.

"I'll ask you all to form a chain as I seek to connect with the immortal soul of Samuel Higgins," instructed Reynaldo,

holding out both of his hands for the men on either side of
him.

I'm not much for this sort of touchy-feely spirituality, but
it was Reynaldo's show so I followed his lead, offering my
own hands. We all linked up, four grown men sitting in the
dark around a candle-lit table, holding hands and feeling
vaguely foolish. Or maybe I was just projecting. Maybe I was
the only one who felt like a fool, but whatever our general
state of embarrassment, all would be forgiven if we got what
we wanted out of this ritual.

"Our minds are one, our thoughts united, as we reach
out into the afterworld together and seek communion with
the spirit. Hear our plea, Samuel Higgins, and reveal yourself
to us."

Reynaldo's eyes closed and his head leaned back limply
on his shoulders as he entered his self-induced trance. It all
seemed like a bunch of hokum to me, but who I am I to
criticize? I do my best shtick in pidgin Latin. He ran through
his monologue a couple more times, switching up words
here and there, drifting deeper and deeper into a state of
reverie. This dreamy repetition had a hypnotic effect, and the
eyes of the other men at the table, myself included, grew
heavy. I had to make a conscious effort to stay alert.

"He's here," announced Reynaldo, opening a single eye
and glancing at me, his trance not so deep after all. That was
my cue.

Without any physical remains at hand, I couldn't sense
the presence and had to take Reynaldo at his word. I bit
down on the tiny glass vial, shattering it between my molars
and releasing the cyanide inside. I hardly had time to wonder
if it had gone stale and become inert before I felt my lungs
seize up and my heart flutter to a halt. Good stuff, that cyanide.
Fast and effective. I wish I had a truckload.

My body pitched forward and face-slammed into the table top. I was almost instantly dead, but my main concern was that I hadn't broken my nose. Or re-fractured my bullet-abused skull.

"Ignore him," Reynaldo told the others. "He's meditating. Don't break the circle."

Hands remained clasped together, including the ones holding my own dead palms. Reynaldo knew I was gone, but Saunders and Andre hadn't clued in. My plan was to be back before they realized I had flatlined. No need to disturb them. Their own body heat would keep my hands from dipping towards room temperature too quickly and they'd be none the wiser.

I stood up. Or, more accurately, I rose from my body. It took a moment to get my bearings. I was still in the same room, but everything looks different from the other side. I could still hear Reynaldo blathering on, but his voice was a distant echo and the surroundings appeared unfocused and malleable. It takes time to adjust, to sharpen images and turn up the volume, but right now I wasn't interested in what was happening with Reynaldo's séance. The ghost of Samuel Higgins was somewhere nearby and I had to find him, corner him, and pump him for information. I looked around, trying to filter out the noise of the living world and see what other consciousness might be present in this land of the dead.

"What a bunch of bullcrap," was the first sentiment to reach me.

I shifted my attention to the end of the room, trying to zero in on the source. I could make out a figure in a vacant ornamental chair. The figure was the shape of a man, the chair functioned as a place to sit. Typical recent-ghost behaviour. It takes them a while to discover they don't really need to cling to any sort of humanoid shape, don't need to sit down and rest, and wouldn't need a chair for such a banal purpose if they did. I suppose they find that sort of behaviour familiar, comforting. They can hardly interact with the physical world at all anymore, but behaving like they can helps ease the transition.

"You must be Sam Higgins," I said, adding, "At last."

He hardly acknowledged my presence. Sam Higgins was too busy observing the men involved in the ceremony designed to bridge the space between their world and his.

"Look at these asshats, making with the hocus-pocus. It's like a circus sideshow."

"It usually is," I agreed.

"What in the hell do they expect to accomplish with this sort of charade?"

"Well, you're here," I pointed out, "so I guess it worked."

"Here, there, doesn't count for much when you're dead. I can be damn near anywhere I please. I heard my name, so I stopped by. And what do I see? This fat idiot trying to badger me about nonsense that doesn't concern me anymore. Bank accounts and deposit boxes. What do I care if I'm dead? I wish they'd just forget about it. I know I have."

"Maybe if you threw them a bone, they'd let it drop," I suggested helpfully.

From what I'd read about him in life, I didn't peg Sam Higgins for a cantankerous old man. But he was certainly a cantankerous dead man. Despite my efforts to keep him on topic, he was already complaining about something else to do with his demise.

"Go into the light, they told me. And I tried. I think the light was just the flashlight the doctor on duty was shining into my eyes."

"Believe me, I've heard that one before."

"You haven't seen this great light around anywhere, have you?"

"Never," I said. "Not even once."

Now that he'd actually taken notice of my presence, he was curious about me. Dead for days, maybe he'd encountered other spirits, maybe not. I might have been his first.

"How long you been on the wrong side of the grass?" he asked.

It wasn't my favourite euphemism for death. I'd been dead many times, but I'd never been on the wrong side of the grass as such. Burials were always best avoided.

"Me? Dead? Oh, about two minutes," I estimated. "My watch is on my body over there."

I looked back towards the table where I could see my own body slumped over, down for the count.

"New guy, huh? Well don't sweat it. Death isn't so bad once you get used to it."

I let him offer those words meant to comfort, pointless though they were. At least he was engaging with me.

"Why would you want to spend the last moments of life involving yourself in such nonsense?" he asked, his attention centering to the events unfolding at the table. He drifted over for a closer look.

"I was trying to earn a favour," I explained.

"With this guy?" he asked, hovering over the meditative form of Reynaldo. "Dropping dead, you did yourself a favour. At least it got you away from him."

I saw Reynaldo flinch slightly, perhaps in reaction to the proximity of Samuel Higgins's spirit. He said something I couldn't quite make out, trying to talk to him, I expect. But the contact was mine. Higgins was listening to me now, not Reynaldo.

"This one's been bothering me," he said of Reynaldo. "No rest for the dead with this guy calling on you day and night."

"You know, there's a way to make him stop," I began, trying to lead Higgins towards the point of our meeting.

He ignored me and instead asked, "Say, want to have some fun with them?"

I wasn't sure what sort of fun Higgins had in mind, but it almost certainly meant communication. It was what we were aiming for, so I went with it.

"What do you have in mind?" I asked, letting him take the lead. Ghosts like to have their way, and whenever possible I indulge them. It puts them in a better frame of mind.

"Let's move something."

In all my time dead, I'd never tried to move something in the physical world I'd left behind. I didn't really think it was possible. Or, if it was, I had assumed it required a very long time deceased and much practice. Apparently that was wrong if Higgins was claiming an ability to manipulate matter after only a week dead.

"You can do that?" I asked.

"A little," he said. "Not much and nothing big, but I've managed to scare the bejesus out of a few people. It's great fun!"

Higgins leaned over the table to the point of hovering. A pad of paper and a pencil had been left in the light of the flickering candle in case there were messages from the beyond that needed to be jotted down.

"Watch this," said Higgins and swept his ethereal hands over the pencil in a repeating motion like someone trying to make waves in a bathtub of water. He strained with effort, a physical strain from a non-physical entity, but at last the pencil moved, imperceptibly at first. The lead tip quivered ever so slightly. It took a moment to decide on a direction, ticking back and forth between clockwise and counter clockwise, before it chose one and began rotating in place.

The men at the table all leaned in, taking notice of this manifestation of a supernatural presence in the room. I could hear Reynaldo in the distance, reminding them to maintain focus and not break the circle.

"That's pretty good," I commented. It wasn't very practical, but I could see where that sort of thing would trouble someone who wasn't expecting it and couldn't explain it.

"Want to try?" he suggested. "We could move something bigger together."

"Sure. Why not?"

Higgins let his wispy fingers drift around the base of the candle, going through the motions of gripping it, even if he couldn't literally touch it. I joined him and seized this same physical object in a mutual effort to lift it. The candle was thick, with the burning wick sunk deep into a melting well of wax. In real terms, it weighed about a pound. For a couple of disembodied spirits, it felt like a ton. But the real heavy lifting was done with our minds. Together, acting out the motions of raising the candle, we summoned the will to levitate it. I wouldn't have though it was possible until I saw the candle waver in place and eventually defy gravity, rising several inches off the table. Suddenly I had promoted myself from ghost to poltergeist.

In spirit form, the dense candle was unwieldy, even for the both of us. After provoking as many astonished expressions from the three surviving members of the séance as we could, it finally slipped out of our grasp and landed back on the tabletop, tipping over and rolling towards the edge, leaving a trail of melted wax behind it as the wick continued to burn. I felt drained after manipulating the physical world from an entire other plane of existence, but I couldn't resist the urge to give the candle one final push. Mustering my strength, I prodded it along, helping it roll all the way to the end, right under Reynaldo's nose. I wasn't quite able to drop it into his lap, but the guttering candle spilled a steady stream of hot wax directly onto his crotch, so all was not lost.

Reynaldo winced, but bore the pain.

"Don't break the circle!" I heard him demand again, although I could tell the others were eager to withdraw their hands as Reynaldo squeezed them too hard in reaction to his groinal agony.

"Good shot," Higgins complimented me. "Shame you couldn't set him alight, but not bad. You'll be haunting with the best of them before long."

Fun and games over, I tried to steer us back to the more pressing matter.

"You understand what it is they're after, don't you?"

"Aren't the terms of the will enough for them? I remember paying perfectly good lawyers a lot of money to write it up."

"They think there's more."

"Who thinks there's more?"

"This one," I said, poking my ghostly finger through the back of Saunders's head. He shivered slightly, like my touch, imperceptible otherwise, gave him a sudden chill. "Jeremy Saunders."

"Oh, him," said Higgins, swooping in to scrutinize the source of his afterlife harassment. "I hardly even recognized the pissant, it's been so long since I laid eyes on him."

"Your nephew, I believe."

"My ass!" he declared. "Nephew-in-law. Relation by marriage only, and an ill-conceived marriage at that. Don't know what that girl saw in the gold digger. The gleam in his eye wasn't charm or wit. It was dollar signs."

"It still is, I'm afraid."

"I gave them a silver tea service the day of the wedding, I recall. My wife picked it out. Still waiting on a thank-you note. Bit late now, don't you think? Glad I didn't hold my breath, I would have died a lot sooner."

"He claims there's another bank account. A secret one, somewhere abroad."

"Oh, that old thing. It's in Zurich. Just a bit of mad money, tucked away from the taxman. There's hardly anything left, as I recall. Chump change and some interest."

"He seems to be under the impression that there's a tidy sum waiting for him if only he can get the numbers he needs to access it. Enough of a sum that he was willing to hire a medium to bother you about it."

"What kind of a lowlife makes a career out of troubling the dead?" Higgins pondered, observing Reynaldo as he would dog shit under his boot.

"It takes all kinds, I guess."

"All kinds," agreed Higgins. "Few of them any damn good."

"Throw them an account number and I bet they'll let it drop."

"You think?"

"I'm positive."

Higgins considered this for a long time. Too long. He had eternity lying in front of him, but time was wasting and I was concerned about my plummeting body temperature giving me away to my hand-holding companions at the table.

"Ah well," he concluded finally, "what's it to me? You can't take it with you, they say, and I've certainly proved them right. If it buys me some peace, they can help themselves and see if they can't piss it all away before they wind up just as dead as me."

"Do you remember the account number?"

"Committed to memory years ago, but it's long."

"I'll have to write it down for them," I said, and set myself to figuring out how I was going to do that.

I only had a dim notion of how automatic writing worked. I'd seen it from the live end of the spectrum, but had never witnessed it from the opposite side. I suspected there was no set trick to it. It was up to the individual spirit to decide how best to communicate through a proxy. Whatever got the job done was fair game, so I went with what I thought might work for me. I selected Andre as my stooge. He seemed more malleable, more susceptible to suggestion than the others.

I'm right-handed, but I let my translucent ghost limb sink into Andre's left arm instead. With Reynaldo so keen to keep the circle unbroken, I figured it would be easier to disengage Andre's grip from my dead, unresisting hand than his. Plus I wanted both of Reynaldo's hands to remain full so he couldn't do anything about the scorching hot wax that was still dripping into his lap.

Andre's jaw dropped in frozen terror the moment his left hand opened and began scrambling across the table on its fingertips as though it had a mind of its own. I'd taken possession of his entire arm and he no longer had any conscious command over it. I maneuvered it over to the loose pencil and grabbed hold, making a fist. Controlling his left arm with my right was like attempting surgery while looking in a mirror, so I tried to keep things simple. With the lead tip jutting out of his clenched fist, I stabbed it into the pad of paper and waited to take dictation.

"Okay, let me have it," I told Higgins.

"Remember, I'm doing this as a one-off just so Porky over there will leave me be."

"Hit me," I prompted him.

Higgins slowly stated a long string of numbers which I dutifully transcribed onto paper. I had to concentrate on each digit intensely in order to recreate it on the page, but one by one they began to appear. My wrong-handed writing through Andre's fist-held pencil looked like chicken scratch copied by a myopic child with a severe mental disability, but I decided it was legible enough to comprehend with close study. At last I was able to release Andre and return control of his arm to him. Once this momentous event had played itself out, the table erupted in activity and excitement. Reynaldo blew out the fallen candle that had been tormenting him and leapt to his feet. The others followed in an instant. I ignored the commotion as I bid farewell to Sam Higgins.

"If that wraps it up, I'll be on my way," he said to me. "I have a busy retirement planned for heaven once I find my way there."

"I'm sure they'll leave you in peace now."

"Yeah," he said, gazing into eternity, "I guess it's about time I get back to looking for this damn light I'm supposed to go to. I don't suppose you know the way, do you? I wouldn't want to take a wrong turn at limbo and end up with a new address in the seventh circle of hell."

"I wouldn't worry about that," I assured him. "There's no hell."

"Good to know," he nodded as he faded away beyond my reach.

There was no heaven either. I'd looked for that place as well during my spare time dead and found no trace. Spirits, like that of Sam Higgins, drifted aimlessly for years until they stagnated and faded away like footprints on the beach. Hardly the eternal reward they thought they'd earned. I was tempted to tell him what lay in store, but why spoil the surprise?

I few moments later, I lifted my head from the table top, alive again. I took in a sharp breath, reinflating lungs that had been paralyzed by cyanide. One coughing fit later, I was able to breathe semi-normally and the blood flowed once more. No one else in the room was paying any attention to me. Reynaldo and Saunders were nearly tearing the top page of the notepad in two as they struggled to both read it at the same time. Andre, however, was in the corner having what was, as best I could assess, a panic attack.

"What the hell was that?" he gasped. "It took control, like it was inside my mind!"

I considered telling him it was only me during the brief time I'd just spent dead, but I didn't think that was really going to soothe him any.

"Doctor Dupont, compose yourself," Reynaldo snapped at Andre before returning to his paper tug-o-war with Saunders. They continued to bicker and argue over the correct interpretation of my terrible writing.

"Is that a four or a seven?" asked Saunders.

"I believe it's an inverted six," concluded Reynaldo, transcribing their findings onto a fresh sheet of paper each time they made some headway.

"I don't care how much you paid me last night, it doesn't cover any of this crazy shit today!" shouted Andre and bolted from the room.

"Oh Reynaldo, you're not paying for it, are you?" were my first words upon rising from the dead. They were ignored.

"Now Andre..." Reynaldo began and then corrected himself, "Doctor Dupont, a little spiritual hijacking isn't as bad as all that."

But Andre needed more comforting—comforting and reassurance that wasn't forthcoming from Reynaldo while he was distracted deciphering the key to Samuel Higgins's hidden fortune. Andre was out of there, going and nearly gone.

"Thanks for the hand," I said unironically.

Reynaldo shouted a promise after his departing gigolo, "I'll call you!"

"Dammit," Reynaldo said a moment later, "I didn't get his phone number."

Reynaldo raised a finger to his temple, trying to read his paramour's mind for the relevant contact information, but Andre was already through the door and too distant. Reynaldo waved it off when he realized he'd been too slow on the psychic draw. As numbers he was trying to score that day went, Andre's was a distant second.

Reynaldo returned to his figures and arrived at a final extrapolation that matched the bank account Higgins had fed me. I didn't congratulate him.

"The bank in Switzerland will be closed by now, but I'll make a call first thing in the morning," said Saunders.

One step at a time, I was regaining my balance and recovering. I slowly headed for the door, following Andre out.

"Reynaldo," I said, "I'll see you at my place tomorrow at seven."

"Don't go trying to make any fund transfers behind our backs," he cautioned me, ever suspicious.

"He can't do anything without the old man's PIN number anyway," said Saunders.

"You have it?" asked Reynaldo.

"It was the same code for everything else in the estate. I doubt this is any different. His memory was going towards the end, so he liked to keep things simple. We should be all set."

Content I couldn't do anything with the information I'd extracted from the ghost of Sam Higgins, Reynaldo saw me out. I noted his robe was thoroughly caked with melted wax. I'd probably ruined it and that made me smile. Reynaldo immediately knew what I found so amusing.

"Thank you for that," he said ungratefully.

"You mean for making you rich? Or should I say richer? Yeah, you're welcome."

"I'll admit you came through in the end. I shall honour our agreement."

"Do you have a tissue or something handy?" I asked him.

Reynaldo reached into his ornate cloak's pocket and pulled out an almost as ornate silk handkerchief, hand-embroidered with a monogram I recognized from his website and business cards.

"Nice," I commented as I took it.

I spat the gritty remains of the crushed cyanide capsule into the handkerchief, along with a fair amount of bloody saliva from my cut gums. I folded the fabric back into a tidy square and returned it to Reynaldo.

"Thanks," I said.

"No," he said coldly, "thank *you*."

There was a waste-paper basket nearby into which Reynaldo dropped his soiled handkerchief.

"Handy little things, those capsules. If only they didn't make them out of glass," I commented, crushing a few tiny leftover shards between my teeth until they were reduced to an unabrasive powder.

"I'll be sure to alert the manufacturers of your complaint, although somehow I expect this will be the first piece of customer feedback they've ever received."

I spared Reynaldo a parting grin through blood-stained teeth.

He shook his head and said, "And you wonder why nobody likes you."

"I never wonder that," I said as he shut the door in my face.

The party was a day away. I doubted that would be enough time for Reynaldo to discover that he'd been ethereally lied to and that the windfall he was expecting was nothing but hot air and spare change. There's an old saying that dead men tell no tales, which I routinely demonstrate to be false. They tell plenty of tales. Some of them are tall tales. And some of them are complete and utter bullshit.

Chapter Eleven

The Life of the Party

REYNALDO SURVEYED MY ABODE for the very first time, soaking it all in like a sommelier judging a new vintage and finding it wanting.

"Bit dreary," he finally concluded. It was an opening salvo, a mission statement. He'd get specific as the night dragged on.

"You invited Reynaldo the Fuckhead?" Rebecca asked me incredulously, not particularly concerned if the fuckhead in question heard her call him by his choice nickname. She was well-versed in my opinion of the man, and had been privy to every bitter anecdote and encounter he'd ever subjected me to—usually within a few hours of the incident when it was still fresh and infuriating.

"Like I said, this party is about business, not fun times."

"The rest of us are allowed to have fun, though. Right?"

"By all means, pour yourself another drink."

"You read my mind."

"If I could do that, I wouldn't need the fuckhead," I muttered. I don't think Rebecca heard me. She was already trying to decide which bottle should be her next victim.

Reynaldo was either acquainted with or aware of most of the people I'd invited. He made a point of not making the social rounds, and instead busied himself with a self-guided tour of my home, poking his unwanted nose into each room in succession before turning it up at whatever he found. When he arrived at my bedroom, he couldn't help but comment.

"A coffin? In your home?" He said this like it was the ultimate decor faux pas.

"Casket," I corrected.

"You can't be serious. Whatever for?"

"I sleep in it."

"Oh, you do not!" he said, giving me a playful and inappropriately familiar slap on the shoulder. He assumed I was kidding him. I let him assume away.

Reynaldo made his way back to the living room and observed my sad attempt at a dining table.

"Is this where it's happening?" he asked, unimpressed with the setup, but resigned to the fact that this was what I was giving him to work with. "Well, let's not dally. I have so many better places to be."

"I figure once we have everyone seated for dinner..." I began.

Reynaldo sniffed at the air, like he was expecting a foul odour, but instead discovered nothing to smell at all.

"Is there something on the stove? Or is the evening's edification cooling in the fridge?"

The door buzzer announced a third option.

"Who's that now?" wondered Rebecca aloud.

Reynaldo didn't wait for me to respond. Finger to temple, he searched the psychic plane to identify the newcomer downstairs.

"Ah," he announced with a dose above and beyond his usual level of contemptuous sarcasm, "the caterer has arrived."

Reynaldo spared me a sad, disappointed glance—disappointed in me, saddened for his own palate—but said nothing. Why spoil it for everyone else before they've had a chance to be disappointed all on their own?

I had called ahead and arranged delivery for a specific time. The kid who brought the stack of boxes to my door was punctual, but that didn't improve his tip. This was a budget party.

Rebecca threw her head back and downed the last of her current glass rather than watch the exchange at the door. I couldn't tell which she disapproved of more—my choice of meal, or my choice of pizzeria.

"If I'd thought about it beforehand, I might have expected you to go take-out. But pizza? Seriously, Rip."

"Did anyone really expect me to cook?" I said, kicking the door shut and setting down the stack of boxes. "Did anyone really *want* me to cook, given the sort of ingredients I have lying around?"

"Please tell me we're eating off real dishes with utensils at least."

Rebecca was the only one impolite enough to openly disparage dinner. I'd like to say it was the booze, but she'd be no different sober.

"Of course," I chuckled. "What sort of barbarian do you think I am?"

I went into the kitchen to retrieve a stack of dishes and a fistful of knives and forks. I threw the bag of paper plates under the sink where nobody would see them and then joined the others so we could carve up our greasy feast.

Tracy was peeking under the box lids, one after the other.

"Don't you have any vegan options?" she asked me.

"Vegan?"

"Yeah."

"It's pizza," I said, figuring, incorrectly, that that would answer any culinary questions.

"So, no?"

Tracy looked crestfallen. And hungry. Mostly hungry.

"I've gone vegan, you know," she informed me as I went over the cut lines of the first pizza, freshly parting the gelatinous melted cheese.

"Again?"

Tracy gave me a look that suggested I should be up-to-date on all her dietary developments. Or at least sympathetic towards them. I was neither.

"There's one Hawaiian somewhere in the mix," I told her. I had selected from the menu randomly, hoping to strike upon a variety that would suit all needs and was fated to suit nobody's.

"Rip, those have ham all over them. Not to mention cheese."

"Pineapple and ham on a pizza?" declared Reynaldo. "Truly we have descended into a pit of madness!"

"Ham pizza, ham hors d'oeuvres," Tracy grumbled.

"The nerve!" declared Reynaldo, hoping to inspire open revolt.

"Ham guest-of-honour," Tracy muttered, not nearly far enough under her breath to keep anyone else from hearing—least of all Reynaldo the Ham himself.

Θ

Twenty minutes later, the first and only course of the dinner was reduced to soiled cardboard and crumbs. Despite the bitching and complaining, the pizzas vanished so quickly, Wilbur barely had time to wave a fork over the empty boxes, say a magic word, and pretend he had accomplished the deed by sleight of hand. Tracy proved to be a strict vegan right up until the pizza smell filled the room and she saw everyone else eating. Only then did her firm ethical stand wilt and keel over under the relentless assault of a slight peckishness. By the end, she had probably disposed of more slices than anyone else.

Gladys was the only one sitting at the table who didn't eat, for obvious reasons. Technically she wasn't sitting at the table so much as placed upon it. Louie had set her down in the middle where she served as the meal's centrepiece. I'd adorned her with a festive cardboard party hat and stuck a streamer she'd never be able to blow between her teeth. There had been some debate whether it made her look cheerful or was another unspeakable indignity.

With the feeding frenzy over, it was time for my guests to digest and relax. For me, it was time to get to business. I called for attention, clinking on a glass with a steak knife, silencing the chatter. I tried to ease everyone into my true agenda.

"Now that we're all gathered and fed, I thought I might say something gracious," I began.

I heard a derisive snort in response. It was Rebecca, her final slice of pizza in one hand, a stiff drink in the other, having a hard time deciding which to finish first. I ignored her.

"I'm glad I could get all six of you together for this soiree."

"Seevan!" corrected Gladys.

"Seven counting Gladys, of course," I conceded.

"Eight!" insisted the voice from inside Tom's breast pocket. Tom pulled out the harbinger and let it dangle from the end of his chain.

"You weren't even invited, Moby-Dick. You don't count."

"You will count me and tremble, necromancer! For I am..."

"Yeah, yeah, fine." I didn't want to argue. "Let's not suffer through that mouthful of a name again. Eight it is."

"That is better," said the fish. I was about to continue, but he interrupted once more.

"Minion, feed me some chips and dip. I hunger!"

I guess now that it had a physical body, the harbinger was capable of getting the munchies like the rest of us.

"Tom, feed your fish and keep it quiet, will you?"

Tom nodded and grabbed a potato chip from the open bag on the table.

"And some dip," added Moby-Dick.

Tom made for one of the open containers of dip.

"No!" Moby-Dick shouted. "Not garlic onion! Qixxiqottltoq demands creamy dill!"

Tom dipped accordingly.

Reynaldo lit a post-meal cigarette, though he'd hardly touched the food that was so beneath his usual gourmet standards. He'd indelicately helped himself to a few choice morsels of topping off a couple of the pizzas, never excusing his intrusive fingers of course, and waited for everyone else to finish eating. His idea of waiting patiently was to chain smoke throughout the meal despite the looks of annoyance he got from the predominantly non-smoking guest list. By my count, this first post-meal smoke was cigarette number four.

"Could we maybe let the air in here clear a bit?" I suggested to him.

"Before we clear the air, so to speak?" he asked.

"Yeah."

"Very well," he reluctantly conceded, and stubbed his butt out in the nearest mound of coagulated cheese he could find stuck to a box top.

"Wadda fak-heed," declared Gladys indiscreetly.

"Solidarity, sister," Rebecca agreed, fist-bumping Gladys's skull.

"I was takkin abat Reep."

Rebecca shrugged and issued another bump of her knuckles to Gladys's bony plate.

"Solidarity, sister," she repeated.

"You may be wondering why I asked Reynaldo here tonight," I began.

"Reynaldo the Wise," Reynaldo corrected, nodding to the table as though they should all be acquainted with his full title.

"Right—the wise guy here—despite certain past disagreements we've had."

"We're all wondering that," said Rebecca on everyone's behalf.

Wilbur blurted out a bit of speculation.

"You're putting an act together and taking it on the road!"

I couldn't tell if Wilbur was being sarcastic or genuine. There's something about old age that masks intent and mixes the snide and the heartfelt in an uncertain middle ground of dotage.

"Good guess, but no. Reynaldo, as you all know, brings a certain skill set into play. His ability to read minds and motivations is unmatched by any other medium in the business. And I've invited him because there is a certain specific truth that needs to be brought to light."

Reynaldo raised a hand, a signal for me to be silent. I was all too willing to shut up and stop flattering him for the sake of building up expectation in the room.

"If I may," he said, and slowly drew the fingertips of both hands to his cranium. Reynaldo rolled his eyes back in his head and held this pose for a few uncomfortable moments. Then he abruptly waved his arms around and snapped his eyes into a sudden intense stare that seemed to focus on everyone at once, but fixed on no specific individual.

"Someone here," he said with the kind of dramatic bravado that would make Hercule Poirot tell him to dial it down, "is a murderer."

There was a long, ponderous silence at the table as eyes darted from face to face, searching for signs of guilt or looks of accusation. Reynaldo seemed frozen, as if waiting for one of the guests to instantly break down and confess all in the face of his ridiculous theatricality. That didn't seem to be forthcoming, so I picked up where I had left off.

"You know Reynaldo's reputation," I told the table. "He's spent decades solving all sorts of cases for the police. Murders, missing persons, even a few high-profile kidnappings. Not only here, but in other cities across the country. They turn to him for answers because they know he's never steered them wrong. His success rate is unparalleled. And now he's here tonight to point his unwavering finger at one of you."

Extolling the virtues of Reynaldo's extensive curriculum vitae nearly stuck in my throat, but I wanted to remind everyone of his legendary track record. I wanted the murderer—if he or she was indeed among us—to feel cornered. I wanted them to know exposure was inevitable and to just come out with it and save us the bother of having Reynaldo probe their minds one by one.

Tom slowly raised his hand, a hang-dog expression on his face.

"I guess that's me. I didn't mean to do it. It was an accident."

I was, I'll admit, surprised. It took a moment for this confession to sink in. He was a suspect, sure. But I hadn't pegged Tom for the murdering kind. Certainly not the sort of fellow to blow the head off some poor semi-innocent necromancer he'd just met, simply because he'd been made to look foolish over drinks one night.

"Wait, are you talking about your goddamn fish?" I asked, realizing where this sudden public display of culpability was coming from.

"Well, yeah. Obviously."

"Forget the fish. Fish don't count as murder."

"You will be wise to hold your tongue, necromancer!" bellowed our aquatic gate-crasher from his sealed chamber inside Tom's vest pocket.

"Oh, shut up!" I barked, concerned he and Tom may have already deflated the necessary drama of the moment.

But there was still guilt hanging over the table. Louie spoke next. There was a dark cloud hanging over him, and his usual light mood and upbeat manner was stripped away. He looked laid bare, more so than I'd ever seen him. When he spoke, his voice was hoarse and halting.

"I may have once been involved in a hit-and-run. I'm not trying to incriminate myself. It was a long time ago, and I never found out what the end results were. Injury, fatality? I just don't know. I checked the papers for weeks but there was never any mention. So yeah, me. Maybe."

It was a heartfelt confession. You could feel the years of regret and pain in his voice. Touching I'm sure.

"Nope, wrong answer," I declared, quashing the moment. "Not what I'm looking for."

My eyes fell on another suspect at the table. Tracy was a good actor, superb when it came to grief. But I'd never seen her do guilt before, and it was guilt etched across her face.

"Tracy?"

Her eyes stared down at the pizza bones on her chipped plate, looking right through it. She was far, far away, but glanced up at me when I said her name.

"Remember that sister I told you about?" she said. "The one who used to invent games that were designed to suffocate me? Well one time I convinced her to play a different game. Tea party. Much easier to play, fewer rules. Except I spiked her tea with a deadly mix of common household cleaning products. It was self-defence, pure and simple. She always wanted to be an only child. She never imagined it would be shy little baby sister who would end up being the solo act."

"I'm not talking about childhood traumas better discussed in a therapy session," I said, cutting off the emotional disclosure.

Wilbur raised his hand and volunteered, "I smothered my wife with a pillow."

"Or mercy killings," I snapped.

Wilbur looked offended. Not by my abruptness, but my downgrading of his crime.

"It wasn't a mercy killing," he huffed. "It was murder. You said so yourself."

Wilbur's wife had never mentioned anything to me about homicidal marital troubles, before or after this alleged murder.

"I said no such thing. I thought she was terminally ill."

Wilbur shook his head, "Healthy as a horse."

"Stage four cancer, I heard," Rebecca weighed in.

"Rumours," said Wilbur.

"Didn't she have dementia?" asked Tracy.

"Sharp as a tack she was," disagreed Wilbur.

"But she died in her sleep," said Louie from a better informed perspective. "I saw the police report."

"She was sleeping all right," confirmed Wilbur. "Never woke up because I held a pillow over her face until she stopped breathing."

The table fell silent. Wilbur looked satisfied that he had at last convinced them all that he was capable of murder.

Once we passed the threshold of awkward and had entered the territory of deeply uncomfortable, I stepped up to ask the question that was on everybody's mind.

"So what the fuck, Wilbur?"

"That woman snored like a jet engine, I tell you. And it only got worse with age. I hardly slept a wink the last ten years of our marriage. I had to do something."

Wilbur's explanation was matter of fact, with no hint of bitterness or anger. This was not a crime of passion, then or now. This was merely a crime of convenience, of personal comfort.

"How about divorce?" I suggested pointlessly, years too late to make a difference.

"And let lawyers eat my retirement savings? Nah, much simpler and easier this way. Anyhoo, I sleep fine now. It took a little bit to get used to the silence. And the guilt. But now I wake up refreshed every morning and I'm a new man."

Nobody knew how to deal with the revelation that Wilbur the Wizard, beloved entertainer of children, was an unrepentant murderer, so nobody did. We moved on.

"Am I the only one here who isn't a killer?" I asked, scanning the table for someone who might yet hold some sort of moral high ground. "Rebecca?"

"I've been known to kill a bottle or two. Oh hey, look, another dead soldier," she said, realizing she'd just squeezed the last drops out of the last bottle. With that accomplishment behind her, Rebecca used her plate as a pillow, laying the side of her face down in the oily pizza film, and dozed off.

"Can you narrow this down for us?" I asked Reynaldo, figuring it was time for him to step up and dazzle us with his amazing psychic insights.

Reynaldo had been silent during the barrage of confessions. He was way ahead of me, with his eyes clamped shut and a look of intense concentration lining his reddening face. He was trying to read the room and was straining against so much feedback, he looked like he'd burst a blood vessel before dessert was served. Dessert, incidentally, was a bag of grocery-store cookies that likely wouldn't divide evenly among the guests.

Reynaldo exhaled sharply, like a pearl diver who had just spent the last few minutes scrounging the ocean bed and had come up empty for his efforts. It took him a few gulps of air to catch his breath again and for his face to return to its normal pallidness.

"It's too much," he gasped as soon as he was able. "So much violence and pain and killer instincts in this room!"

Reynaldo looked around at my table of associates with a whole new perspective.

"You people should be ashamed of yourselves!" he declared. "Such selfishness and immorality. I am appalled!"

I took my own look at the others seated at the table. They all stared back looking rather clueless and without blame, I thought. Everyone except Rebecca. She was passed out.

"You must be getting something," I said. But Reynaldo's usual hubris was absent. He looked bewildered by a puzzle too complex for him to solve. It had thrown him off his game so much, he couldn't even muster his usual degree of bullshit to save face.

"I can't focus," he said, trying to rise from his seat. "Too many threads to unravel. All these impressions and intents are wound around each other like a knotted coil."

Reynaldo gave up on his attempt to stand and flopped back down into his chair, exhausted.

"I just...no," were his last words on the matter. I wasn't about to accept that after coming through for him—or at least pretending to.

"So sort it out!" I demanded. "Unwind them, one by one. Do it if it takes all night, because nobody is walking out of here until I find out which one of them did it!"

"Did what?" asked Tracy, who sounded exasperated by this whole unfortunate bit of dinner theatre.

"The murder!" I explained poorly.

"Which murder?" Louie asked, lost.

"Mine!"

"But you're right here," said Tom.

"Alive and well," added Wilbur.

"But I wasn't," I tried to elaborate. "A few days ago, somebody showed up at my door and blew my head off! I want to know who!"

"Oh dat? I do dat."

All eyes turned to the disembodied skull sitting in the middle of the table. If Gladys had been capable of making any expression at all, I would have called this one smug.

"And how, exactly, did you accomplish this premeditated assassination?" I asked, not even trying to keep my sarcasm in check.

"Wid gon, dammy!"

"Do I really have to remind you that you don't have a gun, that you don't even have hands to shoot a gun, or that you were inside the apartment with me when it happened?"

"I hiar guy to do thees for me."

I took a moment to let that sink in.

"You hired a hitman to take me out?"

"Ya. I call nambar on da cad."

"Card? What card?"

I had to think. It must have been one of the cards I'd stuffed in Gladys's skull since she came to work for me. I hardly ever looked at any of them. Supposedly Gladys was transcribing their contents and contact information to an easily searchable database on the computer, but I had no idea how that busywork project was going. I'd never looked once since I set her to it. Apparently, somewhere in the mix, was a name and a number of a hitman for hire, and it gave Gladys some bad ideas.

"Jeez, Gladys. I know we've had our differences, but why would you go and do a thing like that?" I asked. I probably sounded wounded, my feelings hurt, but Gladys was having none of it.

She spat out a cherry bon-bon contemptuously and yelled, "Yoo yoos my heed as a fakkin candee deesh an yoo ask why I fakkin hate yoo?"

Reynaldo had recovered his senses enough to successfully climb out of his chair.

"Well, it's been a lovely evening of fine food and fine company," he said, neglecting to even taint that sentiment with his usual dose of obvious insincerity. "I'm glad I could assist in solving this perplexing mystery, but I really must be going now."

"You didn't solve shit," I informed him.

"Nevertheless, the culprit has been apprehended and the hour grows late."

Reynaldo fumbled with the lock of the apartment door.

"You still owe me," I reminded him.

"Do we have a written contract to that effect? No, I thought not. Nevertheless, my difficulties have been sorted out, as have yours. I'll take my leave. You needn't see me out."

He was right, I needn't. He'd figured out the lock and was already standing in the hall. I was at a loss.

"What am I supposed to do about this?" I said to no one specific. "My secretary has just confessed to arranging to have me whacked."

"I a fakkin skall on da tabble! Wat yoo do? Arrist me? Call palice? Yoo explan me to dem! Les see dat, asshool!"

"A parting word of advice: Just bin the bitch," said Reynaldo, and slammed the door behind him.

"Easy for you to say," I shouted after him. "I shelled out a thousand bucks for that skull, plus shipping."

The room fell silent as everyone waited for me to collect myself. Once I'd taken a moment to calm down, I addressed the whole table, searching for words of advice, "I don't know how to respond to this."

The search was futile.

"You respond by serving dessert," said Louie.

"There's dessert, right?" Tom wanted to know.

"I guess it's too much to hope you baked a cake," Tracy speculated correctly.

Θ

The guests thinned out quickly as soon as the final drink was drunk and the last cookie crumbled. I burned through an hour that might have been better spent cleaning up picking through old business cards instead. The complete collection was still on the desk where I'd dumped it before refilling Gladys's skull with sweets. There were a couple hundred of them in absolutely no order. I sorted them one by one, taking a moment or two to try to remember a time and a context for each.

In the end, only one stood out as a promising anomaly. I went to bed at last, determined to get in touch with the people who had done me in and have it out with them.

Chapter Twelve

The Business of Death

LIKE CLOCKWORK, my credit-card statement arrived in the next morning's post. Another bill I couldn't afford to pay. Mixed in with the usual throng of charges was one I didn't recognize for DDINC. I consulted the card I had picked out the night before—the one it had been my fatal error to store inside Gladys's skull.

Death Dealers Incorporated

That would be it. Nice of them to list themselves under a more discreet acronym. I guess murder is a purchase you don't want to be quite so obvious on your list of charges. Like pornography or political campaign donations. It could get embarrassing if anyone went snooping through your statements.

If I'd looked at the card a little more carefully when it first came to me, I might have read between the lines. With a name like that, I had assumed they dealt in death. I didn't realize, until I had a closer look following my assassination, that they actually dealt *out* death. Live and learn, die and learn. A quick internet search would have enlightened me if I'd been interested. It certainly enlightened Gladys. They even had talkback reviews posted online. But of course she had nothing better to do all day and all night than surf the web, research strange business cards, and plot revenge against me.

I couldn't even remember where the card originally came from, where I might have picked it up, or who may have passed it to me. My best bet was that it came from the Necronomi-Con, a convention for all things dead, dying or otherwise grim. So many cards and pamphlets and fliers get handed out there, it would have been lost in the shuffle. I sometimes think that convention has more to do with the death of trees—to print all that shit—than any other form of demise.

I read the charge that had been applied to my account by DDINC. My murder came at a surprisingly economic rate. I wondered if they were offering a sale, or maybe Gladys took the time to find a discount code. Considerate of her if she did. Still, bargain price or not, I couldn't afford to eat the expense. I wanted a refund. I wasn't happy with the product and I was living proof that the services rendered were lacking.

Although branches in other major cities, East and West Coast, were listed, the head office was local. Situated in the upper reaches of one of the glass towers of the financial district, it was in the only corner of the city that seemed to reach for the future rather than dwell in the past. According to the card, they had an entire floor to themselves in a building that must have charged astronomical rent for a single suite. Apparently there was money in death after all, despite my best efforts to prove otherwise. I suppose my approach was backwards. I kept raising the dead against the financial flow that indicated more money was to be made filling graves.

Anticipating a complex voice-mail system would bounce me around between multiple lines of multiple departments for hours if I let it, I decided a personal appearance would prove more productive. It's so much harder to transfer a real person taking up real space at the reception desk. Someone would have to talk to me, even if it was only a security guard summoned to drive me off the property.

I went to grab my jacket in the closet on the way out. That's when I found Rebecca asleep on my couch. She'd never gone home and I hadn't noticed. I nudged her, seeing if she would stir. When that didn't work, I tried shaking her awake. Eventually, that got results.

"That was a shit party," were her first words upon regaining consciousness.

"Glad you enjoyed yourself," I said.

Noticing it was daylight, she laboriously set her feet on the floor and assumed a sitting position on the edge of one of the couch cushions.

"Trust me as an expert," she said, rubbing her eyes. "I'm a notorious party girl and that was one shit party."

"How much of it do you even remember?"

"Too much. That's why I got blackout drunk. So I could block out the rest before it got any worse."

I took a visual inventory of the various empty bottles I would have to clean up later.

"Did you drink the green stuff?" I said, not spotting the unidentified bottle.

"I think so."

"What was it?" I asked, purely out of academic interest.

"It's what finished me off is what it was."

"I was just curious. It's been my mystery bottle for years. Nobody has been brave enough to try it and see what it was."

"Disinfectant is my best guess."

"Was it any good?"

"I didn't go blind so, yeah, it was swell."

"If we ever find out what it was, I'll mention that review to the distillery. I'm sure they'll put it on the label."

Deciding she'd spent more than enough time semi-vertical, Rebecca flopped back down and buried her face in an armrest.

"I feel like death," she groaned.

"You look like death. And I should know."

"Did you slip me a roofie last night?"

"I should have," I said. "It might have stopped you from finishing every bottle in the place."

Rebecca turned her head to one side and set her eyes on the coffee table.

"Not quite every one."

Rebecca reached out for a glass within arm's reach. There was still something stagnating at the bottom.

"What are you doing?" I asked.

"Hair of the dog that bit me," she said, and brought the glass to her lips so she could tip the contents into her mouth.

"I think that dog had rabies and ate your face clean off."

Rebecca winced like she was both disgusted and offended. She lowered the glass so she could look inside, but didn't try to spit out what she just drank.

"Gah, what the hell is this?"

"I bit of everything," I told her. "I was tidying up last night and dumped the dregs of everyone else's drink in that glass."

Rebecca took another swig.

"Not so bad once you get used to it."

"I think Reynaldo was using one of them as an ashtray."

"That would account for the burnt, woodsie bouquet," commented the connoisseur.

She finished her morning cocktail and asked, "Did anyone try to cop a feel while I was out?"

"No."

Rebecca let the empty glass fall to the floor—not far enough to break it—and face-planted back into the soothing cushion.

"Like I said, shit party."

"I think Tom's evil aquatic companion was trying to encourage him to misbehave, but decency won out in the end."

"Here's to decency," she said, raising her hand as if to toast. Rebecca gave up on her toast in the name of decency when she realized her hand was empty and her stomach was already home to the last drop in the apartment.

"I have to go out for a bit," I told her. "You want to use the shower and freshen up before finding your way home?"

There was no answer from the hung-over blob on the couch. When I looked again, I saw Rebecca had passed out once more.

"Or you can just crash. Again."

Rebecca didn't answer, couldn't hear, but seemed to accept that option.

Θ

There was no mention of the actual name of the company on the lobby directory, nor on the 18th floor where the elevators let out across from a wall of clear-glass panels that encased the place of business. There was only a company logo—an acronym of two stylized capital-Ds, one within the other. They might have been selling any goods or services. There was no way of knowing unless you arrived with foreknowledge.

Through the elegant dark wood-grain door, unmarked but for the number 1801 in high-polished brass, lay a spacious workspace that was sparsely furnished, but arranged in a calming feng shui configuration that kept visitors relaxed and workers energized. The occasional tie-and-loafer drone flittered about, shuttling files and coffee to their middle-management superiors, each in their own glass-box office, taking calls and pushing product. Every time I saw one of them hang up the phone, I could sense the life that was being snuffed out along with the connection.

I approached the main desk to speak with the secretary. Or the receptionist. Whatever she was, there was money enough to afford to hire multiple underlings to fill every position. She was chipper and efficient and greeted me with a smile, which I suppose was how the job was supposed to be done. Working with Gladys, I kept forgetting how places of business normally dealt with customers, current or potential. They were like a crop to be cultivated, not sliced down. At Death Dealers Incorporated, the reaping was reserved exclusively for targets specified and paid for by their clients.

"Hello, how can I help you?" asked the receptionist, like she genuinely wanted to help and that it would be her pleasure to do so. Perverse. Alien. Oh well.

"I have a complaint about your services."

She didn't seem fazed at all, only more willing and determined to be of assistance.

"Are you a client?"

"No, I'm a victim."

At least that seemed to throw her off her game.

I gave her some pertinent personal details. It took a few minutes of mouse clicking and keyboard tapping to bring up my file and compare it with my credit-card information.

"According to this," she told me after checking, double-checking and triple-checking, "your contract is still open."

"Trust me on this one, I've already been murdered," I insisted.

She took a closer look.

"You don't look very murdered to me."

"It didn't take," I explained. "So I'm looking for a refund on my card."

"You contracted your own murder?"

"Of course not. Why would I do that?"

"We deal with those sorts of cases all the time. Professional suicide, we call it," she explained casually. "It's usually for insurance purposes, or for clients who lack the nerve to kill themselves."

"Suicide isn't a problem. I do it all the time. This job was contracted by my secretary and she used my card."

"I see. So it's more of an identify-theft issue. In that case, I'd recommend calling your credit-card company and filing a fraud claim."

"That could take a while. In the meantime, I've got this balance I need to pay off and I can't really swing it this month."

"You could make the minimum payment until the claim is resolved," she suggested.

"I can't really swing that either. Especially at these interest rates."

I didn't want to get into my troubled finances with a stranger. Especially one involved in a conspiracy to bump me off, sweet though she may have been.

"Perhaps you'd care to change the method of payment. We could switch the contract to your secretary's card and issue you a refund then."

"No, you see it was a misunderstanding. Water under the bridge. I'll order her some flowers or something and all will be forgiven."

The look I got back was blank. Death Dealers Incorporated wasn't in the business of forgiveness and reconciliation. It was bad for the balance sheet.

"Look, there must be some way to cancel everything. The charge, the hit, all of it," I protested. "Obviously, I don't want to pay for my own murder."

"I'm sorry, but all contracts are non-refundable."

"Even if they failed?"

"Success is guaranteed. If our agent missed the first time, I'm sure he'll remedy the situation in short order."

"But he didn't miss," I began, but thought better of it when my words were met with another blank stare. "Never mind."

"Our contracts are also irrevocable. We can't put a stop on them once they're issued. Agents are assigned individual files through a network of contacts designed to assure anonymity and hinder any legal culpability. Once the wheels are set in motion, it's out of our hands."

"So what then? This asshole is going to keep murdering me until I stay dead?"

"Satisfaction is guaranteed," she said like she was reading out of a brochure.

"You guys are about as liberal with your guarantees as you are with your bullets."

"The means of disposal is entirely up to the client. It doesn't have to be a bullet. We also offer a garrotting for the same fee. Your secretary had no specific instructions on how the contract was to be executed, so it was left to the agent's discretion. Guns tend to be the default."

She was very informative, I'll give her that. Helpful, no, but she covered the logistics well.

"I guess I should be grateful she didn't opt to have all my finger- and toenails pulled out before the hit."

The receptionist cut her way right through my derision.

"We don't offer that sort of package deal, sir," she informed me. "But I can refer you to an affiliate. Thumbscrews-R-Us."

Θ

I might have lingered, insisted on speaking to a boss or a supervisor, somebody higher up in the chain who could recall their cutthroat and set things straight. But I'd quickly grown weary of the runaround a well-oiled corporate structure was able to inflict on any less-than-satisfied customer. I could die again—this time of old age—before I got my money back. It would be more fruitful to follow the receptionist's first suggestion and take it up with my credit-card company directly. Claiming identity theft and reporting the card stolen would be the fastest way to sort it out, and was only half a lie. I'd have a new card issued and in the mail in a week or two, at which point I could activate the number and never ever trust Gladys with it again.

So far as their hitman was concerned, his first attempt had succeeded. There was no reason to think he'd hear about my miraculous recovery and come back for a second go at it. Just because the contract was still open didn't mean my head remained on the chopping block. My assassin was probably just slow filing his paperwork. I knew how it was. The bodies stack up and you realize you haven't gotten around to invoicing for the last pile of corpses yet. He didn't have my sympathy, but I could spare a little empathy.

The round trip proved to be a complete waste of too many hours that probably should have been used more productively. I came home to a ringing phone. If I'd been as clairvoyant as my caller, I would have known not to pick up.

"You execrable bastard," said Reynaldo the moment I raised the receiver to my ear.

"How'd you know I'd be the one to answer?" I asked, pretty certain Reynaldo didn't mean to call Gladys an execrable bastard.

"I'm psychic," he reminded me. "How did you know you were the execrable bastard in question?"

"It's a common enough sentiment," I said. "So is this meant as a general insult, or is there something specific that's pissed you off?"

"You know perfectly well what's put me in this mood."

I didn't. Not for sure. But I could guess.

"The Higgins account turned out to be a piggy bank full of pennies?"

"If only! There's no such account at the Swiss bank. Or any of its branches. Or any other bank, owned, associated or affiliated. The number you gave me is a dud!"

"Well so was your reading at the party last night, so I guess that makes us even."

"I may not have determined which of your business associates killed you, but I can tell you which one wants you dead now."

"Yeah? Who's that?"

"Me!" Reynaldo spat across the phone connection.

"Are we officially business associates now, Reynaldo? That's so nice of you to say. We should do lunch, never."

There was a lot of noise on the other end of the line. It took me a moment to realize Reynaldo was no longer listening. He was trying to hang up on me as angrily as he could manage, but had missed the cradle on his first attempt to slam the handset into its dock. After some more frustrated fumbling, he finally disconnected. I listened to the dial tone with some measure of satisfaction before hanging up my end. The dial tone was replaced by a different monotonous drone. The sound was coming from the couch. It was snoring. Rebecca was still there, still crashing.

I was considering waking her up to make sure she wasn't in a coma when the phone rang again. It was probably Reynaldo calling back to give me another mouthful. He'd had a few minutes to think up all sorts of additional insults.

"Rip, I need you down here."

The voice was Louie's. It was getting late and he must have only just begun his evening shift.

"What's up?"

"Something's not kosher with the rabbi."

"Could you be more specific?"

"He's not making like a coat rack in the corner anymore. He's moving on his own."

"Have you tried telling him to stand still?"

"I've tried telling him all sorts of things. He's not listening. He's stomping around the morgue like he's looking for something."

"For what?"

"As if he's going to tell me."

Louie kept vigil while I contemplated what might be causing this unexpected anomaly with my reanimation. Before I could come up with a single suggestion, Louie gave me another update.

"Oh wait, I think he's found something."

"Found what?" I asked.

"Whatever it was he was tearing the place apart looking for. He's checking it out now. Seems satisfied."

"So what is it?"

"It's a trocar."

"You use trocars in the morgue?" I was more familiar with embalming trocars.

"Sure. All the time. You don't want to know about some of the fluids or gas we have to drain in a pinch just so we can do our job. Nasty stuff."

"What does a reanimated rabbi corpse want with a trocar, I wonder?"

"Beats me, but he's on his way over with it."

"Well what else are they used for, other than draining fluids or laparoscopic surgery?"

"Nothing leaps to mind," said Louie

"They must be good for something."

"Cavity access mostly."

"Piercing skin?" I asked.

"I suppose. Most of them end with a fairly sharp point."

"Enough to be used as a weapon?"

"Could be. Why do you ask?"

It was the last thing I heard Louie say before the phone disconnected.

Chapter Thirteen

Dead Meat

I'D GOTTEN SLOPPY.

Okay, perhaps I'm being hard on myself. Complacent. I'd grown complacent. Maybe it was the dwindling work situation. The jobs, what few there were, hadn't been taxing my abilities, and I'd been showing up to gigs ill-prepared for anything more challenging than a post-mortem chat or a partial reanimation. There had been no dangers to contend with—not even a night watchman at a graveyard. Tellingly, the last time I'd gone out with my complete kit had been my night raiding the ashen remains of Csaba Szabo with Rabbi Reubenski. This time I was going to bring the complete arsenal. There was no other choice. I didn't even know what I was dealing with, so I had to be prepared for anything.

Sometime while I'd been out running my errand of futility with Death Dealers Incorporated, Rebecca had gotten up, grabbed a shower, and thrown on my bathrobe. She was sound asleep again. It looked like real sleep this time, rather than alcohol-induced oblivion, so I didn't wake her. She didn't need something new to worry about, and I didn't need to hear her try to talk me out of going to the morgue to investigate—or worse, talk me into letting her come along to watch my back.

I packed my gear, taking careful inventory to make sure I wouldn't be caught short. The wallet-sized mini kit was stuffed in a deep pocket inside my jacket, which I left unbuttoned despite the chilly wind blowing through the streets. Quick access trumped comfort. The big kit was loaded in the satchel over my shoulder, burdensome but reassuringly heavy and substantial. I doubted I'd need more than a select few items from either, but there was confidence in having plenty of choices at hand.

This night marked nearly a week since I'd been shot through the head. Plenty of time to heal up and be back in top physical form. Minus the damn eye, of course. I'd never had a permanent scar before. Cuts, scrapes or broken bones would linger, but a new demise and recovery always wiped the slate clean. Everything mended itself in short order each time I rose from the dead. Everything except my one milky eye. I guess I'd have to see if the colour returned after the next time I snuffed it in some brutal, damaging way. I hoped that wouldn't be tonight.

I'd tried raising Louie on the phone again, but there had been no answer. Whatever was going on at the morgue was keeping him occupied. I hoped it was only the line that had gone dead. Louie was a valuable asset, a competent business associate and, if I may permit myself to get a bit sappy for a moment, a good friend. I didn't want to lose him, but I wasn't reassured by what I knew so far. A mindless zombie corpse—literally brainless—doesn't start walking around without direct commands to do so, doesn't move about with its own agenda, doesn't arm itself.

The sun was all the way down by the time I arrived at Hillside General. I'd tipped the cabbie extra to drive fast, but now that I was there, I didn't rush straight in. Whatever the situation was, I wasn't going to help Louie by kicking in the door and dealing with what I found on the other side off the cuff. I hadn't been able to diagnose the problem based on the scant facts, which meant I was in store for some surprises. I don't like surprises. It's hard to guess which of my kit essentials I should have ready when I'm facing a surprise.

Not everything in my bag of tricks involved the dark arts. Much of my kit was made up of all-purpose tools that served a variety of basic functions, often multiple functions. Kit Essential Number One was my key ring. Casket key, niche key, and hospital service-elevator key, among others. I kept them all on a single steel loop that was never designed to be a key ring, but served its purpose when trying to hook non-standard in-name-only "keys" together for easy access.

I stepped into the Emergency Room, weaving through the casualties of the day—head wounds and heart attacks, concerned family, crying victims—until I came to one of the staff-only elevators. There was too much triage and suffering, bureaucracy and blood to notice one stray civilian pass by who looked like he knew where he was going. I hit the call button and when the first empty lift arrived, I took it. Key in the panel, I unlocked access to the lower levels and rode the elevator all the way down to the bottom of the shaft. The E.R. cacophony of patients coming and going, coughing their lungs out or getting their wounds stitched closed, receded until there was stillness and silence, broken only by the gear-grind of the cables that lowered me to B8.

The elevator doors opened onto an empty corridor. There was no sign of anything alive or dead. I could hear the tumbling washers and driers down at one end, behind the laundry room doors, but that was it. The morgue side was appropriately lifeless, but even the hall-desk post was unattended, which was unusual. I slowly walked towards the morgue entrance, keeping my footsteps silent. The elevator doors shut behind me so the car could return to its default position and answer staff needs. I'd considered blocking the doors open in case I needed to make an abrupt exit, but that would only set off an alarm after a few minutes. I would just have to trust that I could handle the situation, whatever that situation was, without having to make a hurried retreat.

There was a cup of black coffee sitting on the hall desk, full and untouched. I couldn't see any steam rising off it. I dipped my finger inside, breaking the surface tension and sending ripples to the rim. It was stone cold. The temperature of the morgue itself was kept cool, but the corridor was heated. The coffee had to have been sitting there for quite a while to lose all hint of warmth.

I pushed the swinging door in without knocking. I didn't want to announce my arrival. My attempt at stealth proved pointless. There was no one inside—no one living, no one mobile. One of the autopsy tables was occupied, but a peek under the sheet and a glance at the toe tag revealed a palliative-care cancer case who had expired that day. The corpse waited patiently for an autopsy that would only confirm the obvious, but no one was stepping up to attend to this final formality. I expected the rest of the night-shift skeleton crew to be slacking off somewhere, but Louie would never wander away from his station with a body left unfiled and nobody else on duty.

I took a slow tour of the room, checking each cupboard and closet, looking under tables and desks. There weren't many conceivable hiding spots if anybody was trying to hide from me. I quickly narrowed the possibilities down to the body drawers. Alive or undead, the drawers offered the only shelter. One by one, I began to pull them out and confirm the contents. As usual, it was a full house. Louie hadn't made much progress in clearing his roster since I'd been by to identify Rabbi Reubenski and free up one drawer. There were thirty drawers total, ten rows stacked three high. Only two were empty, though one of those would have been earmarked for the autopsy case on the table. Of the occupied drawers, three were stuffed inside body bags. For the sake of being thorough, I unzipped each to make sure it wasn't hiding somebody I knew. I regretted it each time. One was burned beyond recognition, another badly decomposed, complete with plenty of maggoty stowaways. The final one was fresh but filthy, possibly homeless, and stank horribly even before the rot set in.

Only one drawer remained a mystery after I'd pulled open and resealed all the others, each in turn. Drawer Number Twenty-Eight, the topmost spot on the right, wouldn't budge. Rather than try to force it, I decided to be cautious and find the ledger I knew Louie kept of the various comings and goings of the drawers and their occupants. The archive of years past had been digitized and tucked away in a computer file somewhere, and I didn't have anywhere near the sort of hacking skills I would need to find them, but the year-to-date was written down in a notebook I didn't have to hunt for too long to find. "Power-failure proof," is what Louie called his record of current and recent arrivals and departures. He wasn't willing to let a blackout, a system crash, or a software upgrade-gone-wrong interrupt the ebb and flow of the deceased in his tightly run morgue. His notebook read more like a motel registry than a clear and simple chart. I flipped through dozens of pages, scanning each one top to bottom, ignoring names and dates, focusing only on drawer numbers. By the end of page three, I already knew what I needed to know, but I went through the rest of the book just to be sure. Drawer Twenty-Eight was unoccupied. It had always been unoccupied. And I was sure if I could pick through the computer archives, I would discover that drawer had gone unused for years, all the way back to whenever the morgue records first began.

This was more than a stuck drawer. With corpse space in short supply at Hillside General, there was no way somebody in maintenance wouldn't have been summoned to fix number twenty-eight in short order. Louie had never mentioned it. Not to me, maybe not to anyone. Perhaps it was just one of those hospital secrets that was never openly discussed, like the anaesthesiologist who developed grabby hands the moment a surgical patient went under; the nurse who "helped" demanding and troublesome terminal patients die in a timely fashion much to the entire ward's relief; or the supply room with the comfy cot that was host to innumerable staff liaisons and potentially actionable harassment suits. The sealed drawer might have been nothing more sinister than a drop box for an intern who was paying off his student loans by skimming pharmaceuticals and dealing on weekends. I hoped somebody's secret drug stash was the worst thing I would find inside. That hope was thin, nebulous, and easily shattered by the next weapon in my arsenal.

Kit Essential Number Two was a standard flat-head screwdriver. The heftiest one I could find. Not that there was a lot I needed to unscrew on the job. The casket key usually had that covered. But there was no room in the satchel for an entire crowbar. A large flat-head, however, provided enough leverage in most instances to pry open whatever crack I could jam the bladed head into. An oversized steel drawer was a tailor-made target.

I worked the blade of the screwdriver into one side of the drawer and hammered it deeper with the palm of my hand until it was in far enough to start wrenching it open. The drawer fought me, but there was a little more give with each push, allowing me to work the screwdriver deeper and get more leverage. At last I heard something snap. Broken metal pieces tumbled down into the inner workings of the drawer and I could see the remains of a latch that had locked the drawer shut from the inside. The latch wasn't part of the basic design. None of the drawers could be locked. The latch and bolt had been installed sometime after the morgue and its wall of drawers had been built. And it hadn't been installed by someone on the outside. It could only have been installed and hooked by someone or something inside the drawer itself.

Drawer twenty-eight was vacant. There was nothing there, not even dust. It looked pristine and brand new. Hardly surprising since it never got used. I dragged a stool over so I could step up and inspect the interior more closely. That's when I saw the scuff marks. Subtle scratches in the metal base and slightly rougher spots on an otherwise polished steel surface told the tale of past movement inside. Movement in or out was hard to say. Maybe both. Given the marks and the installation of a locking mechanism, I guessed that the drawer was being used not for storage, but as a passage. To where, I had no clue.

I looked at the inside back of the drawer, which was a solid metal plate. That wasn't locked or hooked or clamped into place. It was welded solid. But there was another mark down the side of it—a streak. I put a finger to it and the tip came back red. It was tacky, but still moist. I didn't need to send it to the hospital pathology lab to determine it was blood.

From my vantage point atop the stool, I looked back at the morgue. Other than the complete lack of staff, nothing seemed amiss. There were certainly no pools of blood. No spatter, no droplets, no smears. But from the higher angle, I was offered a different view of how the lighting in the place reflected off all the smooth, polished surfaces—table tops and tiles, counters and cabinets. And the floor. The floor told me something had happened here recently. A janitor came by at least once a day to mop and scrub, keeping a place that processed corpses—some of them mangled, decayed, diseased—as sanitized as possible. A yellow sandwich board would be left behind for ten or twenty minutes while the tiled floor dried, to warn about the slippery, hazardous surface. No use needlessly filling another drawer by having some unfortunate lab technician go flying and break his neck. Once the remnants of soapy disinfectant evaporated, the tiles would be left with a uniformly clean surface that would dry to a dull matte. What I saw from above, caught by the light, were several swirly spots where a spill had been wiped up, probably with moistened paper towels.

Someone had covered up a crime in this room. It was a slap-dash job, but with no apparent victim, who would notice? I was the only one who knew Louie was missing from his post. His co-workers would check in from their perpetual break at some point and realize he was gone, but there would be no reason for them to suspect foul play. And if he never turned up again? There was no reason to think anything had happened in the morgue. As far as anyone else knew, Louie had left the hospital of his own accord.

Abducted, wounded, murdered—whatever his state— taking Louie out by the elevator wouldn't go unnoticed. And that was before I even factored in the zombie rabbi we'd been lucky to spirit away last time. They both might have been stashed in the laundry room, but cleaning staff was in and out of there regularly. The suspicious drawer twenty- eight volunteered itself as the likeliest place to dispose of multiple bodies. I only had to figure out how it was done. And there was only one way to do that.

Swinging one leg high, I stepped off the stool and climbed into the drawer. I lay down with my head to the back, the opposite direction bodies were laid out. Setting my foot on the upper rim of the drawer's cavernous slot, I pushed off and let the drawer roll closed on its tracks. It shut with a loud metallic clang, plunging me into darkness.

Kit Essential Number Three is the biggest no-brainer on the list. The one thing nobody has when then need it the most, and the one thing everybody, not just a necromancer, needs to have handy when they find themselves in the darkest corners of life. A flashlight. Mine was in the bag, easy to find, right near the top. I go scrounging around in the dark more than most, so the flashlight gets plenty of use—too much for it to sink very deep into my kit. Whether I needed to find the bolt holes in a casket lying at the bottom of an open grave on a moonless night, or I wanted to read the expiry date on a carton of milk in my fridge during a power failure, my trusty all-purpose extra-durable flashlight was there for me.

I switched it on and the interior of the metal drawer lit up as the beam reflected off the six steel surfaces. Or perhaps I should count them as six and a half. Once drawer twenty-eight was shut, I could see a large section of the inside roof had been torn out. I shined my flashlight through the ragged hole of rent metal and found a concrete ceiling several feet above the top of the drawer, corresponding to the height of the ceiling proper in the morgue. I grabbed hold of the edge of the hole above me, careful to select a spot that wasn't quite so jagged, and hoisted myself up into a sitting position with my head and light poking out the top.

I pivoted as much as I could, looking all around. The back wall of the morgue was connected to a vast, cavernous chamber. Concrete slab walls and exposed rusty rebar revealed it as a planned portion of the hospital's muti-level basement sub-structure, but this section had gone unfinished. Poking out of the single excavated morgue drawer, I was up near the very top of the chamber, the majority of which dropped down an entire additional floor below Hillside General's lowest level. This was the aborted and forgotten B9. Whatever was planned for the space back when the foundation was first dug had been walled away and erased from living memory.

Crouching to avoid hitting my head on the crumbling ceiling, I was able to stand up and step out of the hole in the top of the drawer. A corroded steel-rung ladder was built into the wall close enough for me to reach. Once upon a time, the ladder would have allowed maintenance crews access to whatever vents and ducts and plumbing were planned to run down to B9, but construction of that behind-the-scenes clutter had never gotten further than the ladder. Step by careful step, I climbed down the sheer drop to the floor far below. I tested each rung before committing my weight to it, but they all held, firmly anchored into the concrete and the iron netting beneath its surface that helped maintain its integrity.

The floor, like the rest of the chamber and the entire final basement level, was unfinished. There was an inch of stagnant, filthy water pooled nearly everywhere I could step. Occasional piles of rubble and long-abandoned construction materials offered the only dry surfaces, but they were all dangerously uneven, unstable, and riddled with sharp edges and pointy shards that promised tetanus or worse with every scratch. I avoided them as I searched the dark with the beam of my flashlight, looking for any landmark to guide myself by, or trail to pursue the suspected body snatcher.

B9 seemed to be a catch-all for everything above. The walls were streaked with pathways where rain water leaked in, brown patches that I hoped were only rust spots, and stalactites of white lime that had filtered through the earth from the surrounding would-be mountain. As I crept deeper inside, past the point where the first probing sweeps of my light could reach, I began to sense that more than the elements had soaked into this unwitting septic tank. It was cold down there but humid, and an increasingly distinct stench of necrotic tissue hung in the air like a tangible barrier I had to push my way through.

Up ahead, somewhere in the dark, I heard something—a sudden moist noise that echoed through that cathedral hall of truncated engineering. It wasn't the dripping sound of a leaky roof over pooled water, but the wet thud of something soggy landing on a saturated base from a great height. I pointed my flashlight up and searched the distant ceiling with my narrow spotlight. I followed a tendril of cracked concrete until I found a gap—a series of them—running the length of one of the walls. Even as my light played over this row of square holes, I saw something fall from one of them. I didn't see where it first landed, but it bounced several times and came to rest not a dozen feet away. I found it with my light, but had to approach before I could see what it was for certain.

It was a foot. A human foot. Cleanly severed, nearly bloodless, and wrapped in clear plastic to keep it tidy on its way to disposal. I recognized a professional amputation when I saw one. It had come from somewhere upstairs—the results of a recent procedure, perhaps on a diabetic whose peripheral artery disease had finally cost him a foot or two. A common enough surgical by-product of daily hospital life, but how had it ended up all the way down here? I turned my beam of light to the wall, the area immediately under where the shafts in the ceiling let out. As I looked at the pile of refuse before me, more dropped from above to add to it. I was immediately reminded of the linen spilling out of the chutes in the laundry room on B8. But these weren't soiled sheets and pillowcases and hospital gowns. This was the total sum of biohazard material milled out by every test, sample, biopsy, study, and extraction performed anywhere in Hillside General. And yes, autopsies too. All those spare organs removed and weighed and never put back in their bodies of origin. They were all down here too, in one single grotesque pile that included everything from urine-sample tubes, to latex gloves that had been used once and once only for a quick prostate exam, to tumours malignant and benign that had been studied and cleared by pathology, to stitches recently cut and pulled free of healing wounds and incisions.

It was a horrid mountain of offal, vast and overwhelming in sight and stench, yet not nearly copious enough to account for all the years Hillside General had been in service. I don't often see things on the job that give me a purely visceral reaction, but this one made me take a step back, literally. I didn't even consciously realize I was doing it until I tried to put weight on one heel and found there was no support under it. I barely caught my balance before I went tumbling backwards into a pit behind me that I had walked right past in the dark and never noticed. I pointed my flashlight down into the abyss to see what I'd nearly fallen into and found myself looking into a rolling sea of pornographic horror. It took several long moments for my mind to accept what I was looking at and consciously acknowledge it. My intellect needed the time to reboot and do a safety check to make sure I hadn't gone suddenly insane.

This ten-foot-square divot cut into the concrete floor would have given me quite a fall, but the landing would have been cushioned by breasts. Hundreds of them, perhaps thousands. I had no way of knowing how deep they were stacked. Many were rotting, grey mounds of bulbous flesh, but the fresh ones on top were easily identifiable for that they were. Once I knew what I was looking at, my mind started doing calculations. How many mastectomies did Hillside General perform in a week, a month, a year? How many were singles, how many were doubles, and how many would it take to account for the collection I saw below me?

Before I could ask myself, "Why breasts?" I saw that it didn't end there. There were other pits stretching out in the dark, spaced at regular intervals—a checkerboard pattern of identical cuts in the concrete that were probably meant for pillars or columns to help hold up the rest of the hospital until the B9 excavation was called off and additional support was deemed unnecessary. Left empty to be filled by nothing more than runoff and dirt, they'd been pressed into service as a series of holding tanks. Each hole I shone light into revealed a different assortment of surgical waste. Arms filled one, legs another. There were individual holes dedicated to housing livers, lengths of extracted bowel, even eyeballs. A few of them didn't contain solids, but instead functioned as cauldrons brimming with suctioned liquids from any numbers of chest cavities and infected abscesses. As much as possible, the fluids seemed to have been separated by colour rather than consistency. The red pit was full of blood, no doubt. The white one, I gathered, was pus. I didn't want to guess at the green or the brown ones, and held my breath near them to avoid confirming my worst suspicions.

There had been a concerted effort to separate and group, sort and file. Little of it was fresh, much seemed to have been left to decay and putrefy, like an aging cheese. It was that notion of a mouldy cheese, turning blue over time, getting better with age—at least to some tastes—that helped me see this place for what it was. It was a gigantic cafeteria—much larger than the official hospital cafeteria somewhere upstairs—catering to an inhuman taste for all things shed from humanity. These pits were like the divots on a serving tray, each one holding its own specific variety of mushy slop. The result was a smorgasbord of filth, constantly being replenished by the discarded flesh from above, lost in the effort to cure or heal.

And it was why the hall, immense though it was, wasn't already completely stuffed wall to wall, ceiling to floor, with the medical waste of years and decades gone by. It was all getting eaten.

"More meat in through the drawer, I sees," said a deep voice in the deeper dark. "Not the usual way for deliveries to come and now twice in one day, like Lump ain't got enough to chew on."

I turned the beam of the flashlight towards the voice, though I didn't relish the idea of discovering what it belonged to. Even with the light directly aimed, it took time to find the outline of the grey creature in the landscape of grey concrete ruins. What caught me off guard was the size of it. If it had been human once, or at least humanoid, it was now so grotesquely obese it seemed like just another hill of rubble piled on the floor amidst all the others. It was only once the light caught its eyes, and reflected back at me through the saucer pupils as a cold glowing white, that I could determine where the head lay atop all the rolls of pale fat. It didn't react to the light as a living thing might, didn't shy away, didn't shelter eyes that had grown so accustomed to the dark. Instead it stared back at me, sizing me up with its acute night vision.

"Fresher than I like, but make it dead and give it time, I always say. Then it gets soft and tasty, more to Lump's likin'."

It raised one of its claws to its face—three or four thick stumpy fingers, capped with split blackened nails. Grasping somebody's cystic uterus, it took a bite out of it like an apple and swallowed without chewing.

There was a good twenty feet between us. Too close for my liking, but far enough that I doubted something so bloated could charge at me and narrow the distance before I was able to react. I decided to try for a formal introduction.

"Lump, is it? That's your name?"

"Lump is what I am, Lump is what I do. Just a big ol' Lump, downstairs, feedin' in the dark."

"Hello, Lump. I'm Rip."

"Rip he says? Rip I does. I rip and I gnash and I chew and I swallows," rumbled Lump. "Meat is what you is, what they all is in the end. Meat and bone to pick me teeth with once the meat's been stripped."

That's when I knew what it was. A ghoul. Fucking ghouls, I hate them. Usually you'll find them, if you're unlucky enough to come across one at all, skulking around cemeteries, looking for a loose grave to dig up and dine on. They're gluttons and they make a mess of everything. When I have to disturb a grave, I try to do a tidy job and clean up after myself. If I do my job right, no one, not even a particularly anal groundskeeper, will know I've been there. But ghouls don't give a shit. They'll leave turned-up earth, splinters of caskets, and gnawed bones everywhere. This sort of desecration usually gets written off as vandalism. The papers never report all the gory details so as not to upset the families of the deceased who got dined on. But this one wasn't a grave robber. This one had stumbled upon the motherlode of feasts down here on the final forgotten floor of Hillside General. Alone for years, supplied with an all-you-can-eat menu inadvertently catered right to him, it had been able to overindulge itself into the rolling mass of flesh before me now.

"How long have you been down here, Lump?"

"Don't count the days, don't sum the years. But it's been a long time. A thousand legs ago or more, about half as many arms. Hundreds of hearts, hundreds of livers, and kidneys by the bucketload. That's how long."

Lump chased his next bite of uterus with a crunchy handful of crisps. Crispy whats, I wasn't sure until I swung my light to the pile of microscope test slides, each flavoured with a single drop of blood. Lump didn't seem to care they were mostly glass, and crushed them to sand between his teeth. Even ghouls like empty-calorie snacks.

"Brick'd us up, they did, lo these many years ago. Forgot we was down here. Don't know, don't care. That's how it goes on the doctors' salary. Paid and paid well to cut and saw and not to think what happens to all them bits and pieces they pull out and cast away. Last they seen 'em, they was taken away on a shiny silver tray and that was the only time they gave it a never-you-mind. Dumped and disposed and who gives a cunt where, eh?"

Lump was chatty for a ghoul. Usually when they encounter a living person, they simply hiss and run away. I supposed Lump's running days were over given the size of him. Maybe even ghouls get lonely for conversation if you leave them buried in a deep dark hole long enough.

"Wherezit all go they wonders not a bit," he lamented. "Doctors don't know, nurses don't know, orderlies don't know. Don't know, don't care a bit of it! Down here it all goes, down to the very bottom with Lump."

Lump washed his mouth out with the contents of a fast-food 12-ounce cup someone must have once thrown down a disposal chute. The straw made a long slurping noise, sucking mostly air as he reached the bottom. I couldn't guess what the liquid inside had been, but I didn't want to be around to watch him get a refill.

"And does we burn 'em all up? The big book says we do. The big book with all the regulations and all the laws about proper disposin' has a lot to say on the subject, it does. But you ever seen any chimneys stickin' outta the roof of this here hospital? Have you now? I don't think so, an' you need the chimneys if you're gonna do some burning, yeh? Of course you do."

Some hospitals incinerate medical waste on site, others seal it in drums and ship it to another location. I'd never thought about whether Hillside did one or the other, and didn't consider there was a third possibility hidden away under the morgue.

"You said I'm not the first to come in through the morgue drawer today," I said, trying to steer Lump towards the point of my visit.

"Nah, you be number three. Three so far. Lump never knew he was so popular."

"What did the other two look like?" I asked.

"Dead," said Lump. "One of 'em dead, draggin' another one. Also dead. Not-moving-at-all dead."

"What kind of not-moving dead do you mean?"

"Bloody he was, and fresh. Too fresh for Lump. Meat from the drawer usually ain't so fresh. But then, Lump don't eat from it no more. Used to be, I'd come and go through the drawer after I dug a hole and put on the bolt. Lump weren't quite so lumpy back then and could fit easy. Pop out, grab a bite, pop back in. No one knew, no one bothered. But why go out when all the tasty goodies come spillin' in here on their own?"

Why indeed? No need to take the risk when the entire hospital staff above keeps tossing you your fill of leftovers, fresh off the stump.

"What happened to the fresh one that was bleeding?" I asked, fearing this description could only refer to Louie.

"Pulls it apart and tucks it away, Lump did. Don't get bodies whole no more, not since Lump stopped making one or two disappear from the slabs upstairs. But it all comes back, it does. Lump remembered how it's done. Arms go there, legs go there, guts all got their own places. And the head? The head I cracks open like a nut to get the brains out."

So much for finding Louie alive and well, or even dead and resurrectable. It sounded like he was scattered all over the place already. But the mention of brains made me hopeful there were still answers to be had.

"Like brains, do you?" I asked Lump. "Me too."

Lump nodded at the mention of our common interest.

"Lump gots a special spot just for them."

"One of the pits is just for brains, I bet. Which one?"

"Nyuh-uh," said Lump, wagging a single scolding claw at me. "We don't share the brains. Them's too tasty."

Let it never be said Lump the ghoul wasn't completely without manners.

"But Lump shares with his guests, he does. Three in one day, and shares is only polite, yeh? There be plenty drops down the chutes Lump won't eat. Sit down, help yerself."

There was still information I needed from Lump, and I didn't want to be rude, so I excused myself as gently as I could.

"You know, I'm not really all that hungry at the moment."

But Lump was already taking inventory of what he could offer me from his pantry.

"Gloves I don't like, plasma bags ain't good eatin' for Lump. Soft they is, and a cozy bed they make. But there always be more gloves, every day. Does the meat eat gloves?"

"No, I can't say I've ever made a meal of a latex glove."

"How does it know it's not good eatin' if it won't try?"

Lump gathered up a fistful of used latex gloves and offered them to me like a wilting bouquet of disposable medical waste. I refused them delicately.

"Pass. I guess we just have similar tastes. Neither of us likes to eat latex gloves."

Lump nodded knowingly.

"Aye, half of 'em taste like ass, they do. Well then, if it be a matter of taste, I suppose I could offer a nibble of liver. Liver ain't Lump's favourite. The meat-guest can have a bit of liver from the visitor what was just here. Very fresh, that is."

I didn't fancy a taste of Louie, either. My face betrayed enough disgust for Lump to pick up on it. He tried to be accommodating.

"Cooked?" he asked. "Does it want it cooked? Sometimes Lump cooks his meat. Just to be different."

Lump waved his arm, sagging and rippling with fat, towards the back wall.

"I got me a little toaster oven that does the job. Upstairs they think all the meat gets burned, but the only burning happens 'round here is when I overcooks the meat."

Lump snorted at his own joke.

"Snatched it we did, back when Lump could fit through the drawer and help hisself. Liver set on broil for a few minutes comes out tasty, even if the liver's too fresh."

Talking cuisine with a ghoul was turning my stomach. I probed for more information about my missing zombie rabbi who may have turned into a killer zombie rabbi.

"Were you this generous with your other guest?" I asked.

"What other guest?"

Lump seemed preoccupied by his cooking tips.

"The other one," I reminded him. "The dead one who was walking around."

"Oh, him. Walking and talking he was."

That was news to me. I knew the rabbi's corpse had apparently self-animated without command, which was highly unlikely, but speaking should have been impossible. He was an empty shell with no brain.

"He was talking? Really? What did he have to say?"

"Lots and lots he said," recalled the ghoul. "Even before he came down hisself with a whole body of meat for Lump. He used to whisper to me through the drawer, like he knew I was down here all the time. When no one else was in the morgue, he'd whisper at the cracks and tell me he'd bring me meat if I let him in. So reach up, Lump did. Reach way up for the first time in years and unlocked the latch. And the dead one didn't lie. He made some fresh meat for Lump and dragged it down. Lump already has plenty to eat, but he won't refuse a gift, yeh?"

"Where is he now? The dead one who walks and talks."

"Lump let him go. Lump wanted to pick him apart and eat him too, but like that one said, he be all skin and bones, so why the bother? He left the back way, but he made Lump a promise before he went."

"A promise? What sort of promise?"

"The dead one says there'd be more fresh meat along in no time at all. Says it was already on the way, and here you is. Meat so fresh it still lives and breathes. The dead one said the meat would call itself Rip and that I should make sure to tear it into little bitty pieces, just to be sure it stayed dead long enough to make a lunch for Lump."

I heard a noise that sounded like car tires inching their way up a gravel driveway. With my beam of light fixed on Lump's face, I didn't immediately notice him drawing closer, but what I heard was his mass of blubber slithering forward across the gritty concrete. His progress was slow, but I decided to speak fast.

"Why bother with meat this fresh when you have all this wonderful spoiled flesh? So tender and rotten."

Lump's advance paused and he looked around at his empire of waste with relish.

"Ain't it, though? So sweet, so tasty."

But like anyone with an empire—even one of waste and ruin—he wanted more of it. His gaze returned to me, and the consuming greed of a bottomless hunger returned to his face.

"But fresh meat don't stay fresh long. Especially not when Lump pulls it all to pieces. You sure you won't have a bite to fatten up before I start ripping and tearing and gnashing?"

I doubted Lump was interested in giving me enough time to fatten up on his generosity, but I wouldn't put it past him to force feed me my own weight in tripe in an effort to create some vile form of ghoulish foie gras. He resumed his steady ooze towards me and I went through my mental list of kit essentials that might dissuade him from scattering my various limbs throughout his lair to ferment over the coming weeks and months. That's when Kit Essential Number Three decided to flicker and die on me. The flashlight illumination faded away, leaving me with only a final glimpse of the approaching wall of fatty grey flab, no more than a dozen feet away and narrowing the distance surprisingly fast.

Kit Essential Number Four is spare batteries. Without them, Number Three can be rendered useless at the most inopportune moments. Moments just like this one. If I had any spares in the satchel, I wasn't going to find them in a timely fashion in the pitch-black, with a gigantically obese ghoul breathing down my neck.

His breath. I could feel it, close and getting closer. I'd been in many dark places before, but none so dark as this. My eyes were wide open and I saw nothing but black upon black. My other senses reached out for any bearings, but the echoing sounds of the creature coming for me were no help. There was only one conceivable source of light in that dank sub-basement slaughterhouse and I ran for it, even though I couldn't see the path, and the route there was a blind obstacle course of treacherous rubble and pits brimming with diseased innards waiting to swallow me up even more readily than the horror on my heels.

With hands stretched in front of me, I ran towards the back wall Lump had gestured towards when he was talking about his skills as a chef. Several times my feet slid across loose stones, and stray strands of rebar nipped at my pant legs. They very nearly tripped me up, but I remained on my feet and made it all the way to the wall without tumbling to the floor or falling into a hole. My hands found the cold concrete surface first and kept me from slamming my face into it. I'd put some distance between the ghoul and myself, but I could hear him coming, and I knew he could see me in the dark just fine. I didn't know which way my hopeful salvation lay, left or right, so I chose left and wondered if my coin-flip chance would keep me from suffering Louie's fate.

Feeling my way along the wall, I found the wire first, running down from a socket somewhere above, insulated with a thick rubber coating. An extension cord. There had to have been one. And somewhere on the other end, Lump's prized toaster oven. I grabbed the cord and started reeling it in rather than try to follow it. Somewhere, out in the dark, I heard the metallic crash and rattle as the toaster oven was yanked off of wherever it was perched. Hand over hand, I drew it to me, hoping I hadn't broken it.

The kitchen-counter appliance arrived at my feet, banging into the toe of my shoe. I felt around the front of the machine until I found the buttons and began pressing them randomly. Each one made a beep, but there was no indication I got it working until I saw the first hint of orange illumination when the coils inside started to heat up. As these first slivers of light shone out the front window of the miniature oven, I held up my palm to reflect them back on the control panel and read the settings. I had set the oven on bake mode. I turned the dial all the way up for maximum heat, maximum light, and the coils responded, glowing stronger.

There was now just enough light to see, and I set down my dead flashlight and kit. Lump was still out there, still coming as fast as his bulk would let him, and I needed more light to fight him off. I rummaged through my satchel, searching for those spare batteries I always kept at the ready. But no amount of illumination from a toaster oven was going to help me find them, no amount of time feeling around inside the bag. There was nothing. Not a single spare. I must have forgotten to restock. I take back what I said earlier about merely growing complacent. This was sloppy work. And it was going to get me killed.

That's when I saw Lump's face, faint, dimly lit, but bright enough in the glow let off by the oven for me to see he was salivating. And why not? He was close enough to smell my fleshy goodness, and very nearly close enough to have his first taste.

People always ask me, whenever they see my all-purpose extra-durable flashlight, why I don't go with something more compact. There are plenty of models out there a fraction the size and weight that cast just as much light in just as wide an arc. Surely one of those would take up less room in the kit, would be easier to carry around, wouldn't suck so much battery power. True, all. But what they don't understand is that a flashlight this big and heavy has a secondary purpose. If it ever fails at the wrong moment, if the bulb breaks or the batteries die or water gets inside and spoils the wiring, it has another use—an emergency backup raison d'être.

It makes a damn good cudgel.

Blackened teeth yawned at me, reaching for the closest extremity to clamp down on. I swung the flashlight hard and knocked as many out as I could with a single blow. I heard a dozen fragments of shattered enamel rattle across the floor and into the dark and the ghoul howled at their loss. That was a dozen fewer teeth he had to bite me with.

Lump staggered back from the blow, but shrugged it off and picked himself up a moment later.

"That weren't nice, that weren't polite!" he roared. "Guests ought be nice, meat ought be polite, lest Lump eats them slow and makes them suffer morsel by morsel, one nibble at a time!"

I didn't feel like discussing dinner etiquette with him any further and slammed my cudgel into his face again. And again for good measure. There was little chance I could knock him out, no chance I could kill him, but I kept at it, forcing him back a few more steps with each impact. Perhaps I could drive him away for a time if I managed to hurt him badly enough, but I didn't place much hope in that. Ghouls can ignore pain, but they can't ignore hunger. And they're always hungry. It's the one preoccupying drive that motivates everything they exist for and it will keep them coming back for more, even if there's an ocean of pain lying between their appetite and their food.

I was exhausting myself. Beating Lump was like hitting a punching bag. The punching bag may reel from the blows, but it will always outlast any opponent. I swung one more time, as hard as I could, because there was nothing else I could do. And on that final mighty swing I hit nothing but air and almost spun myself off balance and into the floor. Even by such dim light, how could I miss a target so big? I looked, but there was no sign of Lump at all. It was like he had disintegrated in the blink of an eye.

"Owwww," I heard Lump howl, a split second later.

That was the most distinct thing I heard him say. The rest were groans and snarls of pain and anger that bounced off the ceiling and between the walls. It took me a while to realize they were coming from deep below me. I looked down and could make out the thinnest outline of one of the empty column pits just before me. Lump had spilled down into it, but I couldn't see him at all. I could only hear him, and the crackling, crunching noise of whatever he'd landed on.

I returned to the toaster oven and picked it up by the base. It was running hot, but I could avoid burning myself if I held it by the insulated legs. Walking with it on the end of its extension-cord tether, I approached the pit Lump had fallen in and pointed the windowed coils down so I could see what state he was in and if he still posed a danger.

"Pricks an' pins and all over Lump they is! Why's the meat treat us so? Don't like bein' et, does it? Well Lump don't care for bein' poked and pricked and pointificated all over hisself!"

Past his initial shock and pain, the ghoul was now better able to articulate his suffering. And he must have been suffering horribly. After untold years developing his filing system, deciding which medical waste earned its own pit and which was left to accumulate haphazardly around the lair and under the drop chutes, Lump had fallen into the abyss he used to cast away every hypodermic needle that had ever landed in his lair. I don't expect he'd put them down there for snacking purposes. These were the discards of medical waste even a gluttonous ghoul didn't see value in. He had probably considered it a safe spot to contain the stinging prongs so he wouldn't accidentally stick himself as he plodded around his open buffet trying to decide if he was more in the mood for lungs, hearts, spleens or, more likely, all of the above. Well he was certainly stuck now. Lump resembled the world's largest pin cushion, with many hundreds of needles jabbed into each roll of flesh, and thousands more lying in wait, primed to pierce him with every shift of his weight, every movement, every attempt to pull himself out of his predicament.

The toaster oven cast scant light, but in an otherwise vast black space, my eyes quickly adjusted and were able to make out more details. I was able to trace my path from where I first encountered Lump, to where I had fled through literal blind luck. I shuddered when I realized how close I had come to plunging into the needle pit myself.

Lump's prospects of ever being able to reach high enough and pull his enormous mass out of that prickly trap were poor. I left him to his complaining and bellowing that would probably keep him occupied until the relentless rain of body parts and organs from above finally filled the hollow hall of B9 and smothered him, burying him under so many immovable tons of gore. It would happen eventually. I estimated it would take a few years at least. Maybe as many as ten.

Ignoring the ongoing racket of ghoul misery, I wandered in the dark, lighting the way with the humming toaster oven held out in front of me. The extension cord allowed me a long leash to explore the immediate area, but it was too short to let me hunt through every hole, every rut, every pit where Lump had stashed his sustenance. I was looking for Louie's brain. There was much it could tell me about what exactly had happened with the rabbi. I just hoped he wouldn't be too pissed at me, having left him in charge of a homicidal zombie. But I needed more details. Something had gone very wrong, and without more facts I was at a loss to say what.

Manually searching for a single brain in all that mess and darkness was fruitless. I was going to have to try a more spiritual pursuit. Concentrating, setting my consciousness free and letting it flow through the necrotic collection, I called out to the one piece in this impossibly shattered meat-mosaic I could use.

"Louie? You in here? Speak up!"

I only got dim, confused mutterings from assorted amputations. The arms and legs and random breasts called out for the bodies they were once attached to, hoping I was it, longing for me to find them and reattach them and bring them home. There was no distinct thought or emotion to it, just a soulless hollow want. The tumors were worse. Malignant or benign, they yelped and chattered, hungering for more flesh to corrupt now that they found themselves cut off from any warm, nurturing bodies by wads of plastic wrap. The absolute worst were the abortions and the miscarriages. Somewhere, out in the dark, they had a pit to themselves, alone and forgotten, some intact, many not. And unlike all the other morsels, they had minds of their own. Immature, undeveloped, but present nevertheless. None of them had language yet, but they knew pain, they knew the most primitive emotions, and collectively they cried out in a single unified protest that could only be translated as, "Why?" The sound was deafening and I was the only one who could hear it. It was overwhelming and I was about to disengage when I heard a familiar tone.

"Rip, is that you?"

Out of the mess of scattered thoughts and vague notions, I had picked up the one I could recognize and focus on. It was Louie. Or whatever was left of him.

"Where are you?" he asked. "Where am I?"

A good question. He was all over the place, but I was able to pick up on the location of his brain, like a single radar ping. It was coming from a pit close by, within the extension cord's range. I made my way towards it and came, at last, to the edge of a drop that let down into a well of squiggly lobes and cortices. If you've seen the inside of enough bodies, you can recognize what's what, even out of context. Even when it's a mess of picked over, pulled apart, chewed on leftovers. The colour and texture is distinct from any other organ, and I knew at once I had discovered Lump's brain drain—a repository of lost intellect, but a wealth of connections and byways to someone like me, looking to make contact with the former inhabiting soul.

I set the oven down and sat on the lip, my feet dangling over the edge. It wasn't far to the spongy surface, but I wanted to let myself down easily without causing any more damage to all those abused neurons and synapses than I had to. I didn't know how well the densely packed neural tissue would support my weight, and I didn't want to jump in and end up sinking to the bottom.

Kit Essential Number Five is a pair of rubber gloves. Thick, substantial, difficult to pierce, impossible to tear. If you wouldn't be willing to scrub out a toilet with them, they're not substantial enough. In the field of necromancy, you need to stick your hands in far worse things than a toilet. You never know when you might have to excavate a muddy hole by hand, move a body that's riddled with toxic mould or, for instance, go picking through a pile of rotting human brains stacked ten feet deep. I pulled mine on and prepared to get to work.

I didn't expect a ghoul to do a tidy job of cracking Louie's skull open and scraping his brain out with its gnarled claws, but this was more of a confused mess than I had anticipated. I couldn't tell for sure where Louie's grey matter began or ended and which pieces were mixed with other brains that had been dumped on the pile before him. I tried to narrow it down by getting Louie talking as I went digging through the mire, trying to find something that was recognizably part of my fallen friend.

"It's okay, Louie," I assured him. "I found you. More or less."

"What happened?"

"That's what I came to ask you."

"Weren't we just talking on the phone?"

"That's right. And then there was an incident. Can you remember?"

"The rabbi. I remember the rabbi was walking around on his own. And then..."

Louie's consciousness fell silent. He was confused, still in shock and likely to remain so for a long time. Violent demises will do that. Dismemberment doesn't help.

"It's okay, take your time."

"I'm sorry, I'm feeling a little scattered right now."

"I don't doubt it," I told him, setting aside promising chunks of brain, discarding others.

"There was something sharp. I felt it. Sharp and deep."

"You mentioned a trocar."

"Yes, that was it."

"What then?"

"He spoke. The rabbi spoke."

"What did he tell you?"

"'Die,'" Louie said. "He told me to die. Is that what happened? Am I dead?"

I didn't know how to break the news to Louie, so I just said, "Yes." And then added, "Very."

The more of Louie's brain I was able to gather together into a coherent whole, the more self-aware he became, but his mind was jumbled. I would have to take it away with me to give him time to focus his thoughts.

Kit Essential Number Six is a selection of re-sealable plastic storage bags. There are a variety of brand names, but I buy whatever's on sale. All I care is that they have a good air-tight zipper to seal in the freshness, or the not-so-freshness, or (more often than not) the putrid rottenness. They come in many sizes, from tiny samplers to jumbo. I like to have an assortment on hand. In this case, I needed something large enough to hold a grown man's brain. Or as much of a grown man's brain as I was able to cobble together in the near dark at the bottom of a smelly pit rank with decomposing minds.

"You can bring me back, right? I mean, that's the sort of thing you do, isn't it?"

"Your case presents certain difficulties," I said, soft peddling Louie's current state.

"Wait a minute. Is my body intact?" he asked, catching on.

"Not as such, no."

I stuffed the plastic bag full of all the fresh brain matter I could spot. I was sure most of it belonged to Louie but there was bound to be a fair amount of accidental by-products and contamination in there. I'd have to figure out a way to sort and separate later.

"Fuck, Rip! I mean, fuck! Fuck!"

Louie was losing it. And he didn't have much left to lose.

"Calm down," I told him.

"Easy for you to say. You're not lying in pieces at the bottom of a medical-waste bin."

"This isn't exactly a medical-waste bin."

"Are we even still in the hospital?"

"Debatable."

"Where then?"

I took a final look around, considered my answer, and came to a firm conclusion.

"Probably the single worst place I've ever been in. So let's get the hell out of here."

I zipped the plastic bag shut. There was no way I'd found every last crumb of Louie's brain, but I was confident I'd recovered a solid eighty percent. Far from perfect, not even close to great, but good enough considering the trying circumstances. I tucked the bag into my satchel and then slung my kit over the lip of the hole. I grabbed onto the edge and hauled myself back up. Once I was back on solid concrete, I ditched my soiled rubber gloves, grabbed my toaster-oven light source, and headed back to the far wall. Lump had mentioned another way out, the path Rabbi Reubenski—or whatever he'd become—had taken to escape. I began to search for it, waving the oven around to illuminate the monolithic concrete surface.

The ghoul's howls of anguish had subsided during my gathering of brain matter. Scanning the wall for the way out, I lost track of how close I was to the trap that had snared Lump until I felt a sudden sharp pain in my shoulder. I dropped the toaster oven and instinctively reached for the source. Something had struck me, pierced me. When my hand found it, still hanging out of my shoulder blade, I pulled it out and discovered I was holding a hypodermic needle.

Even as I wondered where it had come from, more syringes landed near my feet and clattered across the floor. I looked behind me and saw another bunch of needles come flying out of one of the pits. I dodged just in time to avoid stopping them with my face.

"Prick me, you prick?" bellowed the voice from below. "Lump'll stick 'em in the meat and make it squeal!"

It was raining hypodermic needles, all of them far from sterile, many of them infected with who-knows-what. Lump was chucking them at me by the clawful, ignoring how much more damage he was doing to himself with each grab. He was in pain, but all he cared about now was spreading the misery. He was throwing them blind, unable to see his target, but was managing great accuracy by the sound of my footsteps alone. I looked for shelter, but the nearest rubble offered little. Instead, what I saw by the light of the fallen oven's coils was a mound unlike all the rest of the debris in the hall.

It looked more like a nest—a ghoul's idea of a nest. There were many thousands of discarded latex gloves, empty plasma bags, and plastic sheets the amputations from above came wrapped in—all of it swept into a corner and then permanently indented by Lump's bulk. This was the cozy bed he'd spoken of, a place for rest and relaxation between meals. Although, judging from the nasty state of it, Lump liked breakfast, lunch, and dinner in bed before venturing out for another snack, quick bite, or full meal.

It was behind the bedding that I saw the crack. Long and narrow, high on the wall, it split wider and wider as it stretched to the floor, offering a tight passage into the uncertain space beyond. This had to be Lump's original point of entry, too tiny for the now-bloated ghoul to squeeze back out—not that he would ever be tempted to leave behind the endless supply of fresh trimmings. It also had to be the means of my zombie rabbi's departure. At the moment, it was my best bet to escape the assault of flying barbs that were still being launched at me in waves.

Trying not to think of all the filthy places those gloves may have been before they arrived in this even filthier place, I dove into them and wormed my way into the crevasse they half-concealed. The fissure was too tight for me to pass through, and I realized it was my satchel that was making me an impossible fit. I was trying to decide how to lighten the load when another flying needled pierced my exposed calf. Thinning my inventory became easier in that moment, and I decided there was little I couldn't replace at a later date, so long as I held onto Louie's brain. I ditched most of my tools, including my heavy entrencher. Once the satchel became more malleable, I was able to slither away from the stabbing barrage.

The split in the wall became a tunnel, tight and dark, but simple enough to navigate once I was beyond the modest light range of the toaster-oven in the other chamber. Plunged back into total darkness, I crawled along the jagged path, feeling my way through a long vent of eroded concrete that had never set correctly, until I came spilling out into another man-made subterranean structure. I felt around some more and soon realized I had landed, bruisingly, on a stone staircase that offered no hint whether my best option lay up or down.

That's when I saw a slit of light, razor thin, only a dozen or so steps below me. Slowly I rose to my feet. My hand found a railing set in the wall and I carefully stepped down towards that tiny ray of promising artificial brightness. When I arrived at its source, I could see it was down by the floor. It was shining out from beneath a grimy and disused door. I strained to push it open several times before it became unstuck and let me through.

After so much time in so little light, the space behind the door felt like the afternoon sun. In fact it was only another dark tunnel, lit by caged bulbs at thirty-foot intervals, but they seemed as warm and welcoming as a crackling fire in a hearth. Once I saw the tracks, I knew I had come out inside a subway tunnel. The door was there to offer access to maintenance crews, and probably saw use no more than once or twice a decade.

A narrow walkway against the tunnel wall would lead me to the nearest station. I didn't like how little space it offered between me and any passing trains, so I decided to stay in the doorway until after the next one passed. I wanted the most amount of time possible to make my way to the safety of a platform. I'd had my fill of danger for one night and didn't want to needlessly invite more peril.

Kit Essential Number Seven is a public transit schedule. After a long, hard day of work and not much to show for it, it's good to know when the next bus or train is due so I can make the commute home. I can't cab it everywhere. It really adds up. Especially when no one's paying me.

I only had to wait a few minutes before I heard the wheels of the next train screeching on the tracks as it took a curve down the tunnel. It rounded the turn and I sheltered my eyes from the oncoming headlights. The lead car roared by and I was blasted by a hot wind. Able to see again, I looked up at the windows of the cars as they flickered by. It was long past rush hour and getting late. The train was empty of commuters, the seats unoccupied. But in the final car, I saw one rider. Just one. He was standing despite all the free seating. There was no time to make out much detail, but in the brief moment I saw him, I could tell he had a bushy grey beard.

And he was wearing a shower cap.

Chapter Fourteen

The Man in Black

"**Y**OU'RE STILL HERE?"

This I asked Rebecca about forty minutes later when I let myself into my apartment. She was dressed again in her previous night's outfit. The TV was on and my stash of snack food had been raided.

"You stink," was the only greeting I got.

"I know."

"No, I mean you really stink," Rebecca elaborated. "What have you been up to?"

"Working hard," I said, setting down what was left of my satchel kit and shrugging off my jacket. I let it fall to the floor.

"Where?" she asked, sniffing the air around me, determined to place the scent despite her obvious disgust. "A slaughter-house?"

"As near as."

Never before in my life have I so looked forward to a bath. And a shower. Followed by another shower. Even then I was wondering if I would ever be able to feel clean again. I kicked off my shoes, pulled off my shirt, and tossed them onto my crumpled jacket.

Rebecca went to find the remote and shut off the television, making a slap-dash effort to tidy up her mess and conceal the fact that she'd spent most of the day raiding my cupboards and chain smoking. By the time she turned around again, I'd stripped off the rest of my clothes. As far as I was concerned, they were ruined. Some smells will never wash out.

"And you're naked," commented Rebecca, averting her eyes in some semblance of modesty that didn't suit her.

"Don't get any ideas."

"The way you smell? The only one that crosses my mind is throwing up."

"Believe me, I'm planning to wear every bar of soap in the place down to a nub. But first I have a special project I need to set Gladys to.

"Do me a favour," I added.

"What?" she asked suspiciously, knowing all too well the sort of favours naked men usually ask.

"Burn those," I said, pointing at the pile of clothes on the floor.

I ran a bath while Rebecca transferred my discarded garments to a garbage bag for me, touching them as little as possible before sealing them and their stink in with a twist tie.

"I think it's time to retire the murse as well," she called to me over the sound of running water as I poured a bath.

"Leave my satchel alone," I called back. "I have to sort through it and decide what can be salvaged."

Rebecca took the bag of spoiled clothes straight down to the dumpster in the basement, eager to see it gone. As I let the tub fill, I walked over to the hall closet, opened the door, and pulled the chain on the light. The skull on the upper-most shelf stared back at me. Gladys looked cross, but to my eye she always did.

"Are you going to be a good girl?"

"Fffff!" she hissed, forming her first word after a long day isolated in time-out.

"I know, I know," I said, cutting her off. "Fak me. But seriously, no more hitmen. Promise me that much."

Gladys was silent, as though internally debating this issue. Finally she agreed, "No mar heetman."

With that assurance I reached up and retrieved her from the shelf.

"I radder keel yoo mysef," she muttered.

"That's the spirit."

I set Gladys down on the coffee table and went to my satchel to retrieve the plastic bag full of brains. I'd have to do something about my kit. The satchel reeked of ghoul as well.

There was far too much brain matter scattered around the apartment these days, my own included. After getting stuck with multiple corpses with nothing in their heads to chat with, I was now experiencing an embarrassment of riches. Something needed to be done with the mess that was made of Louie if I was going to get any straight answers out of him. I needed to separate the wheat from the chaff or, more accurately, what was Louie and what were bits of contaminating other. It would be a long, laborious process, like trying to take apart the gears of a finely tuned machine that had been assembled wrong, and rebuild it to its original factory settings. So rather than try to do it myself, I was going to delegate.

"Open wide," I told Gladys, as I unhooked her skull cap and swung it open on its hinge.

I left the plastic bag sealed and crammed the whole thing into Gladys's empty cranium. She didn't care for the intrusion.

"Wat da fak is thees?" she demanded.

"Brains," I said. "I know it's been a long time since you had one in your skull, but you're going to sort this out for me. Figure out what belongs to who and separate them accordingly."

"Wat am I? A fakkin bleendar?"

"No, you're not a blender. You're an unblender."

"I doont no how to do thees sheet!" she protested.

"It's like filing. You're a secretary, so file."

"I no seecritarry. I a fakkin sleeve is wat I am," grumbled Gladys.

"See? Now you even sound like a real secretary."

"I no do thees!" she insisted.

"You want to go back in the closet? Alone, in the dark?"

Gladys considered this alternative.

"No," she said quietly.

"Then behave."

I considered how I'd played or misplayed the evening, second-guessing myself as I soaked, rinsed, and repeated in the tub. Spotting my quarry flash by me, almost close enough to reach out and touch—if I wanted to get my arm clipped off by a speeding subway train that is—was vexing. I might have given chase, but he had too much of a head start and who knew where he was going to get off or transfer. I'd decided to call it quits for the night and grab a train heading in the opposite direction, towards home. I didn't buy a ticket, having inadvertently hopped the turnstile in the most round-about way possible. I figured after the evening I'd just had, the world owed me a free ride.

I got out of my second consecutive shower and towelled off. As far as I could tell, the smell had departed with all the scrubbing and I was sterile enough to perform surgery. Even then, I could still see a distinct impression of that damn green smiley-face stamped on the back of my hand at Gallery Nowhere a week ago. Soap was no match for the permanent-ink. Even dying and coming back from the dead three times failed to get my branded skin to regenerate normally. It made me wonder if I was equally stuck with my milky eye. I considered what sort of death and regeneration would reset these marks and wipe the slate clean. None that came to mind held any appeal, so I decided the wait-and-fade approach was best.

I found my bathrobe hanging from a hook on the back of the door and put it on before emerging from the steamy bathroom. Rebecca was back from taking out the trash, so I asked for her verdict.

"Better?"

She sniffed at the air around me and declared, "You smell a bit...girlie."

I raised the sleeve to my nose to judge for myself.

"That's your perfume. You spent half the day sleeping off the party in my robe."

"So I did."

Rebecca looked back to the couch she had been surfing on for the last twenty-four hours and spotted Gladys on the coffee table in front of it.

"I see you pulled Gladys out of mothballs," she commented.

"You knew about that?" I asked, surprised. "I thought you were passed out by the time I threw her in jail."

"I was in and out. I was going to parole her early if you didn't come home soon, poor thing."

"Poor thing? She hired a hitman to bump me off. And charged it to me!"

"Smart, too. You should be pleased. It's not like you hired her for her distracting good looks."

"I'd be happy if she was that clever about her secretarial duties."

"Hey, Gladys," Rebecca greeted the skull, sitting back down on the couch. There was no answer.

"Gladys?" Rebecca asked again, knocking on her skull cap. "Anyone home?"

Noticing Gladys didn't sound like her usual hollowed-out self, Rebecca unhooked the cap and swung it open, revealing the sack of brains stuffed inside.

"What the hell did you fill poor Gladys with now?"

"Leftovers," I said vaguely.

"What is that goop?" Rebecca asked, poking the bag with a finger and making the grey neural tissue squish over to one side.

"I gave her a project. She's actually earning her keep for a change, so let her be. She needs to concentrate."

I gently but firmly removed Rebecca's prodding finger from the skull and shut the cap back in place.

Rebecca fell back into the couch cushions and groaned, "I'm starved! And I've already eaten every potato chip you had stashed away."

"I could open a can of soup," I suggested.

"Don't you have any real food in the place?"

"Apparently nothing that will satisfy you."

"So let's order something," she said, and pre-emptively added, "Not pizza again."

As if commanded, the doorbell rang.

"You read my mind and ordered already! Just tell me it's not pizza."

"I didn't order anything," I told her.

"Are you expecting someone?"

"No," I said, not sure if that was true. How many entities, demons, and living-dead creatures of the night had I run afoul of recently? And how many of them knew exactly where to look me up? Too many.

I hit the intercom button and asked, "Yes?" tentatively.

"I come in peace, before you get any ideas about leaving me out here in the cold," said the crackling voice over the speaker.

I was actually relieved it was only Reynaldo at the lobby door. But I still considered whether or not I should buzz him in before I ultimately did. He sounded unusually conciliatory, and that alone piqued my curiosity.

"Reynaldo the Fuckhead coming to visit again," Rebecca commented skeptically. "When did you two become besties?"

"We seem to keep falling under the illusion that we can use the other's services to our benefit. We've been proven wrong repeatedly, but here we are again, it seems."

"What does he want this time?"

"I don't know, but it must be something good if he's back so soon after our last exchange."

I cracked the door when I heard the elevator arrive on my floor. Reynaldo opened the gate and let himself out. He sauntered down the hall, raising a hand in greeting. He was alone.

"You should get that fixed," Reynaldo commented, rapping a knuckle on the door just beneath my shot-out spyhole as he stepped inside. I noted that sometime during her day-long stay, Rebecca had done a cursory repair job, taping over the hole with a conspicuous "X" of masking tape. Better than nothing I suppose, and probably better than the superintendent would ever get around to.

Rebecca excused herself and disappeared into another room to avoid interacting with Reynaldo—something she found impossible to accomplish sober. After a few moments of impolite greetings, he took a seat without being asked to and I, as his host, offered him nothing whatsoever.

"I have a confession to make," Reynaldo announced.

"You're coming out?" I said, stealing his thunder as rudely as I could. "This will surprise absolutely no one."

"I'll have you know my dear mother still clings to certain delusions that I'm reluctant to strip from her. In any case, it's nothing so personal as that. It's more of a confession in regards to a matter of ethics."

"Oh, don't worry about it, Reynaldo," I assured him. "We've already established you have none."

Oddly, Reynaldo didn't seem as eager as usual to engage in tit-for-tat banter. Something was genuinely bothering him.

"There was a man—if you can call him that—who contacted me, oh, let's see..." He trailed off, counting the days. "I guess it was a little over a week ago now."

That's when I knew where this was going. Charlie Nocturne had made the rounds. And he'd been thorough, hitting up all my associates. Even the ones I didn't want to associate with.

"This man, let me guess, was all in black. And you never could quite make out his face, could you?"

"And they call *me* psychic."

"He was looking for a certain necromancer by the name of Rip Eulogy," I said, a statement not a question.

"He was indeed. And I must confess I put him off. I thought he might be a client, interested in hiring your services for some bit of skullduggery. Terrible of me, I know, but I feigned ignorance as to your whereabouts and sent him on his way. A touch of competitor subterfuge on my part. Nothing personal, you understand."

"No, just dickish. Which is fine. I expect you to be dickish."

"The thing is, I find myself feeling a teensy bit bad about my lacking performance at your party the other night."

"Failure. I think the word 'failure' best sums it up."

"Let us simply agree my results were inconclusive. Disappointingly so. And I want to make amends."

"Really? Even after the séance? I figured you would have written it off as payback."

"In retrospect, your failure was something I should have anticipated. My..." the word stuck in Reynaldo's throat, "...failure—that was doubtless a shock to everyone."

"I'm sure we all took it in stride."

"No, no! No need to soft-pedal it," he exclaimed, apparently misconstruing my sarcasm for a genuine attempt at reassurance. "Everyone was thoroughly disillusioned, I'm sure."

"So you want to make amends for screwing me out of a job again. Well that's real big of you Reynaldo. I'll accept a personal cheque. Certified preferably. Cash is king, of course."

Reynaldo offered a sigh in lieu of financial compensation.

"Not *quite* what I had in mind."

"So why are you here, then?"

Reynaldo reached into his coat and retrieved his wallet. He unfolded it and pulled a slip of paper from one of the leather pockets.

"This fellow who wants to meet with you left a card."

Before he could even show it to me, I cut him off.

"I already have one. He left it with Wilbur. Solid black, with a name laminated in black."

"That's the one," confirmed Reynaldo.

"Useless, really."

"To you, perhaps. Whereas someone of my considerable talent can use such a personal item to establish a connection."

He held the rectangle of black card stock to his forehead and closed his eyes, making a theatrical demonstration of the clairvoyance involved. It was only for show. I'm sure the real technique was vastly different, but Reynaldo would have considered that a trade secret not to be performed in front of anyone, least of all me.

"I made contact again, tonight, not more than an hour ago. We exchanged words, thoughts. He left me with a very indistinct psychic impression. So much clutter and calamity. I've never experienced anything quite like it. The noise in my head was unbearable."

Reynaldo wasn't just making small talk. Chatting with Charlie Nocturne across the psychic plane had disturbed him. If this had just happened, he must have run straight here to see me. Reynaldo talked to plenty of weirdos, living and dead. It took a lot to shake him, and I'd never seen him shaken before. Not like this.

"Have you ever sat in the middle of a crowded theatre and just listened?" he continued. "All those individual voices chatting with each other impatiently as they wait for the show to start. And the closer it gets to the curtain rising, the louder and more desperate the chatter grows. No individual voice is discernable and it becomes a burbling white noise, like a waterfall, waves on a beach, or pouring rain. It's a natural, organic sound, and I actually find it quite soothing. I close my eyes and listen, and sometimes it's so relaxing I'm disappointed when the show begins and the crowd hushes itself to a respectful silence."

I let Reynaldo muse and said nothing.

"This fellow—thing, being, creature—whatever it is, reminds me of that. Even as he spoke to me in clear, distinct terms, there was that background noise present, that chatter. But it wasn't soothing, wasn't natural, wasn't like anything I've ever heard in this world or the next. And I don't mind telling you it made me afraid."

This wasn't what I ever expected to hear from Reynaldo.

"Afraid? Why afraid?"

"Because I knew, whatever it is, whatever it wants, I can't deal with it. Some things are beyond even me. And some things, I'm reluctant to admit, fall exclusively into your purview."

I knew that couldn't have been easy for him to admit. This wasn't Reynaldo the Wise who had come to see me this night, or even Reynaldo the Fuckhead. This was Reynaldo the Fearful. Confronted at last with a bit of business from the beyond he couldn't handle, he'd come to me with his tail between his legs. As much as he downplayed it, something had frightened him more than any ghost or vengeful spirit he'd ever encountered before, and he wanted me to take care of it and make it go away. Despite his facile attempts to bullshit and belittle, I didn't feel like kicking him when he was down. There was no sport in it.

"You know where Charlie Nocturne is?" I asked.

"At the moment, no. But I know where he'll be. You see, I've taken the liberty of setting up a rendezvous between the two of you."

Not only was Reynaldo looking to me to deal with the situation, he wanted to know it was being dealt with immediately.

"Where and when?" was all I needed to know. I was done dancing around with Nocturne. It was time to meet.

"He told me he would await you in the Stutterson Furnace at midnight. You know it?"

"Yeah. But won't it be closed at that time?"

"I think that's the idea. Privacy."

"He mention why he hasn't just come up to see me himself? He has my address."

"Perhaps he's shy."

"So much for a relaxing evening in," I announced, getting up. Some fresh clothes and I'd be on my way out again. Reynaldo got up too, eager to leave now that he'd passed the baton.

"I don't suppose you could give me a lift, save me cab fare," I said.

"I felt I owed you something," he said. "Brokering a meeting was it. I'm afraid a lift across town exceeds my feelings of remorse."

Reynaldo the Fuckhead was back. I was almost glad to meet his acquaintance again.

"Well, I'll be sure to say 'hi' on your behalf."

"No need," he assured me.

"It's only polite."

"Please don't," he said more firmly. "Having communicated with this—I'll say person for lack of a better term—twice now, I have no desire for any further contact."

Reynaldo tossed his copy of Charlie Nocturne's card onto my coffee table, wanting no further contact with that either. Before tucking his wallet away, he pulled a stack of papers out of the billfold.

"Oh, and if you could see your way to distributing these to your party guests."

I took the slips from him, half a dozen photocopied designs on note-sized purple paper.

"What are they?"

"Vouchers. For a reading. Let us call them a rain cheque for my misfire at the party."

"That's really generous of you, Reynaldo."

But of course I spoke too soon.

"Five percent off. Ten if they schedule a weekly session."

"I'll tell them Christmas came early," I said, and saw him out the door.

I made sure to feed Reynaldo's vouchers to the paper shredder while he was still within earshot. Once she was sure we were alone again, Rebecca reappeared.

"You heard?" I asked her.

"Enough," she said. "Don't go."

"Why not?"

"Because I'm telling you, don't go. For once just listen to me!"

"He's been working his way through everybody I know, one by one," I told Rebecca. "He went by to see Wilbur, Tracy. Even Reynaldo as it turns out. Possibly Louie, but I can't be sure yet. Maybe others."

"Me," she said softly.

"You?"

Rebecca started pacing as she spoke, never looking at me once.

"He came to me first, like he already knew me. He said he wanted me to set up a meeting. I thought you'd be interested because...well...if you saw him, you'd know why. So I called you that night to come down to Gallery Nowhere. He wanted to meet you there, specifically there for some reason. You're always complaining about how all the real players have gone underground. I thought I did good."

"So what happened? You bait and switch me into a meet-and-greet with The Amazing Barfo instead?"

She nodded.

"I caught Tom's act a couple of times around town. We spoke once, briefly. I mentioned you, but I was never planning on making the introduction."

"Is that so?" I said, unconvinced.

"What am I, stupid? I knew you'd turn your nose up at a vomiting magician."

"You're right. I'm a snob that way."

"I had someone else in mind. Some*thing* else. This Charlie Nocturne *thing*."

"So what happened?"

"I saw..." she tapered off and grew evasive. "Stuff. I saw some weird stuff and I got cold feet, so I introduced you to Tom when he came out of the back and pretended he was the one I got you out of bed to meet."

"*You* got cold feet from seeing something weird?"

She looked me in the eye once more and confirmed, "Yeah."

"Weird stuff?"

"Yeah."

"So what was this stuff, and what was so weird about it that it was weird even by the high standards I've set?"

I could see Rebecca weighing it in her mind, but finally she walked away and would only say, "I don't want to talk about it."

I let it go. Knowing Rebecca, she'd tell me when she was ready or not at all. There'd be no squeezing it out of her.

"I think he's trying to show me he can get to anybody I know," I said. "And in case that message wasn't clear enough, now he might be showing me he can kill anybody I know."

"What do you mean?" Rebecca sounded alarmed, but it was only fair to give her a heads up.

"Louie's dead."

Rebecca sat down heavily in the nearest chair.

"Fuck me. He was just here last night."

"You saw him more recently than that. What's left of him."

I gestured towards Gladys's skull.

"Oh my God," she said, making the connection with the bag of goop she'd been poking at not ten minutes before. And sitting right next to the skull was Charlie Nocturne's thick black card, looking heavy enough to break straight through the glass top like a stone.

"I recovered what I could," I explained, "but it's a muddled mess. Gladys is working on the jigsaw puzzle for me now. I need to know what happened, but it's going to take her time to put Louie's marbles back together in proper working order. If Charlie Nocturne thinks he's arranged for another meeting with me, I don't want to stand him up again. The last time I did, I wound up dead."

"I thought we established that was Gladys's doing."

"Except maybe it wasn't. I visited the company in charge of the hit today. They said the contract was still open, incomplete. So my mystery shooter is still a mystery."

Rebecca said nothing.

"It keeps coming back to Charlie Nocturne. I think Louie was meant as a message. I don't want him sending any more."

Θ

I couldn't be positive it was this Charlie Nocturne who reprogrammed the rabbi and issued new orders, but it was a fair guess. How many more of my recent misfortunes he was responsible for also remained to be seen, but he was the prime suspect across the board. Leaving the apartment, I had a tough debate with myself about how much I needed to prepare for this meet and greet and how well armed I ought to be. My satchel still stank of the charnel pits below Hillside General, and most of the essentials had been left behind as ballast. I very much doubted any of my usual tools of the trade would have proved at all helpful in the event of an ambush anyway. I couldn't even diagnose what I was about to come face to face with despite what I already knew from eyewitnesses. This was a whole other sort of unknown. Much different than, for instance, breaking into a hitherto-lost catacomb beneath a hospital morgue. I was certain I wouldn't be digging any holes, for one, so my missing entrenching tool would have been useless weight. And my trusty flashlight was out of commission until I bought new batteries. Even then, it might well be broken beyond repair after being repeatedly smashed into a ghoul's ugly mug. As for the rest, it mostly seemed pointless for what was supposed to be a formal introduction and hopefully civil conversation.

In the end, I opted for only a couple of leftover items. I put on a fresh jacket and stuck my picks in one pocket just in case I had to open a locked door or two to get to the meet. In another I placed the derringer. Whatever Charlie Nocturne was, I didn't expect shooting him would do any good, but according to Death Dealers Incorporated there was still an open contract on my head, and an anonymous hitman who would get around to closing it someday. A gun might persuade him otherwise.

Rebecca shared the cab ride with me as far as her place.

"Are you sure you don't want me to come with you," she asked, like she didn't want to come along at all but felt obliged to make the offer.

"I'll be all right. It sounds like just about everybody else who ran into him made out fine. At least at their first meeting. I mean, he didn't hurt you, did he?"

"No. But the things I saw..."

"The weird things. So you've mentioned. I don't suppose you'd care to elaborate?"

Rebecca wouldn't look at me. She just shook her head no.

"You'd tell me if it was anything that would prevent me from, say, getting eviscerated tonight?"

"Just be careful," said Rebecca as she got out of the car. "And keep your distance."

"He wants to talk," I assured her. "I'll listen."

"Just be sure it's not the listening that gets you in trouble," she said and shut the door.

The cab pulled away from the curb, on its way to the second destination I'd given the driver, before Rebecca could offer any additional advice.

Θ

In theory, at least according to the posted signs, the park closed at 11:00 pm. But that rule only applied to civilians. By midnight the place was thick with junkies and pushers, hookers and johns. Anyone looking for any sort of illicit exchange. They kept off the paths, creeping around in the shadows cast by trees that stood guard for them in front of intrusive street lights, always on the lookout for cops who knew damn well what went on in Stutterson Park after hours and would swing by for an easy arrest when things were slow.

"I got what you need," I was told three separate times by three different solicitors as I made my way to the heart of the park. Sex or drugs, they never specified. Perhaps either, perhaps both if the price was right. I had deep concerns about this meeting, but to linger or delay was to invite a mugging. And so, despite my misgivings, I kept my pace brisk.

The four major pathways in the park all converged on what was known locally as The Furnace. It was actually a public greenhouse with two wings and a central entry topped by a glass-paneled dome. It was home to palm trees and other non-indigenous tropical plants that wouldn't stand a chance if they'd been planted outdoors in a climate that could swing between extremes over the course of an average year. Built a century ago, the idea was to give trapped urbanites a place to go to experience some of the flora they might never be able to see firsthand otherwise. It had made for a popular weekend excursion the first few years it was open, but it soon developed its reputation as The Furnace due to the high temperatures it would reach inside on any warm summer day. With little ventilation, there were many fainting incidents, plenty of dehydrations, and at least a few heat-stroke-induced deaths. Its popularity went into sharp decline, despite the exotic jungle on display, because daytime visits were considered so physically uncomfortable it wasn't worth the effort. In modern times the building was still maintained by the city, but was looking a tad shabby with its peeling white paint exposing the rusty iron framework underneath. Only the garden itself looked as it once did, with a horticulturalist dropping by daily to water and prune. The plants, at least, were able to constantly renew themselves, even as the city around them crumbled from budget cuts and a bad economy.

I was ready to pick my way through the entrance, but found the door already ajar. Break-ins at The Furnace weren't unusual. In the dead of winter, when the thermometer plunged in search of new records lows, doors or windows would be breached by transients and homeless looking for warmth that would keep them alive overnight when none of the shelters would have them. The glass panels in the ceiling caught the sun all day and held the heat in long after it went down. It became known as the toastiest place in town to crash, and probably saved more lives by night than it ever cost by day.

This wasn't a break-in. The lock was intact, the wooden frame around the bolt wasn't splintered. The door was merely open, waiting for me to enter. So that's what I did.

At night, the greenhouse was lit by a few dim halogen bulbs. It was just enough light to allow any patrolling cops to peek inside and see if the building was hosting a shooting gallery that night that needed breaking up. I strolled between the potted plants and counter-top gardens, searching through a jungle of non-sentient life for one sentient being who likely wasn't alive at all. Even with the tiny bulbs illuminating my path, the street lights outside were casting more shadows than they could compete with. I longed for my dearly departed flashlight, but resolved to decipher each irregular shadow cast by alien foliage and twisted tree limbs until I found the one I was looking for.

It was his eyes that gave him away in the end. They were the only feature I could make out, like twin splotches of phosphorous paint that were at the trailing end of their charge. I might not have even noticed if it weren't for the fact that everything else around them was so dark. Once I centred on them, I could trace the outline of a head and a wide-brimmed hat sitting on top of a long coat and a pair of legs. The collection of features suggested a man standing silently in the corner, watching my every move as I hunted through the rows of plants, ducking under the greenery that hung in my way and pawed at my face with the points of rubbery leaves.

I stopped in place and stared at him, letting him know he'd been discovered. I tried to make out any details, but there were none to see. The silhouette may have suggested a man, but the darkness of his entire body only confirmed the absence of a man. Charlie Nocturne was a man-shaped hole in the world, a negative space that promised no escape for anything—not even light.

We faced each other for a long time in that glass-paneled chamber, saying nothing, not moving an inch. I hardly breathed. He didn't breathe at all.

"I got your message," I said at last, and then added, "Messages."

"And you have come at last," he said in voice that sounded hollow, but human enough to pass.

"Do I know you?" is what I chose to say next. It seemed an odd question to ask, but there was a certain familiarity I'd felt from the moment I first saw him. Even before he spoke, his presence, simply standing still and silent, staring in the dark as a statue might, filled me with an eerie sense of déjà vu I wasn't used to and didn't like.

"You do," he confirmed.

"I can't say the face is familiar. You'd need to have a face for it to ring any bells."

He seemed neither insulted nor amused by my observation, so I continued.

"You've been following me. Stalking me."

"I have," he said.

I was a bit taken aback. I didn't expect such a casual admission.

"As you have been following me," he added. "Our paths are intertwined, you and I."

"Have we met?"

"Many times. And yet this is our moment of introduction. I am Charlie Nocturne."

He already wasn't making a lick of sense, but I rolled with it.

"'Charlie Nocturne,' huh? Well, I guess I've heard worse stage names."

"Yours for instance."

"Mine isn't a stage name."

"Nor mine. I was called this name once a long time ago. It stuck."

"Well I hope whoever saddled you with that moniker got a good kick in the ass."

"Actually, it was a bullet in the back," he commented.

"Did you put it there?"

"I do not kill people, Mr. Eulogy. I watch them die. These are very different things."

"Oh yeah? And is that why you wanted me here? To watch me die?"

"No. I have seen you die before, Mr. Eulogy. It is one of the things that brings me to you."

"My death?"

"The lack of hold it has on you."

Charlie Nocturne seemed to know too much about me, and I still didn't know a thing about him. I couldn't even narrow him down to a class of being. In my experience, he— or it—was completely unique. I suppressed a shiver. It wasn't just his overall creepiness. There was a decided chill in the air that seemed to radiate from him. He'd been standing in that spot, awaiting my arrival, long enough to make the plants in his immediate vicinity wilt.

"You keep suggesting we've met, but I'm sure we haven't. I'd remember."

"You will in time. From your current perspective, however, you will not," he said, which was no help at all.

"Cryptic. Great. I can never get my fill of cryptic bullshit spouted by supernatural entities from other planes of existence."

"So you have told me before."

"Oh, I have not!" I shouted in frustration. "We've never met! That much I know!"

"What you think now and what you will come to understand are two very different things."

"What do you want from me?" I asked testily. "And if we've bumped into each other so many times before, what's so special now?"

"Events are aligning, the time is ripe, and you have been marked," he said.

"What do you mean, 'marked?'"

Nocturne raised a hand to his face and pointed at his right eye, or the glowing thing that appeared to be an eye.

"That's not a mark! It's just a loss of pigment in one iris."

"It is a sign. Your recruitment is at hand."

I didn't like the sound of that. I'm not much of a volunteer and I'm stingy with my favours. Any form of recruitment sounded sinister and unwelcome.

"Look," I said, "don't take this personally, Charlie, but just what in the hell are you?"

Again, there was no offence taken. There was barely a reaction to my words. Only a simple statement of fact that seemed to make perfect sense to him and that I couldn't grasp.

"I am a doorway," he told me. "Through me you can pass to any place I have been, at any time I was there."

I looked around at the shabby ruins of a once elegant arboretum with its flaking paint and dirty windows.

"Doesn't sound very handy if you spend your days taking meetings in dumps like this."

"I have walked the earth for ages and travelled to its corners most distant. These places and times are but a step away, if you so wish. Would you like to watch Pompeii be smothered in a blanket of ash? I was there."

I curled my lip dismissively and told him, "Not the Italian vacation I've had in mind."

"Would you like to watch the Lusitania take twelve hundred souls in as many seconds as it sank off the Irish coast? I was there."

I shook my head and said, "I'm not much of a swimmer."

"Would you care to watch Spanish conquistadors destroy an entire ancient empire by sword and cannon fire, enslavement and disease? I was there."

"I think I'll opt for a different travel agent, thanks."

"But of course I would know if you had visited any of those places and times through me. I was there. And you were not."

"It seems you have a real taste for history's trouble spots," I noted.

"You could say so."

"How about recent history? There's been a few murders of late. Me for one. My friend, Louie, for another. I don't suppose you were involved in any way?"

"No," was all he said.

"Right. Of course not. You just like to watch. And how about Rabbi Reubenski?"

"I knew him."

I was surprised he was so forthcoming.

"Did you?" I said stupidly.

"He had been aware of me for years. Devout men often are. I was the one who recommended your services to him."

"So that was you," I pondered aloud. "Why toss me a client? What was in it for you?"

"It accomplished things that needed doing."

"And were you the one who killed him once they got done?"

"I sought to meet with him once more. Back in this city where I was attending to business. There was one more step for him to take before his part in this affair was complete. But no, I did not kill him. I was there when he was murdered. I saw it happen. As did you."

I shook my head. Whatever had happened between Nocturne and the rabbi in that back alley had nothing to do with me.

"I was on the other side of town watching bad bands and gross-out magic tricks when Reubenski got murdered."

"The rabbi was not murdered where and when you think he was. You witnessed it personally, but you do not know it yet."

"He was killed in an alleyway behind a kosher deli a week ago. His own remains told me as much."

"That is where and when he fell. It is not where and when he died."

"More cryptic bullshit," I declared. "If you have something to tell me about the murder, I'm all ears. Otherwise fuck off."

"Explaining it to you, unenlightened as you currently are, is too difficult. It will be better if I just show you. And in showing you, I will set you on your path."

For the first time, Charlie Nocturne moved, stepping forward so smoothly, it felt like he was drifting on a slight draft I couldn't feel.

"Hey, a little distance please," I demanded. "I'm very particular about my personal space when I'm talking with an unknown..."

I was still trying to come up with a term for what sort of unknown Charlie Nocturne was when he threw open his coat—or at least the dark mass that was coat-shaped—and swallowed me whole into the dark void of negative space that constituted what could only loosely be described as his physical body.

Θ

The next sensation I felt was pain. I had passed through the void of Charlie Nocturne and come out the other side, only to land hard on asphalt with no sense of balance, space, or time.

"Ow! What the fuck did you just do to me? Where the hell am I?" I demanded, rolling over onto my back. Charlie Nocturne stood over me in a space I didn't immediately recognize. Somehow we were both suddenly outdoors—still in the city, but nowhere near the park.

"Mr. Eulogy," he said. "I was not expecting you."

"How could you not be expecting me? We were just talking!"

"We were not talking here and now, you and I. It was another man I was just this moment dealing with. An acquaintance of yours, I believe. A client."

I looked around and saw a few familiar points of interest. I had been here before, recently. In fact I'd been discussing this exact place only seconds ago. I was in the alley behind the deli where the rabbi's body had been discovered.

"Reubenski," I said aloud.

"We arranged to meet here, and passage was provided."

"What?" I asked pointlessly, still trying to get up to speed. "Why?"

"To meet his fate," he explained unhelpfully. "He returns from that meeting now."

A second figure came spilling out of the black void of Charlie Nocturne exactly as I just had. I barely had time to roll out of the way before the man smacked into the same patch of pavement I occupied. He landed much harder than I did. There was no instinct to throw his arms out to cushion his fall. He was already dead.

I started to turn the body over, but stopped. I already knew who it was, even though it made no sense to me in the moment. I didn't need to see the face. The missing ring finger on his left hand already identified the man.

"Holy shit!" I said, simply because I had to say something, anything.

"Now I must take my leave," said Nocturne. "You are too early."

"For what?"

"Our appointment."

"What appointment?"

"It is not set for the here and now, but someplace else and soon. I shall see you then."

He turned and strode away briskly. At least it looked like a stride. I heard no footsteps and doubted he was actually walking. It was only the shape of a walk, like Charlie Nocturne was the shape of a man.

"Wait!" I called after him. "If you didn't kill him, who did?"

The street was dark and there were many shadows. He vanished among them without another word. And for the first time in my life, for the first time ever, things had suddenly gotten too weird even for me. I didn't know what the fuck was going on.

Chapter Fifteen

Encore

I FELT THE RABBI'S pulse to confirm he was dead. He was. And very freshly dead, with a large wedge of his skull smashed in. The wound was still bleeding even though his heart had stopped. It could only have been a matter of moments since his soul departed his battered and abused body. Any newly freed consciousness is at its most scattered and confused when it first breaks contact with its body— especially so in the case of violent, sudden deaths. Even with the corpse on hand and the brain intact, I wouldn't be able to make contact with the spirit until it had settled down and came to grips with what had just happened to it. That could take hours, and I didn't have hours if I was going to catch up with Charlie Nocturne and get some answers out of him. Answers to questions like: how the hell did my life just get rewound to the wee hours of last Friday?

I was in a hurry, but was compelled to search Reubenski's body for some clue as to what had happened to him and where he had so suddenly come from. His clothes were dirty, like he'd crawled to the back alley rather than tumbled there through a supernatural portal. There was no wallet or identification in any of his pockets, no way for the police to guess who he might be when they found him. That was consistent with the story as I already knew it. His coat pockets weren't completely empty, however. I had thought I heard a crunch when he landed on the pavement. Sure enough, there was broken glass in one of the side pockets. And mixed in among the shards were two tiny tin jar caps. The two halves of the single bone shard they'd once contained were gone— doubtless fused back together now that they'd been set free. Why he still had them with him months later was unclear, but if he was carrying around Csaba Szabo's remains on this unknown errand he was running, then he must have brought the ashes as well. There was nothing else to find in his clothing, but a clear plastic bag I pulled from his clenched fist troubled me. It was impossible to say for certain if it was the same bag I had vacuumed Szabo's ashes into one night in a columbarium, but it was the same type. This one was torn and empty. No ashes were inside, nor any finger to bind them.

If Csaba Szabo's reanimated cremains had been on Reubenski when he was killed, then they were running free now. Somewhere. Anywhere.

From what I understood about Charlie Nocturne, I had just skipped back through time to this moment. Rabbi Reubenski's corpse had arrived from an entire other time and place. Where or when was beyond me, but if anyone knew it was Charlie Nocturne—the portal—himself. I had to catch up with him. I rose to my feet and ran from the scene of somebody else's crime. I made sure to walk a dozen blocks away from where the corpse lay before catching a cab. It wouldn't help my working relationship with the police if it ever got back to them that I was right at the spot the body was discovered at the exact moment it was dumped there.

Ensconced in the back seat of a taxi, I told the driver to just start rolling while I figured out my destination. If I had arrived on the same night that Rabbi Reubenski was murdered, then there was only one place Charlie Nocturne could be headed. He was going to the appointment Rebecca set up and then broke. With me none the wiser, I'd stood him up that evening. Now, it seemed, I had a second chance to make our meeting. I turned over my options and re-examined them for as long as I dared to. I'd just gained back an entire week of my life, but the clock was still ticking. If I was going to do what I thought had to be done, I needed to make a decision and commit to it.

"You figure out where we're going yet?" the cab driver asked me.

"Do you know Gallery Nowhere?" I asked him.

He did.

Θ

I had the driver let me out a few blocks away from the address. By my watch, reset according to the taxi's digital clock, Rebecca was just stepping outside now to await my arrival and usher me to a meeting she herself would scrap in a short while. I didn't want her to see me approach the building. I wasn't the Rip Eulogy she wanted. She was after a younger, less experienced, less confused model.

The sidewalk in front of Gallery Nowhere was as packed by patrons, coming and going, as I remembered it. The music inside was pounding away, trying to get out. I didn't recognize the tune, but then I probably wouldn't have recognized it if it had been one from the playlist I'd been subjected to the last time I lived out this night. As long as I was early, that was all that mattered.

I spotted Rebecca milling about near the door, bumming a cigarette from one of the many men willing to feed her bad habits. Her back was to me as I approached, but I couldn't linger. I needed to skip the line or she would spot me for sure. That would be bad. If I waited a few minutes longer, I'd show up and spot myself. That would be worse.

I had a look at the back of my left hand and saw that the stamp I'd received a week ago, the first time I'd passed through the entrance, was still in evidence. It was faded, but discernable—enough to try my luck with the doorman. He looked sceptical when I first flashed him my hand, but there was no denying the faint green smiley face was a match for the stamp they were using that night. It vouched for the fact that I'd paid my cover charge and could pop in and out for a smoke, a drug deal, or whatever else went on at the fringes of the venue.

On my way up the stairs I showed my hand to the girl who had rubber stamped it already and would do so again in a moments. I didn't let her get too good of a look at my face. There was no point in blowing her mind unnecessarily.

At the top of the stairs I looked back and saw the next round of line queuers and skippers file in. Rebecca was among them, and with her was a face I wasn't used to seeing outside of a mirror. I ducked into the gallery and got myself lost in the crowd as quickly as possible. Even then, filtering through the throngs, I felt pursued by this echo from my recent past. I knew if I wasn't careful, my incongruous face in the crowd might leap out and alert the last people on earth I wanted to see me there. This was all new territory for me, my very first time-travelling jaunt, and I didn't want to screw things up like a newbie by causing some cataclysmic paradox that might collapse all matter and energy in the universe into a single reality-destroying event-horizon vortex. Or, failing that, I didn't want the embarrassment of that socially awkward moment when you accidentally bump into yourself. I mean, what do you say? "Hi, how were you? How will you be?" Just the effort of getting the tense right made the whole scene seem best avoided.

That's when I saw the passage to the backstage area. It was one space I knew the old me wouldn't occupy, wouldn't look. I slipped in like a stray roadie, stepping over instruments and guitar cases, and trying not to trip on the maze of wires spilling out of sound boards and amplifiers that threatened to start an electrical fire with the first spilled drink. Getting clear of the thick band traffic, I hopped into a narrow holding area reserved for miscellaneous talent to prepare for their turn on stage, and found myself facing a young man in a tuxedo sprinkling flakes into a fish bowl.

"Tom," I said, caught off guard by the accidental meeting I might have anticipated if I hadn't been so busy avoiding an entirely different meeting.

"Hi," he replied, noting the familiarity coming from the unfamiliar face even as he offered his hand. "Have we met?"

I took a moment to consider if we had and remembered we hadn't yet.

"We'll be properly introduced after the show," I told him.

"Are you one of the acts?"

"I'm certainly doing a song and dance right now," I muttered, as I tried to squeeze by and get going before I said something the space-time continuum might regret.

"Are you familiar with regurgitators?" Tom asked me.

"Too familiar."

I noted the goldfish in the bowl, nosed up towards the surface of the water, sucking in one soggy floating flake of fish food at a time.

"Having a quick bite to eat before he gets eaten?" I commented.

"You've seen my act before?"

"I think I may have caught it in the past, yeah."

"Have you seen me do The Fisherman before? I only added it to the act recently. What did you think? I figured I needed a showier climax."

Tom was trying to solicit notes, one performer to another. All I wanted to do was extract myself from this conversation as quickly as possible.

"It ends well, believe me," I assured him.

"It was that or The Fireman. I was torn."

I shouldn't have spent a single moment longer with him than I had to, but I had to ask.

"You've done The Fireman?"

"Nobody's done The Fireman. Not in generations. I could do it—in theory—but I haven't had the nerve to try. The fire's not the dangerous part, it's holding all that water. You can rupture something if you're not careful."

I hadn't considered that. It probably takes years of practice for a regurgitator to distend his stomach far enough to carry that volume of liquid. I was sure, with enough training, Tom could get there in time. It was the one thing in the regurgitator repertoire I might actually be interested in seeing.

"I'm sure we'd all like that routine to make its return to the stage one day."

"Maybe," he said. "One day."

"Have a great show," I told Tom, excusing myself.

"Break a fin," I told his doomed goldfish, and squeezed my way down the rest of the narrow corridor that led to the back of the building.

I passed through a doorway that was blocked off by nothing more substantial than a retro-hippie beaded curtain and found myself by the toilets. There was a regular flow of both men and women in and out of the men's room, but the women's room was shut with an out-of-order sign dangling from the door knob. I remembered there was something up with the women's room that night, but I didn't realize it had been closed for business.

That's when I felt the draft. It came rolling out from under the sealed bathroom door and felt like someone had left a window open, with a winter cold snap blowing in from outside. I stepped closer and the chill penetrated my shoes, making my toes curl. I knew then there was nothing wrong with the women's room plumbing unless the presence of Charlie Nocturne had caused the pipes to freeze. This is where the meeting was to have taken place, a small corner of privacy in a very public venue. The sign was the only barrier on the door keeping people out. It wasn't locked and it opened easily when I turned the knob.

Entering quietly and unseen, I swung the door closed and pushed the dangling out-of-order sign back through the crack before shutting it tight. I was thrown into darkness and left fumbling for the light switch. When I clicked it on, the ugly flickering fluorescents sputtered to life overhead, reflecting their drab light off the chipped white tiles and filthy fixtures. I expected to see Charlie Nocturne standing there waiting for me, but I still jumped when I turned and came face-to-facelessness with him.

"Mr. Eulogy, we may now begin," he said with no further introduction.

"Okay, slow down there, Charlie. I don't know what you think I'm here for, but..."

"You are here now for our arranged meeting."

"No," I corrected. "This meeting was set up, but it never happened. I didn't show."

"And yet here you are."

I didn't have a comeback for that one. I struggled to think of something and failed.

"I see," said Charlie Nocturne sagely. "You have only just started down the path. You are still confused, disoriented. This is understandable."

"All I know is that all this shit happened last week and I didn't know I had an appointment with you back then. I hadn't even heard about you yet. I only meet you for the first time a week from now."

"You may know what will happen in the future, but I do not," he explained. "I am sure we have a great many appointments to come. But right now, you are here for this appointment. And you have been prompt and on time."

"Why would anyone set up a meeting in the women's room of Gallery Nowhere in the middle of the night?" I asked, looking around at the shabby hole we found ourselves in.

"Is it not familiar to you?"

"Not in the slightest. But then, I've never made a habit of hanging around the girls' washroom."

"This was not our mutual acquaintance's choice of time and place. It was mine."

"I'd love to know how you managed to pitch this to Rebecca."

"I believe I made an impression upon her."

Aside from his astonishing command of time and space, Charlie Nocturne also had the gift of understatement.

"Yeah, you make an impression all right," I said under my breath.

But Nocturne wasn't listening to me. He looked up, sensing something. The bands had stopped playing at last and I could hear the shuffling commotion of a crowd filtering out. But that wasn't what had seized his attention.

"Ah, here she comes now," he announced. "If you do not believe you are in the correct time and place, you may wish to keep out of sight to avoid additional confusion."

I didn't have to ask who it was. It could only be Rebecca, at the point in our evening when she had nipped off to confirm the meeting she had arranged, only to return to our seats and introduce me to The Amazing Barfo instead. Had that much time elapsed since I'd stepped into the dark looking for Charlie

Nocturne? It only seemed like a few minutes, not thirty or more. But then, I should hardly expect the passage of time to appear normal in the presence of a being that seemed to exist in all times.

His suggestion to keep out of sight seemed a sound one to me. I darted into one of the stalls and latched the bolt behind me. Stepping up onto the toilet, I peered over the top and saw Rebecca enter, much as I had moments before, shutting the bathroom door behind her and making sure the out-of-order sign remained in place on the other side.

When she saw Charlie Nocturne standing motionless by the sinks, she approached with cautious familiarity.

"He's here," Rebecca announced.

"I know," said Nocturne.

"He's waiting at a table by the stage."

"Are you certain of that?"

"Of course," she said. "Why?"

"How sure are you of anything concerning Rip Eulogy?"

"What do you mean by that?" she asked suspiciously.

"How long have you known him?"

"A long time. Years."

"Not as many as I have, I would say."

"You two know each other already?" asked Rebecca. News to her. News to me.

"We go back quite a way."

"So why did you need me to set you two up?"

"That is difficult to explain. We may have met before, but I need to know more. Much more. Tell me, Ms. Stone, what sort of man is Rip Eulogy?"

"Well, he's a good guy, I guess. A little weird. Kinda cheap," Rebecca summarized.

I felt slightly guilty about eavesdropping on Rebecca's candid opinion of me, but if weird and cheap were the worst she could come up with when put on the spot, I damn near took it as a compliment. Nocturne wasn't satisfied with that assessment, though.

"Do you even know?" he prompted her.

"I know the sorts of the things he can do," Rebecca replied, not sure what he was after.

"Perhaps. But do you know what he is capable of?"

"I've seen him do a lot of crazy stuff if that's what you mean."

"What one does and what one is capable of are two different things. Allow me to enlighten you about the man you know as Rip Eulogy. Simply step inside."

Charlie Nocturne broadened his stance ever so slightly, invitingly. Rebecca peered into the void he outlined, nervous and unsure.

"Inside? Inside you? Inside...there?" she asked.

Rebecca stepped closer for a better view, but there was nothing to see, only the blackest of blacks with the promise of so much more on the other side.

"What's in there?" she said in awe. She might as well have been staring up at the night sky, contemplating the vastness of space.

"Only the truth," stated Nocturne. "See for yourself."

Almost subconsciously, Rebecca took another step forward. I was sorely tempted to leap out of my hiding place and pull her back from the abyss, but a second later she was gone, vanished from sight, transported who-knows-where.

I was about to raise an objection, demand to know where Nocturne had sent her, but before I could do more than draw breath, she was back. Rebecca came spilling out of the empty space that stood in the room, landing on her ass on the grubby toilet floor.

"What the fuck was that?" she demanded of Nocturne. "What the fuck are you?"

"Do not be alarmed, Ms. Stone. I can only show you truth," he assured her. "Things as they have already happened. Things that will happen yet."

Rebecca scrambled to her feet and abruptly retreated from the room.

"Stay the fuck away from me! Stay the fuck away from Rip!" she yelled and was gone.

Before I could even ask what had happened, Charlie Nocturne suddenly doubled over in pain, looking as though he were suffering a severe stomach cramp.

I opened the stall and asked, "What's wrong? You don't look well. You don't look like much of anything, but you kind of look sick."

"Something is coming..." moaned Nocturne. "Something has escaped..."

A hand-sized chunk fell off of or out of him—I couldn't say which—and landed on the floor. There seemed to be no distinct form or features, but it didn't react well to the fluorescents overhead and immediately sprung a number of tendril-like limbs that allowed it to scurry away at a lightning pace. The black splotch dove under the door and squeezed through the narrow space, and I knew at once it was attempting to accomplish two goals. It was seeking shelter from the light and it was following Rebecca. It could only be the harbinger I had dealt with, or rather had yet to deal with. And apparently it had been born of Charlie Nocturne.

"So that's where it came from," I commented academically. I already knew its fate so there was no point troubling myself with it now. "What was it doing in there?"

Charlie Nocturne straightened up again, his momentary discomfort having passed.

"I am a portal," he explained. "But I am also a prison."

"Well don't worry about it. It may have escaped, but it doesn't get far. I deal with the nasty little critter in a few days' time. He gets contained, doesn't cause too much trouble. You don't have many more like that in there, do you?"

"I have a great many more just like it, or as near as. All of them hunger. They wait to feed, but some lose their patience and seek nourishment elsewhere. The wait has been very long."

My confusion wasn't improving and now it was giving me a headache. I wanted answers, sooner rather than later, now rather than never.

"What do you want from me, Charlie? I follow you back here, listen to a bunch of music that was shit the first time around, and watch you cough up demonic entities. What's the point?"

As he had done for Rebecca, Nocturne's stance seemed to swell, beckoning me to merge with the void again.

"Step into me once more," he instructed. "There are things you need to see that have occurred at other times. And other places. And even in this very place. Things that will enlighten you. Things that will answer your questions. And things that will reveal your purpose."

I looked deep into the blackness and saw such absolute nothingness, it was strangely enticing. I found myself leaning towards it.

"You said you can send me to any place and point in time you've been at will," I said, my mind already anticipating the tumble through the dark to a whole other place, a whole other state of being and consciousness.

"No, not at will," he clarified. "I do not decide where the path will take a traveller."

"How am I supposed to know where and when I need to go?"

"You do not decide that either. The path decides. Only the path itself knows. It will take you where you need to be at the moment you need to be there."

It was like standing on the edge of a cliff and feeling compelled to leap off, certain in the knowledge I would fly instead of fall. I rode the moment in time like a wave rolling towards a distant shore it would never reach. It was a mesmerizing feeling, so easy to be swept away by.

And then I abruptly cut it short.

"Nope," I said.

"No?"

Nocturne sounded genuinely surprised and that gave me the upper hand. I liked having the upper hand over incredibly powerful and frightening creatures from the netherworld, even if it never lasted long. It threw them off their game. A bit of self-doubt is good for the soul, especially if that soul is dark and tainted.

"That's right," I told him. "No."

"What do you mean, no?"

Charlie Nocturne's hollow voice wasn't able to express much range of emotion, but he came as close to incredulous as he was likely to get.

"I'm not going through you again, especially if I don't know where and when I'm going to end up. I don't see that working out well for anybody, least of all me. Plus you've just admitted to being chock-full of lesser demons, with maybe a few greater ones stuffed in there for good measure. Screw that, no thanks!"

I turned to leave.

"But you must!" he insisted. "How else will you discover your destiny?"

"Stick my destiny up your black hole. I'm not interested."

I pulled the bathroom door open, but paused before my final exit.

"You may have stranded me in the middle of last week, but that's fine. I don't need you to get back. I'm just going to lie low and live out the week until I catch up with where I'm supposed to be and then it's back to business as usual. No path, no destiny, no earth-shattering revelations about my purpose in life."

"You will pass through me again, Mr. Eulogy," he promised. "I have already seen it."

"Oh, fuck off!" I told him, flicking the light switch and leaving him in the dark as I left. It felt good to tell him to fuck off, even though I was sure he'd prove himself right before long. You have to hate supernatural entities with a near omniscient perspective on things that are unknowable to the rest of us. Smug bastards.

Chapter Sixteen

The Time We Have Left

TIME TRAVEL IS NOT as thrilling as you might assume. I suppose if you're travelling to some glittering future utopia or journeying back to see dinosaurs or historic grandeur in action it might be all right. But reliving a week that was already pretty crap the first time around is dull dull dull. Compounding the problem is the fact that you have to avoid bumping into yourself, or pretty much anyone else you might have interacted with in that same stretch of time. It's no use confusing everybody with a bunch of paradoxes that will never get sorted out to anybody's satisfaction. So I resolved to keep my head down and try to figure out some way I could use my current aggravating circumstances to my advantage. If only I paid attention to the sports page, I might have at least been able to place a bet with a bookie to solve all my financial woes.

After walking out on Charlie Nocturne, I hung around backstage, unnoticed by all, until I was sure Rebecca and I had already left. I only came out of hiding as the last of the staff was mopping up. Passing the stage, I saw Tom sitting on a lone chair, cupping his pulverized co-star in the palm of his hand. He was exhausted and sweaty after the long battle with the undead fish that had ended in the inevitable draw. The fish was still flopping over every few seconds, stubbornly refusing to die again. Tom was crying. For the first time since I played that nasty trick on him, I felt remorse. I walked across the floor to retrieve his shoe and handed it back to him. He never looked up or acknowledged me, and his eyes were too full of tears for him to see who was returning his footwear weapon-of-choice. He took the lone shoe from my hand without a word and returned to cradling the goldfish. I let them share their moment. It was, after all, the beginning of an ugly friendship, and a bonding experience best kept private.

Outside I looked up and down the street to confirm the way was clear. Past-me was gone, in the back of a cab somewhere heading home. Rebecca must have followed soon after in a cab of her own. There was nobody left on the block. I was all alone, lost in last week with nowhere to go. I couldn't return to my apartment since it was obviously occupied, so I considered my other options.

The easiest, smartest thing would have been to check into a hotel and ride out my time there, safely anonymous. But I didn't need a week-long hotel bill added to my already troubled finances. Skipping town sounded similarly expensive. Besides, I thought, this bit of accidental time travel was sure to offer me some opportunity, some do-over I could use to my advantage. I only needed a place to rest and figure it out.

It was unpardonably late to go leaning on somebody's doorbell, but I was willing to add that to the list of unpardonable things I'd done in my life. I didn't know much about Wilbur's sleep habits, but the elderly are rarely deep sleepers in my experience. The closer they get to that final dirt nap, the more easily roused they are—like they're eager to prove they're still present and accounted for, just in case anybody gets any ideas about premature burials. I considered the fact that I'd had some small interaction with Wilbur in the previous/now-current week, and that calling on him might cause confusion and some of those paradoxes I was supposed to be avoiding. But paradoxes be damned, I'd had enough for one evening, and I figured Wilbur was confused at the best of times. A late-night crash on his couch wouldn't muddle things any further than advanced aged and diminished cognitive ability already had. Not likely.

The other advantage Wilbur's townhouse offered was that it was close. I was able to walk there in fifteen minutes flat. It made my very late call even later, but I figured an extra quarter hour of rudeness wouldn't matter as I stood at his door and rang his doorbell repeatedly. At last I saw a light come on. I rang one final time to assure the freshly roused Wilbur that this wasn't a bad dream or some night terror that had woken him at such an ungodly time.

The front door cracked open as far as the flimsy chain lock on the other side would allow.

"Who the hell is it? I have a gun, you know," barked Wilbur through the narrow space.

Had I been a home invader, as opposed to a friendly freeloader, the threat and the chain might have kept me out for as much as two seconds. One good sharp push against the door would have unanchored the chain and put Wilbur on his back. Instead, I decided to disarm him with honesty.

"You don't have a gun, Wilbur. I remember when they turned down your application for a permit."

I assured him at the time that poor eyesight had been the cause, but I expected it had more to do with encroaching senility.

"Maybe I bought one illegally," he countered.

"If you'd had a gun, you would have used it to murder your wife instead of smothering her with a pillow."

It wouldn't have been the smart move, but it would have been the expedient one. It's what guns excel at. Dumb, ill-considered, but quick.

I saw Wilbur peering at me from behind the chain.

"How'd you know I murdered her? Did she say something to you?"

Ah, yes. I'd forgotten I wasn't supposed to know that tidbit yet. Oh well, chalk up one paradox.

"No," I assured him. "She never knew what hit her. I just know—stuff."

Wilbur nodded, satisfied that I did, more often than not, know stuff. He slammed the door in my face, pulled off the chain, and opened it again so I could step inside.

"It's late," he informed me, retying the sash of his housecoat more securely so the night air wouldn't give him a pneumonia-inducing chill through his thin cotton pyjamas.

"Sorry to wake you, but I was in the neighbourhood and I've got nowhere else to go. Mind if I curl up in a chair and take a nap before I pass out? I'm dead on my feet. Or will be soon if I don't get some sleep."

"Trouble with the missus?" he asked me, knowingly.

"There's no missus, Wilbur."

"Kicked you out, did she?"

"No."

"Wouldn't even let you have the couch, huh?"

Wilbur wouldn't be dissuaded from the narrative he'd already invented to explain my arrival.

"Nothing like that," I assured him anyway.

"She sock you one?"

"What?"

Wilbur tapped a finger to his eye in mirror opposite to my own bleached pupil.

"Oh, that," I realized. "No."

"Never seen a shiner like it. She must have really let you have it. Knocked the colour right out."

I moved on.

"So how about it, Wilbur? Is there a sofa or a chair I can curl up on for a few hours?"

"Well..." he began, but then stopped and didn't follow through with the thought.

"I don't want to put you out."

"Oh, it's not that. Not that at all. It's just..."

Wilbur said no more and merely walked away into the next room. I didn't know if that was an invite or not, but I followed him just the same. Once we were inside, I could see what the problem was.

"We used to have a girl who came around once or twice a month to tidy up, but she moved away and I've let things go since Emma's passing."

If you were into kitschy television nostalgia or magician memorabilia, there was enough stacked ceiling to floor to keep you busy for the rest of the decade. Anyone into that sort of thing would have seen the archaeological dig of their dreams. Anyone else would have seen the fire hazard of their nightmares. It would take a dump truck or two to haul it all away to the landfill once the executor of the estate let a select few collectors and antique dealers have their pick in an effort to monetize all that junk.

"It's times like this I hate being a widower. If only Emma were still around. She was a crap housekeeper every bit as much as I am, but it's nice to have someone to share your memories with in your twilight years. Even if those memories are strewn all over the house and threatening to topple over and crush you."

"Maybe you shouldn't have murdered her, then."

"Murder is such a harsh term for it. I helped her pass. She was an unhappy woman. We'd both had enough, really."

"So you're claiming it was a mercy killing."

"A mercy for both of us. I suppose 'murder' is still the correct term since we never openly discussed it. But I like to think an understanding passed between us. A silent understanding, but profound."

"Let's just hope you'll never have to try to explain that to a jury."

"If you can find a clear spot, it's yours," Wilbur offered. "I would say feel free to move some stacks around, but I'm afraid you might cause an avalanche and then I'll never be able to find anything."

Wilbur went back to bed and I ended up pulling down one of the curtains to use it as a blanket once I found an area of exposed carpet wide enough for me to lie on. It was the most uncomfortable sleep I'd ever attempted—and this from a man who calls a casket his bed—but I was still out cold within a minute of setting my head down on the creaky floor. I was exhausted. I'd been up since next week.

Θ

What I'd intended to be a mildly refreshing snooze turned into a long night's sleep. Long enough to stretch well into the next day. It might have kept right on going into the following night, but the light streaming through the window I'd salvaged my curtain bedding from fell across my face as the sun rose higher. I tried squeezing my eyelids shut even tighter, but I could still see the sunbeam shining red right through them. I might have rolled over to seek more darkness and slumber, but my aching back was blocked by half a dozen towers of stacked record albums. They were all brittle, heavy 78s, and I was worried that toppling them might not only break them, but break me as well.

I nearly caused a landslide when I was startled by the doorbell just as I was getting up. My mind raced, trying to figure out who else could possibly be calling on forgotten old Wilbur, and whether he was even there to receive them. He might have already gone to the Wonderama and left me to sleep off my evening, in which case I would have to keep low and pretend no one was home—especially if the visitor was somebody I was actively trying to avoid on this repeat-cycle week.

The front door opened and the caller let themselves in. Keeping away from the windows wasn't going to prevent an awkward encounter at this point.

"Rip?" I heard a voice say. "How'd you beat me here?"

It was Tracy and I froze in place, quickly trying to calculate when I'd last seen her in this timeline and when I was scheduled to see her next. She answered my question for me.

"We just had ice cream all the way over on Noonan Street and you don't drive."

Apparently, from her perspective, I'd just teleported to this neighbourhood when really, right around this time, I was en route to the Wonderama and an uncomfortable drink with Reynaldo. Still, if she could make it to Wilbur's in a timely fashion, so could I.

"I got a cabbie with a lead foot," I explained, hoping that would cover the jump.

"He must have really floored it," she commented. "You had time to go home and change too?"

I realized then that I wasn't wearing any of the same clothes I'd had on the last time I lived through this day.

"I decided my other clothes smelled of old people and funeral homes."

Tracy nodded knowingly, like she knew what I was talking about, but kept with the awkward questions.

"What did you do to your eye?" she asked, sounding genuinely concerned about my new-to-her disfigurement.

"It's nothing."

"Did this just happen now?"

"Pretty much."

"How?" she asked, leaning in for a much closer look.

"I hit my head."

"So it's, like, brain damage or something?"

"I'm fine."

Tracy was still staring into my white eye from only inches away. She took her time.

"Freaky," she breathed.

I took her by the shoulders and moved her back to a more appropriate and comfortable distance.

"Tracy, what are you doing here?"

"I'm here for Wilbur," she said. "Obviously."

"Tracy, dear," I heard Wilbur say as he came downstairs, cleaned and dressed for his Friday afternoon shift.

"You two having a fling I should know about?"

"At my age?" Wilbur asked with a laugh. "Turn the clock back forty years and we'll see."

"You couldn't handle me at half your age, or half that again," Tracy teased.

"No," she told me, "Wilbur gave me a call. He wants to be a pre-need client."

"You want to hire a moirologist? What the hell for?"

Tracy scowled at me.

"Nothing against you or your profession, of course," I assured her, even if she wasn't having any of it. "But Wilbur, you're a local celebrity. Of sorts. There are kids out there who grew up with you. Kids who are adults now. They'll care. They'll remember. They love you."

"That's TV-love, TV-memories," said Wilbur. "It isn't real. They're fond of me because I used to entertain them. But that doesn't mean they know me. If they mourn at all, they'll be mourning their own childhood out of nostalgia. I want someone who knew me to cry for me."

"Even if you have to pay for it?"

"You know I'd be at your funeral regardless," Tracy told him. "I'm not one to turn down a paying gig, but I'd come one way or the other. So would Rip. So would plenty of other people who know you personally."

"Sure sure, I suppose," said Wilbur, who sounded unconvinced. "But nobody's going to twist anybody's arm. An old man, with no family left, kicks off and everybody gets busy all of a sudden. They're young, they're alive, they've got things to do and places to be. And they think to themselves, 'Well if I don't make it, others will. I'll send flowers or a card and that will be good enough.' And what does that get you most times? An empty funeral parlour with a bunch of morticians standing around looking sorrowful and composing their grocery lists in their heads."

Wilbur studied our faces and we had no quick replies to that.

"You know. You're in the business, you've both seen it," he said. "All I'm doing is making sure at least one person I know won't skip it. Tracy will come. Maybe because she's a friend and she wants to, but definitely because she's under contract. Cry or not, that's up to you."

I could see Tracy was already getting a bit weepy.

"Try and stop me," she told Wilbur.

Tracy had Wilbur sign a standard boilerplate contract to retain her future services. Then he was off to do his shift at the store and run into me—past me—again, for a conversation both of us would find mildly mystifying. Once we were all out the door, Tracy excused herself to go home for a nap, followed by an early night. She had a big day ahead of her. There was a double funeral for a suicide pact, and both of the deceased had been pre-needs. Since it was only one service for the two, Tracy figured she'd have to cry twice as hard in order to feel she had upheld her end of the arrangement. I suggested she keep a water bottle strapped to her leg under her mourning attire so she wouldn't get dehydrated, but she was way ahead of me. Spare water was standard issue in her biz. No good running dry at the graveside when the nearest tap, fountain, or coffee machine is half a mile back at the administration building.

"I once ran out of tears at the start of a service and couldn't squeeze a drop through the whole lectionary," she told me, as a parting anecdote. "Luckily it was a church service, so I snuck away to raid the baptismal font. By the last of the eulogies I was able to blubber convincingly, so that saved my ass. But since then, I've always got my spring water within arm's reach to keep the ducts lubricated at all times."

Tracy reached into her purse and produced a litre of brand-name water.

"Want a swig? Maybe some tears will get you your colour back," she said, noting my eye again.

"I'm good," I assured her.

"So you keep telling me."

Θ

So far I had managed to navigate conversations with both Wilbur and Tracy without bringing the space-time continuum crashing down on the universe. Sure it had been awkward, but what in my life wasn't? I can get away with all sorts of awkward, uncomfortable moments because it's expected of me. I always have ample reasons to be inflicting these moments on people. They know there's likely something up and they don't want to ask too many questions for fear of finding out exactly what. Under the present circumstances, it seemed highly improbable that anybody would guess time travel. With that in mind, I decided to press my luck.

I was going to be murdered in a few hours. Someone with a gun would soon be on their way to my apartment looking to blow my head off. There was no use trying to prevent it. I didn't want to fuck around with recent personal history that much. Who knew what it would screw up, or if it was even possible to stop something that had already happened farther down the timeline. What I could do, however, was get a good look at the hitman Death Dealers Incorporated had dispatched to close my file. At least then I'd know who to keep an eye out for in the future once I'd caught up with the present. If circumstances permitted, maybe I could even confront the guy, put a scare into him, get him to quit the case and never try to make good on his first failed attempt.

What does a hitman look like, I wondered. Probably like any other nobody walking around among us. I doubted Death Dealers Incorporated hired any help who looked like a mafia enforcer, a murderous thug, or a crazed psychopath. Their roster of professional murderers was likely blandly mundane, resembling any number of random cubicle drones or telemarketers or fast-food franchise managers. Was there anything about them that made them stand apart from the rest of us? Did they exude a lack of empathy? Could you sense their cold hearts from a safe distance? Probably not. It's why they could get close to their targets, why nobody would think of crossing the street to avoid them, why nobody would refuse directions if they stopped you to ask which way to get there from here. And while you were being a helpful Samaritan, pointing up that street and around that corner, they'd be reaching for the knife, and selecting which two of your ribs to slip it between.

I decided to stake out my own apartment building from the vantage point of a basement walk-down across the street. The half-dozen steps below street level offered me a narrow view between the curb and the flight of steps leading up to the brighter, costlier flats above. I hoped this would provide me enough urban camouflage to remain hidden from anyone else staking out the street, and that my presence would go unnoticed by whoever's dingy rental I was camping out in front of.

Seeing as I had arrived for the main event so early, I risked a trip up to my place to grab a snack. The fridge was stocked with a variety of leftovers that were due to go bad and be thrown out after old-me spent the next few days lying around dead. I already knew from experience that I didn't notice anything missing when I threw out the previous week's Chinese takeout cartons, so I didn't hesitate to bum a meal off my past self.

"Yoo bak errly," Gladys commented when she heard me rummaging through the fridge.

"And I'm going right back out," I told her from the kitchen.

"Beezie beezie beezie."

"No rest for the wicked," I agreed.

"Asshools eeder."

I was reluctant to continue another uncivil conversation with Gladys while we were in two separate rooms, but the thought of my imminent assassination preoccupied me, even though it wouldn't be me taking the bullet this time. Not quite, at least.

"Gladys, do you resent me?"

"Of carse I reseent yoo, yoo my bass."

Ask a stupid question.

"I mean for your present circumstances."

"Wha yoo meen?"

"I brought you back from the dead. Do you consider that a good thing or a bad thing?"

My question seemed to catch Gladys off guard. She thought about it at any rate. Then the phone rang, cutting off whatever answer she may have formed.

"Let the machine get it," I told her.

After the third ring, the machine picked up and recorded a brief "Call me back," from Detective Frenz.

"Yoo call heem bak?"

"Later," I said, not bothering to explain I already had.

Gladys still hadn't answered my question, so I tried again.

"What do you remember about being dead?"

"Natheeng. Bat I mees it."

"You miss it?"

"I mees been deed. I mees been aleeve. I mees haffeng a boody.

I understood her last two points. The first, not so much.

"What do you miss about being dead?"

"I doont remeembar."

"Then how can you miss it?"

"Becass wen I was deed, I doont mees anytheeng elz."

Θ

I'd never seen so much of my neighbours as in those hours leading up to my murder. The comings and goings continued at a steady trickle of unfamiliar faces, and I realized I had no way of knowing which might be my killer. If they let themselves in with a key, I assumed they lived there. If they were buzzed in after a quick exchange at the call box, I assumed they were known to somebody who lived there. All I could do was watch for one who looked like they didn't belong— who had to bullshit their way inside, jimmy the lock, or sneak in behind someone else before the front door swung shut and locked. The only person I recognized for sure was myself, coming home after a bad day, oblivious to the fact that it was about to get much worse.

I lost count of the entries and exits, and as the sky darkened I knew the moment of truth was coming up soon. I didn't know the precise time the shot was fired, but I had to guess the killer was already inside by now, had passed right in front of me, or maybe slipped in through the garage or emergency exit out of my line of sight. I would have to go in for a closer look, catch him in the act, and get a look at his face as he fled the scene.

I came out of my hunting blind and crossed the street. Before I could get to the door, another arrival walked up the steps and blocked my way. I waited for him to produce a key, or ring one of the apartments, but he made no move to do so. At first I thought his back was to me, taking his sweet time reading the list of occupants next to the row of buzzers. As I drew closer, however, I realized he was facing me— staring right at me. It was an easy mistake to make. A pitch-black figure in a coat and hat looks about the same from the front as he does from behind.

"Well, well. Charlie Nocturne. You don't look like a hired gun and I wouldn't have figured firearms were your style."

"You assume I know what you are talking about," he said. "You are mistaken."

"What brings you here at this exact moment, I wonder."

"I have come so that we may resume our discussion. So that you can resume your journey."

"Not interested," I said, "But on the bright side, you're just in time to miss me. I'm about to get murdered upstairs. Want to watch?"

"As you wish," he said. "Invite me in."

Lots of entities need an expressed invite in order to enter your home, which is why I'm stingy with my invites to anybody but clients and close associates. Even then, I usually prefer to meet on neutral ground. Hitmen, on the other hand, don't need an invite. In fact, they tend to always operate without one. They prefer their marks don't know they're coming at all. An official invitation would ruin the surprise.

"If it turns out you were the one who shot me, I'm going to feel damn foolish for letting you in," I said, and turned my key in the lock.

I decided to take the stairs. I didn't want to get caught in the elevator with my killer. Elevator rides with strangers can be awkward enough as it is, but are probably more so if that stranger just blew your brains out. Nocturne was right behind me and I was about to tell him to hurry up when I heard the gunshot farther up the stairwell. My murder had just happened, and my brief reunion with Charlie Nocturne had made me miss it.

I left the shadowy entity behind and sprinted up the steps, three at a time, until I spilled out on my floor. I looked up and down the hall, but there was no sign of anyone. I could see my door, a dozen paces away, with the spyhole missing—replaced with a slightly larger hole and outlined with a gunpowder scorch mark.

There was another dark splotch on the floor. At first I thought it might have been the result of a second gunshot, but then I saw it move, edging towards the door and then sliding right under it. It took me a moment to make the connection, but I knew what I had just spotted by the time Charlie Nocturne arrived behind me.

"Are you shedding more of those things or is that the same one from the club?"

He didn't answer. I approached my apartment door and looked in through the bullet hole. I could see myself spread out on the floor, brain matter trailing behind me, out for the count, dead to the world. And crawling up the chest of my corpse was the harbinger, wallowing in my demise, positioning himself over my face so my escaping breath and body heat could give him his cheap thrill for the day.

"Double-dipping son of a bitch."

If it was the same one, I couldn't imagine what had brought it to my place at such a timely moment. I certainly hadn't seen another one flake off of Nocturne in the last few minutes.

"You seek answers," said Nocturne.

"You're damn right I do!"

"Return to the path and all will be revealed."

"To hell with that and to hell with you," I spat.

I heard a door slam and rapid footsteps descending stairs. The shooter was escaping down the stairwell on the opposite side of the building. I wasn't too far away. If I ran hard, I could still catch up, close the distance, and see the face of my murderer for myself.

I only got three steps before Charlie Nocturne stepped right in front of me. I tried to stop, go around him, avoid a collision, but my momentum carried me forward anyway.

I fell straight through him, through time and space.

Chapter Seventeen

Shallow Grave

I CAME SPILLING OUT, face-down, onto a narrow stretch of floorboards between two benches. It was a small room, cramped, and most of the seating was already occupied by weary men in tattered coats. Some were asleep, the rest were too exhausted or dazed to even acknowledge my arrival, if they even noticed at all.

I braced my hands against the flooring and was trying to push myself up when the floor itself bucked violently beneath me, rising up to smack me in the face once more. It was dark and difficult to orient myself. I began to wonder how hard I'd hit my head when I saw the room continue to jostle and shake. I listened and could hear the unsteady drone of wheels rolling over rough terrain. That's when I realized I wasn't in a room at all, I was in the flatbed of a truck slowly making its way down a dirt road pocked with an abundance of holes and debris. The walls were a loose framework of steel bars covered in canvas. I couldn't hear an engine, but we were moving at a slow, steady pace just the same.

Nocturne. If this was where I had landed, he must be here with me, among these broken men. I rolled over into a sitting position on the floor and looked around, scanning the faces of the others in the truck until I found the one with no face at all.

It was Nocturne all right, but not immediately familiar. His silhouette was somehow different. It took me a moment to spot the major change. It was the hat. In my own time, it had assumed the general shape of a fedora. In this time and place—whatever time and place it was—it was peaked with a brim that put me in mind of a military officer's cap.

"Hey, Charlie," I said. "Where and when is this?"

"Are you addressing me?" he asked.

"How many other Charlie Nocturnes are stuffed in the back of this truck?"

He didn't have a response to my scorn. It was like he really didn't understand what I was saying to him. He might not have been expecting my arrival at this moment, whichever moment in a sea of time we found ourselves in. I was about to bring him up to speed when I was interrupted by a familiar voice.

"Mr. Eulogy? My God! It's you!"

Apparently I knew someone else in the truck. I turned, squinting in the poor light, and was astounded to see Rabbi Reubenski seated on the bench opposite Nocturne. He looked haggard, shaken by his present circumstances, but it was obviously him. I'd missed him among the others, not just because I had no reason to expect to ever see him again, but because he blended in with the rest of the men so well. Most of them were bearded, many wore similar heavy, dark coats, and all of them appeared—if I were pressed to make a geographical gene-pool guess—to be Eastern European or thereabouts.

"How did you get here?" I asked the rabbi.

"The same as you. Through him, about an hour ago," he replied, looking at Nocturne.

Charlie Nocturne had nothing to add, but I wasn't expecting any straight answers from him, and likely no answers at all.

"So where has he dumped us?" I said.

"Right in the middle of a nightmare, I fear."

I had no time to assess the situation further before the truck came to a jolting halt. The canvas flap on the back was pulled aside and soldiers with rifles shouted at us in a language I didn't know, waving for us to get out immediately. I joined the line of men as they hopped off the back, one after the other, splashing down into muddy puddles. There was an entire squad of soldiers who had been marching behind the slow truck, making sure nobody could exit early. I looked around the side and saw the vehicle had been drawn to our present location by two horses hitched to the engine block. Even low on gas, with a motor that refused to start, the war must roll on.

We were in a war zone, that much was sure. It wasn't just the soldiers who gave it away, it was the burning city on the horizon sending columns of smoke high into the overcast skies. Before I could wrap my head around the vision of an entire city ablaze, one of the soldiers shoved me back in line with his rifle so I could be counted.

The one in charge of keeping track of the cargo looked slightly confused. The headcount had grown, increasing by two since the truck was first loaded. It might have troubled him, but as long as the number wasn't going down— indicating escapes—he seemed content to have arrived at the final destination with more prisoners than they had left with.

There was a work crew digging a long trench alongside the road, civilians all.

"What are they digging up?" I asked of nobody, but Reubenski was quick to answer.

"Our graves."

I felt stupid for not guessing straight away.

"At least it saves us the work," I commented grimly.

I realized I'd spoken too soon when I was handed a shovel and pushed to the end of the row to help make a long trench even longer, a shallow grave a few inches deeper. Nobody had searched me, and I remembered the derringer tucked in my pocket. I considered drawing it, but what good would two shots do against an entire death squad? I stabbed the shovel into the ground and started moving earth. There didn't seem to be any better option with so many of our armed hosts keeping a close eye on us.

Second World War, I concluded, definitely. The uniforms weren't as familiar as the ones I'd seen in war movies about the Nazis, but they were most certainly fascist. As was the attitude. If any of the diggers even paused to catch their breath, they got a shouted warning first, a poke with a gun second, and a beating third. The ones who tried the guards' patience that third time were rarely in any shape to continue digging after their punishment. We were worked like dogs long enough for blisters to puff up across my palms and fingers, and for my clothes to get caked in the same mud they meant to cover us over with. All told, we numbered about fifty. Fewer than thirty managed to finish the job. When they were satisfied with the size and depth of the trench, they called for us to climb out of the hole and stand shoulder-to-shoulder. I made sure I grabbed a spot next to Rabbi Reubenski. He was old, but tough, and he'd made it through the last gruelling hour better than men half his age or less, myself included.

"Why did you let Charlie Nocturne send you back here?" I whispered to him.

"Hardly my idea," he said. "He was the one who first suggested I call on you for the work I needed done. Months later, he contacted me again and said there was unfinished business I needed to attend to. A path I had to walk. I suggested a time and place to meet. He agreed, but insisted I bring something with me."

"What was that?"

"Szabo."

At the same moment he invoked Csaba Szabo's name, I saw the very man emerge from the cab of the truck. I'd seen him before in person, of course, but only in dust form. Even then, I would have recognized the face before Reubenski said it aloud. His features were as sharp and harsh as his uniform, and he strode the length of his collection of detainees with an arrogance that left no doubt he was in charge of this operation. I saw Charlie Nocturne standing at the rear of the truck. Szabo nodded to him in recognition, like he was greeting his own shadow. I saw then that Nocturne's current silhouette closely matched that of Szabo, like he was mimicking the same officer outfit. His chameleon efforts to blend in didn't fool any of the soldiers. They all eyed him nervously, knowing they weren't looking at an officer or even a real man, but an otherworldly facsimile. They might have all fled from him if they weren't under the strict orders of someone they feared much more.

"Charming company you keep, Charlie," I said, once Szabo had passed out of immediate earshot.

"The only way I can know he is the one is by observing," he said.

"The one what?" I asked, but never got an answer.

Another officer under Szabo barked a command I didn't understand, but everyone in the line turned and knelt down, facing the trench. I followed their lead, preferring to avoid a beating for not complying. It was only once I was down on the ground that I realized Reubenski had not joined us. He stood where he was, staring daggers at Szabo until he was noticed. Szabo marched over to confront the insolent Jew, opening with a backhanded slap across the rabbi's face. Reubenski recoiled from the blow for only a moment and then straightened right back up, resuming his withering stare into Szabo's eyes.

Szabo was the first to look away, or down more precisely, at the coat Reubenski was wearing. He threw it open, tearing away the buttons as he did, and began rooting through his pockets inside and out. He hissed as he searched the rabbi, maybe something Hungarian, maybe German. I'm not sure,

I'm lousy with languages. All I know was that it was foreign and angry. I don't think Reubenski understood any better than I did, but the meaning was clear enough just the same. He wanted to know who this upstart was and, more specifically, who he thought he was to dare show any defiance towards him. I expect he was looking for papers, identification, something that would give him a name, and perhaps a family to also punish.

Szabo came up with Reubenski's wallet first, but the cards and currency inside were completely unknown to him. He threw it away into the road after scattering its contents everywhere. What he found next interested him more. It was a clear plastic bag stuffed with grey ash and something else. He pulled apart the top and plucked out the rabbi's disembodied finger. Once he recognized what it was, he tossed that away too, like more refuse.

Waving the bag of ashes in Reubenski's face, Szabo demanded information, probably about what sort of Semitic mumbo-jumbo it was supposed to be—never realizing it was necromancer mumbo-jumbo he was looking at. I didn't understand the exact question, but I could guess what it was and so could the rabbi.

"It's you," smirked Reubenski.

I could tell Szabo knew the words, but not their meaning. That was what Nocturne wanted the rabbi to bring back to town with him—the tormented mortal remains of Csaba Szabo. He probably had the two bone fragments on him as well, as yet undiscovered in an unsearched pocket. I began to worry, not just about our immediate mortal peril, but for a sudden reanimation of the cremains. With the finger bind broken, those twin slivers were the only thing keeping the current Csaba Szabo from suddenly becoming acquainted with himself as a vengeful spirit from many decades hence. That was sure to be an ugly reunion.

Szabo threw the torn bag back at Reubenski, who caught it with his maimed but healed hand and held it tightly to his chest, even as it bled ashes down his muddy clothes. Szabo pointed at the ground and growled another order for the rabbi to kneel and accept his fate. I watched over my shoulder as the rabbi took a step forward and refused, without having to say another word. The rest of us remained kneeling at the lip of the ditch, held at gunpoint and not daring to resist, even in the face of certain death. But that one brave old man, from another country, another era, would not go to his grave quietly.

This scene that had played out so many times in so many ways over the course of the war was eerily familiar. I'd seen it in documentaries and books of course, but this specific tableau I'd witnessed before. Every detail. It had all been there in a black and white photograph lying in front of me on my own coffee table. Rabbi Reubenski had shown it to me, years after it happened, months before I would see it first hand. Instinctively I looked back at the spot from which I thought I had already examined this moment in time. Sure enough, there was a young army photographer there, ready to immortalize an instant of violence that was already lost, forgotten, and ignored in the midst of this global bloodbath. He was lining up his shot, framing the crime to suit his aesthetic sensibilities as best he could before the slaughter began in earnest. With the press of a button, he would freeze the image and send this message from history to future generations who would study the horror of this day and many days like it. The rabbi and I would be among them. We would receive the message, we would empathize, but we wouldn't fully understand it. We would recognize victims not unlike ourselves in the photo, but we wouldn't recognize them as literally us. Time and a camera lens can reveal a great many things, but they can also distance us from the harsh reality of past events. Past atrocities.

"I hate to break this to you, rabbi, but I think you're about to be murdered," I said.

I couldn't tell if Rabbi Reubenski had recognized the moment we were living in or not, but he had accepted the inevitable, regardless. Not just accepted, but embraced.

"As are we all, my people," he nodded. "I shall die among them and be proud."

And then he looked straight into Szabo's eyes again, becoming that rebellious face in the photograph. Not blurred or grainy, but razor sharp and in focus.

"From what I know about you, Szabo, even now you understand some English, yes?" he told the uniform in front of him. The war criminal. The Butcher.

Szabo was offended to be questioned in another language, to be questioned at all, but the rabbi was right. He spoke some English. It was broken, accented, far less refined than it would become. But comprehension was there.

"I understand."

"Then understand this," said Reubenski, his voice a low growl. "No matter what happens here, you and I will meet again. In another time, in another place. And when we do, I shall fuck your shit up, you fascist pig."

The rabbi spat contemptuously at Szabo's polished boots and added, with a satisfied sneering smile, "You cannot prevent this. It has already happened."

Szabo stared back at the rabbi for a long moment, but the old man met his gaze with contempt, forcing his murderer to turn away from him. Szabo didn't say another word as he borrowed a rifle from one of his men and swung it. The cameraman exposed his film negative to the moment and the rifle butt smashed into Reubenski's skull, fracturing it on contact and sending him reeling. Before his feet gave way under him, the old man stumbled backwards into Charlie Nocturne, and it appeared as if the dark entity might spare him some dignity by catching his fall. But instead of landing in his waiting arms, the rabbi fell right into the darkness, passing through the conscious void that was Nocturne. He never hit the ground. He was gone, simply gone. Murdered somewhere in war-torn Europe, circa 1944, falling dead a world away and decades later, in a back alley behind a kosher deli. No one knew where he'd vanished to except me. No one else would know for a good seventy years.

"What is happen?" Szabo asked, so confused by what he'd just seen, he forgot to switch back from his broken English.

"You have killed the man, just as you intend to kill all these others," Nocturne told the executioner, quite rationally.

"Where is go?"

"He has passed through me to another place and time. It is no matter. As it concerns you, he is one less body to bury."

I gathered Szabo had been dealing with Charlie Nocturne long enough to have stopped questioning the unknowable. The logic seemed to satisfy him and he returned his attention to the prisoners lined up in the dirt in front of him. Szabo handed off the rifle to the squad member he'd taken it from. The man retrieved a handkerchief from his pocket and proceeded to polish the wooden butt and remove the Jewish blood that had soiled it.

As Szabo approached the line of prisoners, he unclipped his holster and drew his sidearm—a more efficient weapon for systematic murder at close quarters. Resistance was pointless. There was nowhere to run, there were too many armed men to fight. The best these drained, shattered men could hope for was a quick end. And that's what they got, more or less, though I must say that waiting to take a bullet at the far end of a line of people being executed one after the other feels interminable. Especially when the executioner has to stop, not once, but twice, to reload his spent clip.

At last, Szabo arrived behind me. It was my turn. There was no ceremony to it, no hesitation. I was nothing to him, nothing at all. I was scum, hardly even worth his contempt, barely worth the price of a bullet to be rid of me. I never even heard the shot, but I felt the round punch through my back, knocking the wind out of me, knocking the life out of me. A moment later my body flopped face-first into the dirt at the bottom of the trench.

We had all dug our own graves, but the death squad was stuck with the task of filling it in again. They had left no one alive to act as their slave work force. The dirt was tossed haphazardly over our corpses, quickly, shabbily, without care or concern. The shovels were thrown into the back of the flatbed that brought us, and the gang of uniformed thugs continued down the road, marching off to their next war crime.

Θ

Being unable to die, I don't fear death itself. But there are certain types of death I dread. Anything involving a burial is right up there. I could be dead enough when they bury me, but as soon as I try to come back, I'd find myself buried alive. Luckily it had never happened to me before, but I was always wary of the possibility of waking up in a coffin one day, with tons of dirt pinning me in, unable to claw my way out, unable to call for help. I could picture that scenario very clearly. Sometimes it gave me nightmares. Of course, things never happen quite the way you picture them. I certainly didn't expect I'd ever end up buried in a mass grave at the side of a road somewhere in bombed-out Europe many years before I was even born. Nope, I sure didn't picture that one.

I guess I should be thankful Szabo didn't shoot me in the head. One of those a week is enough. A mortal body wound was much easier to come back from, despite the trauma to my heart and the blood loss. I figured it took me about a day to return, put the pieces back into working order, and start clawing my way through the mud and corpses, in a direction I hoped was up. I wasn't sure I was headed the right way until I felt fresh air on my fingertips and knew I'd broken the surface. I wormed my other hand up and parted as much earth as I could until I was able to force my head free and suck huge gulps of air into my lungs. At last I could breathe again, which is an activity too many people take for granted, and is vital for feeling alive— especially after you've just been dead.

I slapped my hands down on either side of me, gripping the dirt as I pushed myself up and out of the grave. It felt like the soil was clinging on, trying to drag me back down into an eternal embrace. I took a break once I had my torso free. The rest could wait until I'd gathered my strength again.

I forced my eyes open, cracking through the layer of caked-on mud. The very first thing I saw was a young boy, maybe six or seven years old, standing just a few feet away from me, staring back with his mouth hanging open in a mix of amazement and fear. He must have been passing by when I first started to rise, and stopped to see what sort of creature was trying to burrow out of the ground. He was probably expecting a rodent, not a human. There was a war on, and even a kid as young as that would have already seen more than his share of dead men—just not any climbing out of their hasty graves.

He was probably trying to figure out what old-world bedtime horror-story he was looking at. Ghost or ghoul, I had paralyzed him with terror. I felt sorry for the boy, but at the same time I wanted him gone. I wasn't in the mood to deal with anybody.

"Boo!" I told the child, and that did the trick. He ran for his life, as fast and as far as his stubby little legs could carry him.

I was muddy, filthy. It had briefly rained while I was underground. Saturated mud had seeped down on me from above while bloody soil pooled around me below. The fires in the distant city were out, but the smoke was still rising, thick and black.

The dirt road was as I had left it, but now both shoulders were strewn with abandoned bags and luggage, bits of furniture and personal possessions. The civilian evacuation must have passed me by in the night—people carrying whatever they could, only to discover their belongings were slowing them down. In the end, most of them had decided it was more important to save themselves than extra clothes, family heirlooms, or valuables that had ceased to have any value in light of the onslaught of total war. Before they were too many miles out of town, they had cast most of it aside rather than let it delay their escape and wear them out. I hoped I might spot a loaf of bread or morsel of food I could snack on to help me regenerate from my recent wound, but there was nothing. Nobody wastes food when there's an apocalypse going on.

And then I saw who else was with me. I almost missed him since he was barely there at all.

Charlie Nocturne was sitting on a chair in the middle of the road. Or at least he was acting like he was sitting in a chair as much as an empty black space can mime such an act.

"Waiting for someone?" I asked him coldly.

"Waiting for you," he said in earnest.

"Bit optimistic, don't you think? You saw me die hours ago."

"And yet I knew you would live again. I have a talent for knowing when life has truly parted and when it lingers still. Since you arrived through me, we are obviously acquainted."

"Yeah, you're the one who sent me on this lovely trip to Europe, though I can't say I expected to land in this particular spot."

"You have used me as a doorway before this."

"Sure," I confirmed.

"Then you would know the destination is always unknown. The path, and the path alone, decides."

"Yeah, well my last excursion was a lot shorter. A lot more local."

"I must have already explained to you that the journey is only limited by my own travels through the many years of my existence."

"You mentioned that. So what were..." I stopped to correct my tense. "What *are* you doing in 1940s Eastern Europe?"

"Recruiting."

"Again with the recruiting. Recruiting for what?" I asked. The obvious question. He offered no answer.

"Can you smell it?" he responded instead.

"What?"

"War."

Sitting half buried in a pit, all I could smell was mud. Stagnant, poisoned water, soaking into the ground. Soil that had been scorched and shelled off and on for weeks and years. And seeping out, there was the odour of blood and the first hint of decomposition. This stench bubbled up and entwined itself in air that stank of distant fires and freshly spent gunpowder. But most pungent of all, mud. I told myself that was all I could sense. It was easier to let it mask the rest.

"Can *you* smell it? Don't you need a nose for that?"

Charlie Nocturne was unfazed, impervious to insult.

"I can perceive it on many levels, process it on many levels. Many more than you. But there is something particular about the smell. Smells, I find, paint a picture so much more vivid

than sights or sounds. You need to smell a war to truly grasp
it."

Nocturne pivoted in his seat so he could look past the
treeline, to the horizon. Plumes of smoke wafted up, not only
from the city, but also burning villages and farm houses, much
closer. There was slaughter all around, just beyond our sight.
But its presence, its proximity was overbearing.

"They said the last war was the one that would end all war,
and for a time I believed them," he said. "Yet here we are, only
a generation later, and the world is at war again. I had such
high hopes for this one. The death and destruction are
unparalleled and promise to get worse still. The players are in
place, but something is not right. Szabo is not ready. You are
not ready either. And this war, even with an ocean of blood yet
to shed, is winding down. The Allied forces have landed in
France, the noose tightens around the neck of the Axis, the
writing is on the wall. No, it is not time. But time is always on
my side, and I must be sure of my players. I must be sure I have
the right ones and that they are ripe to get the job done."

I said nothing. Nocturne seemed intent on answering
questions I hadn't even formed yet. I thought if I listened
closely enough, I might possibly understand what he was
telling me.

"Szabo drew me to this place," he said, at last addressing
my initial query. "I was looking for him, or someone very
much like him. I expected a great warrior. What I found was a
great sadist. No matter. Perhaps sadism is what exemplifies war
best. Mad, rampant sadism."

"He's a twisted fuck," I agreed. "You got that right."

"I found him but there is some missing element. I found
you, and again, I find you wanting."

"Sorry to disappoint."

"You will grow. Szabo will grow. Right now he is just a man—sick and vile, the epitome of war. But he will grow and become so much more."

"Well, I guess I'm going to have to disappoint you again there, Charlie. The only thing Szabo grows into is an old man, hiding from justice in Argentina. That's where he dies, at the bottom of a pool."

Nocturne seemed genuinely taken aback. Whatever he thought he was grooming Csaba Szabo for, that wasn't it.

"Is that so?" he said.

"That's so."

He nodded ever so slightly.

"This I will have to look into. In time."

He rose from the simple wooden dining chair and turned to leave.

"'Charlie Nocturne' you called me. I have been called many names over many years. This one I might like. This one I might keep. I thank you."

I struggled to extract myself the rest of the way from the mass grave.

"Hey, you mind not ditching me in some shitty Second World War mud pit?"

"Of course," he said. "You will want to resume your path. Through me."

I joined him on the road, a little shaky on my feet after my most recent revival, but eager not to get stranded so far in the past. I was okay with reliving the last week of my life, but lingering seventy years to catch up with my own time was not a feat I wanted to try. It might have been appealing if I were more of a history buff, but I didn't like the idea of having to wait decades for my favourite music to be played, my favourite books to be written, and just about everyone I've ever known to be born.

Charlie Nocturne stood in front of me, the door to any-where else.

"Do you know where I'm going?" I asked.

"Do you? The path is yours."

"Cryptic bullshit," I muttered under my breath. "I can never get enough."

I stepped into him and through him.

Chapter Eighteen

Missing Bits and Bites

I WAS BACK IN THE GREENHOUSE and it was still dark out. I'd probably only been gone a few minutes, maybe only a few seconds. I looked back and saw Charlie Nocturne right where I'd left him standing, back in his contemporary configuration that wasn't so suggestive of fascist intent.

"Have you travelled far and seen much?" Nocturne wanted to know.

"I was just with you," I said. "In the war."

"Ah yes, I remember. You met Csaba Szabo for the first time. At least from his perspective."

"So did Rabbi Reubenski. And it was his last time. You lured him back to town and sent him back in time to die, you shit."

"I already knew that was where his path sent him. I merely facilitated it."

I didn't want to get into an argument about the immutability of time I would probably lose anyway.

"I guess that explains how Szabo's essence recognized us at the cemetery."

"Recognized you," Nocturne corrected. And he was right. When Szabo's cremains reanimated, they reacted to me alone.

"How'd you know about that?"

"Rabbi Reubenski told me all about your encounter before I sent him on his way," explained Nocturne. "He painted a vivid picture that was not unexpected."

"You'd think the rabbi would have made more of an impression back at that mass execution. An uppity Jew getting in his face, talking trash, and then vanishing into thin air. But it wasn't Reubenski he recognized when I reeled him in and got his ashes mobile. It was me."

Nocturne said nothing as I tried to work it out in my head.

"Why me?" I asked. "As far as Szabo was concerned, I was just another face in the crowd."

"Perhaps he knew you from another moment in time, somewhere between now and then you have yet to experience yourself."

There was no perhaps about it. Nocturne knew something and he was being as coy as his monotone voice and form would allow. I wanted to probe for more, but I was feeling faint. The blood loss from being shot through the heart was catching up with me. I needed to eat, drink, replenish. My eyelids were drooping and I thought I might fall asleep on my feet.

"We must meet again, in the place I originally intended. All of us. Tomorrow night."

"Which 'all' are you talking about?"

Nocturne drifted towards the door to let himself out.

"You, me, and Csaba Szabo as he exists today, reborn."

I would have chased after him, but my body had better ideas. I flopped to the floor of the greenhouse like a marionette with cut strings, filing myself somewhere between petunias and peonies.

Θ

I won't say I was kicked awake. That's a little dramatic. I was poked awake. By steel-toed boots prodding me in the ribs.

I opened my eyes and immediately threw an arm over them to shelter myself from the bright light streaming in through the hundreds of glass panes set in the roof directly above me.

"Okay, come on, get up," I heard someone say.

I felt two pairs of hands grab me under the arms and pull me to my feet. I opened my eyes again and saw matching uniforms. At least they weren't Axis uniforms this time, they were cops. Fascist lite. I saw they both had latex gloves on. Standard procedure when having to manhandle degenerate junkies in the wild. I guess I can forgive them for making certain insulting assumptions about me. I was caked head to toe, and as far as they knew, it was more than just mud. I knew for a fact it was more than mud. There was a lot of blood in the mix, too. Mine and dozens of others who had died at my side decades earlier, all of it still quite fresh and sticky.

"How did you get in here?" asked one of the policemen.

"The door was open."

"It's locked after hours," said the other. "And after hours, you're trespassing."

"It's not after hours now, so I guess I'm not trespassing."

"Out!" was the end of that debate.

The cops led me to the door and gave me a shove to send me on my way. Despite a good number of hours unconscious and in recovery, I still wasn't feeling quite right. My first breaths of dry morning air sent me into a coughing fit that had me doubled over and hacking into my hand.

"You okay?" asked one of the officers who didn't sound convinced that my distress was genuine.

"I've been shot," I explained between gasps.

The cops looked me up and down, but any obvious holes in me were covered over by dried mud.

"You look fine to me," one concluded. "A fucking mess, but fine."

I'd spat a good deal of fresh blood into my hand, plus the source of the irritant that had been tickling my esophagus.

"Here," I said, "this is for you," and tossed him the bullet that had flattened out on my ribs and heart muscles before lodging in my stomach.

The cop looked down at the bloody slug soaked in my mucus, and seemed to recognize it for what it was. Suddenly they weren't as interested in hassling the vagrant. I'd moved on before they thought to bring me to a hospital, soup kitchen, or homeless shelter.

I wasn't too far down one of the paths when I spotted a familiar face waiting on a bench. I sat down next to the woman who was sharply dressed for public presentation. Looking like a panhandler who was just about to hit up a lady minding her own business, trying to enjoy a day in the park, I almost expected her to not recognize me at all. But I was the one she'd come searching for, and by now she was used to finding me in deplorable states.

"Tough night?" Rebecca asked.

"It felt like it would never end."

"I got worried when I didn't hear from you this morning. I was expecting a full report."

"I thought you were going to stay away. Things could've gotten dangerous," I said, and added, "They did."

"It's broad daylight now. There are children playing. If they can brave the monkey bars, I can brave meeting you. And I'm guessing he's long gone. You did meet him, didn't you?"

"Yeah, I met him."

"And you two went to a spa for a mud bath together?"

"Something like that."

"So what is he?" Rebecca wanted to know. I gave her my best guess.

"Technically, I think he falls under the umbrella term, 'wraith.' But he's got more than that going on. He's also a crossroads. A walking, talking crossroads between times and places. On the bright side, I know where you picked up that harbinger."

"Where?"

"Charlie Nocturne. He sheds them, like fleas off a rat."

"He's covered in them?"

"More than that. I think he may be entirely composed of them. Like a hive. All of them clinging together, forming one community, one consciousness, until they've become something entirely new. Something unique."

"A unique what?"

I thought about Nocturne mentioning how Rabbi Reubenski had been aware of him. That holy men knew of him. And I realized practitioners of the dark arts also knew. They referred to him, discussed him in passing, whispered about him, whether they genuinely had any sense of what they talking about or not.

"It's gone by many names over many centuries," I said, recalling what I had heard at various times throughout my career. "It's The Portent, The Augur, The Shade. 'Charlie Nocturne' is what it calls itself these days."

"Stupid name," declared Rebecca. "Who do you think came up with that?"

"Some idiot who didn't know what he was dealing with."

"And why would so many harbingers hang out together and form a single creature?"

"Because they're waiting for the big one," I said. "The final die-off of everything. The end of the world."

"You hang around for century after century with no end in sight, that's got to get boring."

"Oh, there's plenty of death and destruction for them to enjoy while they wait. But together they're pooling their resources to nudge life itself towards the grand finale. It's a master plan that's been in the works for millennia."

"Are you a part of this plan?" she asked like she already knew.

"Apparently he considers me an essential piece of the puzzle."

"So what are you going to do?"

"Refuse to fit in."

Rebecca sat in silence. Being uncooperative with prophecy isn't much of a plan, but it was all I had.

"Let's get you home and cleaned up," she said at last.

"No one's going to pick me up in this state. Cabbies hate having to hose down the upholstery in the middle of their shift."

"We'll take the ferry back across the bay," she said, and led the way to the commuter dock half a dozen blocks away.

Θ

There were vending machines with snacks and coffee on board, and that helped replenish me and my damaged tissue. A day underground, a night passed out in the greenhouse, and I was on the mend. Some calories and protein would finish the job in short order.

The ticket collector didn't like the look of me, but Rebecca made excuses for my appearance and promised we would stay up on deck rather than make a mess of the seating inside. Together we stood on the bow, letting the sea breeze slap us in the face. It was even more refreshing than the black coffee and egg-salad sandwich the machines had provided. It made me feel alive.

"Do you remember the first time you saw me die?" I asked Rebecca, as we drew closer to the opposite side of the bay.

"How could I forget? It was right over there by the boardwalk. You jumped into the early morning surf and drowned yourself. Just to make a fucking point."

"And you jumped right in after me and pulled me to shore. I'd already sucked in a double-lungful of sea water and my heart was stopped. Drowning is such a romanticized way to die, but in reality it's a shitty, unpleasant way to go."

"I remember screaming for help, but there was no one around that early. I must have performed CPR for half an hour."

"More. I know. I watched you do it. You wouldn't give up on me. Everyone else would have called it a day, but not you. You were so determined to save me."

"Yeah. I was."

"I got sick of watching you trying to breathe life back into me. I wanted you to just admit I was dead, but you wouldn't let go. So I stepped back inside, hacked up a bucket of salty, polluted water, and let you think you'd performed a miracle."

"I couldn't believe it when you stood right up after that coughing fit. No worse for wear."

"Well, not quite."

"What do you mean?"

"I never told you this, but you broke all my ribs trying to get my heart going again."

"I thought you sounded a bit hoarse. I figured it was just a side effect from drowning."

"It hurt like hell for days before all those floating bits of bone fused back to where they were supposed to be."

"Good. I'm glad it hurt. Fucker. You deserved it, scaring me like that."

"You're probably right. Anyway, it was all for nothing. You weren't convinced."

"No. But it was fun going around thinking I was a miracle worker for a few weeks."

"Do you remember the second time you saw me die?"

"That one convinced me," said Rebecca, looking slightly queasy at the memory.

"How could it not? Do you still have the dress?"

"No. I threw it away. You ruined it."

"Sorry."

"If you were really sorry, you would have bought me a new dress."

"I don't know your size."

There was another point of business I was reluctant to bring up, but we were alone on deck and I didn't know when there would be a better opportunity.

"So help me out here," I said, "because I need to know something."

"Shoot."

"Appropriate word choice. Why, Rebecca?"

I could tell her first instinct was to deny it, but when she saw the look on my face—an expression that may have been a little hurt, a little sad—she knew I'd finally figured it out. I'll admit, I was slow on the uptake. I shared how I'd come to the obvious conclusion.

"You're the only one who never commented on my eye."

Rebecca, ever conscious of looks, clothes, and hair, hadn't had one thing to say about my inexplicably white eye. This from a woman who could tell how many hours it had been since my last shave.

"Not to mention your harbinger friend was spotted at the scene of the crime."

"That thing was in your apartment, too?"

"It was just a quick gloat-and-go. He never would have been there to enjoy my murder if he hadn't already been following you."

"I guess saying 'sorry' and 'it was nothing personal' won't cut it."

"Why did you shoot me?" I asked, still fuzzy on her motive. "You of all people would know it wasn't going to stick. That I'd just come back again, good as new, more or less."

"I wasn't trying to murder you," she said, looking back out over the water.

"Firing a gun into my head point-blank sounds like a pretty solid attempt."

"I knew it wouldn't kill you. Not permanently. I had to make a quick decision and I always keep a snub-nose in my purse, just in case."

"Just in case you need to murder a friend?"

"You usually carry a gun, too."

"Only to use on myself."

"I didn't go to your place to kill you," she insisted. "I had decided to tell you what Charlie Nocturne showed me at Gallery Nowhere, but then I passed him on the street and knew he was on the way to your place. I ran ahead and let myself in with the spare key you gave me years ago."

"I'm going to have to ask for that back. I'd rather bug the super next time I lock myself out if the alternative is getting shot."

"I should have figured that after I failed to deliver like he wanted, he'd swing by your apartment personally. I needed to put you down for a day or two, take you out of the loop. I hoped that maybe if this Charlie Nocturne thought you were already dead, he'd go away, leave town, forget about you. One look at you with your brains splattered all over the place and he'd give up."

"He already knows I have a habit of not staying dead, so your plan was never going to work anyway."

"Sorry I fucked up your eye for no reason then."

"I'm getting used to it."

"It's kind of distinguished, I guess," she said, giving it a closer look.

"I didn't mean the eye. I meant you fucking up. Anyway, why was it so vitally important to keep us apart? I'm a big boy and all he wanted was to talk. I'm the first one you call when there's a demon loose in your bedroom, but you try to save me from a conversation?"

"He showed me things. Things that will happen, or already happened, or..." she trailed off, about as confused by time travel as I was.

"So you keep telling me. Are you ever going get specific?"

Rebecca took a deep breath and told me, "I saw you murder a man. It was horrible. You looked like you enjoyed it."

I almost laughed.

"Me? A murderer? I've never killed anyone in my life. Myself excluded, of course. I'm not a killer, I'm a bring-em-back-from-the-dead kind of a guy."

"That's not what I saw."

"Well I've done my share of skipping through time and space with Charlie Nocturne, and all I can say is that, as far as I know, I haven't killed anyone, ever. And I don't intend to. Whatever you think you saw, I won't let that happen. That's not who I am."

Θ

A shower did wonders for me. I reached back as far as I could and felt around. The hole next to my spine had sealed nicely, as did the holes through my heart and stomach. I was no longer experiencing palpitations from the perforated chamber, and I didn't feel like I was leaking gastric juices into my chest cavity anymore. It's always nice not to have your leaking internal organs trying to digest each other.

Once I was in a fresh set of clothes, my priority was to see how Gladys was coming along with her brain-sorting duties. Rebecca had come up with me and was looking at the latest pile of soiled clothes on the floor.

"Throw these out, too?" she asked.

"No. I'm running out of wardrobe fast and it's only mud. Well, mostly mud."

"Your jacket has a big tear in it," Rebecca showed me, poking a finger through the bullet hole in the back.

"Take it all downstairs and get a load of laundry going."

"What am I? Your maid?" she complained.

"No, you're my executioner, remember? You owe me. Doing a bit of laundry while I get to work isn't too much to ask given the circumstances."

Rebecca grunted and rolled her eyes, but she gathered my dirty clothes in a basket just the same. She probably figured this would make us even, but I had plans to guilt her into all sorts of menial favours for a good long time. Mere indentured servitude was hardly a fair exchange for my murder, but I was willing to settle.

Once she was gone, I popped the top of Gladys's skull off to have a look at her progress. The bulk of the plastic bag was filled with a well-centred collection of brain matter that was all Louie. Other bits of incompatible grey matter had been separated and bunched into the corners. I could already feel Louie's presence, much stronger and more focused that it had been in the ghoul's lair.

"Nice work, Gladys. It looks more like raw hamburger meat than a brain, but things seem to be working properly now."

I wouldn't trust the soggy mess to operate heavy equipment—like a human body—ever again, but for conversation purposes we were solid. Louie's brain may not have been all there, but I was hoping the missing bits had only been used to store useless information, like high-school algebra, out-of-date phone numbers, and political opinions expressed on social media.

I lifted the bag out of Gladys's skull and regretted it. It was like pulling a gag out of her mouth and the litany of complaints flew freely.

"Darty darty mind! All da time it tink abat da seex, seex an mar seex. Is peervart!"

I tried to ignore Gladys and tune into Louie's frequency. I honed in on his consciousness and I have to say, for someone who had been so recently and brutally killed and dismembered, he sounded very mellow.

"That was intense," expressed Louie's thoughts. "Having a woman gently massage your consciousness back into shape. It was mind-blowing, literally."

"Should I have left you two with a chaperone?"

"I'm not kidding, Rip. Better than sex."

"Peervart!" Gladys thundered.

"I'm happy you had a good time," I told Louie. "Really, I am. And I'm sorry to interrupt your mental massage, but we have some business to settle. Are you good to go? I tried to scrape together as much brain matter as I could find."

"I think you got most of it," Louie acknowledged. "I can feel parts missing, though. Things I should know that I can't quite remember. I'm also having vocabulary difficulties. Certain words don't seem to exist for me anymore. I can be in the middle of a thought, and I'll notice I just substituted some random word for the proper ointment."

"I think I'll be able to fill in the gaps," I said.

"Did you track down that crazy zombie-rabbi and find out why he got so stabby with me?"

"New information has come to light since I saved your marbles from a ghoul's meat locker. It wasn't Aharon Reubenski puppeteering his own remains. It was Csaba Szabo."

"Who or what is a Csaba Szabo?" I heard Louie wondering.

"You don't know him and you wouldn't want to. He was a very bad man."

"So I gathered from our brief trocar-related encounter."

"The rabbi had Szabo's ashes on him when he wound up dead in the alley. That's where they got loose. There was an unexpected merger."

Freed from the finger bind, and with the bone shards fused together again, Szabo would have been mobile, and his first instinct was to crawl away and hide in the shadows. My being right there probably convinced him to make himself scarce so he wouldn't end up captured and confined all over again. I'm guessing he never got very far. Where do you go, what do you do when you're a collection of dust? He probably hung out in the vicinity for days, considering his options which were few to none. And then I gave him the opportunity of a deathtime.

"When we brought the rabbi's body back to the scene of the crime and left him parked there unattended, that's when it must have happened."

"What happened?" asked Louie.

"The body of Rabbi Reubenski got corpsejacked."

I could picture the likely specifics. The reanimated cremains crawling up the leg of the zombie holy man and finding the hole in his skull Szabo himself had smashed in a lifetime ago. And inside? A nice cozy hollow space to nest. All he had to do was lie low, let Louie bring the corpse back to the hospital, and then take possession at his convenience.

"Do you remember anything else he might have said before, after, or during your dismemberment?" I asked.

"Um, let me think," thought Louie, which is pretty much all a disembodied brain can do.

"Yeah," he said after a long pause. "After he stabbed me, just before my lights went out, I thought I heard him say one more thing. It didn't make any sense, though."

"Try me."

"He said, 'I am become War.' I'm pretty sure that's what it was. Does that mean anything to you?"

I hoped it didn't. Before I could ask anything else, Gladys started bitching again.

"Why yoo tak to bran? Bran gat natheeng intristeng to say. Peervart bran jas say theengs leek 'Oooh babby. Rite der. Dat's da spoot.'"

"He's telling me more important stuff than that," I told her. "But then, I guess I don't have the soft touch like you, Gladys."

"Brans is booreng. Make me glad I doont haff wan no mar."

I thought she was done decrying the banality of brains, but no.

"Adder beets of bran jas tink da sam tot ovah an ovah. 'Wan-aff! Wan-aff!' Dat all it tink."

Translating Gladys's accent was challenging sometimes. I didn't know what a 'wan-aff' was, but apparently this repetitive thought from one of the other random pieces of someone else's brain I netted had been irritating her all the while she was sorting. I wouldn't have guessed there was enough of any other brain in the mix to be able to form a coherent thought, even one that repeated itself like a broken record. I was curious to hear for myself what it was saying, unfiltered through Gladys's broken English.

"Hang on Louie," I said. "I've got somebody else's brain on the other line."

I shifted my focus to the corners of the bag, drifting from one to the next, listening to the discards to see what final notion they were trying to convey to anyone who could listen.

"One-off," I heard from the bottom left corner. "One-off."

It was only a tiny collection of brain cells, but it had a one-track mind. And it was tireless.

"One-off, one-off, one-off..."

The voice of a thought isn't like an actual speaking voice, but it's recognizable just the same. And this one I had heard before, recently, saying those exact words. I was reminded of what the spirit of Sam Higgins had told me at Reynaldo's séance.

"Remember, I'm just doing this as a one-off," is what he'd said just before he gave us a wrong number for a bank account that didn't exist.

Or did it?

I switched back to the main hunk of brain and asked, "Louie, did the body of Sam Higgins cross your slab last week?"

"Sam who?"

"Higgins. Local mover and shaker. Old rich guy with his finger in a lot of pies."

"Uh, yeah, sounds familiar."

"You didn't take his brain out and send it to medical waste, did you?"

"Let me guess," he said, dreading another reprimand, even in death. "I screwed up one of your cases again?"

"No," I said, not trying to conceal my smile. "I think this time you may have solved all my problems."

Θ

I've never shied away from crawling through tombs and graves, picking through human remains or dealing with the desecrated undead, but there's one part of running my modest home business that gives me the willies. The computer. It's my main reason for wanting a secretary and putting up with Gladys's bad attitude and frequent desire to see me dead. It's not that I don't know the basics, I just don't want to be bothered with it. Technology changes so fast, who can keep up anymore, and who would want to? As soon as you learn anything, it's already obsolete. That's one thing I like about necromancy. The tools might improve from time to time, but the basics have stayed the same forever. Probably since the day the first living thing dropped dead. Nevertheless, I decided to set my reticence about computers aside and do what I so rarely did—sit down at the desk and switch the thing on.

Zurich was thick with banks, but in my dealings with Jeremy Saunders he'd mentioned "The Ben" on several occasions in relation to the information he was seeking. One search engine request later brought up a bank called The Benziger-Obrist Kantonalbank. The login page was available in many languages. Once I switched to English, I was asked for an email address and a password. This was information Saunders would have already had and wouldn't be prone to share. But Samuel Higgins was an old man, and probably a lot less tech-savvy than me. He'd have an old-man email address, and an old-man password. Both simple so he could remember, but obscure enough that he wouldn't imagine anyone simply guessing.

I still had a clipping of the Sam Higgins obituary mixed in with the papers on Gladys's desk. There was a URL for his foundation listed at the end for people who wanted to present their condolences online. I doubted Sam Higgins had a personal email account. He was from a generation that wouldn't want to be bothered setting up something technical he'd hardly ever use. But he would have needed one to open his online banking account—an email address that would have trusted people in his employ on the receiving end, just in case a genuinely important message ever needed to be conveyed to him. I took a reasonable guess and entered admin@higginsinstitute.net as the address.

The personal identification number was more challenging, but Saunders said his uncle had memory problems and used the same one for everything. Something he could retain. When in doubt, go with dates. The obituary had a few promising ones. His date of birth accomplished nothing, the year he launched his foundation didn't help, but the day, month and year of his marriage to his late wife clicked.

The system seemed to like that combination of email and PIN well enough. Another box popped up, asking me for the associated account number I wished to access. This was where it got tricky. It was the spot that stopped Reynaldo and Saunders cold when they realized Sam Higgins's final message to them from beyond was "fuck you." They never considered that the apparently incorrect number was just another simple old-man password—an easy cypher he'd created in case anyone ever found where he'd written it down and tried to gain access without his say-so.

The gargantuan effort of transcribing the account number via the possessed arm of the fraudulent Doctor Dupont had seared it into my brain, despite its considerable length. Following the oft-echoed hint of "one-off," I tried re-entering the account number with all the digits raised by one. It didn't work, so I tried them all lowered by one. Strike two. Then I tried alternating the single digits changes, one up, one down. Again, nothing. I started to realize the mathematical possibilities were nearly endless and I could spend the better part of forever manually entering single-digit variations of the account number based only on a stupid hunch.

And then I typed the account number one more time, alternating the digits one down, one up.

Just like that, I was in. It happened so abruptly, I thought I'd broken the system. Technophobe or not, I'd somehow successfully hacked into one of the biggest international banks in Switzerland. There was no skill involved, just guesses and dumb luck, but I felt like the greatest computer prodigy in the world.

I looked at the bank balance and saw what Sam Higgins considered chump change and interest. If it had ever been chump change, it had been tucked away for a long enough time to accumulate plenty of interest. I counted eight digits before I ever made it to a decimal point. And the account was asking me if I wanted to transfer any money.

Why yes, as a matter of fact, I would like to move some funds.

Θ

I put the final physical pieces of Sam Higgins to rest, incinerating the scant grey matter in an ashtray with a match and squirt of lighter fluid. I broke up the charred remains and cast the meager ashes into a warm city breeze through an open window, blowing them away like I was extinguishing candles on a birthday cake. I didn't make a wish. I'd already gotten my wish. My financial problems were over. Sam Higgins, may he rest in peace, had just made me grotesquely wealthy.

There was more brain tissue to deal with in the living room. I had the unfortunate task of asking Louie how he'd like me to dispose of his remaining remains. I figured he'd want to be released from the last ties that were binding him to the pulverized leftovers of his physical mind. He surprised me when he turned down my offer to set him free.

"Put me back," was his request instead.

"Back where?"

"Back in Gladys."

"Are you serious?"

"What can I say? She gives great skull."

"Ew," was my verdict on that.

"Rip, it was awesome," he said, his arousal palpable. "Almost worth dying for."

"Your brain is still just flesh," I informed him. "It's going to go rotten and stink up the place. If you want to hang around, a jar of formaldehyde is the best I can offer. I guess I can file you away on a shelf next to Gladys if you two really want to hang out."

I looked to Gladys for any reaction. She wasn't much of a people person and I didn't figure she'd want the company.

"Is okey, we kin heng oot."

I wasn't expecting that one.

"I thought you said he was a pervert."

"I leek a peervart sumtimes."

It was the first time I ever heard Gladys admit to liking anything. There's no accounting for tastes or attractions, before or after the grave.

It only took a couple of minutes to transfer Louie's brain to a specimen jar and top it off with formaldehyde from a jug I kept under the kitchen sink with my cleaning products and potato bin.

"Just don't bother her with pillow talk when she's supposed to be working," I said, as I placed him on a desk shelf overlooking Gladys's work space.

Rebecca returned from the basement laundry room and informed me, "Your wardrobe will be ready in half an hour, once it comes out of the drier. Is there anything else I can do for you? Make you a sandwich, shine your shoes?"

"Sure, that was would great, thanks," I said.

"Don't make me shoot you again," she said, and plunked herself down on the couch. Not even an hour in and my indentured servant was on strike.

The phone rang and Gladys picked it up on her headset.

"Spake ap, I cunt fakking anderstund yoo," she said after a few moments of listening to the caller.

"Who is it?" I asked.

"Sum guy, he wanna tak to a neecrewmincer."

"Necromancer," I corrected.

"Wat's a neecrewmincer?"

"That's me. It's what I do."

"Yoo do neecrewminceng for wurk?"

"Yes," I said, getting frustrated. "That's what I do for a living."

Gladys huffed disapprovingly.

"Git a rill job."

I picked up the extension. I was too busy to take on any new work at the moment, but I was eager to end the exchange with Gladys. It turns out it wasn't a prospective new client at all.

"Soon necromancer, soon," whispered a voice, sounding like a rustling breeze blowing through dry weeds sprouting from a tomb. I can't honestly say I recognized the voice, filtered through atrophied vocal cords that used to belong to an old man, but it rang enough of a bell to guess.

"Oh, hi Csaba," I said, as casually as I could. "How have you been? Still dead?"

He ignored the flippancy. Alive or dead, he hadn't struck me as big on small talk.

"You will join us and despair," he wheezed.

"I don't know about that," I replied. "I'm not much of a joiner."

"Everyone you love will perish."

"Not much of a lover either."

"Everyone you know or ever knew will die by my hand."

"Good thing I'm not much of a people person."

It's never a good thing to let the hostiles get the upper hand with their threats, but under the glibness I was taking them very seriously. This guy had a tremendous body count to his name, accumulated when he was still merely mortal. Now that he had become whatever it was Charlie Nocturne wanted him to become, I couldn't guess at how much more destruction he was capable of.

"I will see you turned inside out, body and soul."

"Well, it was swell catching up with you. Thanks for giving me a ring. Always a pleasure."

I hung up the phone.

"Who was it?" asked Rebecca, already knowing I hadn't been listening to glad tidings.

"Blast from the past," I said. "We go way back."

"What's he after? Revenge or reunion?"

"Both, probably. A little reunion and lots of revenge."

"Should I be worried?"

"We should all be," I said.

Szabo knew my phone number and he probably didn't call directory service to get it. All he had to do was ask his old pal, Charlie Nocturne, who had all my specifics. They were out there, somewhere in the city. I didn't know where at the moment, but I knew where they would be. And if I stood them up that night, I expected Szabo would be dropping by for a personal visit to make good on his threats.

"Rally the troops," I ordered Gladys, who promptly did nothing.

"How I rilly da tropes?"

"Just call everybody," I elaborated. "Friends and associates. Everybody who was on my last invite list. Get them back here any way you can. Tell them it's an emergency."

"Amarginzee?"

I repeated the word, "Emergency."

"Aymargansee?" she tried again.

"Emergency."

Gladys sounded out the new word, taking her time on each syllable.

"Eemargeencee."

"Practice, okay? That's the key word. Try to get it right."

I could only hope they'd all turn up. The light was fading and I'd need every single one of them before the night was done.

Chapter Nineteen

Short Life Expectancies

"I HAVE A SITUATION," I began, and I could immediately see I was inspiring only dread.

One by one, the others had all responded to my call and reconvened at the apartment. The word "emergency" from someone like me, even second hand and mispronounced, caused enough concern for everybody to haul ass. Even Reynaldo, who was quick to inform me that his only concern was whether or not the emergency endangered him in any way. I assured him it did, and that was enough to convince him to take off his coat and stay awhile.

I began my explanation once they had all arrived and settled. Everyone was already imagining what sort of problem I would dub "a situation" and none of them was coming up with anything less than chilling.

"To varying degrees, you all know what it is I do for a living," I said.

And they did. Thus the dread.

I had asked my indentured servant for one more task—go buy booze. I figured everyone would need a bracing drink before the trials of the night. It was one service Rebecca was quick to agree to.

"As you can see, everyone who was at my party is here now."

"Where's your buddy from the morgue?" asked Tracy, who took quick inventory of the faces.

"Except Louie," I added. "Louie's dead."

"What happened to Louie?" asked Tom.

"That's the situation I mentioned. Part of it. Hopefully all of it. At any rate, we don't want the situation spreading."

"Spreading where?" Wilbur asked, looking around.

"To the rest of you."

"Wait, are we in some kind of danger?" said Tom.

"Yes," Rebecca translated.

"You're scaring me, Rip," said Tracy. "So start making sense or I'm going to freak out."

I tried again.

"Okay, remember that case I told you about? The one with the war criminal?"

"Right," she said, trying to recall the details of what had only been an amusing anecdote at the time. "From back in World War II. Some Nazi SS dude..."

"Hungarian death-squad," I corrected.

"Yeah," she agreed, "Guy named Zibba-Zorba or something, but better known as The Butcher."

"Right. Him," I said. "He called me."

"I thought you told me that guy was just ashes in a bag," said Tracy.

"How do somebody's ashes dial a phone?" asked Tom.

"With great difficulty and a lot of determination, I expect," opined Reynaldo.

"Damn touch tones," weighed in Wilbur. "This wouldn't have happened with a rotary."

"He *was* ashes in a bag," I explained. "Now he's ashes in a reanimated rabbi."

I let that one sink in for a good long while. It mostly inspired looks of confusion, but I saw the corners of Reynaldo's mouth turn up and expand into a broad, delighted smile.

"You botched it," he taunted.

"I didn't botch anything," I began, but the denial felt hollow. "Okay, I fucked up, but through no fault of my own. Things just panned out in ways beyond my control when there was more going on than I was aware of."

"Bad synergy," said Rebecca knowingly.

"I don't know what the stupid buzz-word for it is, but yeah, sure. My synergy went all screwy and now I've got some freaky hybrid entity out there who wants everybody dead."

"A creation like me?" said a hitherto uncounted voice in the room.

We all paused to look for who had spoken. Tom reached deep into the recesses of his pants and pulled out his pocket watch. Moby-Dick remained encapsulated inside.

"No, not like you," I informed the fish.

But everyone else seemed to think it was an apt comparison.

"Freaky? Check," said Rebecca.

"Hybrid? Check," said Tracy.

"Supernatural entity? Check," said Reynaldo.

"Wants everybody dead?" said Tom.

"Check," said the goldfish ominously.

I could have wasted my time explaining to everyone how the harbinger/undead-goldfish merger was completely different from the cremains/zombie-rabbi merger, but the technicalities would have escaped them. It would take another necromancer to understand the subtleties and sympathize with my recent missteps that had inadvertently stitched together different risen forms into new and rather more awful creations.

I tried to summarize the threat.

"What we have is the reanimated corpse of a rabbi imbued with the ashen remains of a mass-murdering war criminal bent on gruesome retribution. Against me, specifically. Against everyone I know, more broadly. That means you. All of you. So, uh, sorry about that."

"So you have some mean bastard who needs getting rid of," offered Wilbur. After years as a children's television host, he had a knack for putting things in terms everyone could understand, even if he himself didn't quite get it.

"Right," I said. "Him, specifically. But also Charlie Nocturne. You've all met him or at least heard of him at this point. Ever since he's come to town, he's been pulling strings, making bad stuff happen, furthering his agenda. He's the real threat."

It took a while to process that. There was something that wasn't sitting right with anybody.

"Wait, I thought you were the bad guy," said Tom. He seemed to express what everyone else had been thinking.

"What, me? I'm the one trying to save everybody!" I protested.

"Well," said Rebecca, reluctant to agree but agreeing nevertheless, "you *are* the one who keeps creating murderous zombies and possessed devil-fish."

"Plus you got poor Louie killed," said Tracy.

"I did not get Louie killed," I said.

"He totally got Louie killed," Rebecca agreed.

"He won't be happy until he gets the rest of us killed," said Reynaldo. "Why can't you just murder strangers like a proper serial killer?"

"For fuck's sake!" I yelled. "I brought you all here to keep anybody else from getting killed."

"What the hell are we supposed to do about it?" asked Tom indignantly. "You're the great and powerful necromancer. I throw up for a living!"

"That's just it!" I said. "You all have your own special abilities. I think if we combine our efforts, we can come out on top of this thing tonight and save lives."

"By vomiting?" said Tom.

"Maybe. It's a skill. We'll make it work."

I went through our pool of talent.

"Reynaldo is psychic, Wilbur does magic."

"Pretend stage magic," Rebecca specified.

"Magic is magic if you don't know the trick," I said.

"What does she do?" asked Reynaldo, referring to Tracy.

"Tracy? Tracy cries. It's like her superpower."

Tracy nodded in agreement. She always found a way to make tears work for her, no matter the situation.

"Uh-huh," said Tom, still skeptical. "And Rebecca? What's her superpower? Getting free drinks? Holding her liquor?"

"Don't be silly," I said. "Rebecca can't hold her liquor."

"Fuck you I can't," said Rebecca, defending her honour.

"Seriously, what does she bring to the table?" Tom wanted to know.

"Asks the Magnificent Puke-o," I countered.

"It's Barfo, and I'm Amazing, not Magnificent," insisted Tom.

"I stand corrected," I conceded. "Rebecca, since you ask, is a regular old civilian. What makes her special, what makes her an asset to us, is that she knows what I can do, all of it, and she's not freaked out."

"Not too freaked out, at least," she said, raising a glass. "Drinks help."

I didn't care to hear Rebecca sell herself short. I was serious when I called her an asset.

"I've seen you keep your shit together in a few cases when other people were running from the room, screaming, fainting, trying to claw their own eyes out."

"I'm a little freaked out," she admitted to everybody. "A smidge."

"Anyway, that's what makes her valuable," I concluded. "She can keep herself together. Not just when the bodies hit the floor, but when they get up again and start walking the earth as cursed cadavers."

"May we assume you have a plan to put all these diverse talents to good use?" asked Reynaldo.

"I'm working on it," I said. "I have a few ideas."

"A few ideas?" mocked Reynaldo. "Consider me instilled with confidence."

But as everyone exchanged looks with each other, I could see they weren't quitting on me. Nobody wanted to be the first to chicken out or bail. Peer pressure was working in my favour. I'd be relying on it.

"One more thing," I added, remembering I hadn't quite made it all the way through my list of mortal perils. "I found out who murdered me."

"Bravo," Reynaldo commended. "Do tell. Whodunnit?"

I didn't dare glance at Rebecca for fear my eyes would give it away. That information was on a need-to-know basis, and nobody else needed to know.

"That's not important," I said. "What's important is that it wasn't the guy Gladys hired to bump me off. Which means there's still an open contract on my head. So be careful. I don't want to catch another bullet, but I don't want anybody getting hit in the crossfire, either."

I clapped my hands together abruptly before anyone could jump ship based on news of this final threat.

"So!" I announced briskly. "We're good to go."

"Wilbur," I added, "You're driving."

"Why me?" he asked.

"Why him?" echoed the rest of the room, concerned whether Wilbur was still permitted to operate a motor vehicle at his age with his declining abilities, physical and mental.

Θ

Why Wilbur was simple enough. He owned a van that could fit us all. It was the delivery van for Wilbur's Wonderama. He drove it as a personal vehicle since there weren't many deliveries to be made by the magic store—only a few each year, when somebody ordered a bulky cabinet trick to help them convincingly saw somebody in half, or dismember them through the power of illusion. I figured if we were all stuffed inside the same vehicle, we'd all get there together, and nobody would have any alone time in their own car or taxi to second-guess themselves out of participating.

By the time we arrived on the same street as Gallery Nowhere, we'd brainstormed a loose shadow of a plan. It sounded thin in theory, but it was nothing weeks of planning and rehearsal couldn't have made plausible. It was too bad we only had a couple of hours, tops, to put it in motion.

I had Wilbur park the van half a block up from the venue. I wanted to make sure no one would be seen or recognized before we were ready to move. I also didn't want to listen to the crappy music that was trying to beat its way out of the walls again that night.

Tracy and Tom remained in the van, helping Wilbur prepare for his role. I was standing outside, getting some air, when Rebecca came to confide in me.

"I'm not getting a good vibe from this one," she said. "I feel like we're not all going to make it."

"Don't be so dramatic," I told her. "You're all here to run interference, nothing more. You'll be fine."

Reynaldo came to me next with a dire warning.

"I've had a terrible premonition about this excursion," he said. "At least one of us is going to die."

"Shit," I said, suddenly worried. "You sure?"

"Him you listen to?" said Rebecca in a huff.

"He's psychic," I said. "For-real pyschic."

"And I have women's intuition."

"Overrated."

"It's not really my concern," said Reynaldo. "So long as it's not me."

"I'm sure you'll act in the best interests of self-preservation," I said to him.

"My premonition didn't suggest I was the one, otherwise I'd be long gone."

"Thanks for your concern, Reynaldo, but with any luck it will just be me."

But he really did look concerned, genuinely so.

"No," he said, "this isn't a bounce-back death I foresee. Someone is staying dead. Maybe several someones. Dead for real. Dead for a very long time."

"Not dead forever?" asked Rebecca with a hefty dose of contempt.

"I can't see into forever," clarified Reynaldo, "so I don't like to speak in absolutes. But being really, truly dead tends to last forever."

"Barring a zombie apocalypse, of course," said Rebecca.

"Let's not go there," I warned her.

"Do you think he's already in position?" wondered Reynaldo of our mutual acquaintance.

"He's punctual, I'll give him that," I said.

The place was hopping with staff and patrons at this hour. Gallery Nowhere was thick with bodies.

"Could he have snuck in?" asked Rebecca.

"I don't see why not," I said. "Keeping to the shadows would be no problem. He practically *is* a shadow."

I saw Reynaldo holding up his end of the plan. His eyes were squeezed shut and he was so focused, he was turning red.

"Reynaldo, are you picking up anything?"

He couldn't have looked more strained if he were taking a crap. Admittedly, I set him to a Herculean task. There were too many individual minds in the building to sort through. He shook his head, but kept at it.

"Anything that feels like a vengeful anti-Semitic genocidal maniac who also happened to go to rabbinical school and won't touch pork?"

Reynaldo gave up and let himself breathe again.

"I appreciate the specificity, but no. Just the usual clutter of dull minds who might gather at this sort of bohemian pseudo-arts centre. There's too many of them to be sure. They could both be up there, Nocturne and this Szabo fellow, but I can't pick them out with so much mental chatter. Perhaps once the place empties."

There was nothing to do but wait for closing, which happened promptly at 3:00 am when the law dictated the flow of alcohol had to be turned off. The music cut out, the last smatterings of applause were offered, and patrons began streaming from the door, dissipating by car, cab, night bus, and foot. Some lingered to smoke or score that last minute hook-up of desperation before the evening became a total wash. We waited another half-hour to let everybody who was leaving get gone. That still left a fair number of staff and hangers-on lingering inside. There was no telling how long it would take them to tidy up and lock the doors and I needed everyone out, if only for their own safety.

"How many?" I asked Reynaldo, who was back to picking through individuals in the ether he could sense inside the building.

"Maybe a dozen civilians at most," he said.

"And our boy?"

Reynaldo nodded grimly as he reacquainted himself with the psychic signature of Charlie Nocturne.

"I recognize the chatter—that same otherworld blather of voices crying out for the same thing at once, yet saying nothing intelligible. Nocturne is definitely present. I detect no sign of the other."

I slapped my hand on the rear doors of the van.

"Wilbur! It's showtime!"

Tom came out the passenger-side door and joined us while Tracy cracked the rear door for last minute instructions.

"Give us a few minutes to get into position and then raise the curtain," I said.

Tom, Rebecca and I walked down the street and then crossed over to the same side as the gallery. There was a narrow lane between buildings a few doors down for us to cram into and remain out of sight.

It was only once we were in position that I saw something hanging out the corner of Tom's mouth. At first I thought it was a piece of string, or dental floss that had become stuck between two tightly spaced teeth and left to dangle. It took me a moment to recognize the links of very small chain.

"Goddammit, Tom," I said impatiently. "I told you to leave him in the van."

There was a silver loop at the end of the chain, used to hook one end through button holes or onto belts. I grabbed it and gave it a tug, reeling in the pocket watch hanging on the other end of the chain and dislodging it from Tom's stomach. He wasn't expecting it and brought up the timepiece case with an uncharacteristically sharp gag.

I held up the pocket watch by its chain, careful not to touch any part of it that had seen the inside of Tom. His undead pet was still sloshing around where the mechanics of the piece used to be. The fish cackled scornfully and blew a bubble of disdain.

Tom wiped off some spittle that was running down his chin following the abrupt extraction.

"He wanted to have a look inside. He said I have stomach cancer," Tom explained.

"He's a lesser demon. They talk a lot of shit. Mostly lies. Just try to ignore it."

I handed the watch case and chain back to Tom, who tried to stuff it in his pocket where it belonged, but the occupant protested.

"No!" it gurgled, "You must permit me to participate!"

I shook my head, "Not a chance. I don't trust you, fish-face."

"That," he said, "is an error. Our purpose is aligned."

"How do you figure that?"

"Why do you think I abandoned the collective, necromancer?"

By "the collective," I gathered he was talking about the harbinger hive that had come together and formed Charlie Nocturne.

"You wanted to run off for a light snack?" I suggested.

"It is true. I desire death the way you mortals desire pancakes."

"Actually, I'm more of a waffle man."

"Silence! I am speaking!" he shouted at me.

"When aren't you?" I said.

"I must feed. But what the collective wants is gluttony. All the death there is, all at once. This cannot come to pass."

"So you're saying you have the munchies all the time, but you're not into binge eating. Gotcha."

"I fed for thousands of years before I joined the collective. I wish to feed for thousands more. What the collective strives for is a single grand feast and then...nothing. Nothing for all eternity. Nothing but the void."

"And you're not on board with that plan?"

"I think it sucks," he confirmed.

"So you'll help us?"

"I will help you," he agreed. "And then, one by one, I shall watch you all die and enjoy your final miserable breaths as your quivering hearts beat their last and the endless ocean that is death swallows you into oblivion!"

Once I was sure he was done, I confirmed, "But you'll help us first, right?"

"Yes," said the fish.

"Okay, deal."

"How's a hunk of seafood on a chain going to help us?" asked Rebecca.

"I'll take new recruits where I can find them. We need every man—or fish—we can get."

"What can I do?" asked Tom.

"Right now? I guess you can put him back where he was for safekeeping."

Tom did as he was told and swallowed the pocket watch again. He slurped down the chain as well for good measure.

"I'll call on him if I need him," I said.

I saw Tracy coming down the street by herself. It was go time.

She arrived at the door of Gallery Nowhere and stopped. There was a brief breathing exercise as she took in quick puffs of air and blew out her cheeks. She shook out her limbs, first her arms and hands, then her legs and feet. Once she was thoroughly prepped, she pushed in the door and let out a blood-curdling wail.

It was as loud as any alarm, and there was no way it could fail to alert the entire building. No one could resist Tracy's siren call to come and see what had inspired such blubbering panic as she proceeded into the building and broke down in a mixture of gushing sobs and screaming fits. We could hear her keen through the walls, louder than any band to have shaken the foundation of late and, dare I say, more melodious.

Once she had hooked every person who remained in the building, Tracy came spilling out with a host of bouncers and bartenders trying to hold her up on wobbly legs that seemed to have turned to noodles in her grief.

Tracy pointed up the street and bleated in an inconsolable quiver, "I hit him! I hit him with my car! He went right under the wheels!"

As the skeleton crew of staff left their stations and poured out onto the sidewalk, they all looked towards the fictional accident Tracy was on about. On cue, Wilbur came walking down the street, or hobbling more accurately. How could he be expected to walk straight with his legs ending with a bloody, intestine-dangling wound at his waist? His severed torso clung to them on one side, like they were trying to hitch a ride. More internal organs dribbled down from within his chest cavity, threatening to flop right out and land on the pavement.

"Help me..." Wilbur gasped, reaching out to his would-be saviours as he continued shambling towards them step after agonizing step.

"Holy fucking shit!" was the first hollered review of Wilbur's farewell tour I heard echoing through the entire block.

The staff that didn't bolt right away were reluctant to go anywhere near the gory dismemberment or the man who was, against all possible odds, still alive and on the move. The few who remained drew their smart phones and started taking pictures. The lone conscientious one of the group dialled 911 and made a desperate request for an ambulance.

Wilbur collapsed in the street, but his one free arm—the one not hanging on to his wayward legs—continued to flop around as a sign of life. Tracy ran to him, leaving the lingering staff no choice but to join her and offer condolences and assistance. Nobody tried to offer triage to Wilbur. Such a massive wound was beyond their ability to cope with. Even the finest doctors and surgeons in the world couldn't hope to keep him alive, and yet he continued to wriggle around and groan, despite a trauma that would have killed anyone else in moments.

"Clear," I announced.

The three of us came out of the lane and shuffled to the gallery's vacant doorway, letting ourselves through and manually locking it behind us. We were in, with the place to ourselves. Just us, Charlie Nocturne, and hopefully no unpleasant surprises.

Wilbur still knew how to sell an illusion. It was far bloodier than any he'd ever done before, particularly for children, but this had to convince adults. I had insisted he use some of the more grotesque Halloween props we'd found in the van in conjunction with a generous dose of hot sauce purchased from an all-night convenience store.

The core trick was performed easily enough with an oversized shirt and pair of pants, both cut off in the back. The waist with its open wound was propped up higher than Wilbur's actual waist, and all he had to do was walk with his knees bent and his body twisted to one side with an arm wrapped around his fake hips. So long as the shirt and dribbling guts hung low enough on the opposite side, he could easily mask the fact that he was still safely attached to the rest of his body.

Like most magic tricks, once you knew how it was done, it seemed ridiculously simple. Viewed from the front, it was unnervingly convincing. From behind, the illusion was all-too obvious. That's why it was necessary for Wilbur to collapse onto his back. I hoped the old wizard hadn't injured himself doing stunt work at his age, but he'd been keen to try it, and once I'd proposed the ruse, I don't think I could have talked him out of it.

Now all Tracy and Wilbur had to do was keep the panic and revulsion going long enough for the rest of us to settle business inside. They had Reynaldo for backup. Before we shut the door on the accident scene, I'd seen him join the crowd as just another observing bystander. He was already taking command of the scene, probably claiming medical expertise and using the power of suggestion to keep our patsies at bay—enough steps back from the performance that they wouldn't immediately spot the fakery.

We climbed the stairs up to the stage level. I'd been reluctant to bring Rebecca and Tom along as backup, but they were more familiar with what we were dealing with than any of the others. Even now, I wasn't so sure it was a great idea, but they had little to offer the histrionic distraction going on in the street. If nothing else, they could at least provide two more sets of eyes to watch for anything that might be lying in ambush. That, at least, could buy me a few extra seconds to act if things got ugly. Just when I'd convinced myself the course of action was sound, Tom expressed his doubts.

"I really don't know what use I can be here," he said.

"You helped me contain one lesser demon, didn't you?" I reminded him.

"You mean..." Tom didn't want to name names, so he tapped his chest, indicating his stomach's current tenant.

"Well Charlie Nocturne is basically a whole bunch of those guys all rolled into one."

"Wouldn't that make him a major demon?" he asked, prudently enough.

"I guess," I admitted. "Maybe. Mathematically."

The bar and stage were vacant, left as they had been in mid clean-up. All the chairs were off the floor and placed on tables. The floor itself looked about half swept and mopped. I checked the corridor that led to the toilets. Once again, the out-of-order sign that had been meant to secure our private meeting spot last week was back, hanging from the doorknob of the women's room.

"That's where he'll be," I said to my companions.

"You want us to go in with you?" asked Rebecca.

"No," I said. "Stay here, keep an eye on things. Shout if we're interrupted by anyone."

Rebecca and Tom both looked relieved that I wasn't asking them to accompany me.

"Or anything," I added.

And suddenly they weren't so keen on the idea of hanging back in the dark, empty nightclub.

I didn't give them a chance to weigh their options. I walked ahead, turned the knob on the door, and stepped into my chilly appointment.

Chapter Twenty

Cradle to Grave

T HE FLUORESCENT OVERHEADS WERE ON, bathing the bathroom in a sickly buzzing light.

Charlie Nocturne was there, neither hiding nor lurking. Just waiting, patient and silent. I couldn't tell if he was facing me until I saw those twin tell-tale spots on his face, pretending to be dimly glowing eyes. I skipped the pleasantries.

"Where's Szabo?" I demanded.

"He is not here," said Nocturne.

"But he was with you."

"He was."

"Which means he could have gone anywhere, any time?"

"You are learning," said Nocturne, sounding more proud than condescending. Either way, I didn't like it.

At least Szabo couldn't be off changing history. I'd learned that much from Charlie Nocturne as well. The time-line, it seemed, was inalterable. What had already happened in the past couldn't have played out any differently, despite intrusions from other times. It was all a straight progression, no matter how much skipping around you did. It probably meant the future was just as written out, unavoidable, inevitable. At least I hadn't seen any of it, so there were still surprises to be had. I found some comfort knowing that, but it made me feel like free will was an illusion.

"Okay," I said. "You got me back here. Again. Are you going to tell me what's so goddamn special about this place?"

"What do you see?" Nocturne asked me, referring to our current surroundings.

"I see a shitty toilet in a shitty art gallery with pretentions of being a shitty nightclub."

"Is it not familiar?"

"Familiar how? The toilets? The sinks? The odour?"

"Look past all of that," Nocturne instructed. "Do not see the function of the room as it stands now. See the room itself that lies underneath the fixtures and has stood here for more than a century. This space, defined by these walls, do you see it?"

I took a longer, more careful look.

"It's still a toilet," I said.

"Focus on this room and step into me. I have been here before and I will take you to this place as it once was. Then you will understand."

I really didn't want to go on another magical mystery tour through Charlie Nocturne's wormhole, but I had been expecting I might have to. If this was the only way to discover why he was so interested in me and why he was stalking me like some crazy, jilted ex, I'd go with it one more time.

I stepped through him and, for a moment, thought I'd missed the target. When I came out the other side, Nocturne was standing right where I'd left him and we were both in the exact same room as before.

"I thought you might come," he said.

Only then did I know there had been a shift in time.

"Right. Future you sent me back to see something. Something special about this room that I'm supposed to remember."

"And do you see it?"

I looked around and realized that while the contours had remained the same, everything else in the room had changed. The walls were papered over instead of tiled. The stalls and sinks were gone. There were no more hand dryers. Even the condom vending machine on the wall had vanished without a trace. Instead, there were some modest furnishings. A chair, a bureau, some shelves.

A crib.

"Okay, so it wasn't always a toilet," I said. "The building wasn't always a club or a gallery or whatever the hell it became. It was a residence. Apartments. A tenement."

"People lived here," said Nocturne.

"I'm sure they did."

"People died here."

"Where they do one, they usually do a lot of the other too."

"You died here," he specified. "For the very first time, and for hundreds of times after that."

I was confused. I may have done a lot of dying, but I remembered all my deaths. And I remembered where they happened.

"When is this?" I asked.

"Your first days, your first weeks, your first months in this world. This is where you were born, Rip Eulogy. In this very flat. In this very room. You have not yet left it."

I knew he was talking about the crib. I didn't approach it, wouldn't look in.

"I was four years old the first time I died," I insisted.

"No. You died many dozens of times before that. Here, in this place, from neglect."

Despite myself, I took a slow step forward, followed by another. I saw the crib grow closer by inches each moment until I was standing over it and could look down inside.

There was a newborn lying at the bottom. Newly born, recently dead. It was emaciated and grey. Lividity had set in, with ugly splotches of dark uncirculated blood staining the inner flesh along the sides and visible back. Flies crawled across the body, hunting for a choice spot to lay eggs and spawn maggots. None had formed yet, and I soon knew why. Their nesting efforts were constantly being interrupted.

The dead baby suddenly gasped, flapped its tiny limbs, and made like it wanted to cry, even though it was too weak to make a sound. I leapt back like it had just screamed at me anyway. The flies took to the air, thwarted again.

"This isn't me!" I shouted at Nocturne. "I'm not even from here! I come from a little town on the other side of the country."

"Your first memories are of that place, but here is where you came from. And it was this city, this crumbling monument, that drew you back when you struck out on your own as a man."

I didn't want to believe it, but I've seen too much delusion and denial from the living and the dead to find it an admirable quality in anyone. Myself least of all. I tried anyway.

"My parents were good people," I said. "They wouldn't leave me to die in this shithole. Over and over again."

"You have seen the future," said Nocturne. "I must arrive there in my own time, step by step. But I can speculate about events to come as much as anyone else. I see before me a child who cannot die. Someone must discover you eventually. What happens then is simple to extrapolate. A hospital, a police report, child protective services, adoption, a new chance at life. Even with death waiting ever in the wings."

"New parents," I said, but only to myself.

Hell of way to find out you're adopted.

"You know, you can do something!" I yelled. "You see a child in distress, he can't live, he can't die. You can do something about it."

"I am doing something," said Nocturne, so cold, so practical. "I am standing vigil."

"How long have you been in this spot, standing vigil? Counting how many times I've lived and died?"

"Six weeks," he said.

I wanted to punch him in his fucking face, if he had one. I felt like going through the motions anyway, but I wondered, once my clenched first penetrated that void he was composed of, if the rest of me might get sucked in as well. And sent to what place, what time? I couldn't know. And I didn't want to leave yet. There was something I had to do.

"Get the fuck out of my way."

Nocturne backed away as I scooped up the infant in my arms. No sooner had I lifted the baby from his crib did he shudder and die all over again. I'd never felt queasy handling human remains before, but this time I felt my stomach turn over and tie itself in a knot.

I pushed through the door to leave and felt like I'd walked straight into a wall. The atmosphere in the nursery had been permeated by decay, but here the stink was thick, overpowering. There was a light switch on the wall, but even before I turned it on, I knew I'd walked into a scene of carnage.

There were two victims, a man and a woman, murdered where they sat in front of a television that was still trying to entertain them. Their throats had been opened so wide, their heads hung over the backs of the chairs they sat in, supported only by spinal cords and some loose remaining threads of tissue. The arterial spray from the two near-decapitations had virtually painted the room red when it first happened. Now, weeks later, it was a foul brown, staining and spotting everything, ceiling included. The flies here had not been shooed away by spasms and flailing. These people were well and truly dead. The rotting meat had been plentiful and the air was filled with generations of flies, the floor densely speckled with their dead ancestors. The windows were closed, the doors shut, and the room had spent many days becoming its own miniature ecosystem of decay. The stench was over-powering.

"Are those my parents?" I asked. "My real parents?"

Nocturne didn't bother to confirm the obvious.

"Who did this?" was my next question. He didn't answer that one either because he knew I'd already guessed.

"You're telling me nobody noticed the smell all this time?"

That one warranted a response.

"The walls are thick and the weather outside has been cold. The building is sparsely populated with a landlord who collects his rent irregularly and does not involve himself."

I considered making contact with these deceased parents I had never known existed. There were so many questions to be asked, too many to think of in the moment. But my mind was elsewhere, and I strongly doubted I could muster the concentration necessary to reach out and pull their spirits to me. Not with this suffering, tiny human in my arms. Not with my very life—my fledgling, halting, earliest life—struggling for a foothold in a cruel world.

I made my choice and left without another word. Hillside General wasn't far. I discovered the neighbourhood looked completely different once I stepped outside. Many buildings long gone in my time were still standing, but the streets remained the same, and navigating away from the block of run-down poverty housing was simple enough. I could feel Nocturne's presence, following me at respectful distance, not attempting to engage, but keeping a close eye on me just the same.

By my best count, I died in my own arms another four times on the way to the hospital. I walked the whole way. Taking a cab was too risky. Aside from carrying a sick and often dead baby in my arms, the only cash I had on hand were new bills that wouldn't see circulation for decades.

I walked in through the emergency-room entrance and beelined for the first nurse I spotted.

"This baby is sick, dehydrated, hungry. You need to do something because nobody else will."

One look from the nurse was all it took for her to spring into action. The baby was breathing shallowly, currently alive but fading fast. She took it from me at once and called to a physician in one of the examination rooms who was busy stitching a nasty cut above a man's eyebrow. I don't know what she said to him, but it was enough to get him to abandon his patient immediately, leaving needle and thread dangling while he ran off to deal with the much more dire emergency.

It would be a long process to get food and fluids into my younger self between declarations of death and miraculous revivals. The baby would be a perplexing medical mystery for the first doctors to handle the case. But once things levelled out and the recovery became permanent, it would be hard to convince anyone outside of the attending staff and first-hand witnesses that the condition had ever been as extreme as they claimed. I wouldn't want to be a doctor trying to publish a paper on the case history.

I watched them rush the baby away to an intensive care unit. I wanted to stay, make sure everything would turn out okay. But, of course, I already knew how things turned out. I'd lived it. It was better to simply leave, avoid the questions from staff and the authorities who would be summoned shortly. There was nothing I could even begin to explain to them.

I felt drained, shut down. I couldn't even be bothered to vent any more anger at Nocturne as he passed through the automatic doors and joined me in the hospital corridor. Instead, I asked him, "Do you know where I'm going next?"

"Yes," he said, "as I understand this fractured sequence of events. I believe I do. I have already seen it."

"And where is that?"

"Where you need to go most of all in this moment."

I turned around and walked straight into him without another word.

Chapter Twenty-One

Getting Away from It All

I T WAS A HELL OF A VIEW I found myself staring at. Majestic, snow-capped mountains stretched across the horizon, and the sky hanging over them was crisp and clean. The rolling, forested hills we were on provided a breathtaking view of a deep blue lake. I would have guessed the Alps based on the Germanic architecture of the chalets and lodges that dotted the vista, but there was a hint of another culture flavouring the designs. Spanish, I decided, Central American perhaps. But the scope of the mountain range suggested the Andes.

"It's nice," I commented, not bothering to turn around and confirm my company. Of course he was with me, he had to be. "You on holiday, Charlie?"

"I do not go on holiday. I travel," I heard Nocturne say, apparently unsurprised by my abrupt arrival through time and space. "And always with a purpose. My purpose today is to reacquaint myself with a promising candidate."

"That wouldn't be me, would it?" A statement more than a question.

"I did not know you were coming. But now that you are here, you are most welcome."

He passed me by, heading to one home of a style that wouldn't have looked out of place in Bavaria, even though it probably qualified as a villa here. I followed him through a wrought-iron gate that was bolted to a tall, stone privacy fence at the side of the house. The path led around to the back of the building where there was a luxurious hourglass swimming pool set into the slate-tiled patio. Next to the pool was a round white table with a sun umbrella set in the middle, opened to offer shade on the warm day. An old man was sitting at this table wearing sunglasses and a bathrobe. A pitcher of lemonade rested in front of him, and an iced glass with a straw was held in his lap. He looked like he was expecting a visitor. Just one. A second glass waited with its own ice and straw, as did a vacant chair.

He greeted Charlie Nocturne warmly when he saw him.

"Hello, my friend. Please rest and have yourself a drink," he said, waving a hand at the spare chair.

"I have no need for food or drink, and rest is something always beyond my grasp," said Nocturne and remained standing.

"These things I already know, but a host must make the effort regardless. Courtesy above all else."

Then he saw me coming through the gate.

"I see you've brought a guest of your own. Good, good! Perhaps he will have a seat at my table and pour himself a drink on so hot a day."

The years had been good to the man. He had lived well. I didn't care to accept any hospitality from him, but I sat down in the free chair anyway.

"This," said Nocturne, "is Rip Eulogy. Another promising candidate for our cause."

Our host laughed in good humour. "He has almost as amusing a name as you've adopted for yourself, my friend!"

"You don't recognize me," I said.

"No, young man, I do not. Have we met before?"

"Briefly, many years ago. More than you would guess from my age, and we didn't interact long. Time enough to pull a trigger, no more."

My words told him that not only did I know who he was, I knew what he was, and it gave him pause. I had him at a disadvantage.

"I don't know you," he said after a second, longer look at my face.

"But I know you, Szabo," I said. "Csaba Szabo."

It wasn't a name he ever wanted to hear again, but he took it in stride. His denial sounded completely plausible and well-practised.

"I have no idea who that is."

"Werner Albers, then?"

"That is my name."

"So you're a Hungarian war criminal in hiding, cleverly disguised as a German war criminal in hiding?"

He could tell the pretense of ignorance wasn't going to wash with me. Whoever I was, I knew too much for my own good or his.

"For those of us fleeing an unpopular past, there is a greater support network here if you happen to be German," he said. "It is a necessary illusion and, once I know a language, I have a gift for accents."

He looked around his refuge-in-exile proudly. Rich men not in hiding, free to roam wherever they wish, rarely had it so good in surroundings so beautiful.

"Not a bad retirement, don't you think, considering how our side came out in the war? Germans started coming here a century ago and paved the way for some of the staunchest Nazi party members who would later rise to power. They fled here once they realized they had to get out or face the hangman—or worse, a Soviet gulag. The culture and taste they brought with them has had such an influence, the whole town feels like a slice of home. Funny thing, I've never even been to Germany, yet I practically feel like I live there today. An idealized, romantic notion of Germany, before two failed wars and a collapsed economy took its toll."

"It's a regular Teutonic theme park," I said.

"I see we share a mutual friend in Mr. Nocturne."

"I wouldn't call him a friend."

"Associate then."

"I don't like associating with him."

"And yet you do. As do I. We met during the war, him and I. Such a dark and mysterious man, if you can think of him as a man. He told me he was recruiting and I said the army already had me. But, of course, he represents larger concerns than national squabbles."

"Or ethnic cleansing, genocide..." I added for good measure.

"Indeed," he said, giving his crimes a pass and lumping them all in with the wider conflict. "Such grander plans than all that. I admire his ambition."

"And what role do you suppose a retired Hungarian war criminal hiding from justice in a remote village in South America can play in this grand plan?"

"Mr. Nocturne has been vague, as I am sure he has been vague with you."

"Neither of you is ready," said Nocturne.

"You see? What must we do to satisfy these unspecified requirements, I wonder? He will not say. Year after year, he only waits. So I wait as well. I sit by my pool, I enjoy a drink—lemonade on a warm afternoon, wine after dark—and I let the years pass me by. I am in no hurry. I have done all I can do."

"Killed all you can kill," I said.

Szabo was offended. Just for a split second, I could see it in his eyes. He took hold of the pitcher of lemonade, and I thought he might throw it in my face. But he remembered himself and returned to being a genial host as if the insult never happened. Instead, he poured me a generous glass.

"Have I not welcomed you into my home as a guest?"

"You have," I agreed.

"Offered you comfort and refreshment?"

"Yes."

"But you do not like me, do you?"

"No, I don't."

"Tell me, what ill have I done you?"

A look of concern crossed his face. Not one that was preoccupied with past sins, but one that was troubled by a possible social faux pas.

I raised a hand and assured him, "You won't remember and I'm not offended. There were extenuating circumstances in our past encounters. We've never met like this before, casually, comfortably, civilly. But here, sitting poolside on a beautiful, sunny day, with a cool drink and a cool breeze, I think we've had a better opportunity to get to know each other as people."

"I suppose so. And what have you concluded?"

"I think you might very well be the most inhuman human being I've ever encountered."

His face dropped when he heard me be so rude in the face of his graciousness.

"We both know the things you've done, the murders you've committed. Your crimes, your butchery. And yet here you sit, like your hands have been washed of it all, a proper country gentleman, comfortable and carefree."

"Do you not expect me to live as well as I am able?" he said. "What use is there to dwell on the past? Should I take a vow of poverty, become a monk, confess my sins and repent daily?"

"A hint of remorse would be nice. A touch of guilt. Those things would make you human. A criminal, with crimes against humanity to answer for, but human. I don't see any there at all. Nothing."

I couldn't tell if what I had said registered with him. He seemed to change the subject almost immediately.

"Your accent I cannot place, but you have come far, yes?"

"Farther than you can possibly imagine."

"You come all this way, and for what? To tell me such nonsense."

"No, that's not it."

"So then what brings you here? What purpose is in it?"

"I didn't know when I first arrived," I said. "But I do now."

When I didn't offer more, he stood up from the table, set his sunglasses down and removed his robe. He was wearing swimming trunks underneath.

"Well then," he said. "That is something. We should all know our purpose."

Szabo walked away from me, testing the water temperature with his toes before stepping in at the shallow end. He waded into deeper water, his arms stroking slowly forward, until he was up to his chest. He splashed a couple of handfuls of water over his shoulders, then dunked his head to cool off. Our conversation was done as far as he was concerned. It was like I was no longer there.

I couldn't have continued talking with the man, anyway. My mouth had gone dry. I picked up my glass of lemonade and took a sip. It was sweet, too sweet, and it didn't help.

I rose from my chair and walked to the pool's edge. The sun reflected off the surface of the water, rippling in the wake of Csaba Szabo. I took the first step down and felt the chill wet seep into my shoes. Two more steps and I was up to my waist and immediately soaked through. The water saturated my clothes and climbed higher as the fabric absorbed it. I took another sip of my drink and continued forward until I was as deep as Szabo and face to face with him.

"If you wish to take a dip I can loan you a bathing suit," he said, once he saw I had joined him. "Or you can swim au naturel, I will not be offended."

He looked amused, as though my fully-clothed swim was a joke for his benefit and his benefit alone. Like I was making amends for my poor manners by purposely dousing myself and acting the fool. That wasn't why I had come into the water with him. I was there because I knew it was this man, or rather an even more twisted future version of him, who had travelled through Charlie Nocturne for the express purpose of murdering two innocent people and leaving an infant to suffer many deaths in turn. All in revenge for things that hadn't even happened yet. And I had decided two could play at that game.

"You killed me once," I said to him. "I'm here to return the favour."

I grabbed Szabo by his thinning grey hair and shoved his head under the water. He splashed and fought me, digging his fingernails into my arm. Instead of letting him back up, I pushed him lower. And then lower still until I could plant a foot on his shoulder and push him all the way down. He struggled fiercely, but he was old and thin and there was no getting me off him once I had him flat on the bottom of the pool. I stepped up and put my other foot on the base of his spine, pinning him to the tiles. It took some balancing, but I managed the move without even spilling my drink.

I sipped some more lemonade and caught myself smiling. It was a good day to be alive, a good day to take a life. And my mouth was no longer dry.

I was slurping up the last drops in my glass when I looked up and saw Rebecca was watching me. She was standing, silently, in front of Charlie Nocturne with a look I had never seen on her face before. Was it disappointment or disillusion? It was hard to say because the moment we locked eyes, it turned to fear and she backed away, straight into Nocturne's void, and was gone.

"Are you done here?" asked Nocturne.

I looked down into the water. There were no more air bubbles breaking the surface. There hadn't been for a while. And my glass of lemonade was empty.

"Yeah, I'm done."

I stepped off of Szabo's back, but his body made no attempt to rise again. With his lungs filled with water, he'd lost all buoyancy. After all that struggling and thrashing about, now it was like he was glued to the bottom.

My wet clothes weighed me down as I waded back towards the steps. Chlorinated water poured from my sleeves and pant legs once I was out, leaving a soaking trail of darkened stone as I walked across the patio.

"Did she see?" I asked Nocturne.

"Everything," he confirmed. "Friend of yours?"

"Years from now, yes."

"Ah, the future. I knew I had not seen her before, but clearly I shall again."

"Right," I agreed. "Of course." I'd gotten the hang of it by now, even though I really didn't want to.

"We spoke—will speak—about this moment," I said. "She tells me I looked like I enjoyed it. Did I?"

"I am not one to judge human emotions."

Then I saw someone else had been watching, and certainly enjoying. The harbinger was there with us, tittering with sadistic glee from its shady vantage point beneath the sun umbrella. Once it had had its fill, it leapt off the table and vanished back into Charlie Nocturne—not to rejoin with him, but to continue its pursuit of Rebecca, hoping she might lead to more watery demises, no doubt. Maybe it sensed she would one day witness my own drowning. The water-fixated harbinger would be disappointed when it discovered it had arrived in the wrong time period to see it for itself.

"You're shedding again," I told Nocturne.

"A defector," he said. "No matter. Some deaths are simply too delicious to keep the collective whole."

I saw Nocturne was missing his left hand—a vacancy left by the harbinger after it flaked off.

"You're looking a tad incomplete, Charlie," I informed him.

He raised the truncated arm and looked at the recent amputation. In an instant, a new hand grew out of the end of his wrist, briefly recognizable as another harbinger or two, but then melting into the black monotony of the rest of his form.

"There are many more within," he said. "Expendable all, and easily replaced."

"Szabo won't be so easily replaced."

"No," he agreed. "But he was not yet ripe. You, on the other hand, are now prepared. You have become exactly what I seek."

"That's the nice thing about working freelance," I said. "I can take a job, or I can turn it down. Whatever you're offering, I don't want it."

I set my glass of melted ice down on the table.

"Now open up," I demanded. "I'm going home."

Nocturne didn't try to stop me as I strode forward and through him. I had dealt with Csaba Szabo in the past and he'd been easy pickings. Now I had to handle what he'd become in the future, and that promised to be a lot more challenging.

My brief sojourn in the sun and clean air was over.

Θ

"How did you fare?" asked Charlie Nocturne as soon as I returned.

We were back in the Gallery Nowhere toilets, back in my correct time period, I hoped. As far as I could guess, I'd only left the spot moments ago.

"You need to ask? You were there. You're always there."

"Yes," he said. "For the first time the sequence of events is clear to me. Your path has become linear."

"Now," I insisted, "where's Szabo. The current version of him. The one you let murder my parents."

"He has returned," said Nocturne.

"What?" I said, alarmed. "He's here now?"

"He has only recently arrived."

"He came back in the two seconds I was away?"

"It has been longer than that," said Nocturne. "You have been gone nearly an hour. He awaits you outside."

My thoughts leapt to Tom and Rebecca. An hour alone with that psycho, he could have done any number of things, all of them horrible. I blew through the bathroom door and rushed back into the club without a thought or a plan. I found my friends sitting together, facing me, their hands set on the table top in front of them. It looked awkward, unnatural. I realized it was because they were both on the same side of the table, not facing each other as two people sitting alone together would. This wasn't a social situation, it was a hostage one.

Csaba Szabo stepped out from behind one of the supporting pillars. He was thin, skeletal enough for it to have concealed him completely. Rabbi Reubenski's flesh had pulled itself tight over the frame of bones since Szabo took possession. He still resembled the rabbi on a superficial level, but there was nothing of real significance left of Reubenski. His own family wouldn't have recognized the remnants. Even his bushy beard had become a twisted tangle that looked more like probing thorns than facial hair.

The hospital clothes Louie and I had dressed the body in were gone, cast away. The thing in front of me didn't bother with clothes at all. There was no cold or shame to be felt, and trying to blend in with the living was pointless now. It was an obscenity, but nudity had nothing to do with it. The obscenity came from the ugly parody of human life he had become. Withered, superfluous genitals swayed pendulously as he moved. They might as well have been a residual tail for all the use they were. Everything about him was emaciated, but never frail. He walked with a power and a confidence that spoke of a mastery of this new body and a strength beyond any measly mortal. I didn't expect to fare well if it came to a physical fight.

"Your companions still live," said Charlie Nocturne, emerging from the bathroom.

"I have searched them very thoroughly," Szabo hissed, running his fingers through Rebecca's hair and stroking Tom's shoulders and arms. "So very thoroughly. Just to be certain the necromancer hasn't hidden any of his toys on them."

"They were most cooperative," he added, cackling.

"Are you two okay?" I asked, ignoring the creepy incarnation pawing at them.

"My skin's crawling," reported Tom, "but I'm fine."

"We're not hurt," confirmed Rebecca. "But I'm going to need a few dozen showers before I ever feel clean again."

Getting patted down by a walking corpse is nobody's idea of a fun evening of non-consensual necrophilia.

"I trust they are unarmed," said Nocturne. "Devoid of anything that might turn the tide of the inevitable."

Szabo held out Rebecca's compact revolver. I recognized it from the time it went off in my face.

"The woman had this inconsequential thing in her purse," he snickered. "Nothing more."

To demonstrate how inconsequential a weapon it was, he crushed it in his hand like a tin can and tossed the bent and broken gun aside as trash.

"And what of the necromancer? Has he brought a totem or spell he thinks can be used against me?"

"I sensed nothing that could cause you harm when last he passed through the void," said Nocturne.

"Splendid," said Szabo, with a broad smile no living face could form without tearing something.

I positioned myself closer to Tom and Rebecca in case I had to intercept him. What I could do if it came to that, I had no idea.

"You're wet," Rebecca noticed. "Where have you been?"

"Swimming," I said.

After only a moment of reflection she seemed to understand exactly what I meant.

"I know what you have been up to, Eulogy. I remember it well," Szabo growled at me. "And I will repay it in full."

"Killing Mr. Eulogy accomplishes nothing," Nocturne reminded him. "You know this."

"I disagree," said Szabo. "It accomplishes much in the way of pain and suffering. And it will give me great pleasure to be able to do it over and over again."

"You know," I interrupted, "now that you're undead and walking the earth again, maybe forever, you should look into getting a better hobby."

"Oh, I do not expect to tire of this one anytime soon," he said. "But first things first. Before I amuse myself with you, I shall let you watch me slay your friends. A hole here, a puncture there, until you beg me to finish them."

Szabo went over to the bar where something had been left poking up. At first I thought it was a beer tap, but then I remembered Gallery Nowhere didn't have beer on tap. Besides, this wasn't behind the bar. It was stuck right into the polished surface. Szabo grabbed it and twisted it back and forth, prying it loose. Once it was free, I recognized it as a trocar. He must have enjoyed killing Louie with it, or maybe he was sentimental about his first murder in his new body. Either way, he'd held onto it and was looking to put it to use again. I don't expect stabbing it into a solid block of wood did wonders for its pointed edge, but I doubt The Butcher cared. Put enough force behind it, and it would pierce flesh just fine, blunted tip or not.

As he came back towards us, trying to decide who to start with and intent on doing some permanent damage, I tried to bring Charlie Nocturne in to act as arbitrator.

"Are you going to let this maniac off his leash to do this?"

"I have done what I must to bring about his current form," explained Nocturne. "I do not control him any more than I control you. You have both been recruited for a purpose, but you act without orders, of your own free will. Only the path guides you. So long as you always return from the dead, I take no issue with the wishes of Csaba Szabo."

"Big help," I muttered.

"Rip, tell me you can deal with this," Rebecca pleaded.

"If you can bring 'em back, you can put 'em down, right?" said Tom, grasping at straws he knew nothing about and could never understand.

At that point, the only thing I figured I could try was to start chucking furniture at Szabo. A table, some chairs. They might slow him down for a couple of seconds. Then the killing would begin in earnest.

"I've got nothing," I had to tell them, and watched their hope, their confidence in me, die.

"Allow me," I heard a voice say.

"Who said that?" asked Rebecca.

I knew. And so did Tom. When Tom didn't respond in a timely fashion, I helped him along, making a fist and pounding it into his chest. Tom wheezed from the impact and coughed up the loop of a chain. I grabbed it and yanked out the rest, freeing Moby-Dick from his stomach-lining lair. The watch dangled, dripping stomach acid. The fish inside burbled at me and flapped his fins.

"Release me," he said.

"Huh?" was my clever reply.

"Cast me back into the void so that I may convince my brethren of their folly!"

Moby-Dick swam back and forth, rocking the watch on the end of its chain like a child on a swing set. Szabo paused to observe the ridiculous pet trick for the pathetic display it was, but it gave me time to realize what the fish intended.

I helped him carry through on his next swing and flung the watch across the room, straight into Charlie Nocturne. The watch, the chain, and the demonic fish all vanished into the void. Would Moby-Dick have time to make his case, I wondered. Perhaps he had all the time in the world in there—years, centuries—to convince an entire hive of harbingers that they were backing the wrong cause, that they'd made a terrible miscalculation, that the grand finale they were after was only going to put an end to their fun once and for all. Maybe time, and the infinity of it contained within Charlie Nocturne, was on our side.

There was no reaction from Nocturne, and at first I thought our goldfish's kamikaze attack had been absorbed by the endless negative space and amounted to nothing. But then there came a sound in the room unlike anything I'd heard before. It was like a stampede of wild animals racing across a frozen glassy lake, their claws or hooves scratching at the ice, cracking it open with each successive wave, destroying it underfoot as their numbers increased and more piled on.

The outline that defined Charlie Nocturne's body, defined him in the shape of a man, began to quiver and shake. The vibration quickened rapidly to such a pace, his edges became a blur. Pieces began to break off him and drop to the floor. He looked like a constructed plaything composed entirely of pitch-black blocks after too many had been pulled out for him to remain stable and standing. All at once, he collapsed, smashing into pieces on the floor—more pieces than I could ever have imagined he was composed of. A mound of harbingers, too many to count by thousands, gushed across the club in a flood of black and scattered everywhere. They found themselves exposed to the gallery lights, probably the first light most of them had seen in centuries or more. No longer sheltered by the perpetual darkness of the collective they had created together, they screeched and panicked, skittering away in all directions at once. The bulk of them surged forward in a rolling wave. Now occupying physical space instead of the black void they called home, their weight was tremendous—too much for the old building to hold up. I heard the floorboards creak and then begin to snap one by one.

In the moment before the floor beneath us gave way, Tom and Rebecca lunged for the support pillars, wrapping their arms around one each. Brilliantly, I grabbed hold of a table leg only to find it wasn't nailed down at all. It didn't make for a suitable anchor, but its bulk kept me from sliding through the sudden gap in the broken floorboards. I heard the mass of harbingers land on the level below us, break through that, and then smash through the street level as well. I looked down and saw they had crashed all the way down to the basement, which was at least dark enough for their liking. Once the basement lay exposed far below, the ones that hadn't already tumbled in jumped of their own accord, seeking shelter. The constant stream of stragglers was enough to topple Szabo as they got underfoot. He fell into the hole with them, only stopping himself by grabbing onto my foot.

Szabo's new body may have been skeletal, but it was heavy enough to drag me down. I would have fallen right through the splintered floor and all the way to the basement if the table I'd been gripping hadn't jammed itself in the hole right next to me.

I could see Szabo's angry face drawing nearer as he scaled my leg, hand over hand, trying to bring himself closer to any part of my body he could rend for maximum effect and pain. It was only when I realized he needed both hands to hold on that I knew he must have dropped his weapon in the fall. I looked around and spotted it on the floor next to Rebecca.

"Give me the trocar," I said, reaching for it.

"The what?" asked Rebecca, like a surgical assistant who didn't know the proper medical names of all the instruments on the tray.

"Pointy thing!" I specified.

That she understood. She snatched it off the floor and tossed it to me. I caught it on the fly and jammed the trocar straight into Szabo's eye—then hammered it home with my open palm. It might have been more helpful if there was still a brain in his skull to damage, but I probably gave the ashes nesting there a good stir. Szabo screamed, but probably not in pain. I think he was beyond pain. Anger, however, he had plenty of that. Pure instinct made him reach for his pierced eye and that was enough to dislodge him. He let go of my pant leg and plummeted all the way to the cellar with nothing to break his fall but an endless supply of disillusioned lesser demons cowering in the dark. I didn't want to know how that meeting of the minds went. Not well, judging by the commotion I heard echoing from below.

I didn't move another inch for fear of causing more structural failure, but the old building held together. It might have been in better shape than I gave it credit for. By the time we all dared to start breathing again, the fuss on the floors below us had died down. The harbingers had all found a safe corner or crevasse to hide in, and Szabo, whatever had become of him after landing in the swarm of demons, was not heard from again.

Tom crossed the room and retrieved his pocket watch from where it had come to rest after Nocturne shattered. He put it to his ear and shook it, as though he were checking if the mechanism still worked. The mechanism—an undead fish—had fallen silent. He put it in his pocket for safe keeping. I don't know where he thought he might get it repaired. I wasn't going to fix it for him.

It was a solid evening's work. As usual, I hadn't been paid a dime for it, but there was the satisfaction of a job well done. Destroying Csaba Szabo twice inside of ten minutes felt fantastic.

"Are we done here?" asked Rebecca.

"We can go, right?" said Tom anxiously. "We're done, so let's go."

"All right," I said. "We've done enough damage for one night. Pull me out of this mess and let's get the hell out of here."

Tom and Rebecca were just about to grab my arms and hoist me free of the hole that had me trapped, dangling between floors, when we heard steps arriving on the top level of the building. We all looked to the exit door that led to the stairs and found our path blocked. There was a man standing in the doorway, between us and the only way out. He held a gun and a gas can.

Chapter Twenty-Two

Funeral Pyre

"SORRY I'M LATE," said the nondescript man. "I had to wait around outside for the ambulance and the cops to leave."

The ambulance would have been for Wilbur. The cops as well, once the paramedics realized they'd been victims of a hoax. I only hoped Tracy and Reynaldo had gone to the police station with him and gotten clear of Gallery Nowhere, which had proved to be nothing but a relentless menace all night.

"And you are?" asked Rebecca, her eye on the handgun and its implied threat.

I didn't recognize the man's face, but I knew the card he handed out to each of us once he set down the gas can and retrieved a few from inside his coat pocket.

Death Dealers Incorporated

He kept the large automatic trained on us even as he went through this common courtesy of a formal introduction.

"I thought we locked the door behind us," commented Tom.

"Back door or window," I said. "There's always another way in when you're up to no good."

"Rip Eulogy," the hired gun said to me, savouring the words. "I've been trying to imagine the man behind such a dumb name. That has to be made up, right?"

"It's a professional alias," I told him.

"Not a stage name," Tom specified on my behalf.

The gunman came over and started to pat Rebecca down.

"We've already been frisked once tonight," said Tom.

"Thoroughly," added Rebecca distastefully.

Apparently Szabo hadn't considered Rebecca's phone any sort of threat because she still had it. While the gunman felt around for any weapon or device that might thwart his mission, Rebecca passed it to Tom behind her back. I could see Tom didn't know what she meant for him to do with it until she nudged him and gave him a harsh glare. Without complaint, Tom did as he was wordlessly ordered, bringing his hand to his mouth and stuffing the phone into it. He'd swallowed before the assassin turned his attention to him and began the second pat-down. I winced, thinking of that wide, hard plastic case working its way down Tom's esophagus, but he managed it like the pro he was. Accordingly, all the search revealed was the pocket watch in his pants.

"What the hell kind of a watch is this?" asked the gunman, observing the fish inside with the flapping gills and gaping mouth.

Moby-Dick said nothing. He was still drained from filibustering all those harbingers into breaking rank.

"It's my goldfish watch," said Tom.

"You got something against Mickey Mouse?" said the gunman, and stuffed it back into Tom's pocket.

I didn't get searched. Precariously pinned in a hole made of splintered floorboards, I wasn't much of a threat to anyone.

"You know why I'm here," the gunman said. "I heard you'd been by our complaints department."

"I was trying to cancel the hit," I said.

He shook his head.

"No cancellations, no refunds. Company policy."

"Yeah, I got that."

"I've been playing catch-up with my schedule all week," he apologized.

"You and me both," I said.

"Death Dealers Incorporated is sorry for any unforeseen delays and will be happy to offer you—or your successors—a ten-percent discount on any future business."

"So, just to be clear," interjected Tom, gesturing at Rebecca and himself, "this has nothing to do with us."

"Oh no," assured the gunman, "I'm only under contract to kill this one guy."

"Then we can go?"

"As far as Death Dealers Incorporated is concerned, you two aren't persons of any interest whatsoever."

Tom smiled in relief. He took Rebecca by the arm and started to steer her towards the door. She was reluctant to leave me behind, but I nodded for her to seize the chance to go. I knew I could take a bullet and live. I wasn't happy about getting shot to death for the third time in one week, but I'd feel better about it if I knew she was safe.

"Unfortunately, there's the other contract I'm here to fill," said the gunman, halting their departure with a wave of his gun. "And that one's very specific. No witnesses."

He tapped the can on the floor with the tip of his loafer. The report from the tin vessel confirmed the container was brimming with fuel.

"I only started following you today, and wouldn't you know it, you led me right here. It's like serendipity."

He bent down and handed me another card, identical in style and stock to the one for Death Dealers Incorporated. It even had much of the same contact information. Apparently this second business was in the same building as Death Dealers, only one floor and one suite number removed. The sole significant difference was the name of the business itself.

Insurance Fires Assured

I could already guess. Just as Death Dealers didn't deal in death so much as deal *out* death, this company didn't offer insurance against fires. They offered assurance. Assurance that a devastating fire would tear through a heavily insured building at a time and address of your choosing.

"Incidentally, that ten-percent discount can also be applied to our sister company," we were informed.

"Good to know," I said, even though none of us would be permitted to live long enough to use it.

Tom winced, contorting his body in small, subtle ways and sucking in his chest and stomach alternately. I thought he was having some sort of seizure—a fit brought on by the stress of the moment. But then I heard a voice, muffled and indistinct. It was coming from Tom—specifically inside Tom. I almost thought it was Moby-Dick trying to weigh in on the situation with some unwelcome comment or dire threat, but he was back in Tom's pocket, not his stomach. Besides, this voice was polite. And female. I listened closely when she repeated herself, and the second time around I could make out the words.

"Nine-one-one, what is your emergency?"

"Did you hear that?" asked the gunman.

I didn't answer him. I was too busy laughing.

"You see," I told Tom, "this is exactly the sort of thing you should have in your act."

"You think?"

"It's a modern twist on an old routine. The kids will love it."

Dialling a phone from inside his own stomach was a winning stunt. Sure, he had to struggle just to get three numbers out, but with practice I was certain he could manage ten-digits, even text messages. It would knock audiences on their ass. The Amazing Barfo could get a booking anywhere. It almost made me want to try my hand at being an agent or a manager after all.

"Is there a phone here? Did you just call the cops?" said the gunman.

Aside from some stomach gurgles, the emergency operator wouldn't be able to hear what was going on. But the call would be traced, police dispatched. Maybe with an ambulance and fire truck in tow.

When he didn't get an answer, the assassin moonlighting as an arsonist hurried to wrap things up. He twisted the cap off the gas can, picked it up by the handle, and started pouring a trail of fuel across the floor in a wide arc.

"At least let the girl go," said Tom considerately, stepping forward to make his case. "She won't talk, I promise."

"The whole point of 'no witnesses,'" explained our assigned assassin patiently, "is that *nobody* talks."

Tom stepped closer.

"Please, if you'll just..."

Before he could continue, the gunman clubbed him on the side of the head with the butt of his pistol. Tom collapsed in an instant and lay still. The hired gun kept pouring gasoline as though the interruption had never even happened.

Rebecca gasped and started to run to Tom's side, but I held up a hand, cautioning her against it. I didn't want her to get knocked cold as well. She was the last of us with any mobility.

Gallons of gasoline seeped into the floorboards until the trail had been poured in a complete circle around us. Tom was lying just outside the ring, unconscious or worse. The man with the can closed the loop of fuel, set the tin back down, and stepped away.

"If it's any consolation, this will be quick," he said. "Pretty quick. Old buildings like this are a tinderbox. It'll be a regular bonfire in about three minutes flat."

"You could just shoot us instead of letting us burn to death," suggested Rebecca practically.

"I could shoot you, sure," he agreed. "But whenever I do that, I have to ditch the gun just in case the ballistics of the slugs ever get matched to it. It's a pain and it adds up. Use a gun once, buy a new one. So I like to keep the shooting to a minimum. Skip it altogether if I can. Like now for instance. I'll shoot you if I have to, but I don't think I'll have to."

He produced a book of matches, tore one out of the pack, and clenched it between his teeth. The move was done single-handedly so the gun remained trained on us the whole time. Very professional. With a jerk of his head, he struck the match on the abrasive pad and set fire to the rest of the match heads in the pack. Once he had his modest torch flaming in his hand, he spat the spent match out of his mouth, away from the fuel so as not to begin the inferno prematurely.

"Any last words?" he asked, holding the blazing match-book over the gasoline pooled in front of him. He wore the smile of someone about to cross a lot of unfinished business off his to-do list.

"No," I told him, pulling the derringer out of my jacket pocket where I'd stashed it the day before when the rest of my kit was out of commission. "But you've just said yours."

It was his mistake for not risking an unstable floor to get close enough to me to at least check my pockets. I'd almost forgotten it was in there myself. I really hadn't expected it to come in handy at all, but this made me appreciate there were reasons to keep it close whenever I could.

I aimed the tiny pistol carefully at his heart. Derringers aren't known for their range, but he was close enough to make my shot count. I'd never shot a gun at anybody but myself before. Of course, until recently, I'd never drowned anyone in a swimming pool either. There's a first time for everything, but I was concerned killing was already becoming a habit.

I squeezed the trigger and heard a loud poof.

It wasn't the bang I was hoping for. It wasn't a jam or a mechanical misfire. The round had fizzled.

"Rebecca," I said suspiciously. "Did you check my pockets when you did the laundry?"

"I think so. Maybe. I don't know," she said, trying to recall the mundane detail under duress.

"You washed my derringer, didn't you? No wonder it won't fire."

"Weren't you the one who just went swimming with it?" she countered.

Good point, but I didn't want to admit responsibility for getting us killed.

The Death Dealers contractor watched with bemusement as we wasted our final moments together bickering.

"I'm sure it's fine," she said. "It might just be a little moist."

"Moist? It's ruined! The bullets are fucked."

"Give it here," she demanded, and snatched it from me.

Rebecca knew more about guns. And shooting people with them. So I let her have it.

She pulled back the hammer and blew into the mechanism, trying to dry it out as a quick fix. She wasn't even aiming when she pulled down on the trigger and fired the second 9mm round. That one worked just fine.

The bullet punched right through the gas can and lodged itself in the gunman's ankle. That wasn't enough to ignite the fuel, but him dropping the burning matches as he fell over was. The gasoline went up in flames, arcing out in two different branches as it followed the circular trail. What was left in the can exploded, licking at the contract killer's clothes and lighting him up. "Any last words?" may have been his final words, but they were far from the last noises he made. Lots of screaming followed, until the flames burned the air right out of his lungs. After that, he was just more kindling in a building full of it.

The initial flames drew close to Tom, and the radiating heat disturbed him. He pushed off the floor and shook his head as he came to.

"Tom! Tom!" Rebecca and I yelled in unison, trying to get his attention and make him aware of our predicament.

Tom looked around and saw the room was on fire and that we were separated by flames. Rebecca and I were caught in the blazing ring that was spreading. Already, the fire was crawling up the nearest supports, on its way to the ceiling, and our modest sanctuary of floor space was getting smaller as the flames inched closer.

"I can't get to you!" Tom shouted back at us when he realized there was no path through the rising wall of fire.

"There's a sink behind the bar!" I called to him. "Get water!"

Tom nodded his head in agreement and vaulted over the bar. He ran a tap, grabbed a glass, filled it, and pitched the contents towards the flames, trying to extinguish them.

It was a shot glass.

"For fuck's sake, Tom, at least use a pint glass!"

"There's nothing but shot glasses back here!" he protested, looking around again and finding nothing better. He might as well have been using a thimble for all the good it was doing.

The fire continued to eat through what structural integrity had been spared over the building's years of ill-advised renovation via demolition. I saw Tom on the other side of the tall licks of flame. He had run back around the bar to pour two well-placed shots of water more strategically. It did absolutely nothing to help. I shouted to be heard over the crackling roar of wood beams being consumed.

"Tom!"

He turned towards the sound of my voice, terror in his eyes. He found me amidst the smoke and the flames. Our eyes locked and I had his attention.

"We need The Fireman!" I yelled at him.

It took a moment for the meaning of my words to register. Then Tom nodded solemnly and ran off. He understood. If he was up to it, there was still a chance. Rebecca, however, didn't know what I was talking about.

"Of course we need a fucking fireman! We need the whole fucking fire department! Why do you think he called 911?"

"They won't get here in time," I told her grimly.

Our salvation would not be found with the emergency equipment speeding to our aid. The building wouldn't last another two minutes.

Low to the floor, my leg trapped by split wood and toothy splinters, I couldn't get much of a view of the bar over the wall of fire in front of me. But by the light of the orange flame, I would catch the occasional glimpse of Tom throwing his head back over and over and over again, two-fisted drinking with the twin shot glasses he kept refilling under the running faucet. He didn't bother to swallow, he just poured it all straight down until he was full. Fuller than full. Then he came lumbering out from behind the bar, his belly noticeably distended and round.

Tom stepped as close to the flames as he dared, set his hands on his hips, and squeezed inward and upward. For the first time anywhere in at least a century, The Fireman was performed for a captive audience of two. Had I not been so distracted by our peril, I might have even applauded.

Sometimes I wish my mind wasn't polluted by so many of the things I know. This wasn't one of those times.

Copious amounts of water and gastric juices fountained out of him like a hose, dousing one section of floor between us and him. The scorched wood sizzled and smoked, but for a moment the fire retreated from the short extinguished path, allowing safe passage. Tom emptied himself completely, down to the last drop. I knew he was done when Rebecca's ruined phone came up for a final bow and clattered across the floor.

"Go!" I told Rebecca, pushing her forward. I stayed behind, too pinned to follow.

"Rip, I can't leave you here, you'll die!"

"Don't worry about me. I've done it before, I'll do it again."

"Not like this," she said.

It was true. I'd never burned to death. There are some truly awful ways to go, ways that scare even me. Painful, nasty, miserable deaths I never wanted to put myself though, even knowing I could come back from anything. Burning to death was one of them. It was right at the top of the list.

"I didn't say it wouldn't suck. Go!"

Rebecca seized the moment and ran across the blackened floorboards that barely held firm under her modest weight, weakened as they were. She passed through the gap in the flames and into Tom's arms. He gave me a parting glance that looked like concern but may have even been respect. I waved goodbye. There was nothing else to do. A moment later, they were out the door and racing down the stairs to get clear of the building before the whole thing collapsed in on itself.

I realized Rebecca had run off with my derringer, but it was no good to me anyway. Given a choice, I would have gladly fired a shot through my head to put myself out of misery and spare me the burns. But one round had been fired, the other spoiled, and I was out of ammo.

Dying is easy, I reminded myself. It's staying dead that's hard.

The flames grew closer and I could feel them picking at my sleeves, my hair, testing out new fuel to consume. The heat was unbearable and my skin was blistering. I closed my eyes, tried to distance myself from the pain, and waited for it all to be over.

I heard beams cracking, breaking. Weakened by fire gnawing at them, they started to snap one by one. The few supporting walls that had been left standing began to buckle. Masonry, cemented together for a century or more, peeled away from the mortar and leaned inward on wooden struts and supports that were no longer fit to back them.

My burns were second degree, working on a third, when the top floor caved in and pancaked through the other levels, crushing everything, myself included. I was dead and done before the flames had their chance to torture me to death.

At least that was something.

Chapter Twenty-Three

Last Rites

"I'M AFRAID THE BODY has been cremated."

"Cremated? Who authorized that?"

Rebecca had been given the runaround for weeks, trying to find out what happened to my body after the fire was put out and the rubble of Gallery Nowhere—my place of birth and site of my first and latest deaths—had been bulldozed and picked through. After dozens of phone calls and as many personal visits to police stations, hospitals, and morgues, she had finally discovered a tin box of grey soot that used to be me, numbered and filed on a shelf filled with the city's deceased nameless.

"Was he Jewish, Catholic?" asked the attendant, once a file number and the box had been successfully linked to the fatal fire.

"I have no idea," said Rebecca.

"Did he have some moral or religious objection to cremation?"

"More of a physical one."

I'd tagged along on the hunt, having lost track of where my remains had vanished into the system as well. I'd watched Rebecca's growing distress as the days ticked by, with no sign of me or my promised return. I could see she was starting to wonder if I was gone for good this time, and I was beginning to wonder the same thing, even as I hovered, unseen, right next to her.

Burned beyond recognition is what the nightly news had to say about my body before it was lost in rolls of red tape. Since I was already halfway there, one of the paper-pushers at the coroner's office rubber-stamped the necessary form to get my remains roasted and pulverized at a crematorium for municipal dispensation. Maybe Louie, plugged into that whole system, might have been able to intervene, but he'd been reduced to a brain in a jar and had lost any sway he ever had in the process. By the time anyone found out what they'd done with me, it was too late to stop it. All Rebecca could do was complain to bureaucratic minions and listen to their polite but insincere apologies. And all I could do was watch her growing frustration from the spirit world.

If not for Rebecca's persistent pestering, my unidentified ashes would have ended up in the same cemetery landfill as the thousands of dead homeless, addicts, and drifters who'd had their own misfortune of dying within the city limits with no identification. Rebecca may not have been next of kin, but in these cases the municipality was perfectly happy to hand over unclaimed cremains to whoever expressed interest in footing the bill for disposal.

The hitman from Death Dealers Incorporated had also been dug out of the ruins, but his identification went smoothly thanks to dental records, which, once again, makes the case for keeping current with your oral hygiene. I'd always relied on post-mortem regeneration to keep my teeth in good shape, so I had no records to match. As I'd guessed, the contract killer was an anonymous everyman. Nobody ever figured out what he'd been doing in some dingy art-gallery/music-club in the middle of the night after closing, his wholesome suburban family least of all.

Other than him and me, that was it as far as victims of the fire were concerned. No trace of Csaba Szabo or Rabbi Reubenski was ever uncovered. Not them, nor any other unnatural presence.

"I'm so sorry," said the custodian, who wasn't, but was trained to express sympathy whenever appropriate.

"What does it matter now?" said Rebecca, looking down at the simple container she'd been handed. "Dead is dead."

Of course Rebecca knew better than that, but as days turned into weeks that turned into months, her expectations were steadily lowered. There was no sign of life from the ashes. She dutifully checked them every day for the first four weeks. Then it was every second day. Then hardly ever. The box of cremains sat on a shelf and slowly became part of the scenery in Rebecca's apartment.

Not that I wasn't trying to come back. Even though I had never had to reconstitute myself from remains as meagre as dust, I had always assumed I could. But despite all the spiritual straining and focus I mustered from the other side of death, I couldn't get back in. The ashes wouldn't budge, wouldn't accept me. They were too far gone, too dried out, and there were no organic building blocks to work with.

It didn't surprise me when I found Rebecca making the rounds on social media, calling people, sending emails. She was planning my funeral. The invite list was short, exclusive, like one of my parties.

One day, I'd lost track which, Rebecca dressed up in something drab and tasteful and retrieved my box of ashes from the shelf. I followed her as she cabbed it down to the Bay Area and met my gang of associates at the end of a publicly accessible pier that was usually only frequented by photographers looking for a view, or suicides looking for a quick current to sweep them out to sea.

I'd never expressed my preferences for a funeral for obvious reasons. Why waste my time working out the details of something purely theoretical? Had I any wishes in the matter, I thought they were reasonably anticipated in this Spartan ceremony. No funeral home, no preacher, no undertaker running up a bill for a rented room, thin coffee, and tasteless biscuits.

There were a lot of long faces and even a few tears. Tracy cried of course, but it wasn't her usual theatrical wailing. I don't want to sound narcissistic, but it might have been genuine. I like to think I know when a woman's faking it.

Tom, one of the long faces, had made a point of rounding up Gladys and Louie and bringing them to the ceremony. With no faces, their level of grief was unreadable, but I noted that Gladys remained unusually quiet and didn't swear once. I decided to take it as a compliment.

Moby-Dick insisted on coming out of his pocket hovel for a look. He was swimming excited laps around his watch encasement. Shadowing Rebecca had paid off big for him. Szabo's drowning had delighted the aqua-harbinger, but now he was witnessing a burial-at-sea for The Man Who Could Not Die. He'd waited thousands of years for a fix this good and he was one very happy fish. It was hard to resent him for it.

Wilbur said some kind words. As the oldest of the bunch, he'd been to many funerals and wakes and memorials—almost as many as Tracy, and all for people he genuinely knew. He'd seen them done well and done poorly and apparently had taken notes. Still a showman, he was good at that sort of thing. In the publicity aftermath of his arrest for public mischief, he'd been offered a one-hour special on local prime-time television to perform some of his old magic tricks. If I couldn't make a comeback, I was glad he could.

Even Reynaldo the Wise made an appearance to show proper reverence by not behaving like a fuckhead. He looked appropriately solemn, refrained from all sarcasm, and said very little—which must have been a huge sacrifice for him. I appreciated it.

As I listened to anecdotes, amusing and troubling, about my various misdeeds and accomplishments, I became aware of someone else present for the fond farewell. A man was standing at the entry to the pier, far from the rest of my modest crowd of mourners. I didn't recognize the face. There was no face to recognize. But by then I knew the outline well.

I approached and, as I expected, the collective that called itself Charlie Nocturne sensed my presence and spoke.

"They have given up."

"No," I corrected him. "They gave me every chance. I'm not coming back. Not this time."

"Pity," he said. "It seems my search must continue."

"I'm surprised you made it back in one piece. Last I saw, your whole harbinger crew was jumping ship."

"There were many defections," he acknowledged. "I have been left in a much-weakened state. But many chose to remain—enough to reconstruct myself. The others will return in time. The day of the grand feast will come yet, and they will all want a front-row seat."

"Good luck with that," I said insincerely. "And your talent hunt. How many do you need to bag for your pet project?"

"I have had my eye on Famine for quite some time. Pestilence as well."

Those names rung a bell I didn't care to hear.

"Szabo was to be the third. Alone, he could not be all that I needed him to be. Only once he merged with Rabbi Reubenski did he become the perfect personification of War— both the violence and the victim."

"And that only left me."

"You, I was certain, would become Death. When we first met, I saw your potential as one who could cheat mortality and never stay still in your grave. But you, too, were lacking. It was not until you also took a life of your own free will that you became my Death Incarnate."

But then he paused, and when he spoke again he sounded disappointed.

"In this state, however, you hardly seem up to the task."

I turned to look back at my informal funeral and saw the contents of the tin box being upended over the pier railing. The wind caught my ashes as they came spilling out and cast them into the sea. The grey cloud dissipated and was barely perceptible by the time the particles rained down into the water and were lost.

"Yeah," I agreed. "I'm feeling spread a little thin these days."

"I must reconcile that you are not the Death I have been searching for. I thought all the pieces of the puzzle were in play at last, but another delay seems inevitable. No matter. One day, sooner rather than later, the four shall ride across the continents of the earth and usher in the apocalypse. All life shall be snuffed out before them, and this world will be still at last."

"So everybody dies. All at once. That how you get your kicks?"

"That is how I fulfill my purpose, my destiny. Our purpose, our destiny. We are Legion."

It all sounded unsettlingly biblical. I was just as glad to have no part in it.

"Sorry to disappoint you. All of you. But if you want to bring about the end of the world, go find somebody else to be your stooge. That's not my scene. I still have friends here and I'm sure they'd like to keep the apocalypse on hold. At least until they've had a fair shake at life."

Charlie Nocturne had nothing more to say to me. He was gone by the time I looked back.

Rebecca was the first to leave, to disengage from the ceremony. She didn't look like she was coping well, but a cigarette helped. At least it wasn't a swig from a flask. Tom came after her, stuffing Gladys and Louie back in their carrying case before trying to console her. I wished there was some way to tip her off that I'd left those account numbers and passwords—the keys to an overseas fortune—on a slip of paper filed inside Gladys's skull. Maybe she'd take a look one day.

A hug and a hankie got Rebecca shored up. She left with Tom and I couldn't help but notice they were holding hands.

The rest of my friends came marching off the pier in a downcast procession. On some level, I'm sure they were all glad to be rid of me. The new normal would seem very normal indeed without Rip Eulogy raising the dead, raising hell. They could use a break. I resolved not to impose myself any further. Why hang around and haunt them? That's what memories are for.

I was alone, left with nothing to do but what I always do in these circumstances. Rebuild.

The ocean was vast, impossibly huge. It could take years, even centuries to find enough pieces to start with. A fragment of bone or two might rest at the bottom of the bay. Maybe some bits of soggy ash lay trapped in a clump of seaweed. Or perhaps it was all swept out to sea already, gone forever. I could search until the end of time and never find myself.

Couldn't we all?

The building blocks of my remains were infinitesimal and lost, at the mercy of waves that didn't care where they were washed to, in water that seemed limitless. But it was water filled with salts and nutrients, and the average human body is over fifty percent water. I consoled myself that, in a way, I was already halfway there.

My spirit, my soul, my intangible self, hovered at the water's edge. I didn't know what to call it anymore. The term "ghost" seemed shallow now. "Consciousness" was as accurate as I could get using a tool as blunt as words.

I let whatever was left of myself drift out to sea.

THE STORY CONTINUES IN...

EPITAPH

THE NECROMANCER THANATOGRAPHY
BOOK TWO

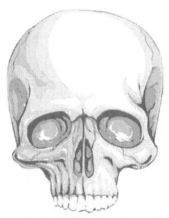

COMING SOON FROM

SHANE SIMMONS

AND EYESTRAIN PRODUCTIONS

Visit eyestrainproductions.com and subscribe to the
newsletter for other free tales from the Necropolis.

Acknowledgements

The author wishes to thank Kathryn Presner, Ellie Presner, Michael Brodie, Kirsten LM, and Peter Taylor for the early reads, and for catching errors and typos that might have otherwise exposed him as a moron.

About the Author

Shane Simmons is an award-winning screenwriter and graphic novelist whose work has appeared in international film festivals, museums and lectures about design and structure. His art has been discussed in multiple books and academic journals about sequential storytelling, and his short stories have been printed in critically praised anthologies of history, crime and horror. He lives in Montreal with his wife and too many cats.

Also by Shane Simmons

Novels

Sex Tape
Filmography

Collections

Raw and Other Stories

Booklets

Carrion Luggage
Hot Pennies
Choke the Chicken
The Red Baron: An Ace for the Ages

Graphic Novels

The Long and Unlearned Life of Roland Gethers
The Failed Promise of Bradley Gethers
The Inauspicious Adventures of Filson Gethers

Last Words

Small-press publishers rely on reviews from readers like you to help get the word out about their books. Whether it's a simple star rating or a written critique, every bit of feedback helps convince the impersonal computer algorithms of Amazon, and other literary outlets, that the book you just read has merit and deserves more exposure. Please support independent authors, editors and publishers by taking a few moments to share your thoughts and opinions with other potential readers who may be sitting on the fence about trying an intriguing novel or collection. Your suggestions or comments can make all the difference when it comes to helping them find a new writer they'll like, or matching a struggling author with the readership he or she deserves. Thank you.